P9-BYS-929

JANE LANGTON'S HOMER KELLY
MYSTERIES

Divine Inspiration

God in Concord

The Dante Game

Murder at the Gardner

Good and Dead

Emily Dickinson Is Dead

Natural Enemy

The Memorial Hall Murder

Dark Nantucket Noon

The Transcendental Murder

PENGUIN CRIME FICTION

GOD IN CONCORD

Jane Langton is the author of nine other Homer Kelly mysteries, including *Divine Inspiration*. She lives in Lincoln, Massachusetts.

God in
Concord

Jane Langton

Illustrations by the author

Penguin Books

PENGUIN BOOKS
Published by the Penguin Group
Penguin Books USA Inc., 375 Hudson Street, New York,
New York 10014, U.S.A.
Penguin Books Ltd, 27 Wrights Lane, London W8 5TZ, England
Penguin Books Australia Ltd, Ringwood, Victoria, Australia
Penguin Books Canada Ltd, 10 Alcorn Avenue,
Toronto, Ontario, Canada M4V 3B2
Penguin Books (N.Z.) Ltd, 182–190 Wairau Road,
Auckland 10, New Zealand

Penguin Books Ltd, Registered Offices: Harmondsworth,
Middlesex, England

First published in the United States of America by Viking Penguin,
a division of Penguin Books USA Inc., 1992
Published in Penguin Books 1993

10 9 8 7 6 5

THE LIBRARY OF CONGRESS HAS CATALOGUED THE HARDCOVER
AS FOLLOWS:
Langton, Jane.
God in Concord/Jane Langton.
p. cm.
ISBN 0-670-84260-5 (hc.)
ISBN 0 14 01.6594 0 (pbk.)
I. Title.
PS 3562.A515G58 1992
813´.54—dc20 91-42940

Printed in the United States of America
Set in Caslon Old Face
Designed by Ann Gold

For David and
Patty Garrison

The wood thrush's is no opera music . . .
He deepens the significance of all things seen
in the light of his strain.

Henry Thoreau's Journal
July 5, 1852

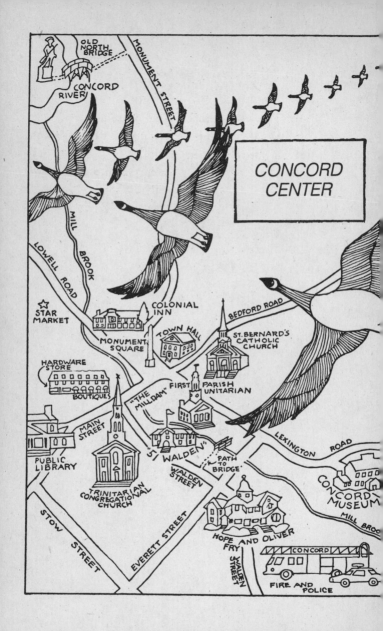

CONCORD CENTER

OLD NORTH BRIDGE

MONUMENT STREET

CONCORD RIVER

MILL BROOK

LOWELL ROAD

STAR MARKET

COLONIAL INN

BEDFORD ROAD

MONUMENT SQUARE

TOWN HALL

ST. BERNARD'S CATHOLIC CHURCH

HARDWARE STORE

BOUTIQUES

"THE MILLDAM"

FIRST PARISH UNITARIAN

MAIN STREET

"WALDEN"

PATH TO BRIDGE

LEXINGTON ROAD

PUBLIC LIBRARY

TRINITARIAN CONGREGATIONAL CHURCH

WALDEN STREET

CONCORD MUSEUM

MILL BROOK

STOW STREET

EVERETT STREET

HOPE AND OLIVER FRY

WALDEN STREET

CONCORD

FIRE AND POLICE

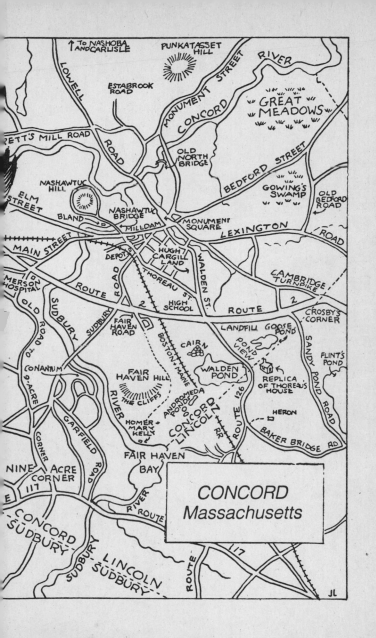

CONCORD
Massachusetts

1

*See what a life the gods have given us, set round
with pain and pleasure. It is too strange for sorrow;
it is too strange for joy.*
Thoreau's *Journal* March 27, 1842

In the forest of oak and white pine beyond the Pond View
Trailer Park, a wood thrush began to sing. Nobody heard
it. All the residents of Pond View were inside their Belvederes
and Skylines and Caravelles except for Stu LaDue, who sat
on his lawn chair beside Route 126 just as usual. If Stu
heard the song of the wood thrush above the noise of the
passing traffic, he paid it no heed.

Inside the mobile homes several impulsive things were
happening that June morning.

Norman Peck suddenly decided to put his collection of
snapshots into an album. Pulling open a drawer, he rum-
maged in it for pictures of his deceased wife.

Mavis and Bernie Buonfesto began yelling at each other
over their breakfast coffee.

Shirley Mills pitched out the leggy geranium she had been
keeping alive for five years.

Charlotte Harris threw herself down at her desk and wrote
a letter.

Of all these impetuous events, the only one that made any
real difference afterward was Charlotte's letter:

Dear Julian, I want to say three things.
   1. I've been unhappy as Pete's wife my whole mar-
      ried life.
   2. Getting a divorce is awful. You know, such a
      mess.

3. I wouldn't ever do it unless I thought you'd marry
    me someday.

If you think this is silly, forget it. I'd rather keep on
with Pete. This isn't a big deal. It's just that I've always
loved you.

Charlotte

She soon regretted the letter with all her heart.

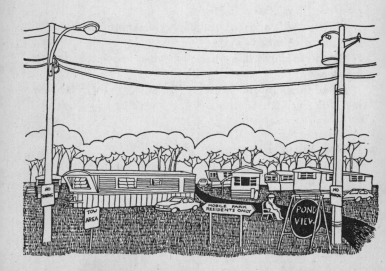

2

. . . I have been anxious to improve the nick of time
. . . to stand on the meeting of two eternities . . .
to toe that line.
Walden, "Economy"

Charlotte's letter was a critical point like a change of state, like the instant when a kettle of water starts to boil, or a swelling balloon bursts with a loud report, or an accumulating pile of gravel steepens until the stones rattle thunderously downhill.

In human affairs there are similar critical points, hours when small things mount to a crisis, moments when anger erupts or tears flow, days when marriages fail. Even the instant when understanding floods the mind can be a crucial turning point.

Long before the morning when Charlotte wrote her letter the simmering had begun in the kettle, the balloon had begun to expand, the steepening slope of the pile of gravel was becoming more acute.

If there was a single moment of beginning, it was the day Jack Markey rode up in the elevator to the seventieth floor of the Grandison Building on Huntington Avenue in Boston to receive a new assignment from Jefferson Grandison.

Jack was already immersed in one commercial project for his chief. He was working hard, throwing into it all his enthusiasm, all his skill in matching buildings to a particular site. Flying up in the elevator, he didn't know how he'd find time for a second undertaking.

The elevator was attached to the outside of the building, and it was made of glass. It occurred to Jack as he rushed up from the dark canyon of Huntington Avenue into the light-filled upper air that Grandison's office was not on the seventieth floor at all—it was somewhere in the upper reaches of the sky. Understanding Mr. Grandison's exalted loftiness was like grasping the concept of infinity. No matter how far away you envisioned the end of space, there was infinite expanse beyond, and no matter how high you imagined Grandison's dwelling place, he was higher still. Empires rose when Jefferson Grandison nodded his head. He shook it and they fell.

This morning Mr. Grandison had completed the details of an important contract by telephone. The other party was unctuously grateful. "That is thoroughly satisfactory, Mr. Grandison, sir. I'll send a messenger directly with the papers and the check, transferring to you the possession of Lot Seventeen. I trust you'll take it off our hands in the very near future?"

"Of course."

"I'm sorry, Mr. Grandison, sir, I don't want to trouble you, but I wonder if you might be just a little more specific, as far as the timetable?"

"Not at this time."

"I see. Well, now, sir—"

"I bid you good morning."

When Jack walked into the office, still a little dizzy from his upward flight, Grandison beckoned him to the map table. It was a very large table, but it was dwarfed by the space around it, a room that was made even larger by the immense views surrounding it on three sides. Oversize maps could be spread out on the table, then swept off to be replaced by others. There were small-scale maps of the entire North Shore, the Berkshires, the Cape, there were mid-scale maps of towns and cities and large-scale maps of single streets and individual parcels of real estate. Jefferson Grandison could focus the zoom lens of his interest swiftly, rushing down from far away to stare at single souls laid bare. In the company of Jack Markey, he often looked down on the creation in this way, gazing at the land of Judah, the river Jordan, the waters of Nimron, the wilderness of Moab.

Today their attention was directed at Concord, Massachusetts, and the intersection of Route 2 with the Walden Pond road, Route 126. Jack's current project was nearby, Walden Green, a mixed-use complex on a parcel belonging to the local high school on the northwest side of the intersection.

Grandison touched with his pencil the forty-acre site of the Concord landfill on the other side of the highway. "It's being phased out, you say, the landfill?"

"Right. They don't have much room left for that old-fashioned kind of refuse-disposal. Oh, they're doing what they can. They're recycling. But pretty soon their only choice will be a transfer station in the same place. Well, you know what that's like. Big expense. Everything sorted and trucked away."

"The landfill belongs to the town of Concord?"

"That's right. To the town."

"Which is, I believe, in a state of fiscal crisis?" Grandison's pencil drifted slowly down Route 126 and stopped. "And this, what's this next door?"

"Pond View. It's a trailer park."

"Surprising, a landfill and a trailer park so near to Walden Pond."

"Yes, but the trailer park is being phased out, too. Those people only have a life tenancy. When they die, nobody else can come in."

"According to this map, the trailer park belongs to the commonwealth of Massachusetts, which is also in a perilous financial condition. How old are the tenants, roughly speaking?"

"I don't know." Jack made a joke. "Somebody might set a few of those mobile homes on fire."

Grandison twiddled his pencil and said nothing. The pencil made meaningless scrawls across the parcel known as Pond View.

When the interview was over, Jack entered the glass elevator, pushed the button, and fell out of the sky, plunging earthward, emerging on Huntington Avenue breathless after his headlong descent.

On the sidewalk he had to step around the scattered possessions of a bag lady who was sitting just outside the glassy entrance of the office tower. Jack tossed a quarter in her direction and walked quickly away.

Sarah Peel reached for the quarter and zipped it into her coin purse, but she was not grateful. Sarah knew that no kindly Lord kept watch over this sparrow's fall. Only the cold March wind, blustering down the narrow shaft of one Boston street or another, affected the course of her days. Sometimes it blew dust into her face, sometimes sleet and snow, and sometimes money. It was a random process, entirely without intention to help or to harm.

3

There were two visitors to the Pond View Trailer Park on the day Charlotte Harris rushed out of her mobile home to toss her letter into the cab of the small truck belonging to Julian Snow.

The first was Homer Kelly. When Homer set out on that June morning he had no intention of visiting the trailer park. His destination was Goose Pond, a miniature body of water lying in a deep kettle hole just east of Pond View.

Actually he wasn't approaching the real Goose Pond. Homer was seeking a vision in his mind, a wild place described in the journals of Henry Thoreau. Like Jack Markey and Jefferson Grandison, Homer was studying a map of Concord. His was an old one. The forking rivers ran across it from lower left to upper right, lined with little symbols meaning marshy places—the Sudbury Meadows, the Great Meadows, Gowing's Swamp. Converging lines were hills—Annursnac, Curly Pate, and Thoreau's favorite lookout over the Sudbury River, the rocky ledge he called the Cliffs. The ponds were marked on the map, too—Walden, Bateman's, Flint's, and the wide bend of the river called Fair Haven Bay where Homer lived with his wife, Mary, in a small house on the shore.

There was no Route 2 on Homer's old map, there were no housing developments, no hospital complex, no regional high school, no correctional facility, no fashionable shops. In those days Walden Pond had not been afflicted with a

7

highway, a landfill, a trailer park, and a thousand visitors a
day on hot summer Sundays. The railroad, it was true, ran
past the pond, and there had been mills and a leadworks in
the southwest part of town. But mostly Concord had been a
network of woodlots and farms, with a few stores on the
main street called the Milldam.

Looking at the map, consulting Thoreau's journal, Homer
could imagine the mid-nineteenth-century town. Daily he
studied the record of Thoreau's explorations of his native
village. Daily he set off to see the places for himself, looking
for the wellsprings of Thoreau's prose. The words had been

written down on paper, but to Homer they were attached to the landscape, stuck to the clapboards of houses, written on the leaves of trees, growing like lichen on the stone walls, ground into the soil by Thoreau's stout boots. Homer didn't know what he would learn by his explorations, but he was convinced that he couldn't understand the words without seeing the landscape from which they had come.

It was good to be back. During the last academic year, Homer and Mary Kelly had abandoned New England for Italy. They had taken a sabbatical from their teaching jobs in Cambridge and their transcendental heroes in Concord, to go whoring after foreign gods. Now they were burrowing back into the nest.

For Homer this morning the goal was Goose Pond. Henry Thoreau had once scared up a pair of black ducks at Goose Pond. He had seen waterbugs dimpling the surface. Perhaps on this warm June morning a century and a half later there would still be ducks on the water and a new race of waterbugs, the remote descendants of Henry Thoreau's.

"And who knows?" said Homer, putting a banana in his pocket as he walked out of the house. "I might hear my first wood thrush."

"Not there," said Mary. "Not at Goose Pond. You'll never hear a wood thrush so close to Route Two."

Mary was wrong, but by the time Homer found his way to the shore of the pond, coming in from the housing development on the eastern side, the local wood thrush had stopped singing. Homer could hear only the roar of traffic on Route 2 and the drone of mosquitoes diving in for the kill as he splashed around the pond in his rubber boots.

Soon the mosquitoes were floating vials of Homer Kelly's blood.

*How many a man has dated a new era in his life
from the reading of a book.*
Walden, "Reading"

The second visitor to Pond View that morning was Ananda
Singh.

Ananda was a young pilgrim from India. Supercharged
with emotion, he got off the Boston-to-Fitchburg train at
the Concord depot and looked at his watch. He had been in
the United States only two and a half hours, and here he was
already, setting foot in the village of his dreams.

He knew he should have been sensible and given in to his
weariness after the twenty-four-hour flight from New Delhi.
He should have settled in at the airport motel and gone to
bed. But it had been so enticing, the knowledge that he was
only fifteen miles from the destination of his pilgrimage,
Walden Pond. At Logan Airport Ananda reclaimed his suitcase, cashed in his traveler's checks, inquired how to get to
Concord, hopped into a cab, and caught a train at North
Station just as it was pulling out. And here he was in Concord, Massachusetts, wide awake at eleven o'clock in the
morning instead of fast asleep at midnight in his father's
house in the foothills of the Himalayas.

For a moment Ananda stood motionless on the Concord
platform, watching the train pull away with a long, slow
jerk. The other passengers who had traveled with him from
Boston were moving off purposefully, as if Concord were
just an ordinary place on the surface of the earth. Eagerly
Ananda carried his suitcase around the depot and looked
curiously at the street. It was an American street, not very
different from the village streets of England where Ananda

had spent two years of his life at university. There was a pizza parlor, a liquor store, a cleaning establishment. Where would he find Walden, the pond that to Thoreau had been "sacred as the Ganges, a gem of the first water which Concord wears in her coronet"?

A girl was standing on the sidewalk. "Excuse me," said Ananda, "can you tell me how to get to Walden Pond?"

The girl laughed. Her laugh was musical, and Ananda laughed, too. She pointed to the right. "That way. You just walk straight for a mile or so, and you'll come to it on the other side of Route Two."

She was as tall as he was, but built on a grand scale, whereas Ananda was lank and thin. His mother often teased him by saying he was a pair of brown eyes on the end of a plank.

The girl reminded him of the Statue of Liberty. It seemed appropriate that the first young female person he spoke to in the United States should be like the symbol of the country. She had the same round jaw and long straight nose and huge rectangular eyes. Her teeth were dazzling, like those of the girls at home.

Ananda looked excitedly down the street in the direction of the pond. "Thank you," he said. And then he couldn't help himself, he had to tell her. "I've come ten thousand miles to see Henry Thoreau's Walden Pond."

"Have you really?" The girl seemed impressed.

Some people, Ananda thought admiringly, were more transparent than others. The girl's light voice and open face were a revealing whole, and he caught her up in his mind as if she were an object on a table. For a moment he held her in his hand. Were all Americans like this?

Now the girl pursed her lips and looked doubtful. "A lot of people think Walden isn't true to Thoreau's memory anymore." Her brow darkened, as if the Statue of Liberty were beholding thunderclouds over Kansas. "But they overdo it, those people. My father, for instance." Then she groaned. "Oh, there he is, and there's the car. I should have seen it. Oh, isn't that typical."

She drifted away in the direction of a tall sandy-haired man who was shouting at a woman in uniform.

"Two minutes," bellowed the man, "that's all. I'm only two minutes late."

"Well, okay, Mr. Fry," said the woman in uniform. "I'll take your word for it." And she took his parking ticket out from under the windshield wiper.

The girl looked back at Ananda and waved good-bye. "I hope you like the pond," she said.

Ananda set off, marching with his long loose stride in the direction of his dream. For a moment he thought about the splendid girl and her angry father, Mr. Fry, and then he forgot them, enchanted by the clapboard buildings on either side of the street. They reminded him of the big houses in Simla, shaded by trees and wrapped in verandas.

The wooden houses petered out. So did the sidewalk. The street broadened. Cars rushed past him, and Ananda had to walk carefully to avoid being run down.

At the base of a long hill he stopped to rest, a little disturbed by the busy street. It was not the idyllic country road he had imagined.

A car pulled over, wobbling to a stop. The left front tire was flat. The driver looked at Ananda and said, "Shit."

"Can I help you?" Ananda said politely.

Jack Markey said, "Sure," and grinned at him. He got out and opened the trunk and lifted out the spare. "You're from somewhere else, right?"

"Oh, yes, I'm from India. This is my first day in this country." Ananda put down his suitcase, accepted the socket wrench, and looked at it doubtfully. He had never changed a tire in all his life.

Jack looked at him and laughed. "Here, you twist off the

lug nuts." He took back the socket wrench and showed Ananda how. Ananda knelt and unscrewed them successfully while his new friend jacked up the front bumper.

When the job was done, Jack Markey thanked Ananda and looked at him inquisitively. "I don't suppose you've got time to do something else for me? Ten minutes, that's all it'll take."

Ananda hesitated, then said politely, "Well, I don't see why I should not."

"Good." Jack opened the car door and waved him onto the front seat. "It's my assistant, he's sick today, so I need somebody to hold the stick for me. I'm doing some surveying right here, just up the hill."

Ananda's tiredness vanished. Henry Thoreau too had been a surveyor. He beamed at this reincarnation. "I would be most happy."

The car whizzed around in a U-turn and started up a broad drive. "This is the high school," said Jack. "We'll park the car and walk up. You can leave your suitcase on the seat."

Ananda soon found himself standing on a playing field at the top of a wooded ridge, holding a long graduated stick while the man with the curly yellow hair peered through a telescope mounted on a tripod and shouted at him to stand a little to the left, a little to the right. Through the trees Ananda could see a broad highway. Cars flooded by, trucks made huge accelerating noises. Below him people were playing tennis. "Up to the net, Jarvis," shouted the coach. "Get a move on, Kenny, get a move on."

"Great, great," said Jack, looking up from his telescope. "Now, hey, how about standing over there in front of that tree?"

Ananda moved quickly to the tree and held the stick again. He couldn't admit that he was in a hurry. It would be impossible to explain that after flying ten thousand miles he couldn't wait another moment to see Walden Pond. Obediently he moved from place to place, wondering why the surveyor was mapping this bit of countryside so close to the sacred water. Was it a geodetic survey? Perhaps the map would show flora and fauna or the nature of the geological substratum.

At last the yellow-haired surveyor was satisfied. "Gee, thanks. You're a real sport."

"It was no trouble. May I ask what sort of cartographic study you are making?"

"Cartographic?" Jack Markey looked at the skinny foreign kid in surprise. "Oh, we're not mapping anything. We're planning a shopping mall. You know, with a condo complex on the side. Grandison Enterprises. I work for Jefferson Grandison."

Ananda was dismayed. "But is it not too near to Walden Pond?"

"Walden Pond?" Jack grinned. "Oh, you mean because of the book. There's a book called *Walden Pond*."

Ananda began to explain, but a backhoe came up noisily beside them, and his words were drowned out. Jack went up to the driver. "You see those orange sticks? Dig there, and there, and there."

Ananda walked back to the car with a sinking heart. Extracting his suitcase, he continued his pilgrimage.

In a moment he stood at a highway intersection. A huge eighteen-wheeler thundered past him, and then another and another. The high scream of the colossal tires rose above the immense roar of the diesel engines grinding into gear.

Confused, Ananda misunderstood the traffic light. Dodging across from one lane to the next, he forgot to look left instead of right and was nearly run down. The furious driver blasted his horn and shouted at him.

Shaken, Ananda hurried along the granite curbing on the other side while another tide of cars rushed toward him along the secondary road, plunging up to the stoplight, surging around the corner, and speeding in the direction of Boston.

Then Ananda's steps faltered. What was that vast hole, that enormous pit gouged out of the landscape?

Stumbling up to the fence, he stared in horror at the Concord landfill, gaping at the distant mountain of trash and the muddy hollow with its pile of old washing machines rising skyward, interspersed with crumpled stoves and bent refrigerators. Heavy machinery was parked on a hilltop. A couple of giant dumpsters glittered with broken glass.

Turning away, Ananda tottered back along the road, looking for a glint of blue water, that "perfect forest mirror, the work of a brave man surely, in whom there was no guile." It was nowhere in sight. Instead he came upon a trailer park. A swinging metal sign read "Pond View." Behind it boxy dwellings were parked at angles to one another, white and turquoise.

An old man sat on an aluminum lawn chair beside the

road and stared at Ananda as he trudged by. Ananda gave him a feeble smile.

Another foreigner, decided Stu LaDue, looking back at him coldly. Christ, they were everywhere, like cockroaches.

5

"There, marriage is like that." (Thoreau, kicking a skunk cabbage)
Frank Preston Stearns

Julian and Alice Snow had lived at Pond View for thirty years. They had been married for thirty-two. By now you'd think they'd be used to each other, but they weren't. Their long union had rubbed them both raw, and the rough places chafed and chafed, scouring bleeding grooves.

Why had they stayed married so long? In the daytime, exasperated, Julian wondered why. In bed at night he didn't wonder, although it wasn't sex that kept them together. Sex was only another reason for irritation. It was their two warm bodies lying closely enfolded all night long, every night, year in and year out. In the dark their outer selves fell away, leaving only the deepest core. Clinging together in sleep, they forgot their bitterness, their fuming resentment.

But now it was daytime. It was the end of Julian's vacation. He didn't enjoy vacations. He felt trapped. Alice was too much of a muchness. Lying there in bed—Alice was an invalid—she never stopped talking and eating and spilling crumbs and laughing and crying and crocheting and giving orders and picking fights and wanting things. God, how Alice wanted things. She was always ordering useless gimcracks from catalogs, although Julian railed at her that they couldn't afford it. Next thing he knew, something else would arrive in a United Parcel van, a monogrammed doormat, a skirt for the bathroom sink, a hideous lamp with a ruffled shade, a furry blue scatter rug.

For himself Julian wanted nothing. His job at the landfill next door was just a job, but it was all right. He pumped

18

out the leaching tank, he operated the Trashmaster, the big roller that flattened the rubbish, and sometimes he ran the crawl dozer that buried everything in dirt. On weekends when Alice agreed to spare him, he took his boat out on Walden Pond and fished for trout. Or else he descended the steep slope of the kettle hole behind his mobile home and looked for waterfowl in Goose Pond.

This morning Alice said she needed him. But whatever it was she wanted, it had to wait. A bunch of her friends dropped in and sat around her bed and billowed over into the kitchen, helping themselves to coffee, passing around their homemade goodies, talking loudly while Alice's television chattered in the background. Then they all stopped talking to watch the next episode of "The Young and the Reckless," which was everybody's favorite. Julian, cramped into a corner of the kitchen with the morning paper, heard the sudden quiet as Vanessa confronted Dirk with his infidelity, and Dirk said, "I hoped and prayed my relationship with Angelica would not become a factor here," and Vanessa screamed at him.

Julian stood up and looked out the window, staring at

Goose Pond. Somebody was down there, tramping around, a big guy in rubber boots, flailing around clumsily, batting at mosquitoes. What was he up to? Julian watched him while Vanessa sobbed, "You used me, you lied to me."

"Well, so long, Alice dear," said Mavis when the program was over. Shirley left, too. Honey Mooney stayed, loyally cleaning up the kitchen, offering Julian a coconut brownie, at last fussing down the trailer steps with her bundle of leftovers.

"Julian, hey, Julian," Alice called from the bedroom. "Hey, listen, I want you should go to the store. I want some of that cookie ice cream, okay? And I need some more purple yarn from the dime store, okay? And get me some stamps, all right? I want to order something."

Julian was glad to get out of the house. His spirits rose like a kite, lifting free from Alice's clutching fingers. Climbing into his Chevy Blazer, he took off up the driveway.

As he slowed down to make the right turn onto the street, he was surprised to see Charlotte Harris run out of her house and wave at him. She must have been looking out her window. He waited as she ran nimbly across her pretty garden, holding up a white envelope. Without a word she dropped it into his open window and ran back.

Stu LaDue was sitting beside the road as always, keeping an eye on everything and everybody. From under his visored cap his thick glasses flashed at Julian's truck. Julian didn't want to read Charlotte's note under the prying gaze of that bastard, so he left it lying on the seat and drove across Route 2 to the center of Concord and parked behind the post office.

Turning off the engine, he picked up the envelope and read the note.

He read it three times. His eyes kept going back to the last line, "It's just that I've always loved you."

Julian was touched and dismayed at the same time. What did Charlotte mean by "someday"? Someday after Alice died? Alice wasn't about to die. Someday after he got a divorce? A divorce! Julian could imagine what people would say, "His wife got sick, so he divorced her." Oh, that would be just great.

And what about Charlotte's husband, Pete? It was true that Pete was a nonentity and a slob, but so what? Julian couldn't ruin Pete's life. And yet—for a moment Julian allowed himself to imagine what it would be like to be married to Charlotte, to live with a woman like that.

But it was impossible. Julian left the letter on the seat and went to look for Alice's purple yarn. But he couldn't get Charlotte out of his mind as he walked out of the parking lot and into the dime store.

Whoops, wrong store. This wasn't Woolworth's. It was some kind of fancy little shop selling perfume. A pretty girl with a fancy haircut was standing behind the counter, looking at him sharply.

Julian went back out to the sidewalk and looked up and down the street. The dime store was gone. Instead there were three other shops with snappy hemispherical awnings. They all had magnificent hand-carved signs in gold leaf—Corporate Gifts, the Den of Teddies, the Parfumerie. There were expensive-looking crystal bottles in the window of the Parfumerie, a giant toy moose in the Den of Teddies, and a lamp shaped like a golf club in the window of Corporate Gifts. It was obvious to Julian that none of these stores could supply him with Alice's yarn.

At least the post office was still there. Julian walked down the street and found it just where it had always been.

He had to stand in line to buy stamps. In front of him a couple of well-dressed women were discussing their winter vacations in the Caribbean. Julian Snow, who had never been to the Caribbean, couldn't help overhearing them, and neither could the garage mechanic behind him or the old couple behind the mechanic who were living on a pension.

"You might try Nassau next year," said Mimi Pink, the woman with the weird hairdo and the football shoulders.

"Roger and I are really mad about St. John," said Marjorie Bland, who was entirely outfitted in lavender, from sporty sweatshirt to running shoes. "We had a little house on the shore, and the houseboys brought in our meals, and there were the nicest people in the next cottage. She was in my class at Sweet Briar."

Back at Pond View Charlotte Harris was already regretting her impulsive action. Oh, dear God, the letter was a dreadful mistake. But this morning something had boiled up inside her. How many times in her married life had Pete said the same good-bye—"Don't take any wooden nickels"—when he left for work? How many times? But today it had set off something uncontrollable in Charlotte, something violent. She had snatched up a piece of paper and driven down the words with a smoking pen, and then, no sooner had she stuffed it into an envelope than she had seen Julian's truck slowing down, preparing to turn out onto the street. Without stopping to think, in all the turmoil of her feelings, she'd run out and thrust the envelope at Julian through the window of the cab.

She shouldn't have done it. Watching the big vehicle lurch into a pothole as it turned out onto the road, Charlotte felt her heart lurch in the same way. What had she let loose on the world, what havoc had she wrought? Her letter might go on blundering through her life for years to come—and through Julian's, Pete's, and Alice's. Oh, God, if only she could snatch it back. If only she hadn't written it at all.

6

ADVANCE TO ST. CHARLES PLACE.
IF YOU PASS GO, COLLECT $200.
Chance card, Monopoly

Mimi Pink left the post office and strolled up Walden Street, her high heels wobbling on the sidewalk, her eyes studying the shop windows. Her glance was proprietary. Mimi owned the Den of Teddies, the Parfumerie, and Corporate Gifts, and she was negotiating right now for properties on Main Street around the corner. She had an idea for another gift shop, the Unique Boutique, and she had acquired the franchise for a new Porcelain Parlor.

Mimi was on her way to a business lunch with Jefferson Grandison's first lieutenant, Jack Markey. It wasn't their first meeting. The first had been initiated by Mimi, with her usual gift for grasping at opportunity.

She had heard privately from Judy Bowman, the chairperson of the Concord School Committee, that Jefferson Grandison was conducting a feasibility study at the high school. "It's the old lacrosse field," said Judy, "right next to the highway. He can have it, as far as I'm concerned. We could certainly use the money."

Jefferson Grandison in Concord! Mimi had her reasons for being intrigued, and it didn't take her long to get on board. "You need me," she told Jack Markey. "I know the ropes. I know how things work in Concord. You don't."

Jack had been a pushover. And in an unguarded moment, he had gone so far as to inquire about Pond View, the moribund trailer park. "I understand the occupants have only a life tenancy. How many of those old folks are left?"

"Oh, hardly any. I mean, they're all at death's door. Trust

23

me." Jokingly Mimi flexed her hands over the table. Her long red fingernails raked the air. "I know this town."

Today they were discussing money. Mimi had already rendered important services, and it was time to get down to business. "Oh, I don't want a fee," she said modestly. "A percentage, that's all I ask."

"A percentage?" Jack was outraged. "How much, for Christ's sake?"

They haggled. Mimi won her point. Jack got up from the table and said an angry good-bye.

Mimi got up, too, and looked at him in triumph. "How's your boss?" she said sweetly.

"My boss? You mean Mr. Grandison?" Sullenly Jack picked up the check and turned away, leaving Mimi to pay the tip. "He's okay, I guess."

"And his wife," Mimi called after him, "how's his darling wife?"

Jack was not aware that Grandison had a wife. He looked back at Mimi and shrugged his shoulders.

Mimi smiled and watched him go. Then she walked back up Walden Street to her favorite shop, the Parfumerie. "You can break for lunch now, Bonnie," she told the girl behind the counter.

Nearly every day Mimi spent an hour or two in her perfume shop. She loved watching her manicured hands remove the crystal stoppers from the elegant bottles, she loved the heavy scents that hung in the air.

A woman entered the shop, a fashionably dressed older woman with a hairstyle just like Mimi's, cut close at the nape, bushing out above the ears. She knew just what she wanted. Mimi opened the little flask of Parisian perfume and stroked the woman's wrist with the stopper.

"Oh, but it's so expensive," the customer whispered, looking longingly at the pretty bottle.

"Here, try this one, Odalisque. It's a trifle warmer, don't you think? A little exotic?"

A heavy fragrance rose around them, enclosing them in the atmosphere of a seraglio in the Arabian Nights—while a mile away at Goose Pond a ray of sunshine slanted into the deep kettle hole and stroked the petals of a thousand blossoms on an elderberry bush. At once the blossoms opened and released their delicate scent into the June air, free of charge.

Homer Kelly inhaled it gratefully as he lifted his boots out of the wet rim of the pond and began walking in the direction of the place where he had left his car.

But then another sound rose above the steady hum of traffic, a woman's shriek.

It was very near, just up the slope, where one of the mobile homes of Pond View was visible through the trees.

And someone was crashing along the steep incline, heading away from Route 2. Homer could see the undergrowth shake, as though a gust of wind were running across the hillside. Small saplings and honeysuckle bushes waved to and fro.

Slowly Homer began to climb the hill. "Hey," he shouted, "what's going on up there?"

. . . Walden, is it you?
Walden, "The Ponds"

Ananda Singh had lost track of himself. What was he doing here? His pilgrimage to Walden Pond was a failure. He had found the pond, he had seen the replica of Thoreau's house in the parking lot, and he had walked down to the beach in a crowd of half-naked bathers. Then he had hiked along the beaten path to the place where Thoreau had lived for two years in a house he had built himself. The house was gone. There were stone markers and a sign. Four teenage boys were horsing around, pushing each other and shouting. Embarrassed, Ananda extracted from his suitcase the specimen of manganese from Jamshedpur and dropped it on the cairn of stones, a silent witness to the presence of a devotee from the other side of the world. Then he turned, exhausted, and found his way back to the road.

He was in a state of shock. Through a haze of heat and dust he saw the caravans at the place called Pond View, and the old man sitting on a chair beside the road.

Stuart LaDue saw him coming and prepared himself for a peevish exchange. The kid had those dangerous-looking foreign eyes with that liquid look, like he could mesmerize you. His skin was dark and ashen at the same time. He looked sick, like he had some tropical disease.

"Excuse me," said Ananda, pausing in front of him, desperate for enlightenment. "I have come ten thousand miles to see Walden Pond. I am surprised to find it so different from what I had imagined."

"Hey, listen," said Stu LaDue, "you should of knowed better. That Henry Thoreau, he wasn't no great shakes. Womanizer. He used to have women every night while he was here, that's what I heard. Drinker, too, that's what they tell me." Stu watched with satisfaction as the foreigner blinked and winced. "Hey, I tell you what. You should talk to Norman Peck. Real Thoreau freak." He pointed. "Blue home, down the driveway. You can't miss it."

Stu watched the foreign kid start down the drive, congratulating himself on spoiling Norman's day.

Ananda's suitcase weighed him down. In the last hour it had grown very heavy. Which place was Mr. Peck's? Staring ahead, Ananda heard a woman scream, and then beyond the last of the caravans he saw the bushes swaying wildly left and right. Ananda had once seen a herd of elephants crashing through a forest in southern India, and now for a moment he imagined an elephant trampling this American woodland. It amused him to think how pleased Henry Thoreau would have been to see an elephant in Walden Woods. Thoreau had played with the conceit that someday he would find every kind of flora and fauna within the confines of the town of Concord, even the alpine edelweiss. If the edelweiss, why not the elephant?

There was another cry, a different voice, a man shouting, "Hey, what's going on up there?"

Ananda walked around the last caravan to the far side and looked down at the ground in consternation. A woman in a pink wrapper lay on the steps before the open door. Her feet were on the top step, her head rested on the cement slab below. Her eyes were open and unblinking.

Dropping his suitcase, Ananda knelt beside the woman and lifted her wrist to feel for a pulse. There was none.

A shadow fell across the woman's face. Ananda looked up to see a big man standing beside him, breathing heavily, looking down.

"I fear she is dead," said Ananda.

Homer Kelly got down on his knees. "There's a terrible wound on the back of her head," he said softly.

"Perhaps she fell and her head struck the step."

"Perhaps."

They both turned at the sound of breaking crockery. A small round woman stood staring at them. At her feet lay a broken pitcher and a scattering of ice cubes.

"Oh, poor Alice," cried Honey Mooney. Waving her arms, she ran away, screaming along the driveway. In a moment she was back, trailing a parade of elderly men and women.

"Jesus," puffed Stu LaDue. He looked accusingly at Homer Kelly. "Who the hell are you?" Narrowing his eyes, he pointed a finger at Ananda Singh. "I knew this kid was up to no good. Somebody call the police."

The others ignored him. They ignored Ananda Singh and Homer Kelly. With exclamations of sorrow they bent over Alice Snow. One of the women was crying.

"Where's Julian?" said Norman Peck.

"He went off in his truck," said Stu. "Kind of funny. His wife dies and he drives off. I call that mighty peculiar, if you ask me."

"Nobody's asking you," said Norman.

Charlotte Harris was the last to arrive, running awkwardly along the driveway, her arms and legs stiff, her head forward. At the sight of Alice's body on the ground she stopped short and put her hand to her face. Norman Peck put an arm around her, but Charlotte pulled free and stalked away as though she didn't trust herself to speak.

"You know," Honey Mooney said sorrowfully, "it's like I had a premonition. We were watching TV in Alice's bedroom this morning, and I remember thinking, Maybe we'll never be all together like this, watching 'The Young and the Reckless,' not ever again."

"Now she'll never know how it comes out," said Shirley Mills.

"How what comes out?" said Norman Peck.

"Vanessa and Angelica. They're both in love with Dirk, only Dirk can't make up his mind. But I think Angelica——"

"Shirley, honestly," said Honey. "At a time like this."

Then Homer Kelly touched Ananda's arm and nodded at the truck that was pulling up beside them. "The husband, I think."

Julian Snow got out of the truck with the bag containing Alice's ice cream and looked at the neighbors gathered beside his house.

They stood back sorrowfully so that he could see Alice lying on the steps of the trailer in her pink bathrobe.

Thereafter, for the rest of his days, Julian Snow associated the death of his wife with the scent of elder flowers opening in the woods around Goose Pond.

8

*If a man does not keep pace with his companions,
perhaps it is because he hears a different drummer.
Let him step to the music which he hears. . .*
        Walden, "Conclusion"

As Hope Fry climbed into her father's car at the depot, she glanced back at the man who had come ten thousand miles to visit Walden Pond.

There he was with his suitcase, striding along the sidewalk, smiling, full of eager anticipation. The poor guy, he was bound to be disappointed. Her father should send out a world-wide notice, Beware! Concord is going to the dogs.

Hope was living at home for the summer with her widowed father after her junior year at Boston University. She liked the house on Walden Street, which had been in the family since the turn of the century, but she was sick and tired of living there with Oliver Fry. His testy affection was almost more than she could bear.

Her father was spending his middle age in a state of wrath. Hope was bored to death with the hissing steam of his anger against the Concord selectmen, the planning board, the finance committee, the world at large. Oliver Fry was a steam locomotive stoked with burning coals, driving at full tilt with shrieking whistle against all the other trains on the track. Hope had heard her father's friend Homer Kelly offer him useful advice—"Listen, Oliver, you've got to be more tactful. You should come up behind those people and go through the little door at the back."

Hope knew it was useless. For her father there was no little door at the back, it was front-end collisions every time.

She had fought many a battle with him herself. "Listen, Father, you can't save all the land in Concord. Just because

Henry Thoreau walked on some field or waded in some swamp, my God, he walked on every field and swamp in town. You can't save it all."

And then her father would pound his fist on the table and glare at her. "Why not? Why ever not? It's sacred ground, the whole entire town."

Today it was the Burroughs farm, on Monument Street. "George Burroughs is subdividing it into fifteen lots. He ought to be strangled." Oliver Fry bared his teeth. His eyes bulged. "Fifteen houses down there by the river. It's sacrilege."

Fortunately there were three things that kept Oliver Fry's boiler from blowing up altogether.

The first was strong drink. Oliver took a dollop of cheap

Oliver Fry's house

whiskey every single night before supper—a measured amount, four ounces, more or less.

The second was his job. Oliver taught natural science at the high school. Even this was a source of disagreement with his daughter, because the house had become a zoo of living creatures. Opening a kitchen drawer, Hope would find it full of mealworms, white and wriggling in a nest of bran. There were frozen frogs in the freezer, garden snakes tangled in an aquarium on the kitchen counter, a cage of shrews on a shelf over the radiator, and a wasp nest above the living room mantel. One of the pantries was crowded with a failed skunk cabbage experiment. All the little snoutlike plants were deliquescing in their pots. As a small child Hope had accompanied her father on field trips, catching butterflies, scooping up pollywogs in Fairyland Pond, paddling down the river to catch turtles. She had loved those expeditions, but now she had forgotten how closely they had bound her to her father.

Oliver had not forgotten, and his heart was bruised whenever Hope complained about his collection of living things.

For Hope the worst was the caged barn owl. Sometimes when she went out on the back porch it was disemboweling a live mouse. The owl had a broken wing. Oliver had tried to set it, but the owl had cruelly torn his hand, and the wound had festered. "It's making a fool of you," said Hope.

The owl was still there, awaiting repair.

The third saving passion in Oliver's life was his tender feeling for his daughter. It was a strained affection, because of the way Hope combated him at every turn. But he adored her. Except for a few silly notions, the girl was perfect. Oliver worried about the unknown young man who was out there somewhere, waiting for Hope, the one who would carry her off someday. How could anyone be worthy of her? None of the callow young men she brought home ever seemed good enough.

Oliver had sense enough not to discuss her marriage prospects out loud. He knew what Hope would say· "What makes you think I want to get married? What's the matter with being single?"

But the truth was, Hope did cast a careless glance around, whenever she was in a crowd of miscellaneous strangers, looking for someone, sifting and rejecting.

Today, after his fury about the Burroughs farm, Oliver tried to calm down. "Well, Hopey, dear, I'll make lunch. That chicken I boiled yesterday is in the refrigerator. I'm going to take it apart and wire the bones together."

"Oh, good," said Hope, "I'll make a chicken salad." Running to the refrigerator, she threw open the door, then yelped and jumped back. Something was heaving on the bottom shelf.

"Oh, sorry," said Oliver. "It's that big snapping turtle Homer Kelly gave me. It's all right, it's dead. They go on wriggling like that for a day or two. Here, I'll get the chicken."

The moment of calm was over. Adrenaline pulsed through Hope as she stirred mayonnaise into the shredded chicken. Her father had started in again on Mr. Burroughs, and soon he was attacking the chairperson of the planning board, Roger Bland, for permitting this vile molestation of Henry Thoreau's countryside. "I'll sue them," he said. "I'll sue the whole board for failing in its duty."

Hope mashed the chicken and mayonnaise together and tried not to listen. Who cared about famous people after they were dead? Henry Thoreau was dead, Ralph Waldo Emerson was dead, they were all dead, dead, dead, and she, Hope Fry, was alive, alive, alive! And she meant to wring the most from this fact, right here and now. Turning on her father, Hope cried, "I'm leaving," and snatched up her pocketbook.

Openmouthed, chagrined, Oliver watched his beloved child storm out of the house. What had he said? Nothing that wasn't true! Solidly, factually true!

The Frys' house on Walden Street was near the center of

town, only two blocks from the Milldam. Hope stalked to the intersection of Walden and Main and plumped herself down on a stool in Melanie's Lunch Room.

"Oh, hello, dear," said Melanie, slapping down a knife and fork. "Liverwurst as usual?"

"Yes, please," said Hope.

Melanie's was a down-to-earth lunch room with an old-fashioned menu of sandwiches with coleslaw and pale tomato slices served on thick plates. The jar of mustard and the bottle of ketchup stood on the counter next to the paper-napkin holder. There were no fashionable vegetable salads or oatmeal croissants or spinach soup at Melanie's, no alfalfa sprouts or arugula.

"I love this place," said Hope. "It ought to be a national landmark."

Melanie was working fast, slathering Wonder Bread with mayonnaise. She looked worried. "Well, I'm sorry, Hopey, but I don't know how long I can hold out. That Mimi Pink, she's bought the whole building."

"Mimi Pink?"

"You know. She runs those stores with the awnings, the gift shops. And you know what? She don't like this place. She came in here one day, looked around, read the menu, and flounced out."

"What does she look like?"

"Shrink-wrapped. You know, sort of shiny." Melanie shook her head. "She don't like me. And you know what? The feeling is mutual."

"Well, hang in there, Melanie. Everybody loves your place." Then, as Hope bit into her sandwich, someone sat down beside her.

"Hey," said Jack Markey, turning to her at once, picking up the menu, "what's good to eat in this place?"

"Everything," Hope said, smiling at him and flourishing her sandwich. "I happen to be partial to liverwurst."

"Local girl?" said Jack, looking at her. "I'm a stranger

here myself. I'm out here working for Grandison Enterprises."

Hope couldn't help being intrigued by Jack's bright blue
eyes and curly yellow hair. And he looked old enough to
have done things, accomplished things, beyond the narrow
little world of Concord, Massachusetts. "Grandison Enterprises," she said, "what's that?"

"Oh, you know. Big development firm. We're doing a
feasibility study on some of the high school property out by
Route Two. Walden Green, that's what we want to call it.
Shopping mall, condos. You know."

Hope stared at him. She couldn't believe it. "But can you
do that? Have you got permits—you know, from the town
fathers?"

"Permits? Christ, no. Oh, the school committee says we
can do the study. I mean, of course we have to do the study
first. No point in trying to change the town zoning if the
soil won't perc."

"Perc?"

"If the percolation tests show that rainwater won't drain
away. Got to look into that before we even make an offer."

Hope put her sandwich down and began to laugh. She had
a hearty laugh, and the other people in the lunch room glanced
at her and smiled. "My father," she said, hardly able to
speak, "he'll have apoplexy. You should see him when he
drives past that intersection where the high school is. He
shakes his fist at the landfill. He curses that trailer park called
Pond View. Sometimes I think he's going to run down the
people crossing the road to the beach at Walden Pond."

"My God," said Jack, looking worried, "is your father a
member of town government around here?"

"Oh, no, just the reverse. If he's opposed to it, the town
boards will love it, I swear. But I'm surprised you're even
thinking of building over there. Listen, it isn't just my father.
A lot of people won't like the idea of changing the zoning
so close to Walden Pond."

"Walden Pond? Hey, you're the second person today who's brought that up. I know, you don't have to tell me. It's a book. I should have read it in school."

Hope was drawn to the healthy ignorance of this outlander. "What a nitwit," she said, grinning at him.

Jack looked at the way Hope's sunburned throat ran down into the neck of her shirt and wondered how much more of her had been exposed to the sun.

They sat companionably side by side on Melanie's stools, and before they finished their sandwiches they were exchanging phone numbers. Before they began eating their lemon meringue pie Hope was promising to help Jack Markey persuade the town boards to accept Jefferson Grandison's development project, the mixed-use complex to be called Walden Green.

For Jack it was a stroke of luck, a bonanza, free of charge this time, unlike the costly expertise he was hiring from Mimi Pink.

For Hope it was an excitement charged with guilt. She saw herself with perfect clarity. She knew what she was doing. She was agreeing to be an informer, a spy in the camp of this new enemy of her father's, an enemy he didn't even know existed.

"I'm just so sick of it all," she told Jack. "I don't care if I never again in all my life hear the name of Henry David Thoreau."

9

What if you or I be dead! God is alive still.
Journal, March 13, 1842

Julian Snow stared down at the body of his wife. When Homer spoke to him, Julian looked up, and Homer saw in the pale irises of his eyes the reflection of the moving treetops like landscapes rushing away. One of the men put his arm around Julian's shoulders.

There were murmured introductions. "My name's Homer Kelly," said Homer. "I was bird-watching down there at Goose Pond." He looked questioningly at Ananda.

Ananda raised his eyebrows, feeling too insignificant to be a person at all. "Ananda Singh," he whispered, and Homer noted the name in his mind. It sounded familiar to him, but probably thousands of young men in India were called Ananda Singh.

"The police," said Stu LaDue again. "Why don't somebody call the police?"

"We don't need the police," said Norman Peck sorrowfully. "She fell, that's all. She fell down the steps."

"She shouldn't have got out of bed," said Honey Mooney. "I told her, over and over, I told her she should stay in bed."

"Let's take her inside," said Homer softly.

Alice Snow was too heavy to be carried by one person. Julian Snow picked up his wife's shoulders, and Ananda grasped her by the ankles.

"Wait," said Homer. "Back up." Bending over the metal steps, he looked at the treads, examining them swiftly for splashes of red, for clots of blood and hair. He could see none, but he took off his jacket and draped it over the side of the steps where Alice's body had fallen. Then he snatched up a folding lawn chair and set it over the bloody patch of concrete where her head had lain. "All right," he said softly, "you can go in now."

Alice's friends pressed forward. Homer shook his head. "I think you people better wait outside."

Stuart LaDue was incensed. "What right have you got to tell us what to do?"

Homer pulled out his wallet and removed the worn card that had once identified him as a lieutenant detective in the office of the district attorney for Middlesex County. He flaunted it in front of Stu LaDue. His thumb was well accustomed to covering up the date.

Stu was mollified. But Honey Mooney wasn't about to be put off. "I was Alice's best friend," she said firmly. Pushing in front of Homer, she bustled up the steps after Julian and Ananda and followed them along the narrow corridor as they struggled to carry the body into the bedroom.

Alice Snow weighed nearly two hundred pounds. Sweat poured down Julian's face and Ananda gasped with effort as they lugged her to the bed. Honey ducked ahead of them to straighten the tumble of flowered sheets and ruffled pillows. Breathing hard, they laid Alice down. At once Honey tugged the puffy comforter over her head.

They had all seen it in the movies, the pronouncement of death with a white sheet pulled slowly over the face. Homer glanced at Julian Snow. Julian looked drawn but expressionless. For the thousandth time Homer wondered why husbands and wives were often so ill matched. This skinny man in the plaid shirt and jeans was completely at odds with his cluttered setting. It was as though a stork had settled down with a bird of paradise. The place was flouncy with cushions and doilies, jumbled with pictures and ornaments and statuettes, fuzzy with afghans. On the wall a doll held a basket of plastic flowers. There seemed no place for Julian Snow in his wife's plush-lined nest.

Dumbly they moved back along the hall to the living room, which doubled as a kitchen. Ananda Singh paused at the outside door and nodded to Homer in farewell.

"Wait," said Homer. "Don't go."

"Oh," said Ananda. "Well, I'll just get my suitcase." Carefully he walked down the steps, retrieved the suitcase from the grass, and brought it inside.

On the little lawn around Julian Snow's mobile home, Shirley Mills, Mavis and Bernie Buonfesto and Norman Peck had been joined by Dot and Scottie Ryan, Eugene Beaver, Porter McAdoo and Madeline Raymond. They all looked up sorrowfully at Homer as he grasped the handle to close the door. "Sorry," he said, pulling it shut.

Honey Mooney and Julian Snow were looking expectantly at Homer, too. He sighed. Why did everybody always put him in charge? Because he was bigger and taller by a foot or two? It wasn't a good enough reason. Homer cleared his throat and began. "Down there at Goose Pond I heard a woman's cry. It seemed to be coming from up here. It wasn't a scream exactly. It must have been Mrs. Snow. And then I think I saw someone hurrying away. Did you hear anything, or see anything like that, either of you?" Homer looked at Honey Mooney and Ananda Singh. "Did you see anyone nearby?"

Honey looked blank. Ananda spoke up. "I heard it, the cry. And I too saw a movement in the bushes." He wanted to say he had been reminded of elephants, but he knew it would sound absurd.

At that moment the door burst open. Stu LaDue slammed it behind him, pushed past Ananda, and marched importantly into the middle of the room. "Hey, look at this," he said loudly, holding up a piece of paper and glaring at Julian Snow. "I found it on the front seat of his truck. It's a love letter from a married woman. I saw her give it to him. It's from Charlotte Harris, a married woman, right here in Pond View."

Julian recognized Charlotte's letter at once, and he woke from his stupor. "That's mine," he said, reaching out a long arm.

But Stu gave it to Homer, who took it reluctantly, recognizing it for the bombshell it was. For a moment he struggled with his sympathy for the grieving husband on the one hand and his curiosity on the other, but by the time he had decided not to read it, he already had.

It was profoundly personal. Homer winced, and held the letter out to Julian Snow. But Stu wasn't going to allow this sensational opportunity to pass. Snatching the letter back, he cleared his throat and read it aloud:

Dear Julian, I want to say three things.
1. I've been unhappy as Pete's wife my whole married life.
2. Getting a divorce is awful. You know, such a mess.
3. I wouldn't ever do it unless I thought you'd marry me someday.
If you think this is silly, forget it. I'd rather keep on with Pete. This isn't a big deal. It's just that I've always loved you.

Charlotte

The words crashed painfully among them. Ananda turned away, ashamed to be hearing what had not been meant for his ears. Honey Mooney's eyes were enormous. Julian stared at the table, his face scarlet.

Homer felt sorry for him. Reaching out, he plucked the letter from Stu's fingers.

"So there's your motive," said Stu malevolently. "Julian pushed his wife downstairs so he could marry Charlotte. Her husband, Pete, he's gonna be next."

"But Mr. Snow was not here," said Ananda, eager to

refute this accusation by the mean little man in the thick glasses. "He was somewhere else in his lorry."

"But maybe he was just parked somewhere," said Stu, "and then he ran back to his truck and drove here like he'd been someplace else all the time."

"Where were you, Mr. Snow?" said Homer.

Julian made a feeble gesture in the direction of Concord center. "I was doing errands. Alice wanted some yarn."

"You had a bag in your hand," said Homer, remembering. "You must have left it outside. Would they remember you, where you bought the yarn?"

Julian stared at him. "Store's gone. Dime store's gone. The bag is ice cream. Alice, she wanted some ice cream."

"Ice cream?" said Homer. Then Honey Mooney nipped outside and hurried back with the sopping bag. Before Homer could caution her, she pulled out the sticky quart container and popped it in the freezing compartment of Julian's refrigerator.

"Where did you buy the ice cream?" said Homer.

"Star Market," murmured Julian.

Homer was fascinated. "Well, you couldn't very well have been committing a crime and executing a complicated maneuver of deception, not with a quart of melting ice cream on your hands." He looked around, beaming.

"I know where he could've got the ice cream," said Stu evilly. "From Charlotte's icebox, that's where he could've got it."

Homer's face fell. Stuart LaDue was a foul specimen of humankind, but of course he was right. The ice cream could have come from any of the refrigerators right here at Pond View. "A receipt," he said. "Have you got a receipt from the Star Market?"

Julian shook his head. "I always throw those things away."

Stu snorted, then turned his venom on Ananda Singh. "This kid, what's he doing here, anyhow? He saw his chance, sick old lady, lots of stuff he could rip off."

Homer glanced sympathetically at Ananda's startled face, then turned to Julian Snow. "Did you have anything valuable that someone might have wanted to steal? Is anything missing?"

Julian looked at him blankly, and then he moved across the room and climbed up on the built-in bench under the little bay window. Reaching up, he took down a small metal file box from the shelf over the window. Getting down again, he flipped open the lid of the box, then set it down heavily on the table.

The box was empty. "It was all my savings," said Julian, his voice choked. "Two thousand dollars. Somebody must have taken it."

"Look in the kid's suitcase," bawled Stu. "He was here, he helped himself, I bet."

Ananda couldn't believe what was happening. The nightmare was getting worse. The United States was a terrible place. Humbly he picked up the suitcase. The handle was strung with tags from Heathrow and Indira Gandhi airport, and on the lid Ananda had attached a couple of vainglorious stickers from the University of London and New Hall College, Cambridge.

He lifted out the contents and dumped them on the table. There were white muslin shirts of a long Indian cut, a cheap-looking cotton suit, some gray underwear, a pair of denim jeans, a framed picture of his sister, and a paperback book.

Homer's eyes fastened on the book. "Ah," he said, recognizing *The Heart of Thoreau's Journals*.

Then Ananda groped in the elastic pocket of the suitcase and pulled out something else, a thin folder of blue plastic. "The money from my traveler's checks," he said, explaining. "I cashed them at the airport this morning. I bought them just yesterday, or perhaps it was the day before, at the Bank of India in New Delhi."

"You cashed all of them at the airport?" said Homer. "How much was it?"

"Thirty-six thousand rupees. I forget how much that is in your money."

"Count it," said Stu LaDue. "Go ahead, count it."

Silently Homer counted the hundreds and twenties in the folder. "It comes to two thousand and twenty dollars," he said uncomfortably.

"What'd I tell you!" cried Stu in triumph. "He was here, he took Julian's cash money."

"But I have the receipts, the whole list." Ananda pulled an Air India envelope out of his pocket. "I have just come from New Delhi. I came because of the book *Walden*."

"Bullshit." Stu looked at Homer angrily. "You going to call the police or ain't you going to call the police?"

"Rest assured, I'll take care of it," said Homer ambiguously. "Look here," he said, suddenly brisk, pushing Honey and Stu toward the door, "I'm sure Mr. Snow needs a little peace and quiet."

In a moment he had them all outside. Ananda put his suitcase on the ground and stuffed his belongings back into it.

"Wait for me," said Homer to Ananda, and then he turned to Julian, who was standing silently in the doorway. "Goodbye, Mr. Snow. I'll talk to Chief Flower in the police department. Would you like me to ask Mr. Pettigrew to come for her? People around here mostly use Mr. Pettigrew. He'll take care of her until she's turned over to the medical examiner."

"The medical examiner?" Julian looked bewildered.

"In a case like this, when the cause of death isn't certain, there has to be an examination by a pathologist." Homer reached up his hand.

Julian, who never did anything without thinking it over first, let a moment go by before taking it. "I see," he said. "Thank you."

The other residents of Pond View had vanished, except for Norman Peck, who still lingered by the steps. "Julian?" he said.

"Come on in," said Julian gruffly.

The door closed. Homer, turning away, could hear the gasping sobs of someone who apparently had no experience in crying.

"Listen here," said Homer, turning to Ananda, "where are you staying?"

Ananda misinterpreted the question. "Ah, you will want to keep track of me." He shrugged. "I don't know. I must find a place."

Homer was amused. "Is it true you came straight to Concord from the airport to see Walden Pond?"

"Yes," said Ananda with melancholy dignity. "I came to this country to see the place of Henry Thoreau."

Homer threw back his head with a shout of laughter, then covered his mouth, remembering the bereaved husband nearby. He clapped Ananda on the back. "Good Lord, do you know what I was doing before all this happened? I was down there at Goose Pond, hoping to hear a wood thrush. You know, Thoreau's famous wood thrush."

" 'He sings to amend our institutions,' " recited Ananda, his face brightening in a brilliant smile.

" 'He sings to amend our institutions,' " repeated Homer in ecstasy. "Right, right. That's what he does." He took Ananda by his thin shoulders and bounced him up and down. "Listen, you can stay with us. Oh, I've got so much to show you. Forget Walden Pond. Wait till you see the river. Wait till I show you—listen here, don't move. I've got to talk to that woman Charlotte Harris." He looked around. "Now where does she live?"

Homer ambled along the driveway. Almost at once he ran into Honey Mooney, who had been lurking beside her own mobile home, a large Roycraft with pale green shutters. "Oh, Mrs. Mooney," said Homer politely, "can you tell me which is Mrs. Harris's home?"

Honey pointed, and then she came forward a few steps and said in a loud whisper, "She was there this morning."

"She? You mean Mrs. Harris? Where was she?"

"With Alice Snow. She was there before it happened. I saw her knock on the door and go inside."

"Did you see her come out?"

"No." Honey pursed her lips sanctimoniously. "I have better things to do than spy on my neighbors."

The mobile home belonging to Charlotte and Pete Harris was at the other end of Pond View, right next to Route 126. It was surrounded by a garden of bright flowers. They were ordinary annuals, just beginning to bloom in the June sun, but Homer could see that the colors had been chosen with care.

He knocked, and the door was opened at once, as though Charlotte had been expecting him. She was an angular woman with fading red hair and an anxious face as freckled as a child's. He remembered seeing her before. She had run up to them as they were gathered around the body of Alice Snow, and then she had turned and hurried away again.

The interior of her house was different from the over-crowded stuffiness of the mobile home inhabited by Alice and Julian Snow. It had a shipshape feeling, like the cabin of a seagoing vessel. There was a bookcase on the wall, and it had real literature in it, Homer decided, giving it a swift glance. Thomas Hardy was there, and Willa Cather.

Charlotte looked at her visitor with dread. Something awful was about to happen, she could feel it.

Homer wasted no time in producing the awful thing. He took Charlotte's letter out of his pocket. "Can you tell me when you wrote this?"

Charlotte dropped onto a chair and put her face in her hands. "Oh, I'm so ashamed." She lowered her hands and looked at him in anguish. Her cheeks were flaming. "Julian showed it to you?"

"No. Stuart LaDue found it in that truck of Julian's."

Charlotte closed her eyes and shook her head slightly. "Stuart! Then everyone will know. My husband—"

"I'll speak to Mr. LaDue," said Homer grimly.

"Oh, I've been such a fool."

"You wrote the letter recently?"

"Yes, this morning. I don't know what came over me. I dashed off the letter, just getting something out of my system. But then I saw Julian in his truck, and I rushed out without thinking and tossed it in the window. Afterward I was sorry." Charlotte stood up, too tormented to sit still.

"Honey Mooney tells me you visited Alice Snow this morning," said Homer softly, as though he were merely making conversation.

"Yes. I was feeling so horrible at what I'd done." Charlotte gazed miserably at the letter in Homer's hand. "In that letter I said it wasn't a big deal. Well, it was a big deal. It was the kind of thing that could be very destructive, I saw that at once. I was in despair." Charlotte clutched her arms against her breast and began walking up and down the narrow room. "I brought Alice some flowers. I didn't stay long. She was in bed watching television and I felt in the way, so I just put the flowers in water and said good-bye."

"You saw no one else? Alice Snow seemed perfectly well? What time was it?"

"I don't know. It was only about ten minutes after that when Honey came running up the driveway, shouting that Alice was dead."

Homer stood up and handed her the letter. "Here. It's nobody else's business." He went to the door. "I'll go talk to Mr. LaDue. Where does he live?"

"Right across the way." Charlotte looked at Homer soberly. "Thank you," she said with formal dignity.

From her window she watched Homer walk across the driveway and knock on Stu LaDue's door. Then she went quickly to her desk and cut her terrible letter into small pieces with a pair of scissors.

As the pieces fluttered from her fingers into the wastebasket, she tried not to think of Julian, who was all alone now, as though in answer to her dangerous desire. And she tried not to think of Pete, but he loomed very large in her mind, overwhelming in his obesity, in his rude good health, in the monotony of his dullness. The last scrap of paper sifted from her fingers, and she turned away abruptly. She mustn't think such things. She mustn't think them ever again.

Across the driveway in the mobile home belonging to Stuart LaDue, Homer was a different man from the one who had interviewed Charlotte Harris. He towered over Stu, he loomed. A few minutes later he left him cowed and subdued, swearing to say nothing about Charlotte's letter to Julian Snow.

Then Homer went off to entreat Honey Mooney to keep quiet about it, too. If the police interviewed her, well and good, she was to tell the truth. But there was no point in embarrassing Mrs. Harris unless it was absolutely necessary.

Stu LaDue watched Homer Kelly come out of Honey's house and walk back down the drive to where the foreign kid was lying asleep on the grass. Stu snickered to himself. Oh, so he wasn't supposed to tell on Charlotte Harris? Well, what if he'd already blabbed it to one or two people? Jesus, it was a free country. A filthy thing like that, what the hell, people had a right to know what was going on under their noses. That stuck-up Charlotte Harris, everybody thought she was so fine, but, Christ, she was just another scheming woman, a fucking home wrecker, maybe even a murderer, so, Jesus, what the hell?

10

*We check and repress the divinity that stirs within
us, to fall down and worship the divinity that is
dead without us.*
Journal, November 16, 1851

The unctuous voice was back on the line. "Good morning,
Mr. Grandison, sir. How are you this morning?"

Jefferson Grandison bared his teeth. What right did this
interfering fool have to ask him how he was? "I am in good
health."

"Good! What I was calling about, Mr. Grandison, sir, I
was calling to ask if you could tell us when you will be
taking Lot Seventeen off our hands. I mean, when they
stopped burning these things down in Connecticut because
of the smell and the air pollution, we relied on you to fulfill
your contract, because you said you'd take away anything and
dispose of it, right? Anything, you said. And you said it
would be soon."

"I will be calling shortly to announce a date."

"Thank you, Mr. Grandison, sir. That's all we ask. Thank
you so very much, sir. Good-bye, sir."

Grandison put the receiver down softly. "Idiot," he said,
enraged.

Jack Markey laughed. "Lot Seventeen?"

"Look here," said Grandison, summoning Jack to the map
table, "this is the only place." He pointed. "It makes perfect
sense. I mean, look at it. It's right next to the landfill. We
dig a pit, a deep pit."

"Right you are."

"So keep working on it."

"I am. Oh, I am."

"Those other people out there in Concord, they're doing what they can?"

"Oh, you bet. Don't worry about it."

"Well, let's get on with the other thing." Together they bowed over the assessors' map, quadrant H16 of the town of Concord, Massachusetts, and after that Jack displayed his preliminary sketches of Walden Green. "Good," said Grandison, well pleased. "But this part of the complex doesn't look right to me. Look at this access road, the grade's too steep." Stretching out his arm over the map, Jefferson Grandison separated the light from the darkness. He had never actually set foot in Concord, Massachusetts, and Jack sometimes wondered about his intense interest in the town. Whimsically it occurred to him that a man like Grandison didn't actually have to appear on the scene in person. After all, wasn't he universally omnipresent at every moment at every point in the universe? All he had to do was dispatch someone like Jack to take his place on the spot, to carry out his will as a local avatar of the deity.

So Jack went back and forth between Concord and the glassy high rise on Huntington Avenue, riding up and down in the glass elevator, zooming up into the sky and plunging earthward again as if on wings. Sometimes he couldn't believe his own good fortune. Why had Grandison chosen him as his confidant and principal assistant?

His rise had been so rapid! Jack had begun at Grandison Enterprises as a mere draftsman, but soon he was designing bathrooms and closets, and before long he was a full-fledged architect of suburban malls and urban high rises, and finally he had become a senior planner, privileged to sit at a huge table with the others at meetings attended by Grandison himself. And at last he had been plucked from all the rest to sit at Grandison's right hand. How on earth had it happened?

The truth was beyond Jack's power of guessing. At the planning meetings around the big table, Jefferson Grandison had noticed a certain audacity and brashness in the good-looking kid whose name was Markey. The boy had a way of running a bold finger across the plan of a shopping mall and saying, "Scrap it. Turn all the units the other way." Or he would suggest something crazy—"Why not put it in the water? Build it on pilings, the whole thing, with islands and bridges and catwalks"—and everybody would gasp and laugh and say, "Why not?"

There was something in Jack Markey's eye that Grandison was drawn to, a certain wildness, as though he had been brought up by wolves in the forest.

Actually Jack had been reared in a respectable working-class household as the son of a fundamentalist minister. Respectable was certainly the right word for the Markeys of Chester, Pennsylvania, but there had been wildness there as well, a boisterous delirium that came straight from the last book of the Bible.

The book of Revelation had been the holy of holies to Jack's father. Its intoxicating prophecies had enlivened all his sermons with a savage vitality. Little Jack had grown up with them. The passionate phrases were as normal to his life as sofa cushions, the Mother of Harlots was as comfortable as Mother Goose, the wild poetry of the blood from the winepress no more shocking than the pail of water fetched by Jack and Jill.

As a pudgy little child Jack had been precocious, a quick learner. He had stood on a table at the front of the church in his tiny white suit, and the mad verses had come out of his innocent mouth, and everyone had smiled and clapped and praised him.

It couldn't last, his acceptance of the world he had been born into. In adulthood he had come to his senses, he had repudiated church, mother, father, Bible, and his own little white-suited self.

And yet that childhood had branded him. Perhaps the odd fervor that Grandison saw in Jack's eyes was a light put there by the falling stars of the Apocalypse, and the star called

Wormwood, and the scorching fire. Jack's logical adult mind had long since put aside the stars and the fire and the beast that spake as a dragon and the terrifying horsemen, but they were engraved on his collarbone and his elbow. They were coiled within liver and spleen.

Now, working for Jefferson Grandison, riding up in the glass elevator to the seventieth floor, Jack Markey couldn't help seeing the door that was opened in heaven, he couldn't help hearing the voice of a trumpet talking, which said, "Come up hither, and I will show thee things which must be hereafter."

And whenever he rode down again and walked once more on the lowly ground where others walked, whenever he saw someone like the bag lady in the doorway of the Grandison Building, Jack remembered the bottomless chasm and the smoke rising out of the pit, "as the smoke of a great furnace. And there came out of the smoke locusts upon the earth."

11

ADVANCE TOKEN TO NEAREST UTILITY.
IF UNOWNED YOU MAY BUY IT FROM THE BANK.
Chance card, Monopoly

The little world of Mimi Pink was very different from the powers and principalities of the seventieth floor of the Grandison Building. Instead of an immense landscape spreading to the horizon, Mimi's universe was a miniature playing board.

The commanding myth of Mimi's childhood had not come from the Bible. Her own girlish obsession had been the game of Monopoly, that great right-angled odyssey, that pilgrim's progress to the celestial city of Park Place and Boardwalk. For Mimi the journey out of Egypt to the promised land of Go (COLLECT $200) had been fabulous enough. Her wandering fortunes had been subject to chance bolts of fate, sometimes a shattering blow—*YOU ARE ASSESSED FOR STREET REPAIRS*—and sometimes a glorious windfall—*BANK ERROR IN YOUR FAVOR.* Her business career was a reliving of those summer days of long ago, those endless afternoons with her sister, Lee-Ann, and the kids from the neighborhood, Annie Finney and Buzzie. But today's game was happier. Mimi was winning. In the awful days of her childhood she had never won. Her sister had won, Buzzie had won, but never Annie Finney and never, never Mimi.

"Boardwalk," shrieked Lee-Ann, "you landed on Boardwalk. That's mine. You owe me a thousand dollars." And Lee-Ann screeched with gloating laughter and snatched at Mimi's yellow hundred-dollar bills.

"I hate you, I hate you!" screamed Mimi. She couldn't stand

53

*it: she picked up the Monopoly board and threw it at her sister.
Little green houses and red plastic hotels were scattered all over
the floor.*

"Stop it, you dumb kid, stop it," cried Buzzie.

"Oh, Mimi, no," cried Annie Finney.

*But Lee-Ann was still laughing at Mimi, still taunting her
sister. "You're ugly and fat and dumb. You'll never win. You're
just too dumb."*

*So what could Mimi do? Sobbing, she threw herself at Lee-
Ann and shoved her hard and made her fall down, and then
Lee-Ann shrieked and jumped up and clawed at Mimi, and
Annie tried to help, and Buzzie dragged them apart, and then
Mimi's mother came running in and sent Annie and Buzzie
home, and Lee-Ann wept pitifully and blamed Mimi, and Mimi
couldn't explain her rage and frustration, so her mother slapped
her and sent her bawling to her room and took her little honey-
child to the movies.*

*Next time they played the game, Buzzie cheated, and he won,
and Mimi got mad again, and he jeered at her, and so did Lee-
Ann, and after that it was Lee-Ann's turn to win, and Mimi
cried and cried, but it never did any good because Lee-Ann and
Buzzie always won, and when Lee-Ann grew up she got in the
movies because she was a whole lot cuter than Mimi.*

But now Lee-Ann wasn't working in films anymore. She
had lost her looks and her money. She had married some
old fart, and she was a nobody now, just a nobody. She had
come crawling for help to Mimi.

Mimi had married, too, but she soon discovered her mistake and shucked Dickie Pink. Now there was nobody to
slow her down as she surged out of the sleazy back lots of
the Monopoly board, throwing the dice and throwing the
dice, working her way tirelessly in the direction of Boardwalk
and Park Place. Mimi was a hell of a businesswoman, that
was what everybody said.

In Concord she had begun with the cheap down-market

purple properties, the Mediterranean and Baltic avenues of the town, and then she had gone on to acquire the middle-market parcels, the plum-colored St. Charles Places of Concord and the orange Tennessee Avenues. Now she hungered for Pennsylvania and North Carolina and Pacific avenues, those choice green pieces of real estate that Mimi identified with the Milldam, the up-market commercial section of Main Street.

And now there was the exciting prospect opened up by Jack Markey, the new shopping center he wanted to build across Route 2 from Walden Pond. That would be the final Eldorado, Mimi's true Park Place and Boardwalk.

She had certainly chosen the right town at the right time. She had selected Concord only after shrewd investigation of a number of suburban centers west of Boston. The place had seemed so unspoiled. It didn't occur to Mimi that she herself might spoil it, that her proprietary takeover was an invasion like that of some shrieking horde of barbarians galloping down on the huddled village, burning, raping, and pillaging. No indeed. She was intensely proud of her transformation of Walden Street and Main. She prided herself on the new look she was giving to the town.

Others were not so sure. People complained that they couldn't get anything useful in Concord anymore. They couldn't buy a yard of fabric or a book or a pair of shoes or a set of pillowcases, they couldn't find any of the necessities once supplied by the dime store—a length of ribbon, a bag of potting soil, a pancake turner, a skein of embroidery thread, a set of jelly jars, a plastic bag of goldfish, a pair of cotton panties.

Therefore it was not the local citizenry who frequented Concord center. It was wealthy women from suburban towns like Weston and Newton and Wellesley. They strolled along the Milldam in pairs, looking sharply left and right for something to want. They didn't really need anything. They were well fed, well housed, and well clothed. But they had a gnawing inside them, a longing to buy something. Their pocketbooks trembled with eagerness, their checkbooks were at the ready, to pay for a brocaded fireplace fan, a Toby jug, a pillow embroidered with chickadees—something, anything they could bring home in a smart shopping bag puffy with tissue paper.

Mimi's stores were doing well. They were just what these women wanted.

But Mimi wasn't satisfied. Among the shops there were holdouts, merchants who were stubborn, who failed to see the handwriting on the wall. That pathetic little lunch room, for instance. Unfortunately there was nothing Mimi could do about the hardware store, because the proprietor owned the building and refused to sell. The Cape Verdean barber owned his place, too. He, too, was being stubborn. But Mimi was determined to win him over, to make him give up. His grubby establishment was a blot on the landscape. She had to do something about it.

On the day of Alice Snow's death at Pond View, Mimi walked boldly into the barbershop to try again.

There wasn't a single customer in either of the old-fashioned barber chairs. Alphonso Domingo was occupying one of them, reading the paper. Mimi knew that his only patrons were old geezers who had been coming to him for years. Alphonso didn't even notice the new haircutting fashions. Younger men had to go elsewhere to be properly styled.

Wrinkling her nose at the smell of cheap hair tonic, Mimi made Alphonso another offer, half again bigger than the first.

Once again he refused. It was a lot of money, he agreed, but no sale. "If I retire, what do I get? My wife, twenty-four hours a day. Don't get me wrong, she's a fine woman, but, holy Jesus, twenty-four hours a day?"

Well, Mimi had failed again. But she would keep at it. Alphonso Domingo's barbershop had to go. Sooner or later she would find a way.

Angrily she walked out and strode around the corner to

the Den of Teddies. It was a good place to find comfort. The shelves were lined with cuddly animals, puppy dogs with pink felt tongues, kittens with green glass eyes, pigs with curly tails.

"I adore this shop, don't you?" said Mimi, confiding in the new girl she had hired as resident zookeeper.

"Well, it's okay," said the girl, "but subtibes the fuzz gets up by doze. I thigk I'b allergic." She sneezed and blew her nose, then sneezed again.

"Try not to do that in front of the customers," said Mimi severely. "Why don't you take care of your health problems in the office? Here, I'll take over for a while."

And then while the new girl was in the back room, Mimi sold a stuffed bunny to a shopper for forty-nine dollars and fifty cents. "For your grandchild?" said Mimi, stroking the bunny's furry back and squeezing it to make it squeak. Its glass eyes were pink, just like the eyes of the animal from which its white fur had been flayed.

"Oh, no, I want it for myself, it's so adorable." The customer held the bunny against her cheek and giggled. "I'm just a great big overgrown baby."

"Oh, look," said Ananda Singh, getting out of Homer's car in the driveway beside the house on Fair Haven Bay.

A rabbit was darting into the woods, bounding lopsided, showing its white tail.

"Did you see?" said Homer. "It's lost a leg." He led Ananda up the porch steps. "Foxes get them. And we've had an outbreak of coyotes lately."

They found Mary in the study, and Homer introduced Ananda. "Look what I found on my trip to Goose Pond, better than a wood thrush any day. Meet Ananda K. Singh, world traveler, disciple of Henry Thoreau, worshiper at the shrine of the transcendent in nature, devotee of beauty, justice, and truth."

"Well, how do you do, Ananda K. Singh," said Mary,

getting up and shaking his hand. "Worshipers and disciples are always welcome in this house. Devotees, too. Make yourself at home."

Back at the Den of Teddies, Mimi Pink took another white bunny out of a box in the storeroom and set it on the shelf, where it peered at her blankly with its pink glass eyes, assuring her that beauty, justice, and truth were hard to come by, but cuddliness was available any moment of the day.

12

Death is that expressive pause in the music of the blast.
Journal, December 29, 1841

Turning to the obituary page of the *Concord Journal*, Roger Bland read about the death of Alice Snow:

Mrs. Alice Snow, a resident of Pond View Trailer Park, died unexpectedly on June 12. She was 59. Mrs. Snow was born in Springfield. She leaves her husband, Julian, and her sister, Delphine, of Los Angeles.

Roger Bland was the chairperson of the Concord Planning Board. He was delighted, on the whole, to learn of the passing of one more of the occupants of the trailers at Pond View. Looking up from the paper at the view of the Concord River beyond his living room window, he caught himself wishing the rest of those old folks would die a little faster. Then he put the paper down, ashamed of himself.

Of course he wouldn't dream of wishing death on any of those old codgers. But he longed for the day—and it would come sooner or later—when the last of the mobile homes would be hauled away. They were eyesores. Jackhammers would reduce their concrete slabs to rubble, the septic tanks would be dug out, the power lines removed, the water pipes disconnected. Then at last the whole place would be plowed up and native trees would be planted and the site would be decent once again. No more Pond View. All of those old geezers would be dead or in nursing homes.

How many of them were left? Roger didn't know. He meant to find out.

On Saturday evening on the way to a Pops concert at Symphony Hall with his wife Marjorie, Roger took a detour to the park and pulled into the driveway. Beside the first trailer a woman was mowing her lawn with an old-fashioned machine, *clickety-clack*.

Roger leaned out the car window and spoke up loudly. "How do you do? My name is Bland. I'm a member of the Concord Planning Board. I just want to say on behalf of the town how sorry we are about the passing of Mrs. Snow."

The woman with the lawn mower was Charlotte Harris. She stopped mowing and looked at him blankly. Then she pointed down the driveway. "Perhaps you should say that to her husband. He lives down at the end." Charlotte turned back to her lawn mower. The clickety-clacks began again.

Roger had no interest in confronting the bereaved husband. All he wanted was an answer to a simple question.

There was an awkward pause. Marjorie Bland came to the rescue. Marjorie often sensed the need to say something, to fill embarrassing gaps with smoothing-over words, covering-up words, nice words. Niceness was Marjorie's stock in trade. Leaning across Roger, she said sweetly, "We're so sorry."

Charlotte went right on mowing her lawn.

Roger adopted a tone of good fellowship. "I remember," he called to Charlotte's back, "when there were dozens of mobile homes in the park. It's sad to see so few of them still here. How many . . . ah, residents are left, I wonder?"

Charlotte gave him a level look. "Fourteen," she said, swooping her lawn mower around and pushing it the other way.

"Only fourteen," breathed Roger, congratulating himself. Leaning out again, he said, "Please convey our sincerest sympathy to Mr. Snow," and backed his car out of Pond View.

13

*The twelve labors of Hercules were trifling in
comparison with those which my neighbors have
undertaken. . . .*
Walden, "Economy"

Julian Snow's two-week vacation was over. He was back at
work at the landfill next to Pond View. His boss at Public
Works had offered to extend his leave, but Julian said no.
"I guess it takes his mind off his loss," said the boss.

So all day long in the mid-June heat, Julian sweltered in
the cab of his big machine, sitting sideways, hurling his two
mighty rollers at the heaped-up mounds of trash, driving
them ahead of him. Plastic bags billowed and tumbled. The
huge teeth of the rollers burst the thin coverings and crushed
them flat. Flotsam and jetsam sailed through the air. A folder
from Saint Bernard's Catholic Church floated into the open
window of the cab and landed in Julian's lap. "FIRST FRI-
DAY," it read, "MEDITATION AND PRAYER FOR THE SANC-
TITY OF LIFE." A pizza box thudded against the windshield,
and Julian could plainly read the penciled word *Pepperoni* on
the cover before the box fell away. Craning his neck left,
then right, he backed and filled while the householders of
Concord drove their cars up to the working face and threw
out their accumulations of rubbish.

In the crawl dozer Eddie Tanner sped toward Julian with
a bucketload of dirt raised high in the air. Sandy dust foamed
around them. The air conditioner in the cab had stopped
working two years ago. Sweat poured down Julian's face.
The back of his shirt was soaked. The two massive machines
made a tremendous throbbing racket as they came together.
Eddie dumped his dirt on the flattened trash and raced away
for more.

After lunch Eddie and Julian changed jobs. Now it was Julian's turn to cover the trash with dirt excavated from the cliff face beside the landfill. It was a state law; everything had to be covered by nightfall. The Concord dump was a model landfill, operated strictly according to the rules laid down by the commonwealth. Deep down under the excavation a lining of clay prevented the contamination of groundwater. Effluent was pumped out every day.

Julian took pride in the way the place worked. Sometimes, it was true, he imagined old Henry Thoreau standing in the line of trees beside the convenience area, looking out over the dumpsters full of newspapers and glass. But then he told himself that Henry Thoreau was dead and gone, while here he was, Julian Snow, doing the best he damn well could to keep the place clean.

So he went home with a good conscience, as the sun disappeared behind the white pines in a transport of pink-and-orange cloud. Entering his mobile home, he was aware that his stomach muscles were not tightening with apprehension the way they usually did at this hour. Tonight there

would be no asphyxiating fog of talk, no whimsical demands, no blare of television game shows.

He took a shower, and then in blessed silence he made himself a pan of fried potatoes. After supper he got to work clearing out Alice's stuff. He took down the ruffled curtains, he stuffed her flowered pillows into paper bags, he removed the picture of Willard Scott. He lifted off its hook the thing he detested most, the doll basket with its wicker skirt full of plastic flowers.

Without the pillows and curtains, without Alice's giddy afghans and sentimental pictures, the living spaces were bigger and dirtier. The rosy dusk of the summer solstice filled the trailer with warm light. Julian sat down at the kitchen table and looked around with satisfaction. Then he exclaimed and leaped to his feet, catching sight of a young man staring at him from the next room. But it was only Julian's reflection. The fluffy curtains no longer hid the mirror.

He stared at himself as if at a stranger. He didn't really look all that young. It was just that his stoop was gone. He was sitting more erect.

But when Julian crawled into bed, he missed Alice. At bedtime her motor had always run down. In the dark she stopped talking at last and lay quietly in his arms. Without her, the bed was too wide, too empty. Julian tried lying in the middle, spreading out his arms and legs, but he soon moved over again to his own side, missing his wife.

Next day after work Julian distributed Alice's stuff. Shirley Mills took the comforter. Mavis Buonfesto got the pillows. Honey Mooney was delighted with the ruffled curtains. Since Honey had been so especially kind since Alice's death, Julian asked her to pick out anything else she would like. At once she chose the doll basket. "I've always loved it," she said.

Honey lived alone in the mobile home next to Julian's. She was a widow, one of the youngest residents of the park. Her trailer was fixed up in a style very much like Alice

Snow's, so the ruffly curtains fitted right in. She found a
place for the doll basket right next to the telephone on the
wall beside the door. The plastic flowers in the wicker skirt
looked dusty, so Honey plucked them out and threw them
away. Something else came out with the last of the flowers
—a hundred-dollar bill.

"Oh," said Honey, snatching it. At once she looked in
the basket. It was stuffed with money. Pulling out all the
bills, she counted them and tucked them in her pocketbook.
The total came to sixteen hundred dollars.

Next day she blew the whole wad. She drove to Waltham
and bought an entertainment center. It was a multiunit set
with a twenty-seven-inch TV, a stereo, a radio, and a CD
player, all built into a piece of Spanish-style furniture.

Delivery was prompt. Somehow the two men in the truck
managed to wedge the bulky apparatus through Honey's door
and set it up in her living room. As soon as they left, Honey
turned on the television set. She was just in time for "The
Young and the Reckless."

Honey called Shirley and Mavis, and they came right over.
Sitting down comfortably in front of the entertainment center,
the three of them munched on Shirley's date-nut squares and
stared at Vanessa and Dirk, who filled the screen, twice life-
size.

"Oh, if only Alice could be here," said Mavis tearfully.

"Look," said Shirley, "Vanessa's pregnant. But her husband had a vasectomy, remember? Who do you suppose . . . ?"

Neither Mavis nor Shirley asked how Honey had acquired
the money for her new entertainment center. Honey herself
did not reveal that it was Alice Snow who had helped herself
to the family savings and hidden it all in the doll basket.
Nor did she explain that she had found the money and taken
it for herself.

As a matter of fact, Honey hardly bothered to remember
the source of her good fortune. Julian had given her the doll
basket. It belonged to her. She had found the money in it,

she had taken it, and she had spent it. And that was that.

And if anybody else at Pond View wondered how Honey Mooney could suddenly afford an expensive entertainment center, they never asked her about it. One didn't question a neighbor's extravagance.

14

*Perhaps on that spring morning when Adam and
Eve were driven out of Eden Walden Pond was
already in existence, and even then breaking up
in a gentle spring rain. . . .*
Walden, "The Ponds"

"But how can there be a dump beside Walden Pond?"
Ananda said innocently. "And a public beach? And a park
for caravans?"

"Oh, we get tired of our heroes in the United States," said
Homer dryly. "Granted, there was this man living in our
town who wrote the best American prose of the nineteenth
century, and it's true he was the founder of the conservation
movement, and he taught us how to live the good and simple
life, and he preached a pure religion without cant, and he
invented the idea of civil disobedience that would one day
free the people of India and bring a measure of equality to
American blacks, not to mention the fact that he was the
best surveyor for miles around and made the finest pencils
in the country—granted all those things, what do people say
about him? He was a crank, that's what they say. He stole
Mrs. Emerson's mince pies right off her windowsill."

"But surely they don't say those things here? Not right
here in Concord?"

"Especially in Concord."

Ananda shook his head sadly. "Alas, I know it to be true.
There was a man at the place called Pond View. He said
Thoreau was a drunk, and he had sex with women in his
cabin."

"There," said Homer, laughing. "You see?"

They were sitting on the front porch, looking out over
Fair Haven Bay. Below them the little slope dropped to the

spongy edge of the river. The water was high. Blue flags blossomed in the shallows amid a swarm of mayflies. Ananda jumped up as Mary came running out with a handful of knives and forks. "You must let me help," he said eagerly.

"It's just spaghetti." Mary looked at him curiously. "Can you cook?"

"Cook?" It had never occurred to Ananda that he might ever be asked such a question. "Alas, I fear——"

"That's all right. Here, you can throw these around the table." Mary disappeared, and Ananda fumbled with the cutlery while Homer went back to Thoreau.

"Of course it isn't everybody in town who thinks he was a careless hippie. There are a few of us enlightened souls. There's the Thoreau Lyceum, for one thing, and the Thoreau Society. And there's always Oliver Fry."

"Oliver Fry?" Clumsily Ananda arranged the knives and forks here and there. He remembered the statuesque girl at the railroad station and her angry father. "Does Mr. Fry have a daughter?"

"Hope Fry," said Mary, coming out on the porch with the plates. "A grand girl."

"True," said Homer, "but I don't know if her father is a blessing or a curse. The trouble is, Oliver feels things too strongly. He gets mad and polarizes things."

"But he has a true heart," said Mary stoutly, slapping down the plates.

Ananda followed her back into the kitchen, anxious to be of service. Left in charge of stirring the spaghetti sauce, he burned it, and before the evening was over he broke a wineglass. "Alas," he said while Mary squirted disinfectant on his cut finger, "I fear I am rather clumsy."

"You can't be any clumsier than my husband," said Mary comfortingly. "Tell me, is your bed comfortable? Is it what you're used to back home?"

"It is perfect," said Ananda. "But the rent you have suggested is not enough. I will find work, and then I will pay you more. This is the best place to live in all the world."

Mary looked at him shrewdly as he struggled with a Band-Aid. His clothes were wrinkled and oddly assorted, half western, half Indian. The boy was obviously an impoverished student. His money wouldn't last long. "No, no," she said, "you won't pay us a cent more."

Ananda Singh exclaimed and argued, but Mary was stubborn, and he went to bed without persuading her to raise his rent. It was true that his cash resources would not support him for long, but Ananda was not a poor student. His father was a wealthy sugar planter with thousands of acres of ancestral land in Himachal Pradesh in the high plains of northern India. Ananda's father was also a celebrated cabinet minister in New Delhi. But Ananda's compulsive flight to America had not had his parents' blessing.

"I will not pay for such a thing," his father had said, and Ananda had retorted politely, "Of course not. I shall pay my own way." And then he had shown his father his earnings as a clerk in a London shop.

Ananda's mother had been especially disappointed. Her eldest son was the apple of her eye, and she had in mind a list of clever Brahman girls of good family for him to choose among. They were all university women—a practicing physician in white coat and running shoes, a dietitian in sari and sandals, a social worker in gold bangles and *salwaar-kameez*. There would be a beautiful traditional wedding, with Ananda and his bride sitting together under the bridal canopy.

Instead her austere young son had set aside such things. He had never joined the others of his set at the Green Room in Simla, he had not strolled with the crowd at Scandal Point. "He has his nose in those books of his," his mother complained to his father.

It was true. From the very beginning when Ananda had been captivated by his grandmother's stories of Krishna and the milkmaids, he had been lost in stories. Slowly he had spread the net of his interest farther and farther, from the

Hindu sagas of the *Mahabharata* to the novels of Narayan and Naipaul, from the works of Chaucer and Shakespeare to those of Jane Austen and Melville and Faulkner. At the University of London he had taken a fancy to the mystics, from Tagore and Vivekananda to Thomas a Kempis and St. Francis of Assisi. And then one day his tutor introduced him to Henry Thoreau, and Ananda was stunned. It was the pinnacle of all that had been gathering in his mind. Here was a reverent mysticism based on the natural world, amazingly united with political idealism.

"I will get a job," Ananda repeated to Homer. "I can be a clerk in a shop. I can work in a library. I can sell books."

Homer looked at him doubtfully. "The bookstore is gone, unfortunately. That woman Pink replaced it with a store full of porcelain geegaws."

He glanced at Mary, and she too tried to imagine Ananda as a useful member of the working class. "Try the library," she said firmly.

Next day Homer and Ananda began with the Concord Library. It was one of Homer's favorite places, and he was glad to see that Ananda too was pleased. While Homer asked for the head librarian, Ananda paid worshipful visits to the busts of Thoreau and Hawthorne and the great seated statue of Emerson.

But there was no place there for Ananda. "The truth is, we've been letting people go," said the head librarian. "And the squeeze is getting tighter all the time. I'm sorry."

Homer and Ananda walked up Main Street and looked warily at the smart shops with their bright awnings. In Corporate Gifts on Walden Street they found Mimi Pink herself behind the counter.

Mimi was charmed with Ananda's romantic good looks and his beautiful accent. "You're new in this country?" she asked him. "Do you know American money?"

"Of course he does," said Homer, inwardly vowing to take Ananda aside and explain nickels, dimes, and quarters.

Ananda looked around, puzzled. "What is it you are selling here?" There didn't seem to be any rhyme or reason to the odd objects in the shop. Today Mimi was featuring a large pillow shaped like a sports car, a nine-foot broadloom putting green, and a zebra-striped telephone. Ananda picked up a ceramic object masquerading as a wad of hundred-dollar bills.

"It's a bank," said Mimi. "Isn't it divine?"

Ananda looked sad and put the object down.

"I don't know," said Homer, taking him by the arm. "I suspect a disciple of Henry Thoreau wouldn't do very well selling corporate gifts."

"Oh, you're a Thoreau person, are you?" said Mimi, trying to rescue the situation. The boy was so yummy, she simply had to have him. She knew only one thing about Thoreau, so she trotted it out. "Did you know he used to steal pumpkin pies from Mrs. Emerson?"

Homer glanced at Ananda. "Mince," he said to Mimi Pink.

"Mince?"

"The pies he didn't steal. They weren't pumpkin, they were mince."

Later that afternoon they found an opening for Ananda in the hardware store. Homer was surprised to see Charlotte Harris sitting in a corner under a goosenecked lamp, doing something with invoices and catalogs. "Well, hello there," he said politely, and introduced Ananda.

"Hello," said Charlotte. Blood washed freely through the freckled skin of her face as she remembered her letter to Julian Snow. She pointed to the counter, where the owner of the store was puttying a window.

The proprietor had been looking for a salesperson, and he hired Ananda at once.

Ananda was delighted. "I will learn quickly," he said ardently, picking up a tool from the counter. "Tell me, what is this?"

"That?" Homer was dumbfounded. "It's a screwdriver." He picked up a hammer. "Do you know what this is?"

"Of course. It is a hammer. You see, I will soon know everything."

"Well, I can see that," said the proprietor, somewhat taken aback.

15

*What does the law protect? . . . If I avail myself
of it, it may help my sin; it cannot help my virtue.*
Journal, *March 16, 1842*

The Concord police were only mildly interested in the death of Alice Snow. The pathologist's report that she had died from a traumatic injury to the back of her head accorded so well with the position of her body on the steps of her mobile home that they paid little attention to his insistence that the wound was a rounded cavity, whereas the edges of the steps were sharply right-angled.

Homer made a fuss about it, too. "It didn't happen on the steps, I tell you. I looked and you looked. There wasn't any blood on the steps, just on the concrete where she was lying."

"But you people were all over the place," said Chief James Flower. "You should have cleared the area. You ought to have known better than let people mill around like that."

"I suppose I should have. Listen, did you look for something round that somebody could have hit her with? That trailer was full of baubles. Oh, well, I suppose it was taken away by whoever was running across the hillside afterward. Did I tell you about that?"

Flower listened politely to Homer's description of the movement in the bushes at the time of Alice's death, and he looked curiously at Ananda Singh when Ananda said he had seen the same thing. It was only when Julian Snow reported his missing two thousand dollars that Chief Flower called in a homicide detective from East Cambridge, who interviewed Ananda with cold courtesy. Had Mr. Singh really picked up his two thousand dollars at Logan Airport, or had he stolen it from Julian Snow?

Fortunately the detective pursued the matter further. At Logan he found a woman teller who remembered the darling boy with the traveler's checks from the bank in New Delhi.

At once the Cambridge detective lost interest in Ananda Singh. Probably Alice Snow had tripped over her own feet on the trailer steps. Or maybe it had been a simple break-and-enter with accompanying homicide by some crazy person from Walden Pond, some kid looking for drug money. And how would you track down anybody like that?

The detective's interest flagged, and he went back to the Middlesex County Courthouse, opened a new file in his bulging file drawer, and forgot about Alice Snow.

So Ananda was off the hook. He spent a sparkling Sunday afternoon helping Homer comb the hillside behind Julian Snow's mobile home. They were looking for a round object that could have been used to kill Alice Snow. They found nothing, only a small tube-shaped piece of rubber. "What is this?" said Ananda, holding it up for Homer to see.

"You mean you don't know?" Homer was amused. "You want me to explain?"

"Oh, oh, I see." Embarrassed, Ananda dropped the rubber object and covered it with last year's leaves. "Perhaps someone made love here," he said bravely.

"People make love everywhere. In cemeteries, in coal bins, at the North Pole, even on the steep slopes of glacial kettle holes."

Ananda went on thrashing in the bushes, turning away from Homer. What an innocent child the boy was, thought Homer.

Afterward he passed along to Jimmy Flower the news that he had found nothing on the hillside below Julian Snow's trailer. Jimmy didn't pay much attention. Like the Cambridge detective, he too had filed away Alice Snow.

It wasn't that Jimmy wasn't interested in her case, it was just that so many other things kept coming up. On the day the final report from East Cambridge came in, there was a four-car accident at Crosby's corner with three fatalities. There was also a theft from a parked motor vehicle on Walden Street, possession of a class-D substance at the high school, a woman driving under the influence on Route 2, and a runaway horse on Main Street.

The horse was Marjorie Bland's, and she was deeply apologetic. "Poor old Carmencita, she's so old, I think she's senile. She charges at me whenever I open the gate. This time she got away from me. I'm terribly sorry."

And then there was an embarrassing episode right there on the Milldam, involving a respectable tradesman accused of verbal assault. It was Taylor Baylor, whose shoe store had been part of Concord's commercial community for thirty years. Taylor's accuser was the sharp cookie who was buying up the town, the woman called Pink.

"I was walking quietly down the street," Mimi Pink told the arresting officer indignantly, "when this wild man came up to me and began shouting, accusing me of destroying the town of Concord. He shook me. If my assistant hadn't come to my rescue, I don't know what would have happened next."

And then Taylor Baylor shouted some more and .ranted and raved. Officer Shrubsole might have added a charge of resisting arrest, if Taylor hadn't been an old pal of his from way back. He let the charge go at verbal assault, and Taylor had to appear in court, fuming and unrepentant.

But the thing that was most distracting to the Concord Police Department was the announcement by the Concord Finance Committee that they would not endorse the department's request for two new cruisers and a ten percent pay increase for everybody in Public Safety.

"It's the financial crisis in the state," the chairperson of FinCom explained to Chief Flower. "Local aid has been cut to the bone. At the special town meeting in October we're going to recommend cuts across the board, in every single department."

Chief Flower was angry. His retort was barely polite.

"Oh, I don't blame you," said the long-suffering chair-person. "Everybody else is mad at us, too. It's a fiscal crisis in the commonwealth. Of course our local problem is worse because our town holds so much land in conservation. As you know very well, conservation land yields no taxes to support town services. What this town needs is some giant corporation to take over half the open land and start paying taxes through the nose. Just kidding, of course."

"Jesus," said Jimmy Flower. "I suppose it's Henry Thoreau, right? Bunch of starry-eyed idealists want to save some swamp Henry Thoreau stood in up to his neck once upon a time. Well, I wish to hell he'd drowned in it. Damn Henry Thoreau anyway. Pretending to be so independent there at Walden Pond, when all the time he was stealing squash pies from Mrs. Emerson."

"Apple," said the chairperson of the finance committee gloomily. "It was apple pies he stole."

"Apple? It was? I thought it was squash."

16

Oliver Fry didn't know what to do about his daughter Hope. He felt helpless in the grip of some violent natural force, an avalanche, a tidal wave. Hope was a man-eating tiger, she was eating him alive, spitting out his belt buckle and wristwatch. Sometimes to his relief there seemed to be a truce. She would bring him breakfast in bed, or come up behind him and put her arms around him, or watch television with him and laugh when he laughed. But much of the time she resisted him at every turn, arguing furiously or retreating into angry silence.

"She makes the house shake," said Oliver, complaining to Mary Kelly. "Metaphorically, I mean. She doesn't fit through doorways. She's a grandfather clock, a grand piano. Some moving man should jack her up and take her away."

"She's a dear girl," said Mary.

"Oh, I know she is, of course I know." Oliver smiled fatuously. "But we don't get along. She's pitted herself against me."

Mary told Homer that the trouble with Hope and Oliver Fry was that they were really so much alike. "She's her father's daughter. When she comes into the room you know something extraordinary is going to happen. Maybe not sensible, but you'll remember it afterward."

"Just like Oliver," agreed Homer.

On the last day of June Hope was alone in the house. Her father had gone off on his bike to the high school to spend

the morning making a list of lab materials he would need
in the fall. Hope felt giddily free. She frisked down the porch
steps and walked barefoot in the cool grass. It was a delicious
feeling. She was weightless, released from gravity. Remembering her old ballet class, she ran past the forsythia bushes,
took a huge leap, turned around in midair, and came down
facing the other way.

Someone clapped and cheered. Hope turned in surprise.
It was Jack Markey.

"Oh, hi there," said Hope, grinning at him. "Come on in."

"Nice place," said Jack, looking up at the porches and
the moon-shaped opening in the lattice and the keyhole
window in the peak of the roof and the onion-domed turret.
The house had been built in 1895. On this street of simple
center-entrance four-square houses it was a piece of Victorian
fantasy.

"I'm moving out as soon as I can," said Hope, dismissing
the home of her ancestors with a wave of her hand.

They sat at the kitchen table, deep in conspiracy. Around
them the walls of the kitchen towered in dark varnished
woodwork. Beyond the kitchen a lofty pantry was fitted with
a slate sink. Matched sets of dishes lined the high shelves,
all chipped except the soup plates. There were teapots shaped
like Cotswold cottages, drawers of tangled string, closets with
old croquet sets and dusty golf bags. Upstairs four of the six
bedrooms were unoccupied. An old canvas hammock dating
from 1938 hung on the sleeping porch. Family pictures lined
the staircase wall—grandparents, uncles, aunts, Hope's
mother on her wedding day, her train a swirl of tulle. Another
picture was a holy icon, Hope's mother with baby Hope in
her arms. She had died when Hope was a small child, and
afterward Oliver Fry had done a loving but clumsy job of
bringing up his daughter by himself.

Hope sometimes wondered what the dead people in the
pictures would say if they could see the house now. Would

they be surprised to find it so much the same? Her father had wanted everything to stay just as it had been when his wife was alive. Hope suspected that her mother too had inherited a sentimental fixity in household arrangements.

She didn't care. She was going to leave as soon as she finished her last year at Boston University, where she was concentrating on the history of art. The history of art! What art history was there in Concord, Massachusetts? What was this barren little provincial town compared with Florence and Venice and Rome? What was the First Parish Church com-

pared with Kings College Chapel, or Chartres Cathedral, or St. Peter's Basilica? Concord, Massachusetts! How rustic could you get?

Hope felt a withering scorn for her father's native village. She was ready to give Jack Markey all the advice she could think of. Her father didn't have to know. Nervously Hope put her father out of her mind. Leaping up from the table, she looked for the town report.

She found it among the cookbooks. Like them, it was a little sticky. "Here we are." Hope flung herself back onto her chair and opened the report at the beginning. "Look, here's a complete list of the town boards."

"Jesus, how many are there?" Jack moved his chair closer until their shoulders touched. Together they pored over the pages listing the town officers.

"Well, the important ones are the board of selectmen and the planning board and the board of appeals and—what else?—the natural resources commission, the housing authority, the finance committee. Oh, and the school committee. And maybe the refuse disposal task force and the historical commission. Each one is powerful in its own bailiwick. All those people are volunteers, but there's also a paid town manager and town planner. You've got to line up support among them all. Somehow or other you've got to make them all happy."

"Well, the taxes we pay should certainly make them happy, right?"

"Of course. But I'll bet you can do a lot more." Hope's mind buzzed with ideas. "How about buying another pretty piece of land somewhere and giving it to the town for conservation? You know, sort of an exchange?"

Jack nodded. His employer, Jefferson Grandison, was well accustomed to quids pro quo.

Hope jumped up again and vanished, then returned with a map. Spreading it out on the table, she weighted down the corners with four jars of slimy brown liquid.

"My God," said Jack, "what's that stuff?"

"Gunk from Gowing's Swamp, I think. For my father's biology class. They were looking at algae under the microscope." Briskly Hope smoothed the map and explained. "All these green pieces are already in conservation."

Jack was used to maps. He stood up and spread his hands flat on the table and let his eyes rove over the winding roads and rivers and the contour lines of hills, the imprint of the town of Concord on the white paper. He had seen the map before. "What's this, right near the center? The Hugh Cargill land, what's that?"

"The old poor farm. Hugh Cargill left it for the use of the poor a long time ago. They've sold off most of it, I think, to get money for affordable housing someplace else. Forget the Hugh Cargill land. It's mostly wetland anyway." Then Hope pounded the table, and the jars of swamp water bounced. "Wetland, that's how you can win over the natural resources commission. Offer them a swamp. If there's anything those people love, it's a swamp. There must be one you could buy."

They stared at the map, looking for the little pattern of tufted lines that meant wetland.

"Here's one," said Jack. "Gowing's Swamp, where these jars of bilge came from. How about that?"

Hope's nose wrinkled. "Oh, ugh, Gowing's Swamp. It's a quaking bog. You could be sucked down. Father told me people used to bury animals in Gowing's Swamp. They took horses there and shot them, so they dropped in the hole and disappeared forever. But it's already in conservation. Forget Gowing's Swamp."

They were sitting down again, shoulder to shoulder, yellow hair grazing brown, when Oliver Fry bumped his bicycle up the steps of the back porch and burst into the kitchen, shouting, "Hopey?"

The caged owl screeched. The snakes writhed in their tank. The shrews burrowed deeper in their nest of shavings.

Oliver was in a transport of rage. At the high school he had encountered the chairperson of the school committee, Judy Bowman, and Judy had told him about the percolation tests on the lacrosse field, the possible sale of the land to a development company. Oliver was boiling over. It was unheard of, intolerable, abominable. He had to explode to somebody.

But he stopped short at the sight of Jack Markey and gaped at the map on the table.

Jack sprang to his feet and grinned his sunshiny grin. Hope stood up too and introduced him to her father. In spite of herself, she felt awful. *Father, meet the Devil incarnate.*

"I was just telling Jack about the town," she explained lamely. "He's new around here."

"Oh, you've just moved here?" said Oliver, trying to sound jocular and failing utterly.

Jack sensed the tension in the air. "No, no, I wish I had. It's such a wonderful little historical community." Jack pawed around in his mind for something to say to the old man who was staring at him with such terrible eyes. "I understand, sir, you're a real Thoreau buff."

Buff? A Thoreau buff? Oliver's brow darkened. He was a disciple, an apostle, a worshiper at the shrine, not a buff.

"Of course he is," said Hope, feeling flustered, aware of the heavy-handed mistake. "My father's a pillar of the Thoreau Society."

In his ignorance of anything intelligent to say about Henry Thoreau, Jack tried a light touch. "Is it true he stole pies from Ralph Waldo Emerson?"

Hope closed her eyes. Her father reeled and spluttered. "Thoreau was not a thief, he was a gentleman, devoted to abstinence. He said he could live on board nails."

"I stand corrected," Jack said politely.

"Oh, Father, please." Hope rolled her eyes at Jack. "I told you he'd quote Thoreau."

Oliver's mouth clamped shut. A man forbidden to quote Thoreau was a man struck dumb.

17

Read not the Times. Read the Eternities.
"Life Without Principle"

The battle was joined. The news was out.

**DEVELOPER EYES
HIGH SCHOOL PROPERTY**

announced the *Concord Journal*. And there was a subheading:

Grandison Seeks
Zoning Change

The land in question lay still. The backhoe was parked at the edge of the lacrosse field, awaiting the ultimate decision of the town. Crows cawed in the tops of the white pines and flapped their black wings, but they could not call a meeting of protest. A mockingbird sang all day long, warbling and twittering, composing impulsive arias and recitatives, but it could make no enduring claim to the dead tree on which it was perched. And the red-tailed hawk that glided above the high school and soared over Route 2, gazing down at the sweet-rocket blooming pink and white on the edge of the woods, had no inherited deed of ownership, no binding contract guaranteeing possession to its heirs and assigns forever.

The human citizens of Concord were taking sides. Feeling ran especially high in the breasts of all the Thoreauvians, who had fought the good fight so many times before. They were worn out. They couldn't believe they were in for another battle.

"Look," said Oliver Fry, chivying them unmercifully, urging them to action, "we've got to do something."

"But it's hopeless," said his old friend Elizabeth Bates. "How many times can you fight City Hall?"

Other people in town were tired, too. They didn't want to hear another word about Henry Thoreau and Ralph Waldo Emerson. Like Oliver's daughter, Hope, they were sick of the way those Thoreau people were always hauling out their dead heroes, displaying the mummified bodies in their moldering greatcoats, propping up the grinning skulls. This was the present, it was here and now, they were poised on the brink of a new millennium. The nineteenth century was buried in the dust of the past.

The town was clenched like a fist. And yet there were still a lot of people who hadn't made up their minds one way or another. After all, the matter wouldn't come up until the special town meeting in October. It was now only the first week of July. There would be plenty of time to decide how to vote later on.

Poor Oliver Fry was suffering keenly on another count. His daughter was nursing a viper in her breast. The healthy-looking kid with the golden hair and pink cheeks, the one who had been sitting with Hope in Oliver's very own kitchen, was Jefferson Grandison's representative. He was the enemy.

Against his own better judgment Oliver confronted his daughter with her apostasy. "How can you talk to somebody who's threatening to build all that garbage in Walden Woods?"

Hope was chagrined. She had hoped her father wouldn't find out who Jack Markey was. But now Jack's name was all over town. She put her hand to her stomach, where there was a sudden pain, and blustered back at him. "Walden Woods! It's just a scrawny piece of land next to Route Two. Who cares what happens beside a highway? I bet it will look a lot better with Jack's development on it than it does now. And he's including affordable housing. You're just being snobbish, not letting lower-income people live in Concord."

"Affordable housing!" Oliver looked at his daughter in disbelief. "Affordable for whom? We couldn't afford the rents they'll be charging, I'll tell you that right now."

The Concord Planning Board was not surprised by the news in the *Concord Journal*. Chairman Roger Bland had already been consulted by Judy Bowman of the school committee.

"We're letting them dig test holes, that's all we're doing," said Judy. "But between you and me, it would be a blessing to have some money coming in right now. As it is, we're going to cut back on the language program and slash the biology budget, and if things don't improve, we may have to eliminate football altogether."

"Football!" Roger was shocked. He promised to listen carefully to the Walden Green proposal when it came before the board.

At breakfast the next morning he told his wife Marjorie all about it. Marjorie was not the sort of helpmeet to give Roger sound advice, but she could be depended on to express the opinion of the town's average citizen.

"Goodness," said Marjorie, "a shopping mall in Walden Woods! Those conservation people aren't going to like it."

"They'll talk about our historical heritage, I suppose," said Roger. "No matter what comes up in this town, somebody fastens the word *heritage* to it. It's a pain in the neck."

"Oh, poor Roger. But of course we're lucky to live in a place with so much history. I tell myself that every time I drive around in less fortunate places."

"But there has to be a limit somewhere," protested Roger.

"Oh, of course!" Marjorie stirred her coffee and added a wee dollop of cream. "I must say, those people in the Thoreau Society are just a little bit . . ."

"Far out?" suggested Roger boldly, and Marjorie laughed and agreed.

Far out—it was something no one would ever say about

Roger Bland. Roger could be relied on to stay close to the sensible center of public opinion. He would never crawl out on some nutty limb all by himself. He walked down the narrow path in the middle of every road. His clothes walked down the middle, too, his coat lapels, his necktie, his shirt, his pants. *Oh, let there be no pleating at the waist when I go out to sea!* Something in Roger Bland recoiled, withdrew, shrank back from extreme positions. Unconsciously he dreaded expansiveness. There was a lid within him, controlling, calming, pressing down. It was unimaginable that any large and generous impulse would ever induce him to push up the lid and burst free, shouting "Huzzah!"

"There's one good thing anyway," said Roger, picking up the morning paper. "We don't have to lift a finger to get back another piece of Walden Woods. Those Pond View people are dying off. Remember? There are only fourteen of them left."

"And they're terribly old, I'll bet," his wife said optimistically. Marjorie always looked on the bright side.

When Roger left for the office that morning, Marjorie went to the stable to set out a bucket of feed for her horse, ducking in and out quickly before Carmencita could race across the paddock and plunge at her or bite her or misbehave in some other upsetting way. That job done, she came in again and sat down at her desk to pursue her own personal good cause, her new hobby.

Marjorie had joined the recycling movement. This morning she was writing a letter to the editor of the *Concord Journal*, urging her fellow citizens to bring their old newspapers to the recycling area at the landfill. "And what about saving your grocery bags and using them over again next time? Save, save, recycle! (signed) Marjorie Bland, Musketaquid Road."

Marjorie loved her recycling campaign. It was such fun. But then everything Marjorie did was fun, even her severest duties, even caring for her senile old horse and rolling the tennis court. Marjorie's fun was the pitiful remnant of the sturdy resignation to the will of God on the part of the forefathers, who had endured without complaint death-dealing plague, hunger and privation, and savage spells of bitter winter cold.

18

Talk of heaven! ye disgrace earth.
Walden, "The Ponds"

"Mr. Grandison, sir? I'm calling again about Lot Seventeen. I wonder, sir, if perhaps it's slipped your mind?"

Jefferson Grandison looked at the telephone with disgust. He had given specific instructions to his receptionist that this particular caller was not to be put through. "Of course," he said after a moment's delay, "we will attend to the matter at once."

"I knew you would, Mr. Grandison. I knew it was merely an oversight on your part. I wonder if you could speak in terms of an exact time?"

"Excuse me, but my other phone is ringing." Grandison put down the phone and walked out to the anteroom to speak sharply to Martha Jones.

Later on, when Jack Markey stepped out of the elevator and said good morning, Martha cautioned him, "Watch out. He's in one of his funny moods."

"Right," said Jack, but he felt confident that he knew how to handle his chief in all his funny moods. He smiled conspiratorially at the receptionist. In her white dress she was an astonishingly beautiful girl, but he had given up trying to charm her. There was something, perhaps, about living in the clouds that had unsexed her. Perhaps it was the altitude. Perhaps medical people should look into the effect on the sex drive of height above sea level. Jack wondered if he should stay the hell away from the seventieth floor of the Grandison Building before his own healthy urges slipped away from him.

The woman was right about Grandison. He was indeed in one of his detached stratospheric moods. His vague gaze dodged away from Jack and lost itself in the mist outside the enormous windows. But Jack had long since discovered in that unfocused eye a remote and smoldering point of light. It was like peering into the smoky entrance to a cave, seeing far away within the cavern a bed of burning coals. Grandison was in there all right.

Jack recounted his progress in preparing the Concord groundwork for the development to be called Walden Green. Then they got down to brass tacks, the massive business arrangements that would be necessary whenever the town gave them a binding agreement——the permanent commitment from the Paul Revere Insurance Company, the construction loan, the mortgage, the hard and soft costs, the timing. "There'll be a saving on the design," said Jack, smiling.

"Of course. In-house. Your department."

"Right."

Not until then did they get down to the other Concord matter. "You've found an intermediary, I understand?" murmured Grandison.

"Yes. Two, as a matter of fact. One of them's free of charge." Jack grinned.

"I leave it in your hands entirely." Grandison stared at his right hand, which was doodling in a notebook, leaving only the faintest trace on the white paper.

"Oh, Mr. Grandison," said Martha Jones, putting her head in the door, "Mrs. Grandison is on the phone."

The meeting was over. Jack excused himself and plunged earthward once again in the glass elevator.

It was always a shock to find himself on the ground again, surrounded by the reality of Huntington Avenue with its drab street people. The same sorry-looking bag lady was occupying the glass portico of the Grandison Building.

Once again Jack stumbled over her disordered belongings.

Why didn't the damned woman move out of the way? "Excuse me," he said irritably.

Sarah Peel glanced at him with her ancient reptilian eyes. She saw Jack speak to the guard before turning on his heel and striding away down the street. Slowly she got up.

The guard walked toward her. He was a softhearted man, but he knew he had been too lenient already. "Look here, ma'am," he said, not unkindly, "you've got to move on."

Without a word Sarah collected her possessions, stuffed them into her stroller, and trudged off in the direction of Copley Square.

She had been asleep when Jack Markey tripped over her, or at least she had been lost in the half stupor with which she abolished time. It was the same daydream that had made her childhood bearable, in that sad house in East Boston next to the New England Ring and Flange Company, where the whole neighborhood echoed with the scream of the high-powered saws and the thundering noise of sheet metal racing between rolling drums. Young Sarah had dreamed of a green countryside with farms and trees, she had longed for cows with large soft eyes and ponies with flying manes and tails.

Once a traveling fair had come to the empty lot beyond the Ring and Flange Company, and every day for a week Sarah took a ride on the merry-go-round. Every day she chose the same horse, the white one that looked back at her with a fiery eye. Down the horse plunged, and up, and then it rushed forward with a lovely surging bound, while the calliope wheezed the "Skater's Waltz" and the drums banged magically by themselves, and the cymbals clashed. The horse belonged to her. She gave it a name, Pearl.

The other kids didn't know how to ride, they just sat there, but Sarah knew how. She felt it in her bones.

*. . . put an extra condiment into your dish,
and it will poison you.*
Walden, "Higher Laws"

It had been a month since the death of Alice Snow. Honey
Mooney was up early to get ready for church. First she washed
out the casserole in which she had cooked the pasta for last
night's party. She didn't really need to scrub it so hard. It
wasn't her pasta that would be to blame, if anybody bothered
to investigate. It was Mavis Buonfesto's pecan pie, and Honey
had tucked the stuff neatly into only one serving, the piece
that went to Shirley Mills.

Then she looked in her closet for something suitable to
wear to church, although she doubted she would actually get
to church this morning. Where was her knit blouse? Oh, of
course, she had left it in the dryer in the laundry shack.

Charlotte Harris too had a basket of dirty clothes to take
care of. Carrying it to the laundry shack, she tried to smooth
the sadness from her face. For weeks she had been struggling
with depression. Normally she threw it off by getting mad
and doing something about it, but this time there was nothing
to do, since the only person to be mad at was herself. Charlotte
was still aching with embarrassment about her letter to Julian
Snow.

For the entire month she had scrupulously avoided Julian.
She hadn't even allowed herself to walk to the other end of
the park. But at the same time it was unendurable to be
incarcerated week in and week out with her husband.

This morning even Pete noticed something different.
"What's the matter, baby doll?" he said, getting up from the

table and putting on his cook's white coat, ready for the Sunday morning shift at the hospital.

Baby doll. If anybody in the world was not a baby doll, it was Charlotte Harris. Charlotte was a tall, angular woman with big hands and feet. There was nothing fluffy about her at all. She wanted to strangle him for calling her that. "Oh, I guess I'm just kind of down this morning."

Pete wasn't listening. He gulped down the last of his coffee and tramped out of the kitchen, ready to dismember chickens all day long. Opening the door, he glanced back. Charlotte tensed and closed her eyes. "Don't take any wooden nickels," said Pete. The door banged.

For a moment Charlotte sat very still with her eyes closed, asking herself why she had married him. Well, that was a stupid question. She had been young, that was why. She had been a fool. Pete had been just as dumb, to have picked her from all the rest.

The real question was why she stayed married, why she didn't just walk out. Charlotte knew the answer to that question, too. She was afraid. If she left Pete, she would get sick, or else Pete would get sick. It was what happened to people who abandoned their mates or were abandoned by them. They got sick and died. It had happened to Charlotte's father, who had walked out on her mother and promptly developed prostate cancer. It had happened to Charlotte's older sister, who had left her husband, only to die of liver disease. It had happened to the wife of her cousin George when he went off with a younger woman. Poor Loretta had suffered a fatal stroke.

So Charlotte hung on, timid, superstitious. At least she was able to get away from Pete every day at her job as bookkeeper in the hardware store. She liked the proprietor, she liked his new young clerk, the boy from India. Once in a while she set young Ananda straight about the merchandise. "The customer wants a box of washers," she would say, drawing him aside. "Look, they're in this drawer, in different sizes. They fit between things, like this, you see?"

But at home things were going from bad to worse. It was strange the way Pete never seemed to notice her weary hostility. Well, he wasn't exactly deprived. Pete took what he wanted when he wanted it. The more Charlotte despised him, the more she felt it her duty to go along.

The laundry shack was not her favorite place. The machines were in a basement seven steps below ground level. Opening the door, she inhaled the dank underground smell and heard the buzzing hum of the washing machines and the tumbling noise of the clothes in the dryers.

Julian Snow was there ahead of her, raising the lid of an empty washing machine. It was the only one that was not shaking and sloshing. "Oh, sorry," he said, backing away. "After you."

"No, no, you were here first."

But he insisted. "Go ahead. I'll be back later on. You just go right ahead." And he went away.

When Honey Mooney came in a moment later, she found Charlotte with tears running down her cheeks. "Charlotte, dear, can I do anything? Tell Honey what's the matter."

You're not my honey, Charlotte wanted to say. She rammed a quarter into the machine and turned to look straight at Honey. "Where does it come from, your name?"

Honey giggled. "It was a pet name of my husband's. And my mother used to call me that."

"Because you're so sweet, is that it?" Charlotte said it with ironic intent, but she knew Honey would take it as a compliment.

"Let me know, dear, if I can help in any way," said Honey, smiling, pulling her clothes out of one of the dryers.

Walking back across the driveway, Charlotte couldn't help thinking that there was too much unnecessary love in the

world. Of course it was important to have love between the
sexes at a certain stage, so that people would have children
and reproduce the race. But why should there be all this extra
amount left over? Here she was, a woman past the repro-
ductive age, yet she was still mooning over a person of the
opposite sex. It was part of the overabundance and extravagance of nature. There were too many mosquitoes in the
midsummer air, too many spiders building webs under the
propane tanks of the mobile homes, too many tadpoles in
the shallows of Goose Pond, too many stars in the sky—
and now somebody had found a whole lot more galaxies in
the infinite depths of space.

Charlotte looked back at the woods beyond Julian's house,
where too many trees were vying with each other and too
many leaves were thick on the too many branches. She opened

the door of her own house and went inside. Her own excess of love was part of it. In a tidier universe a woman would die at the end of her hormonal usefulness. She would simply vanish from the earth.

Honey Mooney, Mavis Buonfesto, and Shirley Mills were the only regular churchgoers at Pond View. On Sunday mornings they met at Honey's at nine-thirty and drove in her car to St. Bernard's for ten o'clock mass. They always sat in a pew halfway to the altar beside one of the stations of the cross, Christ falling for the third time. And afterward they went for coffee and sweet rolls at Brigham's on Main Street, and then they liked to wander along the sidewalk and see what all the cute shops were selling— cunning teddies and fancy gift items and funny Garfield greeting cards. And then Mavis would buy a new lipstick at the drugstore and Shirley would pick up a dispenser of hand cream, and Honey would choose a new decorating magazine, because she loved to see all the new ideas for fixing up your home.

This morning Shirley was late. Mavis kept looking out Honey's window, expecting to see Shirley hurry along the driveway in her navy sport jacket and ruffled blouse, but she didn't come, and she didn't come, and finally they went to fetch her.

Her door was locked. They knocked, but there was no answer.

Mavis was tall. Standing on tiptoe, she could see into Shirley's bedroom window. "Oh, for God's sake," said Mavis, "she's still in bed."

Mavis rapped sharply on the window, but Shirley didn't stir. "Shirley," called Mavis, "get up, it's time for church."

Shirley still didn't budge.

"Oh, dear God," said Mavis, turning to Honey with wide eyes. "She looks really strange."

They hurried down the road to the park manager's house, because he had duplicate keys to all the mobile homes. The manager came back with them, and soon they were all standing over Shirley's bed, looking down at her. Honey shook her and called her name.

Shirley didn't respond. She was curled up tight, her eyes squeezed shut, her features pinched together in a grimace.

They looked at each other in horrified surmise. "I think she's dead," said the park manager.

"Oh, no," sobbed Mavis. "She was just fine yesterday."

"She was only fifty-two," wept Honey. "I know, because she was exactly five years older than me, to the very day."

They called Dr. Stefano, the physician who took care of all the people at Pond View. He called them his private zoo.

"But I don't think I ever examined Shirley Mills," he said, looking down at her sadly. "I just saw her once, when she had the flu."

"She had a heart condition," explained Honey. "Didn't she tell you?"

"You know," said Dr. Stefano, looking at Honey severely, "you people shouldn't be living alone. If somebody had called me, I might have been able to save her life. It's dangerous for all of you to be by yourselves. Why don't you women double up and live together?"

"I'm a married woman myself," said Mavis proudly.

"We all keep an eye on each other," said Honey.

"Think about it," said Dr. Stefano, packing up his black bag.

Roger Bland made a habit of reading the obituary page of the *Concord Journal*, and he noted with satisfaction the passing of one more resident of Pond View. "Look," he said, showing the paper to his wife, "another one of them is gone."

Marjorie Bland's face took on its automatic expression of sorrow before the transitory nature of life on earth. "Oh, too bad," she said, sipping her sherry. Then her attention was caught by the birds fluttering around the feeder just outside the living room window. "Oh, Roger, look at the darling chickadees."

"That's thirteen now," said her husband, hardly glancing at the chickadees.

"Oh, no, not as many as that. One, two, three. No, four. Five! Oh, Roger, look!"

Thirteen, thought Roger, smiling to himself. Only thirteen more to go.

20

Instead of noblemen, let us have noble villages of men.
Walden, "Reading"

Under the guidance of Hope Fry, Jack Markey approached the town boards with good luck in his pocket.

Concord was one of the best-run suburbs west of Boston. Dozens of public-spirited citizens devoted their spare time to serving the town without pay, attending endless meetings, submitting themselves to continuous public scrutiny and criticism.

"It's democracy in action," people said when they approved of a decision made by one of the boards.

"Throw them all out," they said, when they didn't.

It was a good system, everybody agreed, and on the whole it worked well.

Jack was especially lucky in the hearings he attended. Not only did he have the shrewd advice of Mimi Pink, he had the keen insider's information supplied by Hope Fry. Best of all, he had the good fortune to follow in the footsteps of the finance committee, which had preceded him and prepared the ground.

FinCom had all the appalling figures at their fingertips. They knew how perilous the town's financial condition really was. Like all the other small municipalities in Massachusetts, Concord had been abandoned by the commonwealth, which had reneged disastrously on its promise of local aid.

"You've got to cut at least ten percent from the budget passed at the spring town meeting," FinCom said to each of

Selectmens room

the boards. "We're sorry, but we won't approve anything less drastic."

"Look, we can always raise taxes a little bit," said one or another anguished member of the personnel board or the public works commission or the school committee.

"Impossible," said FinCom. "We can't ask the elderly or the unemployed or the young to pay any more, and we certainly can't add to the burden of the hardworking professionals who are already paying through the nose. You've got to cut. You've got to cut until you bleed."

One by one the committees came before the judgment seat to plead. FinCom treated them all the same way. They were cruel but fair. Again and again they raised their glittering scythes and slashed the dewy, hopeful grass.

"Look here," said FinCom to the library committee, "why don't you impose a six-month moratorium on the purchase of new books? I mean, you've got a whole lot of books already, right? I'll bet you've got a million books."

The director of the library was scandalized. "Not buy new books? Not buy new books? What's a library for? We can't stop buying books!"

"Well, take your choice," said FinCom heartlessly. "It's either books or staff members."

So in the end a couple of librarians were thrown to the wolves.

FinCom had another money-saving suggestion for the public works commission. "Why not forget about potholes next spring? Just let 'em go. It'll be hard on people's suspension systems, but, what the hell, you've got to cut somewhere. If we have an open winter, you'll be okay."

"Not repair potholes?" exclaimed the chairwoman of Public Works. "You don't know what you're saying. If we don't do simple maintenance on our forty-two miles of public ways this year, we'll have forty-two miles of major reconstruction in years to come. You don't really mean it."

It was the same story in every department of town government. The modernization of the light plant was canceled. The acceptance of new streets was denied. The new telephone system for the high school was postponed. Even the expansion of Sleepy Hollow Cemetery was rejected.

"So what are we going to do with the deceased?" snarled the cemetery committee. "Take them to the dump?"

Everybody was angry. The atmosphere in the Town House was one of testiness and rancor, exacerbated by news of still more million-dollar deficits in the commonwealth, grimly reported by the *Boston Globe*.

For Jack Markey it was all to the good. When his turn came, each of the town boards was in a softened-up condition, ready to clutch at any straw. Some of them caved in reluctantly, some stroked their chins and postponed judgment, some were delighted from the start.

The chairwoman of the Concord Housing Authority was one of the latter. She was a tough-minded down-to-earth woman who had been fighting for low-income housing in Concord for years. She was suspicious of easy excuses based on mere aesthetics or on the town's historic heritage. The hard fact was that the Concord Housing Authority needed more housing. Their waiting list was pathetically long.

She looked over Jack's plans for the condominiums at Walden Green with a practiced eye.

"Three units of low-income rentals," said Jack, getting down to brass tacks. "Seven moderate income."

"Ten low. We don't give a damn about moderate-income housing. Those people can take care of themselves."

Jack didn't promise anything, but he could see that the woman was on his side.

Refuse Disposal was a pushover, too, although the chairperson seemed doubtful at first. He looked at Jack solemnly. "In case you don't know it already, trash disposal is a serious matter in this town. Well, it's a serious matter all over the place." The man was in earnest. He wasn't fooling.

"You're damned right," agreed Jack, who knew a lot about

the subject already. His employer, Jefferson Grandison, was into waste removal in a big way. It was the coming thing, and Grandison knew it. From his lofty perch in the Grandison Building he stretched out his hand not only to create, but to bear away that which had been created. (Jesus, thought Jack, remembering Lot Seventeen.)

"You need a really good transfer station," he told the chairman. "What if we provide you with the equipment?" And then he listed one succulent item after another—a compactor to reduce volume, a complete recycling center with hydraulic lifts, a trammer mill to turn used building materials into wood chips, even an on-site chemist.

The chairman was impressed in spite of himself. "We're putting in a compactor ourselves, just as an experiment," he said. "But those other things, my God, they're so expensive. How can your people afford it?"

"Oh, we hope to make enough from the leasing of our shopping mall and the rental of the condo units to get a substantial return on our investment. And of course we have a vested interest in keeping the intersection of Route Two and Route One Twenty-six as well landscaped as possible. Right now, with that big hole in the ground, it's . . . well, let's just say it's not very attractive."

"It sure isn't very attractive. And it's an insult to Henry Thoreau, the whole damned thing. I just happen to be a Thoreau nut myself. Look here, I'll tell you the truth. I hate what you're doing, but I don't know how else the town of Concord can afford a transfer station."

The next board on the list was tricky, very tricky. Jack approached the natural resources commission cautiously. They were a hard-nosed conservation-minded bunch of people with an affection for swamps, bogs, and thistly wildernesses. But they could find no fault with Jack Markey's plan. The percolation tests had been superb. The thirsty subsoil of the high school site gulped down surface water through thick layers of gravel and sand.

Jack brought forward his hard facts truthfully. The buildings would occupy one hundred thousand square feet, he said, with an effluent of ten thousand gallons a day. And then he talked knowledgeably about wetland buffer zones, catchment basins, and sewage. The entire board leaned forward and pricked up its ears when Jack offered to extend the town's sewer pipes all the way from the county courthouse to Route 2. What a boon that would be!

But his ace in the hole was Titcomb's Bog. Titcomb's Bog would be bought by Grandison Enterprises and given to the town as a free gift. "Titcomb's Bog," said Jack triumphantly, "sacred to the memory of Henry Thoreau."

"I fear not," said the chairperson of the natural resources commission. "You're wrong there, friend. Henry Thoreau never wrote a word about Titcomb's Bog. But I admit we'd be pleased to see it in conservation."

The planning board was the last on Hope's list. It was too important, she said, to be approached head on. So Jack made an appointment for a Saturday morning visit with its chairman, Roger Bland, at his home on Musketaquid Road.

Roger's house was an impressive dwelling, quite new, overlooking the Concord River beside the Nashawtuc bridge. A little pale gray horse looked inquisitively at Jack from a field beside the house and whinnied at him, as if to warn its master. Jack couldn't help thinking at once of the four horsemen of the apocalypse in the book of *Revelation*—"And I saw, and behold a white horse; and he that sat on him had a bow; and a crown was given unto him; and he went forth conquering."

Marjorie Bland opened the door, wearing an apron over her peach-colored turtleneck and lavender trousers. "Oh, come right in," she said gaily, waving a potholder. "Roger will be right down."

And there he was, coming down the stairs, Roger Bland the country squire, in old khakis and a plaid shirt. Jack could see him sitting high on the white horse, going forth to conquer.

"Let's go in here," said Roger, leading the way into his study. It was a rich warm room with an Oriental rug, a computer, and shelves full of books. If Homer Kelly had been there, he would have snorted at the books, which were not like those belonging to Charlotte Harris in her mobile home at Pond View. Roger had inherited his library from an elderly aunt, whose taste had run to Gene Stratton Porter, Faith Baldwin, and Ethel M. Dell.

But Jack didn't know anything about books, and he was impressed. "What do you use the computer for?"

"Investments," said Roger. "I have a direct line to my broker. I've got this software program that sends me information. You know, the daily performance of the Dow, all kinds of stuff. It's kind of a hobby of mine."

"How's your average?" said Jack, daring a jocular intimacy.

"Pretty good, if I do say so myself."

They sat down, and Jack put his roll of maps on the coffee table. Roger knew what Jack had come for, and he spoke bluntly. "You understand, there'll be a lot of opposition to your proposal. A shopping mall across from Walden Pond! Wait till you lock horns with the Thoreau types."

"Oh, I know about the Thoreau types." Jack grinned engagingly. "But I think they may change their tune when they hear what we have to offer." He unrolled one of his maps. "We understand the Burroughs farm on Monument Street is for sale. What if we were to buy it and deed it to the town of Concord for conservation?"

Roger whistled, trying not to show his pleasure. Who cared what happened to a dusty woods right next to a noisy highway, compared with the preservation of a twenty-five-acre farm on the most beautiful street in town?

Outwardly he was careful to remain noncommittal. He gave Jack neither encouragement nor discouragement. But after Jack took his leave, Roger stood dreamily in the hall, thinking about the Burroughs farm and the figures his visitor had tossed off into the air, the amount of money that would flow into the town treasury in taxes every year from Walden Green. "Even suppose," Roger murmured to himself, "that it's only half what he said. Even suppose——"

"What, dear?" shouted Marjorie from the kitchen, where she was bustling about, whipping up a casserole of coq au vin for a dinner party, pouring in a dash of cognac and touching it courageously with a match. *Whoosh*, went the cognac, blazing up, and Marjorie uttered a little shriek. Oh, cooking was such fun!

21

Mimi Pink was thinking big. "What we need," she said to her assistant in the Porcelain Parlor, "is an organization of retailers. All our own people."

"Well," said Bonnie Glover, "there's, you know, the Concord Chamber of Commerce."

Mimi laughed scornfully. "The Chamber of Commerce, what good is that? A lot of old-fashioned people stuffing themselves with pancakes and sausage once a month at the Colonial Inn. No imagination. No creativity. No, we need our own team, our own elite corps."

"Oh, fabulous," murmured Bonnie Glover. "Fabulous" was Bonnie's noncommittal way of saying "Hmmm."

They pondered over names for the new organization. "Coalition of Concord Shops?" suggested Mimi.

"Fantastic," said Bonnie automatically.

But Mimi shot it down herself. The word *coalition* implied equality among the participants, and that was out, because as the owner of all the shops, Mimi herself must be more equal than the rest.

In the end she came up with Consortium of Concord Boutiques.

"Awesome," said Bonnie, clapping her hands, sensing that this was Mimi's choice, this was *it*.

"The Consortium for short," said Mimi.

The first meeting of the Consortium of Concord Boutiques was called for July 17 in the Porcelain Parlor immediately after closing hours.

106

"The meeting will come to order," said Mimi, smiling at her audience, enjoying the way they had all adopted a Mimi Pink look.

Bonnie Glover was the best clone. Bonnie was extremely pretty in her own right, and she had made the most of her endowments. But the others, too, were good demonstrations of the Pink style. Narrow skirts rode high over black nylon knees. That year the fashion was for big football shoulders, and Mimi's were wider than anybody's. There was hardly room along the rows of folding chairs for the bundles of shoulder padding crowded together side by side. Everyone's hair had been blown into fluffy exaggerated shapes like Mimi's and sprayed with a glistening coating. Fingernails were silver, scarlet, baby pink. All Mimi's people were drenched in scent from the Parfumerie. Swooning fragrances blended in an olfactory mishmash.

Reverently they listened as Mimi held forth. "I've got people begging me for space right now, with the darlingest ideas. Potpourris Unlimited has been after me for a year. And Loving Hearts—you know, those specialty shops that sell heart-shaped things—they want a shop here, too, and there's a new little chain, Ladybugs, exclusive knitwear with the ladybug emblem. I'm dickering for more space. And I'm hiring the interior designer for Hyatt Hotels."

Mimi Pink was throwing the dice, throwing the dice, hopping over the less important properties on the Monopoly board, aiming for some ultimate perfection of real estate, some glorious Park Place, some supremely up-market Boardwalk with towers of alabaster.

Everyone in the room felt part of something important. It was especially fantastic to be here in the Porcelain Parlor surrounded by the most expensive merchandise in town. The fabulous price tags on the china figures cast a spell. The track lighting was artfully arranged to shine on the glass shelves with their fragile images of bluebirds among apple blossoms and mothers cuddling babies and nubile girls with windblown skirts. In the place of honor perched a porcelain imitation of azalea twigs adorned with lifelike magenta flowers. Its price tag was seven hundred and fifty dollars.

Across Route 2 on the south side of town, deep in the woods between Walden Pond and the Sudbury River, Homer Kelly and Ananda Singh were ankle deep in the cushiony moss covering the surface of the fourth Andromeda Pond. Above them on the hillside stood a row of oaks, vast round globes of moving leaves, nodding in the soft breeze like dreaming old men who had lost the power of speech.

Swamp azaleas blossomed here and there. No price tags hung from their fragrant branches. They were altogether free.

22

Why should we be in such desperate haste to succeed,
and in such desperate enterprises?
Walden, "Conclusion"

In the dining room of the Colonial Inn at the far end of
Monument Square, the Concord Chamber of Commerce was
enjoying its monthly breakfast. "Enjoying" was perhaps not
the right word. Most of them were suffering, but they ate
their eggs and bacon and their pancakes and sausages with a
will, forking them up hungrily while they exchanged outraged exclamations and shook their heads in bewilderment,
wondering what in the hell to do.

"It's not fair," complained Melanie Dew, proprietor of the
lunch room that was wedged between Mimi Pink's Porcelain
Parlor and her new Bridal Boutique. "She tripled my rent
overnight. I can't possibly pay that much." Melanie's voice
disappeared upward in a little squeak as she started to cry.

The others were embarrassed, but they were intensely
sympathetic. There were growlings and mutterings, and then
Taylor Baylor spoke up. Taylor had been heavily fined in
the county courthouse for his verbal assault on Mimi Pink,
and he was deeply resentful. "I think I speak for all of us
when I say that Melanie is not alone. Mimi Pink is trying
to force all us honest merchants out of town, people who've
been here fifteen or twenty or thirty years. They tell me she's
dickering with that out-of-town real estate firm that owns
my block. If she gets her hands on that, I might as well
give up."

"It's war, that's what it is," said Isabelle Moseley, who
had a small notions shop on Walden Street. "It's the battle
of Concord all over again, only this time it's not the min-

109

utemen and the British, it's us and Mimi Pink. Only this time the enemy is winning."

Taylor Baylor stretched out his fork like a musket. "Fire, fellow soldiers, for God's sake, fire," he cried, quoting Major Buttrick at the North Bridge.

Everybody laughed uneasily, and the breakfast meeting broke up.

Taylor Baylor was too sore in spirit to go back to work in his shoe store. He stayed on at the breakfast table with the barber, Alphonso Domingo, to drink second and third

cups of coffee and indulge in angry gossip about Ms. Pink.

Therefore when Mimi took her usual morning stroll along Walden Street from one shop to another, she noticed that Alphonso Domingo's barbershop was empty.

She paused. The barbershop was the only remaining interruption in her row of pretty stores, a ghastly hole like a missing tooth. Mimi's repeated offers to buy out Alphonso had been steadfastly rejected.

The door of the shop, she noticed, was slightly ajar.

Mimi pushed it open. "Mr. Domingo?" she said loudly.

One of the barber chairs creaked slightly and turned a fraction of a degree. Mimi looked at herself in the big mirror. It seemed strange that an old mirror like that would have the capacity to reflect her modish silhouette, her smart hairstyle, after all those years of giving back only the reflections of Alphonso and his aging customers. Mimi winced at the sagging vinyl-covered couch, the shelves of sticky bottles, she recoiled from the dusty hair clippings on the floor, not yet swept up. What a slob the man was.

"Mr. Domingo?" Mimi said again.

Still no answer. Inquisitively Mimi peeked through the curtains at the back of the shop and pushed through them. The farther room was empty. It was a sort of locker room with a dirty sink, a sloppy desk, a grubby window, a worn linoleum floor, and an overflowing trash barrel—Alphonso Domingo's sanctum sanctorum.

Mimi stared at the heaps of papers on his desk. Without hesitation she slipped her long manicured fingernails among the piles and shuffled them, turning them over, examining them with practiced eyes, reaching deeper down, pulling out buried invoices and bills, surveying them swiftly.

One piece of paper was more interesting than the rest. Mimi plucked it out and read it carefully. It was a bill from the Sonesta Hotel on the Charles River in Cambridge— "Michelle LaFitte, occupancy three weeks, $2,100."

There were other bills clipped to it. Michelle LaFitte's

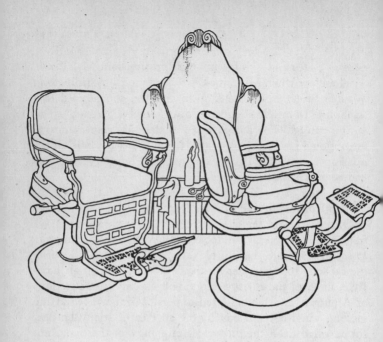

hair had been done, her teeth had been fixed, her corns attended to. She had bought a fur coat.

Alphonso Domingo was a married man. Who was Michelle LaFitte?

With the incriminating papers in her hand, Mimi hurried outside and dodged into Corporate Gifts, where she kept a copy machine. In a trice she was back in Alphonso's office, returning the originals.

Strolling back along the sidewalk to the Parfumerie, Mimi smiled. Perhaps there would soon be no ugly hole in her row of smart shops. Another bright awning might soon be filling the gap.

Later that week Mimi Pink made another assault and captured another enemy fortress. The bank at last came through with her new loan, and she completed the transfer of the commercial building housing Taylor Baylor's shoe store.

Taylor moved out at once, not waiting for his lease to expire. Selling his stock of shoes at a loss to a competitor in Framingham, he moved south, intending to spend the rest of his days ambling around a golf course in Orlando, Florida, flailing glumly at a golfball amid showers of exploding turf, telling himself that this was the life. Day after day Taylor whapped the ball high in the air and watched it bound into the rough, or bury itself in the sand, or plummet into a waterhole. Taylor was bored and disgusted. He was homesick for Concord, Massachusetts.

As for Mimi Pink, she wasted no time in taking over the abandoned ruins of Taylor's shoe store. Standing victorious in the shambles, she looked around in cool disdain at the debris he had left behind.

"We'll take down that wall, I think," she said to her decorator. "A pink carpet, pearl-gray walls. How soon can that woodcarver deliver a new sign?"

The decorator shook his head. "I don't know. He says it's getting harder and harder to get gold leaf. The price is going up. How about plain gold paint?"

But Mimi had her standards. She closed her eyes in disgust and shook her head. "It's gold leaf or nothing. He's probably gouging me. I'll talk him down."

Look at me, Lee-Ann! Look at me, Annie! Look at me, Buzzie! Who's winning now? Me, that's who! Me, me, me, Mimi Pink!

23

It wasn't only the town boards that were meeting in Concord that summer, and the Chamber of Commerce and the Consortium of Concord Boutiques. Down on the shore of Fair Haven Bay where the Sudbury River turned the corner and spread itself out like a lake, another planning session was under way.

Homer and Mary Kelly, Oliver Fry, and Ananda Singh were deep in conspiratorial consultation. They sat on the porch high in the air above the river and put their heads together. Mary's common sense, Oliver's anger, Homer's euphoria, and Ananda's fresh enthusiasm trembled on the verge of possible action.

Ananda recognized Oliver Fry at once as the angry father of the handsome girl at the railroad station. But Ananda was unknown to Oliver Fry. At first Oliver looked at him suspiciously. Was this another Jack Markey, with smoking nostrils and lashing pointed tail? But when Homer related his first conversation with Ananda, Oliver was disarmed.

"Do you know what he said?" reported Homer. "He said, 'The wood thrush sings to amend our institutions,' that's what he said."

Oliver was charmed. He melted at once, and beamed, and shook Ananda's hand.

So that was all right.

Oliver was full of news. He had been inquiring around and attending hearings. He had collared one of the selectmen, he had bawled insults at the chairwoman of the school committee, he had burst into a meeting of the planning board, a wild apparition with sandy hair, inflamed freckles, and bulging eyes. " 'Who hears the fishes when they cry?' " he had shouted, quoting Thoreau in the middle of a request by a petitioner to add a rumpus room to his garage.

"Fishes?" the petitioner had said, bewildered. "What fishes?"

Homer listened to Oliver's tirade and wondered why idealists were often so absurd. Realists were always sober and sensible. They spoke in measured tones and quoted the bylaws and belched discreetly behind their handkerchiefs. They won, that was the trouble, while the frustrated idealists grew more and more ridiculous and cut off their ears and stopped taking baths and adopted a hundred and fifty cats.

Concord was selling out to Jack Markey and Jefferson Grandison, that was the substance of Oliver's story. If nobody did anything about it, there would soon be a mixed-use complex of housing units and commercial properties on land now belonging to the high school, right across the highway from Walden Pond. All that was needed was a slight change of zoning at the special town meeting in October. With the town boards behind it, the motion would probably pass.

"This Jack Markey," said Mary Kelly, "does he live here in town?"

"No," growled Oliver, "he comes from Brookline."

"Then how did he find out about all the boards? How did he know who to talk to? How did he figure out all these trade-offs?"

"There must be a traitor in our midst," said Oliver, glowering. And then he had an excruciating thought. He remembered his first sight of Jack Markey, sitting at the kitchen table with Hope. The two of them had been bowed over a map of the town of Concord.

Oliver groaned aloud. Hope was the traitor, his own beloved daughter.

Then Ananda broke in. "But how can the people of Concord allow such things to happen?"

Homer and Mary looked at each other and made wry faces, but Ananda went on talking. He was like the child before the naked emperor, asking an innocent question. He was not blinded by the pragmatic crudities of local politics, he was not deafened by rote phrases of long custom, nor was his tongue thickened with trite phrases about the sacred heritage of history. His view was large and ample. "All over the world there are disciples of Henry Thoreau. People of every nation will care what happens to this wooded hill near Walden Pond. Surely the people of Concord will wake up, will remember, will be ashamed."

Ananda stopped talking and lowered his eyes.

For a moment no one else said anything. The sun threw shimmering sparkles into their eyes from the river. A pair of white gulls floated high over the water, blown all the way from the landfill where they had been scavenging choice bits of garbage.

Oliver gaped at Ananda. He opened his mouth to say something, then closed it again. Mary smiled. What a darling the boy was.

Then Homer came to his senses and laughed. "Do you know what we've got here? A spokesman. We've got to send him out into the world to carry the flag."

"I know," said Mary promptly, getting to her feet, "the television station. Concord's got one. Why can't he appear on television?"

"Brilliant." Homer thumped the table. "They're always looking for issues and causes, people to talk about something. Anything to use up time. Call them up."

Ananda looked frightened. "You mean I am to make a public speech?"

"Just say what you said just now, that's all. Tell the world. Well, it won't exactly be the world. It will be a few people only half listening because they're getting supper and they forgot to switch channels, or they're looking for the ball game and they can't find it, or they tuned in by mistake. But it's better than nothing."

Mary made the call at once. To her surprise the station manager accepted the idea with enthusiasm. "But we'll have to get somebody to talk on the other side. I mean, we can't just show one side."

"What do you mean, the other side?"

"You know, the side that wants to see Walden Green built on that site. We've got to be fair, after all."

"You mean, you've always got to balance right with wrong, and truth with falsehood?"

The station manager let this sarcasm pass, and they arranged a date for Ananda's appearance.

"Tuesday evening, is that all right, Ananda?" said Mary. "It will be a sort of debate, with somebody speaking for what they call the other side."

Ananda was dismayed. "I know so little about local matters. You must instruct me. I am so ignorant, so uninformed."

"I wonder who they'll get to speak for the developer?" said Oliver Fry darkly.

"Maybe they'll go right to the top," said Homer, "and get Grandison himself."

But it was not Jefferson Grandison. The manager of the television studio called Jack Markey and asked him to do it. But Jack thought of a better candidate.

He discussed his choice with Grandison on the phone. "After all, she's a local citizen. She'll carry more weight than some foreigner. And she's the daughter of that Thoreau nut, Oliver Fry. She'll undercut their side, knock the bottom out of it."

"I see," said Grandison, staring out the window of his vast office in the direction of the blue haze that was the western suburbs, where Jack Markey was an invisible microscopic speck in a tiny telephone booth.

So Jack arranged it with Hope, who was too surprised to say no. Next morning at breakfast she broke the news to her father as he took his container of dead frogs from the freezer. "Oh, by the way," said Hope carelessly, "I'm going to be on television."

"Oh?" said Oliver, prying off the top of the container to inspect the frogs. "What for?"

"Well, the truth is," said Hope with a laugh, as though it were just a joke, "I'm going to be defending Walden Green, the new shopping center. Now, Father, don't get upset. Jack asked me to do it, and I didn't see why not, so I said yes."

Oliver dropped the container. The slippery brick of frozen frogs slid out on the floor. "You didn't see why not?" He gasped and pursued the frogs across the linoleum. "Why not? Because it will make a fool of your father, that's why not."

"You mean, they asked me just because I'm your daughter?" Hope laughed cruelly. "Maybe they think I'm something in my own right, not just the daughter of Oliver Fry."

Oliver was silent. He picked up the frogs, feeling his heart break.

Hope's conscience lashed at her, but she flounced out of the room and ran lightly upstairs. In a moment Oliver could hear her typewriter rattling in her bedroom. The noise battered at him. He couldn't bear it.

Tackety-tackety-tack went Hope's typewriter, clattering without cease. But when she heard the screen door slam she stood up to watch her father ride his bicycle up Walden Street in the direction of the high school.

He was hunched over the handlebars like an old man. For the first time Hope saw how much power she had over him, and she was dismayed. She didn't want his happiness to be dependent on her. People should be free and self-sufficient, as if they lived in separate narrow shafts without connecting doors and windows.

But now, looking through her own bedroom window as

her father pumped his bicycle away around the curve of the street, Hope threw up the sash and called after him. It was too late. His bicycle grew smaller and smaller and disappeared behind the blank wall of the light-plant substation across the road.

24

*Money is not required to buy one necessary
of the soul.*
Walden, "Conclusion"

The United Parcel truck was just pulling up to Julian Snow's door when he got home from the landfill. "For Alice Snow," said the driver, hopping out of the truck with a big box.

Julian took the box inside and opened it suspiciously. Cautiously he felt around in the Styrofoam popcorn for the silly things Alice had ordered. He found a doorknob chime, a plastic whatnot with four triangular shelves, a musical toilet-paper holder, and a praying hands paperweight. Sadly he set them side by side on the table.

Well, Honey and Mavis would take them. Julian picked up the box, intending to carry it to the dumpster behind the laundry shack, when something else fluttered out. It was a handwritten message for Alice Snow: "Please in the future do not send cash."

Alice had paid for all this stuff in cash? Eighty dollars, the invoice said. Where had she got the cash money?

There was only one answer. Julian was so staggered, he dropped the box, and the white popcorn scattered on the floor. Alice had been helping herself to their savings. She had taken all the hundreds and twenties out of the file box over the window and hidden them somewhere, and then she had stuck them in envelopes and sent for things from catalogs. Honey or Mavis or Shirley must have mailed the letters for her.

Julian thought about it. Some people had said that Alice was killed when she caught someone stealing the two thousand dollars. But it wasn't true after all. There was no connection between the disappearance of the money and the death of his wife. Alice had taken it herself and hidden it somewhere.

Julian ransacked every nook and corner. He found nothing.

Oh well, hell, it didn't matter. Julian didn't begrudge Alice her little extravagances. If she'd told him she was taking fifty dollars here and eighty dollars there, he wouldn't have said no. But she would have had a fight on her hands, ordering doorknob chimes and plastic whatnots. Maybe that was why she had been so secretive.

Next day was Saturday. Julian got up early, hauled his aluminum canoe out of the bushes, lifted it into the back of his truck, tossed in the paddles and his rod, and put the bucket of minnows from the bait shop on the floor of the cab. On the way out of Pond View he slowed down at Norman Peck's place, because he'd been planning to ask Norman to go along. Then he didn't stop after all, because he recognized the Toyota belonging to Norman's daughter parked beside Norman's car. So Julian went on by himself, driving down 126 and into the Walden Pond reservation and down the hill to the boat launch on the shore.

Julian was after rainbows. In the summer they were mostly too deep, down there in the cold water in the depths of the pond. But there were cold springs here and there, making chilly columns in which the trout rose closer to the surface. He had a thermometer. He could test for the cooler places.

In the early morning there was a lacy mist on the water. Julian reeled out his line and looked at the mist. He should have felt contented, but he didn't. He felt funny about Alice. The ugly objects on the kitchen table had brought her back so strongly. There she was, Alice Snow, right there in the kitchen. And then in spite of himself Julian thought about the note from Charlotte Harris, "It's just that I've always loved you." No sooner had Charlotte written those words than Alice had died. What about Pete Harris? Would he vanish, too, like Alice, at a single breath of betrayal?

It took Julian two hours to catch his limit. Afterward, on the way back into the trailer park, he was surprised when Stu LaDue stood up from his chair and waved his arms and waddled over importantly to stand beside the cab of the truck and tell him something. "Norman's passed on," Stu said, staring at Julian, his round eyes enlarged by his thick glasses. He was obviously enjoying his role as the deliverer of tragic information. "Brain hemorrhage. The hearse is there now. See, right beside his daughter's car. Fran, she come over from Watertown."

Julian's eyes filled with tears. Norman had been his closest friend at Pond View. They had been fishing companions from day one.

He pulled up beside the hearse just as the men from the funeral parlor emerged from Norman's Landola with a covered object, all that was left of Norman Peck.

Sorrowfully Julian approached Norman's daughter, who was watching from the doorway. He could hardly get the words out as he told her he was sorry.

Norman's daughter was businesslike. "I suppose you people want this thing out of here," she said, jigging her elbows sideways to indicate the trailer. "Well, I can't do it. First I've got to clear out Dad's junk, and then who the hell wants a thirty-five-year-old mobile home? I'll have to advertise. I'm not going to give it away, I'm telling you that. You already got a bunch of empties here. Well, one more won't hurt you."

It was true. People died, and their relatives didn't get around to removing their mobile homes. The old trailers weren't worth much on today's market, that was the trouble. People looking for mobile homes now, they wanted big fancy Burlingtons with cathedral ceilings and fancy kitchens and glamorous bathrooms and wall-to-wall carpeting. Some of the new ones were seventy-two feet long.

Julian watched Norman's daughter get into her car with the trophy Norman's dog had won thirty years ago for being the best pug dog in the state of New Hampshire. He couldn't believe that the man he had joked with yesterday was reduced to a round mound under a tarpaulin, a hardhearted daughter in a Toyota, and a silver-plated trophy for a prize-winning pug.

Another shock was waiting for him. Bernie and Mavis Buonfesto hailed him from their screened porch. Dot and Scottie Ryan were there, too. Julian pulled his truck over and got out and walked up to the porch, looking for sympathy, for tender memories of Norman. "Now there's only twelve of us left," he said, smiling at them wanly.

"Only ten pretty soon," said Bernie.

"Ten?"

"We're leaving," said Mavis. "Moving to Miami. I mean, look, our best friends are gone. Well, not counting you, Julian. And Bernie's got glaucoma. Our daughter's been trying to get us to come down. Everything's cheaper there. And the winters—well, you know what they're like around here. So we're packing up, driving down next week. Dot and Scottie are coming, too. We're going down together."

"It's just a holiday," said Scottie.

Dot looked at him severely. "No, it's not. I'm going to look for someplace nice. You might like it down there better than you think."

"Don't listen to her," said Scottie, grinning at Julian. "She's just kidding. We're not moving away."

"I sure hope not." Julian got back in his truck and drove to his own place. Then he sat in the cab and looked at the sunlight dappling the roof of his mobile home. They had all known it would be like this, ever since the Massachusetts Department of Environmental Management had taken over the property. Oh, sure, they'd all known there would be a slow subtraction of residents until only a few of them were left, and then only two, then one, and at last, some fine day, they would all be gone. But he hadn't expected it to feel so bad.

Next day, the last Sunday in July, Madeline Raymond keeled over with an embolism, as if sudden death were catching. Her nephew didn't come to her funeral, but he arranged long distance from Philadelphia to have her trailer hauled away and sold. Talk about efficiency!

It took Roger Bland a couple of weeks to catch up with the new statistics on the number of living souls remaining at Pond View. He didn't know the Buonfestos had left for Miami, he didn't know the Ryans were arguing between themselves about moving to Florida, too.

But he was pleased. Only eleven! It was wonderful the way nature, left to itself, simply took its course.

25

*In the street and in society I am almost invariably
cheap and dissipated, my life is unspeakably mean.*
Journal, January 7, 1857

Homer had lots of things to look up in the Boston Public
Library. He parked at the Concord depot and went in on the
train.

It was a frustrating morning. The Boston Public was one
of the great libraries of the western world, but it was troubled
by the same spending cuts afflicting the town of Concord.
As a result the computer screen told Homer that the where-
abouts of one of the books he wanted was unknown, and the
other had been stolen from the collection.

Homer gave up and walked out of the library into the
moist heat of late July in Copley Square.

At once his attention was caught by a woman groping in
a trash can on the corner of Dartmouth Street. As he waited
for the light to change he watched her turn over the trash
with the pointed end of an umbrella and fish out a bedraggled
T-shirt. Bulging plastic bags packed into a baby stroller held
her belongings.

Homer had heard a lot about homeless people, but he
rarely saw them in the flesh. Furtively he took a ten-dollar
bill out of his wallet and held it out to her, wondering if it
was the wrong thing to do. Perhaps the woman would be
insulted.

She was not. She accepted it, giving him a piercing look.
Embarrassed, Homer smiled at her and plunged down the
subway stairs. The Green Line took him to Park Street and
the Red Line to Porter Square, where he boarded the train
for Concord. But when the conductor passed through the

Copley Square

train and stood beside him to punch the return half of his round-trip ticket, Homer couldn't find it. It wasn't in his billfold, where it should have been. It wasn't in any of his pockets. "Sorry," he said, rummaging for the price of another. He was short ten cents. The conductor looked at him strangely and let it pass.

The truth was that Homer's ticket had flown out of his billfold when he removed the ten-dollar bill. The ticket landed on the sidewalk in front of Sarah Peel. Homer didn't see it, but Sarah did. She reached down and picked it up, examined it carefully, and tucked it away for safekeeping.

Back at the house on Fair Haven Bay, Homer found Ananda in the cellar. Ananda was examining the household collection of nails and screws. He shook his head sorrowfully at Homer. "I can't get them straight, you see. Some of the screws are flat on top, some are round, some have a cross. People ask me for them in the store, and I don't know which is which. And a six-penny nail does not cost six cents."

Homer tried to imagine the life of a young man who had never used a screwdriver. Patiently he explained, while Ananda made careful notes. "There," said Homer, "that's enough. Let's go out on the river and cool off."

"Oh, yes," said Ananda, his anxious face transformed.

On the river the hot sun poured down, but cool exhalations rose from the slow-moving water, and the gentle ripples slapped against the aluminum canoe. Homer laughed at Ananda's fumbling attempts to handle a paddle. Ananda apologized. He had spent a summer at New Hall College, Cambridge, and there he had become expert at handling a punt on the river Cam, standing up and propelling it with a pole. But canoes were new to him.

"You just dip it straight in and out like this," explained Homer. "Whenever the canoe begins to swerve, just hold the paddle close in on the other side. That's right. Good for you."

Swiftly they moved downriver. By the time they had passed the hospital and skimmed under the whizzing traffic on Route 2, Ananda was paddling strongly. Soon they were moving briskly past the sloping backyards of the big houses along Main Street.

In the shelter of the Nashawtuc bridge they paused to eat their cheese sandwiches. A blue heron flapped up in awkward flight, its huge wings curved to cup the air, its head hanging low. Ananda watched the duckweed swirl in spirals at the edge of the river like galaxies forming and dissolving. Everything was quivering, tossing, trembling. A bird made a snipping noise like scissors.

"Look," said Homer, "that's a new house over there. It wasn't here last year."

"It is very large," said Ananda.

They looked at the new house. It was a complicated structure with decks, terraces, a three-car garage, a greenhouse and outbuildings, and a scattering of the Palladian windows that were so popular that year.

"What a pretty creature," said Ananda, admiring the pale gray horse that looked at them from an enclosure beside the house. Its ears were pricked up, it leaned over the fence to stare at them. They watched as a woman came out of the house with a pail, opened the gate of the paddock, and stopped at a covered bin. They saw her lift the lid and scoop something up.

A small gong went off in Homer's head. Her gesture reminded him of something. Taking the binoculars from Ananda, he watched shamelessly as the woman approached the horse, carrying the pail, calling, "Here, Carmencita, here, girl, good girl."

Carmencita wasn't having any. She sprinted to the other side of the paddock, whinnying in derision. Her mistress gave up and went indoors. But only for a moment. Soon she emerged from another door, carrying a basket.

"Should we not continue?" murmured Ananda, embarrassed by the way Homer was watching the woman so inquisitively.

But Homer was fascinated. "She looks so familiar. Wait, I know who it is. It's Marjorie Bland."

Ananda glanced at her over his shoulder. "Her husband is president of the planning board?" Ananda had been doing his homework, getting ready for his appearance on television.

"Right. He's the chairman. She's Mrs. Roger Bland." Homer went right on staring. Now the woman was kneeling on the grass beside the deck. She was taking little pots out of the basket, transplanting flowers into the ground. Homer could see her profile, her pink nose, her pretty smile. (As usual, Marjorie was having fun.)

Putting down the binoculars, Homer took in the larger scene—Marjorie's house, Marjorie's horse, Marjorie's garden, Marjorie herself with her happy smile and pink shorts. It was like a commercial version of Eve in the Garden of Eden. Marjorie Bland was Eve before the Fall, as pictured on the cover of an L. L. Bean catalog. If somebody had sent a catalog to the original Eve, she wouldn't have had to go naked, she could have worn a beach and town tank top in cornflower blue and walking shorts in cherry pink and flashing white Top-Siders, just like Marjorie's.

Ananda picked up his paddle. "Shall we carry on?"

"Wait. There's something about this woman that gives me a pain. And you know what it is?" Homer picked up the binoculars again and studied Marjorie Bland. "It's her happiness, that's what it is. Her horrible happiness. She's probably the happiest woman in the whole wide world."

"She will see you," murmured Ananda, staring carefully down at his sandwich.

Then Homer knew what he had been reminded of when Marjorie reached into the feed bin with her pail. It was the woman in Copley Square, the homeless woman with all her possessions packed into a child's stroller. She had reached into the trash can in just the same way. For a moment the two images coalesced.

There was a word for it, "doppelgänger." Marjorie Bland and the homeless woman were doppelgängers of one another. They were opposites in every respect, yet Homer knew he would never again catch sight of Marjorie Bland without seeing through her the woman at the library in Copley Square.

Homer and Ananda stuffed their sandwich wrappers under the canoe thwarts, took up their paddles, and headed back up the river. Turning his head, Homer caught a last glimpse of Marjorie Bland. She was standing in an open doorway looking eastward. That way lay the city of Boston, beyond the willows draped with pale green hair, beyond the cloudy trees of French Meadow, beyond all the intervening suburbs, beyond the sprawling city of Cambridge.

Homer guessed that Marjorie's consciousness stopped short at the town line. Beyond the Concord horizon there might be a noise of some sort, an occasional tormented cry, but her ears were stopped up, and she would never hear.

. . . a successful life knows no law—Live free,
child of the mist . . .
Thoreau, "Walking"

When Sarah Peel stepped off the train in Concord, bumping her stroller down the high step, having made the journey with Homer Kelly's lost ticket, she made straight for the house of Marjorie Bland like a homing pigeon, as if she knew all about Homer's doppelgänger theory that there was an ethereal bond between herself and Marjorie.

But Sarah was merely following her nose, heading away from the Concord depot, looking for her imagined landscape of green trees and brown cows and horses with flying manes and tails. At the intersection of Thoreau Street and Main she saw a bridge, and beyond it a light-filled meadow. Pausing on the bridge, she looked down at the water flowing darkly underneath, then lifted her eyes to the green lawn on the other side.

There was a horse on the lawn, standing behind a fence. The horse was looking at Sarah.

Dragging the stroller behind her, she plodded across the bridge and found her way down a bushy slope to the pasture fence. Ducks flew up from the edge of the river. A bird threaded the air, swooping down from a great height and soaring up again.

The horse was waiting for her. It trotted along the fence and stopped, its ears cocked eagerly. It was a small grayish white horse with a fiery eye, just like her own special horse on the merry-go-round. Whiffling gently, it reached its long neck over the fence. Small as it was, it towered above her.

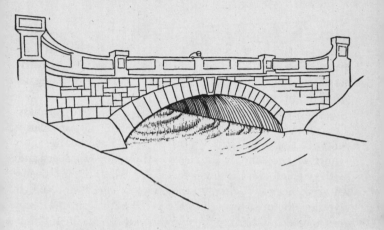

Its belly swelled, its rump was round, its eyes were brown and melting. Crowding up against the fence, it bent its great head to Sarah.

She knew at once what to call it. "Pearl," she said, stroking its nose tenderly. "Your name is Pearl."

All of Sarah's past life welled up in a burst of affection. The white horse in the green field was a gift, a compensation for her impoverished childhood, her pinched adulthood and brutal old age. It was what she hungered for. The horse too had been waiting—waiting for her, for Sarah Peel.

"I'll never go back," said Sarah, whispering in the horse's ear.

Looking around, she saw beyond the pasture a big house and a small shed. The door of the shed was open.

*. . . our foe is the all but universal woodenness of
both head and heart. . . .*
"A Plea for Captain John Brown"

Marjorie Bland's niceness was a golden principle. It was
the rallying cry for her life on earth. She was nice in every
possible way, from getting up in the morning to going to
bed at night.

Since Marjorie was not an imaginative person, her niceness
was confined to fashionable causes like her recycling campaign. But of course it was a truly worthy undertaking. The
banner of her concern for the recycling of newspapers and
bottles rippled over the town of Concord. Many of the citizens
who read her jolly letters to the *Concord Journal* resolved to
save their bottles, separating the green ones from the clear
ones and taking them to the recycling area at the landfill and
tossing them into the green bottle dumpster and the clear
bottle dumpster. Some were diligent about it, some sorted
their bottles when they remembered to do it, a lot of people
threw them carelessly into the ordinary trash in particolored
confusion.

The day Sarah Peel arrived in Concord was the day of the
week when Marjorie Bland sorted her own bottles, tossing
the green wine bottles into one bag, the clear ketchup and
vinegar bottles and the jam and mayonnaise jars into another.
They were rather pretty, separated like that, each bottle lying
among its mates, all matching like the upholstered furniture
in her living room.

Clutching the two bags to her chest, Marjorie walked out
of the house and approached the shed where her horse, Baronesa Carmencita de Granada, had her stall. Nervously Mar-

jorie skirted the side of the shed where Carmencita was munching on a bucket of horse pellets.

Carmencita belonged to Marjorie's son, Wally, who was spending the summer as a camp counselor in Bar Harbor. Actually the horse was too small for Wally now, and it was going through some sort of senile crisis. Marjorie winced and dodged out of the way as Carmencita caught sight of her and laid back her ears dangerously. Surely it was time to have the dear old thing put to sleep? Marjorie vowed to discuss the matter with Roger.

The shed space allotted to her recycling studio was on the other side, safely removed from Wally's impossible horse. Boldly Marjorie pushed the door open and walked in.

At once she shrieked and dropped her bags of bottles with a splintering crash. An old woman was sitting on a pile of newspapers, looking at her.

Homer Kelly would have relished the moment of confrontation between Marjorie Bland and her doppelgänger, Sarah Peel. But Homer was not there. Marjorie and Sarah were alone.

Rallying, Marjorie faced the crisis, recognizing the nature of the problem at once, seeing Sarah for what she was, one of those homeless people she had read about in the paper. Their plight was very much in the public eye. Homelessness was a fashionable topic of conversation in Marjorie's circle of friends. The question was always the same: Why didn't somebody do something about it? Roger said it was the budget crisis in Massachusetts. With money so tight, the legislature couldn't afford to address the situation. It was really a shame.

What was Marjorie to do now? She stared at the weird creature in her shed, and Sarah Peel stared back. It was obvious to Marjorie at once that she couldn't do anything about this pitiful case herself. But on the other hand, she couldn't call the police and have the woman taken away. What if word got out that the Blands had thrown a homeless woman out into the street?

They had to be so careful. Roger was about to run for the office of Concord selectman, and there was an even more important contest on the horizon. He had been asked to be a candidate for the board of overseers at Harvard.

Roger was so excited about it! He was trying to figure out how to write the required self-description, so that the alumni and alumnae could read about him when they received their ballots in the mail. Together Marjorie and Roger had been studying the ballots from previous years. The candidates were always successful in business, but more important they were men and women with deep public concerns. They were dedicated to the YMCA or the Salvation Army or endangered species. They certainly didn't turn homeless people out on their ear.

All these considerations flashed through Marjorie's head in an instant. Then she knew what to do. She remembered her watchword. Niceness was the key. "Good morning," she said brightly to Sarah Peel. "Would you like some lunch?"

Sarah merely looked at her. There was something in her eyes that frightened Marjorie. Turning, she scuttled out the back door of the shed, carefully avoiding the paddock. In the kitchen she bustled around, arranging a pretty tray, and in a few moments she was back in the shed. On the tray lay a watercress sandwich, the crusts daintily removed, apple slices in a rosette, two cookies, and a marigold.

The woman was still sitting on the pile of newspapers. "*Bon appétit!*" said Marjorie, setting the tray down on another stack and trotting away.

For the next twenty minutes she kept looking out the window anxiously, hoping the queer old woman would depart.

She didn't. At last Marjorie popped back into her recycling studio. "All finished?" she said gaily, looking at the empty tray. Even the marigold was gone. The woman must have eaten it. Marjorie was amused to see a yellow petal stuck to her cheek.

"Now!" she said in the tone of one who claps her hands and brings a class to order. "Let's take a ride into town, shall we?"

Swish, swish, poppity-pop. Before Sarah knew what was happening, she was bundled onto the backseat of Marjorie's shiny red Nissan.

It was a short ride to the depot. On Thoreau Street a parking place opened up before them like a miracle, the parting of the Red Sea. Hopping out, Marjorie ran around the car, plucked Sarah and her belongings out onto the sidewalk, and rushed them across the street.

By another miracle the train to Boston was just pulling in. Swing low, sweet chariot! And then at the last minute, just as Sarah dragged her stroller up the high step of the railroad car, Marjorie thrust into one of Sarah's bags all the green dollars in her purse.

"Good-bye, good-bye!" she cried as the train pulled out. Then she stood back, gasping, feeling she had handled the crisis superbly. Niceness had done its utmost. She would tell Roger all about it, and he would congratulate her for quick thinking. Marjorie raced for the car as the first big drops of a summer storm fell out of the sky.

But as the train moved away from the Concord depot on the shining track and rolled past Walden Pond and plunged into the woods, Sarah thought of the horse in Marjorie's stable, the pretty white horse named Pearl, the horse that belonged to Sarah.

"Just you wait," Sarah promised Pearl. "Don't you worry. I'll be back."

Alphonso Domingo, the barber, was also leaving Concord on the train. He sat across the aisle from Sarah Peel, leaning forward, staring at the floor, his hands clasped between his knees.

Alphonso had not intended to leave his shop so early, but after a surprise visit from Mimi Pink, he had hung a Closed sign on the door and locked the place up.

Mimi's visit had been a disaster. She had taken pieces of paper out of her handbag and rattled them at Alphonso. She had proof, she said, of his intimate friendship with a woman. She slapped down her copies of the bill for Michelle LaFitte's three weeks at the Hotel Sonesta, and the bills from Michelle's podiatrist and dentist, and the receipt for Michelle's mink coat.

And then Mimi offered to buy Alphonso out.

Alphonso was cornered. He said yes.

28

There is never an instant's truce between
virtue and vice.
Walden, "Higher Laws"

Jack Markey sat in Hope's kitchen on the morning of the television debate. Before them lay the plans and elevations for Walden Green.

"Where's your father?" said Jack, looking around nervously.

"Don't worry," said Hope. "He'll be gone all day. He's on a collecting expedition. He's looking for pitcher plants in Gowing's Swamp."

Jack shivered. "Isn't that the quaking bog where they used to bury horses? What if he falls in?"

Hope laughed, but Jack had an image of Oliver Fry's mad eyes rolling as he went down, down, down into the swamp. It was a pleasant thought, and Jack smiled as he explained the layout of Walden Green. "This building that looks like a church is really housing for the elderly. The town hall at the other end has shops downstairs and offices above."

"It's nice," said Hope, leaning over to study the plan in detail while Jack looked around the old-fashioned kitchen. He couldn't help thinking how he would transform it. The soapstone sink would go, naturally, and he'd open up that wall with sliding glass doors and eliminate the back porch. Maybe someday he'd get a chance to do a lot of things to this house. Jack looked at Hope's long brown hair trailing over the plans he had drawn with his own hand. He couldn't believe his good luck. This stunning girl had turned up as if by magic and offered herself to him as a spy in the enemy camp. Maybe she would offer herself to him in another way, if he played his cards right.

Hope was impressed by Jack's plan, she couldn't deny it. He had conceived of Walden Green as a village green with white clapboard houses all around it. "It's really pretty."

There was a shriek from the drying porch. "My God, what's that?" said Jack.

Hope laughed. "It's just Father's owl. Don't worry." But the owl's cry was like the voice of her father, it was a warning straight from Oliver Fry. Hope knew very well that he would not be impressed by Jack's charming scheme for the woods across Route 2 from Walden Pond. "Phony," he would say angrily. "The whole thing is completely phony." This morning he had looked at her silently across the breakfast table, his tragic eyes accusing her, and she had felt terrible, really terrible. Somehow she had to get away, she had to move out. It was too painful living with her father, sharing the same house with all that steaming intensity and wrongheaded passion.

Hope felt a constriction in her stomach, and she knew what it was—another Hope, a larger Hope, wedged inside her, crowded up against her skin, all elbows and knees, trying to get out. *Squeeze down*, commanded Hope, *stop shoving*.

She looked anxiously at Jack. "What about this other person on the program, this guy from India? Do you know what he's like? I'm scared."

"Oh, don't worry. He's probably some mystical freak with a yellow robe and a shaved head." Jack did a comic imitation of a generic Oriental, bobbing his head obsequiously, his palms together prayerfully.

But later on, looking out from the control room of the television studio, Jack recognized Ananda Singh at once as the foreign kid he had picked up that day on the road, the one who had held his surveying stick. He laughed. So this was the big expert on conservation and Henry Thoreau! Those people on the other side must be poorly supplied with experts if all they could find to represent them was an ignorant immigrant.

Hope too remembered Ananda at once. He was the pilgrim who had come ten thousand miles to visit Walden Pond. She had forgotten about him, although his dark eyes had haunted her for the rest of the day. He was wearing a suit, of course, not a saffron-colored robe. As he bowed to her gravely, she was flustered. "Oh," she said, "it's you."

Ananda in his turn was astonished that the daughter of Oliver Fry had been chosen to speak for the new development in Walden Woods. How could there be such a difference of opinion in one family? The United States was full of puzzles. "How do you do?" he said formally, waiting until Hope sat down before taking a seat himself.

Their interviewing host was a pretty girl with a mop of red hair. To Ananda's surprise she began the program by reading the local news.

"Heading the news this evening," she said briskly, "is a fire at the Pond View Trailer Park. An unoccupied mobile home was completely destroyed by fire in the small hours of last night. By the time Concord fire fighters arrived on the scene, the home was a burned-out shell. The fire has been attributed to carelessness on the part of the owners, Mr. and Mrs. Scott Ryan, in failing to turn off the electric stove before departing for a vacation in Florida."

Ananda and Hope waited nervously through a sewage-disposal issue in the town of Nashoba and a motor vehicle accident in Bedford. Then the redheaded girl put down her notes and smiled radiantly at the camera. "We turn now to our issue of the day. I know you will enjoy hearing the two sides of an interesting controversy that is shaking the old town of Concord to its very roots, right now as we speak, a little matter of a shopping mall in the woods near Walden Pond." The redheaded girl turned to Hope. "Hope Fry, who was born in Concord, will speak on behalf of the project, which is a mixed-use development by Grandison Enterprises.

Hope, will you kick off by telling us why you, as a Concord citizen, support Walden Green?"

Hope looked sternly at the camera and opened her mouth. A stranger's voice emerged from her lips, uttering crisp sentences. In her own ears it was sharp and hateful. Swiftly she listed her prepared arguments. "The development will increase the percentage of low-income housing in the town. It will not be an eyesore, as people have feared, not at all. It is a tasteful development that will improve the landscape. And it's not on the shore of Walden Pond, it's half a mile away on the other side of a heavily traveled highway. It will be completely invisible from the pond." Hope's face felt frozen. She dug her fingernails into the palms of her hands. She did not look at Ananda Singh.

Nor did Ananda look at Hope when his turn came. He spoke with easy assurance. His words were spontaneous. They did not sound like memorized arguments. Once again he described the excitement he had felt in coming so far to see the place where *Walden* had been written, a book whose fame had spread around the world. Surely such an influential book, one that had changed the lives of millions, a book that was connected so fundamentally with the landscape from which it had sprung, surely that book and that landscape should be more honored in Concord, Massachusetts?

He was winning. Hope could feel it. She stared at him, wordless, unable to muster a reply.

The redheaded woman jumped into the silence to thank them both. She said something amusing, which Hope was too distraught to understand. Ananda laughed. Hope smiled tensely. It was over.

"You were just great," said the redheaded girl to Ananda, tenderly disentangling him from his microphone.

They stood up. Ananda reached out his hand to shake Hope's and say something courteous. She took his hand limply and gazed at him, transfixed.

Confused, he backed away and said good-bye. As he left

the studio he remembered that he had thought of the girl at the depot as the Statue of Liberty. Now, glancing back, he saw her raise her arm to him in impetuous farewell, as though she were holding a flaming torch.

But the torch flamed for the wrong cause, and he put her out of his mind.

"You were sensational," said Jack Markey, appearing out of the control room.

"Oh, I was not," mumbled Hope. "I made a fool of myself."

Jack took her arm and led her to the parking lot. "No, you didn't. You were great, just great. And you looked absolutely marvelous." He handed her something as they got in the car. "Here, they made a copy of the whole thing."

They celebrated with an evening of dinner and dancing. Jack was really attractive, Hope had to admit it. If she hadn't been so flustered by her encounter with Ananda Singh, she would have responded with more pleasure to Jack's embrace when he stopped the car at her door.

But the visitor from India had distracted her. The needles of her gauges were twitching back and forth, refusing to settle down. "Oh, Jack, I'm sorry," she said, pulling away. "Thank you so much. I had a lovely time."

Disappointed, Jack drove away with his fingers trembling on the steering wheel.

Hope felt a little contrite as she ran up the porch steps. But as she opened the door and glanced into the fierce yellow eyes of the caged owl, she forgot Jack Markey and remembered Oliver Fry. Surely her father had seen the television debate. Oh, God, what would he say?

She need not have worried. Oliver was feeling no pain. He had taken his usual evening dose of four ounces of Tennessee sour-mash whiskey, and his soul was soothed. Apoplexy was staved off for one more day.

Liquor was important to Oliver, and he knew it. He told himself he wasn't an alcoholic because he didn't pour his first

jigger into an ice-filled glass until suppertime. And as medicine it worked like a charm. No matter how ferocious the
battle into which he had been charging with lowered lance
and spiked truncheon, it was wonderful the way a couple of
jiggers of eighty-six proof brought peace to his heart. Not
until the fumes cleared from his head around three o'clock
in the morning would Oliver wake up uneasily and remember
the causes of yesterday's disquiet, and begin to thrash his
limbs and throw himself from side to side.

But at this time in the evening he was suffused with
affection for all the world. Especially for his daughter.
"Hello, there, Hopey dear," he said fatuously. "You looked
so pretty on TV. But that boy Ananda did us proud, you'll
have to admit that. Oh, say, somebody's been calling you.
The number's beside the phone. Bonnie somebody."

Bonnie? Hope didn't know any Bonnie. But she remembered her at once as soon as the breathless voice came on the
line. "Hope Fry, how are you? It's Bonnie Glover, remember
me? I used to be Erline. You remember me, Erline Glover,
at Regional?"

"Oh, Erline, of course I remember you." Erline from
high school, Hope couldn't believe it. Erline had been famous
for having the most amazing measurements in the senior
class. Hope couldn't remember them exactly, but they were
huge-tiny-huge. The only other thing Hope could remember
about Erline was her cooing way of establishing intimacy.
"How does it feel to be you?" Erline would say, leaning
forward eagerly as if she really wanted to know.

"Hey," said Erline Bonnie Glover, "like I just caught
your show on TV."

"Oh, that. I'm afraid I didn't do very well. The trouble
is, I was just—"

"Ananda Singh! Tell me about him! Where is he? Did
you see his picture in *Celebrity* magazine? Did you see that
article last week on the most eligible bachelors in the world?
The whole world?"

"*Celebrity* magazine?"

"There he was, getting into a big limousine. His father's something really big and important, and he's one of the richest men in the world." Bonnie Glover was squealing. "And Ananda, he's so good-looking, so sexy. Oh, God!" Bonnie stopped squealing and began to coo. "Tell me where he's staying. I want to sit on his doorstep. Oh, God, I love celebrities!"

Hope told Bonnie she didn't know where Ananda was staying and hung up, feeling stunned.

Her father was clumping cheerfully to bed, whistling, stumbling a little on the stairs. Hope had the kitchen to herself. Against her better judgment, she played the videocassette.

Oh, it was bad. There she was in an unbecoming dress, sounding artificial, stiff, mechanical—and wrong. She could see it with perfect clarity. Ananda Singh, on the other hand, was simple and powerful and overwhelmingly persuasive.

Hope rewound the tape and played it again, turning down the sound whenever it was her turn to speak, turning it up again when her opponent was talking. She played it through three times, mesmerized by the sight and sound of Ananda Singh, *one of the most eligible bachelors in the whole world.*

29

We are children of light—our destiny is dark.
Journal, October 3, 1840

Homer and Mary Kelly watched the television encounter between Hope Fry and Ananda Singh. Mary was shocked to see Oliver Fry's daughter in the role of a defender of Walden Green.

"Her poor father," she said, leaning forward to turn off the set. "How could she do it to Oliver?"

Homer wasn't listening. "Did you hear that, about the fire at the trailer park? One of the mobile homes burned down. You know, it's just one thing after another over there. The place seems to be trying to self-destruct."

"Oliver thinks the world of that girl. I suppose she's got a right to her opinion, but she doesn't have to tell the world about it."

"And three more of them are dead. Three more in two weeks, not counting Alice Snow. I keep reading their obituaries in the paper. Two of them were really old, but Shirley Mills was only fifty-two."

"The trouble is, she was brought up without a mother. You know, a firm maternal guiding hand."

"Who, Shirley Mills?"

"What?"

Bewildered, Homer got up and stared out the window at the fading glimmer of light on the silvery bend of the river. Then he wandered away to the telephone and flipped through the Concord book, looking for Charlotte Harris. What was her husband's name? Pete. Yes, here he was, *Harris, Peter, 801 Walden Street*.

Homer sat down, gripped the phone, and dialed the number.

"Hello?" said Charlotte Harris.

"Mrs. Harris? Charlotte? This is Homer Kelly. I came to see you after the death of Mrs. Snow."

There was a pause, then Charlotte Harris said, "Yes, Mr. Kelly, I remember."

"I wonder if you can tell me something about the people whose mobile home burned last night, Mr. and Mrs. Ryan. I gather they're on vacation in Florida?"

"Yes, they left yesterday morning and flew down with the Buonfestos. That's another couple from here, they're retiring to Miami. The Ryans are just staying with friends for a week or two."

"Has anyone reached the Ryans to tell them what's happened?"

"Yes, Honey Mooney told me she called them."

"They must have been terribly shocked."

"Yes, of course." Charlotte gave a wry laugh. "At least it will settle the argument."

"Argument?"

"About whether to move to Florida for good or not. Scottie didn't want to, and Dorothy did. Now I suppose they have no choice. There's nothing here to come back to."

"Did Mrs. Mooney ask them if they might have left the stove on?"

"Yes, she did, and Dot said she was sure she had turned it off, she was positive, but Honey thinks she has a tendency to be absentminded."

"Do you think she's absentminded, Mrs. Harris?"

There was another pause. "No," said Charlotte, "I don't."

"I see. Well, thank you, Mrs. Harris."

Charlotte's good-bye was cool and polite.

Homer hung up, then dialed the number of the Concord Fire Department. The fire fighter on phone duty turned out to be a friend of his, Melvin Pierce.

"Oh, hi there," said Melvin. "You got a fire to report, Homer?"

"No, sorry, Melvin. I just want to ask about one. Can you tell me anything about the trailer fire at Pond View last night?"

"Not much to tell. It was the middle of the night. Nobody over there woke up to call us until it was too late to do anything."

"Who finally called you?"

"Man named LaDue. His rig is right next to the one that burned, so he was afraid his would catch fire, too. He was all excited. We hosed his place down. No problem."

"Is it true that the stove was on?"

"Sure is. Of course all the electrical systems were burned out, but one of the knobs was turned to the high setting. Pretty careless of those people, if you ask me."

"Did the Ryans leave a key with anybody? Might somebody have come in after they left and turned on the stove?"

"I don't know about anybody else having a key, but the park manager has keys to all those mobile homes. But it doesn't make sense, somebody else burning the place down, unless they were doing it for the Ryans, so they could collect the insurance."

"What's the name of the park manager?"

"Murchison, Guy Murchison. I've got his number right here."

Homer said good-bye and called Murchison at once. As he waited for the park manager to answer the phone, he pictured the two-story suburban house that was the manager's home and office, there beyond the Walden Pond parking lot. In Homer's opinion the house was as painfully out of keeping with Thoreau's Walden Pond as the landfill and the trailer park. "Hello," he said. "Mr. Murchison?"

Guy Murchison was affable and eager to talk about the fire. "Oh, my God, it was a damn good thing those people were away. The thing must have gone up in seconds. All those mobile homes, they've got a fire door in the bedroom, but sometimes it happens so fast, if they'd been there they might not have got out alive."

"Mr. Murchison, I understand you have keys to all the mobile homes. Can you tell me if anyone might have borrowed their key without your knowledge?"

"Wait a sec. All the keys are on a board in the hall. I'll take a look." In a moment he was back. "Yup, it's still there. Of course somebody might have taken it and brought it back again without my knowing it. Not very likely, I'd say."

"Can you tell me who's been in your office lately?"

"Are you kidding? It's summertime. Everybody and his brother's at the beach. We got emergencies, lost kids, stray dogs, drunks, cars won't start, fistfights, people want to park when the lot is full and won't take no for an answer. You name it, we got it."

"I mean somebody from Pond View. Has anyone from the trailer park been in your office recently?"

"Oh, well, let me see. Julian was here, Julian Snow. He had to sign a paper because his old rental agreement was in his wife's name. Mrs. Mooney and Eugene Beaver, they were here to help me get in touch with the relatives of Shirley Mills."

"That's all?"

"It's all I remember. But, hell, why would anybody want to burn down the Ryans' place? Oh, I can see the Ryans doing it themselves, to collect the insurance. Especially Mrs. Ryan, because she didn't want to stay up here, she wanted to move south. But they were decent people. They'd never do a thing like that. Mrs. Ryan was a timid soul anyhow— too timid to start a fire, for sure."

Homer thanked Guy Murchison, hung up, and went out on the front porch with his wife to watch the dainty fluttering silhouette of a bat, gathering up the flying bugs of evening.

There was a roll of thunder. By the time they went to bed it was raining hard.

30

How enduring are our bodies, after all!
Journal, February 3, 1859

Julian Snow was having a hard time waking up. He kept telling himself that something was wrong. He tried to pull himself to a sitting position, but then he fell back on the pillow and sank into a stupor. At last he forced himself to open his eyes and crawl out of bed.

There was an overpowering smell of gas.

The windows! He must open the windows. Last night he had closed them against the driving rain. Thunder was still rumbling, and there were flashes of lightning.

The first window was stuck and wouldn't open. Staggering a little, coughing, Julian tried the next one, but the crank was missing.

By this time he was struggling for breath. He couldn't stand up. Crawling on hands and knees, he made his way to the emergency door on the other side of the bedroom. There was something in the way, Alice's dressing table. Alice had insisted on pushing it right up against the door.

By now the stench of fumes was overwhelming. Julian pulled himself up beside the dressing table and leaned on it for a moment, his chest bursting. Then he took hold and tugged at it with all his failing strength, trying to pull it far enough so that he could squeeze behind it and open the door a crack. By the time he had hauled it far enough his breath was gone. Julian fainted and lay still beside the closed door. But then a thunderclap woke him, and he was able to reach up, turn the handle, open the door, and put his head out into the rain.

For a while he knelt with water running down his face, filling his lungs with the moist fragrance of woodland, the fresh mud-smelling air of Goose Pond in the hollow below.

Before long he felt better. His head cleared. He got to his feet and hurried into the corridor. There was no time to lose. Something was leaking, either the gas-fired water heater or the gas stove. If the mixture of gas from the stove and the oxygen in the air got too rich, the pilot light would set off an explosion.

With trembling hands Julian tested all the knobs on the stove. Then he went to the water heater and knelt to turn off the valve connecting it to the propane tank outside.

What if he had not waked up? Sooner or later, sometime before morning, there would have been a fiery conflagration and he would have been burned alive.

Alarmed, Julian stood up and went to get a flashlight so that he could look for the leak. Leaning over the stove, he aimed the flashlight behind it. Then he transferred his attention to the water heater. Kneeling on the floor, he poked the flashlight behind the big white tank.

Yes, there it was, a round black hole an eighth of an inch across, right next to the soldered joint.

Funny, you'd think it would be the joint itself where the solder would give way, to let out a pinhole stream of gas.

Getting up off his knees, Julian went to the bedside table for his glasses. Putting them on, he knelt again and aimed the flashlight at the small round hole.

After staring at it a moment, he rose shakily to his feet.

The hole had been drilled. The edges were silver, bright in the feeble illumination of the flashlight. Under the pipe lay a scattering of metal shavings spun off by the drill.

Someone was trying to kill him.

31

I did not think so bright a day
Would issue in so dark a night. . . .
Journal, November 7, 1840

"Mr. Kelly? This is Julian Snow. I hope you've got time to talk to me."

"Certainly, Mr. Snow. As a matter of fact, I want to talk to you, too. What if I came over this afternoon after lunch? Are you working today?"

"I'm working this morning. I get off about two o'clock."

"Perfect. I'll be at your place at two-thirty."

Julian hung up and sat looking at the phone. He wasn't sure he was doing the right thing, talking to Homer Kelly. Oh, the guy seemed sympathetic enough. But probably he'd listen to Julian's story about last night and then go away and forget all about it, just like the police. Well, what the hell, what could anybody do, anyhow? Nobody could put hired bodyguards all over Pond View. If somebody was determined to kill Julian Snow, they'd do it sooner or later.

The trouble was, Julian wasn't ready. Last month it might not have mattered so much. He'd been feeling fairly desperate last month. But now, it was funny the way life was opening up. It seemed good to be alive. And he couldn't deny that the last sentence of Charlotte's letter filled him with a curious excitement.

The gristly maleness that had been holding Julian upright for so many years was softening. The steel plates he had erected to shield himself from his wife's excesses were coming down. Every day Julian unbolted another section of sheet iron.

It was time to go to work. Julian made himself a bag

lunch, filled a thermos with ice water, and walked next door to the landfill. He stopped at the ticket house beside the place where incoming trucks were weighed and said good morning to Bill Sawyer. Eddie Tanner was already at work in the crawl dozer, running up the hill with his big bucket full of sewage sludge.

It was another hot day. The air was heavy with humidity. Julian climbed into the cab of the Trashmaster, sat down on the worn sheepskin of the bucket seat, took his sunglasses out of his pocket, and waved at Eddie Tanner.

Below him yesterday's trash lay mounded, partly exposed by the rain of last night, which had washed away much of the covering layer of dirt. Reaching out his bare brown arm, Julian turned the key, pulled the horizontal lever that raised the blade, stepped on the throttle, and shifted into first gear.

At once he knew something was wrong. The turbocharger began to scream. It was revving too fast. The machine lunged forward. It was out of control, plunging downhill.

Julian grasped the emergency lever for the air shutoff, and it came off in his hand. He put his foot on the brake, and nothing happened. He pulled the emergency, and it flopped back and forth. The spiked wheels of the eighteen-ton machine wallowed downhill, and the engine roared. Steering was impossible. Julian's heart was in his mouth. Off to one side he caught a glimpse of Eddie Tanner shouting at him with his mouth open, but Julian couldn't hear. *Christ*, he was going over the edge into the soft fill.

Wrenching at the articulating lever, he tried to keep the two halves of the machine from cocking into an angle that would tip the whole thing sideways. With a bone-jarring wham, the front end dropped six feet. Julian lurched from side to side as the grinding engine gunned through the loose dirt where rocks rose up like boulders in white water. With crash after jarring crash, the machine butted into them and slithered sideways. By a miracle it reached the hard bottom of the landfill without buckling and rolling over, but it still careened wildly out of control. Directly in its way the ticket house loomed up, and Julian saw Bill Sawyer's white face as he dove out the door just in time. In an instant the house was reduced to splinters, crushed beneath the spiked rollers. Now the runaway machine rammed up the driveway. Julian howled out the window at the approaching cars, and they veered left and right, backing up insanely, trying to get out of his way. But now the front end of the machine was yawing sideways, dropping off the road, charging up the steep slope of the cliff below Route 126. As it barged upward at a frightening angle, Julian saw the chance he had been waiting for. Grasping the blade lever, he jerked on it with all his strength, raising the plow as high as it would go, then let it fall. At once it dug itself into the hillside and shuddered there, burying itself deeper and deeper down. The turbocharger was still screaming, the engine was still roaring at four thousand revolutions per minute, the hundred and fifty thousand dollars the town of Concord had paid for the machine was burning up with the engine, but Julian had brought it to a dead stop.

Exhausted, he hung his head and waited for his pounding heart to quiet down. When he looked up again, he saw Bill Sawyer running toward him with his eyes bugging out of his head. Some of the householders whose cars had been threatened were running up, too, wanting to know what the hell. Eddie Tanner leaped up into the cab, shouting, *"Jesus!"* and supported Julian while his shaky legs fumbled for the metal step.

It took only a few minutes more for the engine to seize up. The whole thing suddenly exploded. Pieces of metal rocketed into the air and the side plates blew off.

Eddie and Julian stood beside the machine they had handled day after day, year after year, and watched it die.

32

*While these things are being done, beauty stands
veiled and music is a screeching lie.*
"A Plea for Captain John Brown"

"It was no accident," Julian told Homer Kelly. "Somebody put sand in the oil line that goes to the bearings. And that's not all. They disconnected the air shutoff and cut the brake lines with a pair of tin snips and used bolt cutters on the emergency."

"Good God." Homer stared at Julian's ashen face. For a moment he was too appalled to say anything more. He got up from the table in Julian's kitchen and put his hand on Julian's shoulder. "Listen here," he said, "have you had any lunch?"

Julian shook his head and looked down at the table.

"Low blood sugar," said Homer. He opened Julian's refrigerator and poked around inside. "There's some baloney in here. Have you got any bread?"

Wordlessly Julian pointed at the bread box, then found his voice. "There's something else. It's what I called you about this morning. Something happened last night." In a flat monotone he told Homer about the leaking gas and the drilled hole in the pipe.

Once again Homer was staggered. "Show me," he said.

He was almost too big to wedge himself down on all fours in the narrow hallway and get his head into the closet housing the water heater. But by looking out of the corner of his eye as Julian aimed the flashlight, he was able to see the bright silver of the drilled hole and the scattering of metal shavings.

"Right," he said, backing out, heaving himself to his feet,

and barking his head on the door frame. "It's odd the way somebody has a fondness for fuel lines."

Silently they went back to the kitchen and sat down. Homer looked at Julian gravely. "It isn't just you, it's the whole park. Somebody's going after everybody in the park." He picked up the untouched sandwich on Julian's plate and handed it to him. "Come on, eat up. And tell me about the fire in the Ryans' trailer. Did you see anybody go in there after Mr. and Mrs. Ryan left for Florida?"

"No, but I wasn't exactly standing watch. You'll have to ask the others."

"Well, come on."

They started up the driveway, and at once they came upon Honey Mooney. She was working with a sponge and a bucket of water, cleaning the aluminum siding of her mobile home.

"No," said Honey, "I didn't see anybody go in there. But all their neighbors were hanging around. Porter McAdoo was doing something to his car, Charlotte Harris was working in her garden. Both of them live right across the driveway from Dot and Scottie's place. They could have nipped over when the rest of us were indoors." Honey gestured with her sponge at an old man sleeping on a lawn chair across the way and whispered to Julian, "Eugene was outside, too, just lying there like that. Maybe he was just pretending to be asleep." Honey stared at Eugene Beaver and frowned. "You'd think he'd do something about his lawn."

Homer sauntered over to speak to Eugene, followed by Julian. "Oh, Mr. Beaver," said Homer loudly, bending over to look at him. "I'm sorry to wake you up."

Eugene Beaver jerked awake and looked up at Homer in confusion.

"Mr. Beaver," began Homer, but he was interrupted by a shout.

He turned to see a portly man running toward them, waving his arms. "It's Charlotte! Christ, she's been electrocuted!"

Julian was off like a shot. Homer lumbered after him, following Pete Harris, who was whining and flapping his hands.

By the time Homer and Pete were jammed together in the doorway, Julian was down on his knees in the Harrises' kitchen, trying to resuscitate Charlotte, who lay on her back on the floor.

"It was the iron cord," whimpered Pete. "It's not my fault. I don't know shit about electricity." Pete mopped his perspiring face and stared at Homer with bulging eyes. "She was ironing, right? And all of a sudden it goes zap, and there's this blue light, and there she is on the floor. Christ!"

"Look," said Homer, "call the emergency police number and ask them to send an ambulance." He dropped to his knees beside Julian. "Let me help."

Julian shifted to one side, and soon the two of them were working together, Julian breathing air into Charlotte's lungs, Homer applying pressure to her breastbone.

"Christ," moaned Pete again, struggling past them to the phone, stumbling over the fallen ironing board.

But it was all right. By the time the ambulance came screaming into Pond View, Charlotte's eyelids were fluttering. She was coughing and trying to sit up.

"There now," said Julian, "it's all right now." He smiled at her and allowed himself to stroke her cheek just once, and then he and Homer stood up and backed out of the way. Homer could feel Julian's arm tremble against his own.

The two young guys from the police ambulance knelt beside Charlotte and listened to her heartbeat. They tested her blood pressure and murmured questions.

Charlotte responded weakly, shaking her head as they lifted her onto the sofa. "She'll be okay now," said one of the medical technicians, nodding at Julian and Homer. "That was quick work. Good for you."

Julian looked grimly at Pete. "Show me the iron."

Pete fumbled under the ironing board and brought up the

electric iron, its cord dangling. "It's never done that before," he said defensively. "Looks brand new, right?"

Homer picked up the cord. "Here's the trouble spot," he said, putting his finger on a frayed blackened place.

"Well, don't use it again," said one of the men from the ambulance, looking solemnly at Pete.

"No way."

"Maybe she ought to see a doctor. You got a doctor?"

"Well, naturally we got a doctor." Pete sounded miffed. "Dr. Stefano. We all use Dr. Stefano, everybody here at Pond View."

Walking back down the driveway with Homer, Julian was choking with anger. "It's like my gas leak. Somebody shaved off the plastic sheathing of that iron cord. Pete Harris! Pete did it, I'll bet."

"You mean he wanted to kill his own wife?" Homer shook his head in disbelief. "And you, he wanted to kill you, too?"

"Well, maybe he heard about the letter." Julian gave Homer an embarrassed glance. "You know." They sat down in a couple of Julian's lawn chairs and gazed thoughtfully at the tangled shrubbery around Goose Pond.

"Look here," said Homer, "I've been thinking about people's ages. I understand Norman Peck and Madeline Raymond had genuine heart conditions. They were both in their eighties, and they probably died of natural causes. But your wife and Shirley Mills were younger, isn't that so?"

"Alice was fifty-nine. Shirley was only fifty-two. She had a stroke, everybody said, but she was perfectly healthy before."

"What about you and Charlotte, how old are you two?"

"I'm sixty. Charlotte, I guess she's about fifty-five, fifty-six."

"What about all the rest?"

Julian spread out his fingers and counted. "Stu LaDue, he's eighty-five. Eugene Beaver, I think he's the oldest now. He's over ninety. Porter McAdoo is about sixty-three, I think. Pete Harris must be about Charlotte's age. Honey Mooney, she's the youngest. She's only in her late forties. Her husband was much older. He died last year."

"It looks to me as if the older you are, the safer you are from these so-called accidents." Homer watched a squirrel run along a branch and make a daring leap to another tree. "I think I'll talk to that Dr. Stefano who looks after all you people. I've got a kind of a sort of a hazy idea of the beginnings of a thought." He tapped his forehead. "Doesn't happen often. Congratulate me."

Julian was not amused. The lines framing his mouth deepened. "What about Charlotte?" said Julian. "Do you think she's in danger? I hate to think of her living there with Pete. He could try again, any time at all."

"Oh, God, I don't know. Keep an eye on her, will you?"

Homer went away and left Julian to his fears. He didn't know what else to do. He felt like a heel.

33

Love is a thirst that is never slaked.
Journal, March 28, 1856

"Hello," said Hope Fry, standing at the counter and looking soberly at Ananda Singh. The new fervor that had drawn her to the hardware store poured out of her like bubbles from a bubble pipe, foaming throughout the store. The bubbles of her ardor popped against the racks of pruning shears, the shelves of sandpaper, the toaster-ovens.

"My worthy opponent," said Ananda graciously. He smiled at her. "May I help you?"

"My father needs a box of screws."

After Homer's schooling, Ananda was now an expert on the subject of nails and screws. "Ah, but I must ask you, does he want wood screws? Flat or round-headed screws? Phillips-head screws?"

His strong male expertise added fuel to Hope's fire. Oh, he knew so much. "Wood screws," she said quickly. "About . . . um, an inch long."

When her transaction was completed she lingered only a moment, trying to think of something to say. Failing, she hurried away, too quickly to hear Ananda's puzzled response to another customer, "What is it, please, a socket wrench?"

Next day when she came back to the hardware store to ask for a paring knife, she found Bonnie Glover sitting on the counter. Bonnie had discovered Ananda on her own. One day, looking across the street from the Porcelain Parlor where she was waiting on a woman customer, she had seen him leaning aluminum ladders up against the display windows of the hardware store. She had abandoned the customer in the middle of a sale and barged right across the street to introduce herself.

Now as Hope walked into the hardware store, Bonnie was firmly parked on the counter with her plump silky knees crossed and her high heels dangling over the nested wastebaskets. Her silvery lipstick and blue eyeshadow were in odd contrast with the rack of caulking guns beside her.

Hope dodged out of sight behind the electric drills, then melted out of the store and stalked away up the street, wondering how she could get to know Ananda Singh without inventing phony errands. Her father was acquainted with him, she knew that. Homer and Mary Kelly knew him. In fact, Ananda was living with the Kellys, down there on Fair Haven Bay. What if she dropped in on them on Saturday morning? Probably Ananda didn't work on Saturday. She might find him at home.

But it was only Mary Kelly who answered the door on Saturday morning. "Well, hi, there, Hopey, what a surprise. Come on in."

"I just thought I'd walk along the river," said Hope. "I mean, I thought I ought to ask if it's okay."

"Well, of course you can walk along the river. Would you like a glass of cold cider first?"

"Oh, yes." Hope followed Mary inside and looked eagerly left and right. "Is—anybody else at home?"

"Anyone else? Why, no. Homer's gone to get his hair cut. And then he has a doctor's appointment or something. We have a guest these days, but he's working today."

"A guest?"

"Yes, a young kid from India. He and Homer are in cahoots. He's a real old-fashioned full-blooded transcendentalist. You know, a Thoreau person, like your dear father." Then Mary remembered. "Well, you know him. You were on that television program together."

Hope was disappointed not to find Ananda at home. "We sort of met, that's right."

Mary seized the opportunity to act as a surrogate mother. "Really, Hope, I was surprised at you. How could you support that Walden Green project? It's counter to everything your father believes in."

Hope's feelings were in confusion. She felt guilty and rebellious at the same time. Touched by Mary's maternal

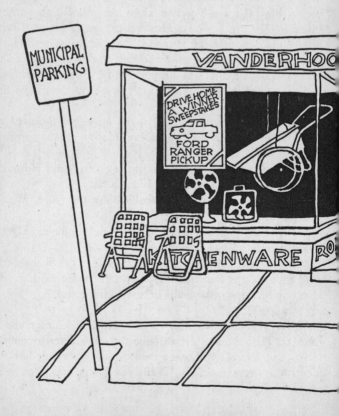

scolding, she wanted to lean on her and cry. Instead she argued back, but her tone was despairing. "My father's so impossible. Oh, I get so sick of the whole thing."

Mary put two glasses of cider on the low table in front of the sofa. Sitting down beside Hope, she tried a new tack. "What did you think of Ananda Singh?"

"Oh—well, he was awfully good." Hope looked at Mary and looked away. "Is he—is he going to stay long?"

"I don't know. I hope so."

Hope took one sip of her cider, then banged down the glass and stood up, knocking over a chair. Absently she righted it, and then she wandered up and down the small living room, staring at the map of the river on the wall, peering at books and magazines, inspecting the pears in a bowl. Then, turning suddenly to Mary, she said, "I didn't know this house was big enough to have a guest room."

"Oh, yes, it has one. It's very small." Mary stood up, too, and opened a door. "You see?"

Hungrily Hope inspected Ananda's room. It was immaculate. The bed was made, although not very well. Books and papers lay on a small table. The pencils were at right angles to the books. There was a small framed picture of an Indian-looking girl on Ananda's dresser. It was Ananda's sister, Maya, but Hope didn't know that. Her heart sank. She turned to the books—*The Maine Woods, The Natural History Essays, Walden, Civil Disobedience*. They were all by Henry Thoreau.

Hope turned to Mary with an anguished face. Her feelings were like a boil on the end of her nose. She was entirely exposed.

Mary took pity on her. Mary herself was not immune to the attractions of Ananda Singh. She had told Homer it was a good thing she was twice Ananda's age, or she'd run away with him to the end of the world. "He's from Simla," she told Hope kindly. "He came here to study Thoreau. He's very poor."

"Poor? He's poor?" Hope was astonished. Then Bonnie Glover had been mistaken. Of course she had been mistaken. The world's richest bachelor wouldn't be working in a hardware store. It was some other Indian person who was so fabulously wealthy. Well, what did it matter? Hope sighed with longing. "Thank you, Mrs. Kelly." She turned away. At the bottom of the porch steps she walked vaguely toward her father's car.

"Aren't you going for a walk?" said Mary, calling down from the porch.

"A walk?" Hope looked back at her blankly. "Oh, a walk. No, I guess not."

Later that afternoon Mary went to the Star Market, and then she picked up Ananda at the hardware store. Triumphantly he showed her his first paycheck. He had worked a full week. "From now on I must pay you more rent. You and Homer are too kind. Truly you must allow me—"

"No, no." Mary glanced at the worn knees of Ananda's jeans. The boy had only a single pair of shoes. And then she had a thought. She remembered Hope Fry and the way she had stared so dolefully into Ananda's room. "I wonder," she said. "Perhaps I've thought of something. Well, we'll talk about it later."

At home in the privacy of her bedroom she called Oliver Fry and asked him if he'd like to rent a room to young Ananda Singh.

Oliver was charmed. "Certainly we'll have him. This place has six bedrooms. It was meant to be a boarding house. And we could use a little extra income. How much do you think the kid can pay?"

"Well, not very much, I'm afraid."

"Well, anything's better than nothing." There was a pause, and then Oliver cleared his throat. Mary could detect his anxiety. "I don't know what Hopey will think. She's been so queer lately."

"Oh, I bet she'll take it in good stride," said Mary comfortably.

34

This is not the figure that I cut. This is the figure the
tailor cuts. That presumptuous and impertinent
fashion whispered in his ear, so that he heard
no word of mine.
Journal, January 14, 1854

Homer Kelly was on his way to the barbershop. His wife
had told him he needed a haircut, and when he looked in
the mirror he had to admit she was right. His hair was
sticking up all over as if struck by lightning.

He hated to take the time. For one thing he was worried
about Julian Snow and Charlotte Harris, and he had a new
idea he wanted to work on. For another, he was falling behind
in his preparations for the fall semester. There was a new
course, new to Homer although it had been part of Harvard's
core curriculum for years. It was one of those fast-moving
lecture courses that wipe away ignorance in huge strokes,
galloping through the centuries at high speed. But, good
God, the broader the stroke, the more full it was of lies.
Before sweeping and swabbing with his big brush, he had to
prepare the way with a private pursuit of niggling detail.
Sometimes Homer envied the specialists, those dry professors
who insert a narrow splinter into the past, then pluck it out
and pick their teeth.

Homer left his car in the Walden Street parking lot and
strode past half a dozen of Mimi Pink's boutiques. Thank
God for Alphonso Domingo. In this desert of sillified merchandise his barbershop was an oasis of dingy reality. Mimi
Pink's shop windows made Homer wince, and he kept his
eyes fixed on the sidewalk.

But at the barbershop he stopped short. It looked different.
There was a barber pole outside, twisting with stripes of pink

and white. And Alphonso had put up a snappy new turquoise awning. The faded lettering on the window, BARBER HOP, was gone, replaced by a hanging wooden sign with words in gold leaf, *HUGO'S HAIR HARMONIES*.

Homer quailed. Who in the hell was Hugo? And where was Alphonso Domingo?

Venturing inside, he was horrified to discover that the old barber chairs had been cleared away. In their places were a couple of turquoise lounge chairs from some interstellar starship. A girl and a guy in matching turquoise jumpsuits were working on a guy and a girl. The girl on the lounge chair was Mimi Pink herself. The guy in the jumpsuit, who was obviously Hugo, was clipping her neck up to the tops of her ears, then bushing out her hair on each side and flattening the top into a sort of mesa. Homer stared at it, imagining tiny Navahos tramping around it in a rain dance.

"I'm ready now," said the jumpsuited girl, glancing at Homer. "Like take a seat."

"Where's Alphonso Domingo?" said Homer, scandalized.

"Oh, he's retired," said Hugo, winking at Mimi Pink.

Mimi tittered. Homer was dismayed. With gingerly caution he lowered himself onto the lounge chair. Twenty minutes later he emerged from Hugo's Hair Harmonies shampooed, shaped, styled, blown dry, and separated from twenty-five dollars. He felt like a fool.

Creeping back into his car, he was careful not to look at himself in the rearview mirror as he drove down Main Street. He was on his way to Emerson Hospital to look for the doctor who took care of all the people at Pond View, Dr. Stefano.

Homer had an old fondness for hospitals. In this one he had proposed to his wife. The signs directing the visitor here and there pullulated with interest—EMERGENCY, X RAY, PHYSICAL THERAPY, OBSTETRICS. It was in these sterile places that people entered the world and left it. Dramatic crises worked themselves out in operating rooms deep underground. Homer wanted to poke his nose into all the rooms and say, "Hey, how are you? What are they doing to you? Wow, no kidding!"

Dr. Stefano's office was in the new wing. Homer found it on the third floor. Opening the door, he recoiled. For the second time in the last hour he was assaulted by interior decoration. Dr. Stefano's waiting room was a cave of gray and pink. Gray louvers hid the glorious view of the river. Huge gray silk flowers rose from a pink vase. Immense airbrushed pictures of opalescent blossoms covered the walls. The carpet was dusty pink, silencing his footsteps as he approached the receptionist.

She was a teenager in a high state of cosmetic finish, but she smiled at Homer in a friendly way, and her corny greeting won him over, "What can I do you for?"

"Is Dr. Stefano in?"

"No, sorry. Hey, that's a really fabulous hairstyle you've got there. Listen, you haven't got an appointment, right? But it's okay. He'll be back soon, and we've had a cancellation. I mean like you're in luck."

"Well, good. But maybe you can help me. My name's Kelly, Homer Kelly. I'm conducting an investigation into the deaths of several people who lived at the trailer park called Pond View. I'm sort of a—"

"Detective!" The girl's eyes widened.

Homer smiled modestly, not wanting to deny an assumption that was, thank God, no longer true. "I have a list here, the names of all the people who live in the park. I wonder if you could look them up and tell me about their general health?"

The receptionist invited him into the doctor's office. "I'm Cheryl," she said with a dazzling smile. With the list between her teeth she squatted on the floor and whipped through a file drawer with nimble fingers. "Oh, shit," she said as one of her pasted-on fingernails came off, revealing a normal girlish nail bitten to the quick. Her pretty fingers went on searching, then paused again, and Cheryl glanced up at Homer. "That's funny. Charlotte and Peter Harris aren't here. Neither are Stuart LaDue or Porter McAdoo." Rapidly she flicked through another drawer. "You know what? I think they've all been taken out, all the ones on your list."

Cheryl teetered to a standing posture on her four-inch heels. "And I remember some of them myself—Mrs. Harris and Mr. Snow and Mr. and Mrs. Ryan and Mrs. Mooney. They certainly were patients of Dr. Stefano's, and their files ought to be here." Then Cheryl beamed. "Oh, here comes Dr. Stefano. Hi, Dr. Stefano! Hey, Dr. Stefano, this is a detective, you know, from the police, and he wants to know about the people at the trailer park, you know, Pond View, and you know what? We can't find their files. I mean like they're all missing."

Dr. Stefano nodded at Homer and sat down at his desk with a groan. He looked tired. Homer was glad to see that he didn't match his office suite. His face wasn't part of any decorating scheme. It was lined and puckered with stillborn babies and burst appendixes and dying men and women. "That's strange," he said.

"Like maybe you took them out yourself?" said Cheryl encouragingly.

"No, but look here, I don't really need the files. I can tell you about all those people. Most of the physicians around here have their memories locked up in their computerized records. I've got them up here." Dr. Stefano tapped his head. "What do you want to know?"

Homer explained his theory. "I may be wrong, but I wonder if someone isn't trying to shorten the life expectancy of the trailer park. Somebody, I think, wants to see the residents die off as soon as possible. They're not doing anything about the oldest ones, because those folks can be depended on to expire before long. But the youngest are being helped into early graves. That's what I think. I admit it's a shaky theory."

The doctor looked shocked. "But that would be terrible.

Are you talking about the deaths of Alice Snow and Shirley Mills?" Dr. Stefano's wan face sagged. "I assumed Mrs. Mills died of a coronary thrombosis, but I admit I didn't call in a pathologist. You're not counting the deaths of Norman Peck and Madeline Raymond? They were very elderly, and they certainly passed away from natural causes."

"No, but since then there have been attempts on the lives of Julian Snow and Charlotte Harris. Failed attempts, thank God."

"Good heavens."

Homer paced the dusty-rose carpet. "Let's start with Alice Snow. I'm puzzled about Mrs. Snow, because she doesn't fit my theory. I understand she was an invalid. I should think this erstwhile killer might have started with some healthier person who could otherwise have been expected to live for years."

"Alice Snow was no invalid," said Dr. Stefano sharply.

Homer was flabbergasted. "She wasn't? But everybody said she was bedridden."

Dr. Stefano smiled grimly. "She might have been bedridden, but she wasn't ill. She was as healthy as you or me."

"Then that means—" Homer brightened. "Somebody knew she wasn't really ill. Somebody knew she might live a long time if she weren't dealt with. They could have found that out from your missing file."

"You mean somebody stole my files in order to establish who was going to die of natural causes and who needed to be finished off?"

"Precisely. So if I could find those files in someone's possession, we'd know who's been creating the nastiness at Pond View."

"Diabolical," said the doctor.

Homer said good-bye and escaped from the new wing of the hospital into the bald sunshine of the out-of-doors, where the flowers were blazing orange marigolds and screaming scarlet salvias rather than pallid blossoms like the ones in Dr. Stefano's office.

He spent the next day doing his duty by Julian Snow, going from one mobile home to another at Pond View, asking about the Ryans' keys, inquiring about tools that might have drilled a hole in Julian's gas pipe, letting his eyes rove inquisitively over the exposed surfaces of tables and counters, looking surreptitiously for Dr. Stefano's missing files. From his great height Homer inspected the tops of refrigerators. He knew from long experience that those belonging to short people were always dusty. He had seen hundreds like that. Sometimes he had even kindly offered to wash them himself. But even the dusty ones at Pond View were not laden with Dr. Stefano's purloined files.

And nobody admitted possessing a key to the Ryans' trailer. It was easier to inspect the collections of tools, looking for one that might have stripped the insulation from the cord of Charlotte's electric iron, or drilled a hole in Julian's gas line, or tinkered malevolently with Julian's machine at the landfill.

All three of these dangerous interferences pointed to the kind of skill that was second nature to most men. But these days, Homer reminded himself, there were plenty of handy women as well.

One glance at Eugene Beaver was enough to eliminate him from the running. He was too old and frail to have managed feats requiring stealth and nimble fingers.

Honey Mooney was different. She was young and quick. But Honey professed a total inability to handle tools. "I always have to get Julian or Porter to help me when anything stops working," she said, retreating into coy helplessness.

"Do you have any equipment in the house?" said Homer. "A toolbox, or anything like that?"

"Oh, well, there's my husband's old set of tools," admitted Honey. She pulled it out from under the sink, and Homer looked at it. There were the usual hammers, pliers, and screwdrivers. There was also a new-looking pair of wire strippers and an electric drill. Homer held up the drill and examined the bit. It looked just about the right size to fit the hole in Julian's gas line. "Do you mind if I borrow this?" he said. And when he took it to Julian's place and thrust it into the hole, it fitted precisely.

But so did the bit in Porter McAdoo's drill. It too was an eighth of an inch in cross section. So was the bit in Julian Snow's. Homer suspected that his own drill at home sported the same size bit. It was a useful size, the one you were apt to choose to make a miscellaneous hole in something.

The fact that Stuart LaDue and Pete Harris didn't own any drills at all didn't eliminate them. Surely any sensible murderer would get rid of the incriminating weapon.

On his way back to Fair Haven Bay, Homer began thinking once again about reasons. Why would anybody want to hasten the end of the Pond View Trailer Park?

He could think of only one answer, and it pained him. It would have to be someone who wanted to see Thoreau's Walden Pond cleared of insults like the sanitary landfill and the trailer park and the public beach and the bathhouse. The beach was ancient history and unassailable, and the landfill would require long-term political action, but the old folks at Pond View were vulnerable. Once they were gone—dead from natural or unnatural causes—the place would probably be returned to nature once again.

Who would like to see that happen? Oliver Fry for one, and a lot of other people Homer admired and respected.

Not to mention that arch-transcendentalist, Homer Kelly.

. . . most legislators, politicians, lawyers, ministers,
and office-holders . . . rarely make any moral
distinctions, they are as likely to serve the Devil,
without intending it, as God.
Thoreau, *Civil Disobedience*

The first August hearing of the Concord Planning Board was held on the hottest night of the summer. As Homer waited for Oliver Fry on the steps of the town hall, his shirt was already clinging to his back.

He was early. He looked out at the Civil War obelisk rising above the round green trees of Monument Square. The trees were hazy with humidity. Their leaves hung limp. The flag on the traffic island drooped on its lofty pole. The long view down Main Street was striped with sun and shadow.

Turning, Homer saw an apparition speeding toward him down Lexington Road. It was Oliver Fry on his bicycle. Even from here there was a sinewy cantankerousness in Oliver's outline against the evening air. Nobody but Oliver Fry would pump a bicycle so furiously forward and drive down the pedals with such violence. Homer grinned, appreciating from afar the essence of his old and valued friend. After the easy laxity of polite ties with other people, there was excitement in the tug of the vibrating string that was Oliver Fry.

Together they mounted the stairs to the public hearing room on the second floor. When Oliver paused on the landing to catch his breath, Homer pressed him gently on the subject of Pond View. Had Oliver heard about the fire?

Oliver didn't seem interested. He had no wrath to spare for anything but the new dragon that was spitting fire and threatening the sanctity of Walden Woods.

Thankfully Homer dropped the notion of Oliver Fry as

murderer and arsonist. But there were other earnest conservationists in Concord who might harbor in their breasts a deadly eagerness to see the abrupt end of the trailer park. Homer vowed to track down a few and talk to them.

The hearing room was a high and handsome chamber. Surely, thought Homer, it was the very room in which American eloquence had reached its peak, when Thoreau delivered his oratorical defense of John Brown. He looked around reverently and took off his jacket. The place was hot. Some of the sweltering heat rose to the ceiling, but no cooling breeze wafted through the tall open windows. A standing fan turned and droned, failing to stir the sodden air. Under the windows the board members arranged themselves behind a long table. Chairman Roger Bland sat in the middle. It was

clear to Homer that there would be no eloquence this evening.

But it was a crucial meeting of the planning board. Homer had seen the agenda. Would the board members support Walden Green? Would they urge the board of appeals to look on it with favor? Would they speak for it in Town Meeting? Homer feared the worst.

Oliver and Homer settled down on two of the folding chairs. "There's the enemy," said Oliver, nudging Homer, glowering at a crowd gathering on the other side of the room. "The young one's Jack Markey."

"I see," murmured Homer. He didn't need an introduction to the bearded older man taking a chair next to Jack's. Jefferson Grandison had a celebrated face. He was accompanied by eager lackeys. They gathered around him and whispered in his ear like the mob of lesser angels buoying up Michelangelo's Jehovah.

Other petitioners were fluttering in, alighting in murmuring flocks on the folding chairs. Homer recognized Mimi Pink as she paused in the doorway, raked the room with a chilly eye, and found a seat behind the numinous sublimity surrounding Jefferson Grandison.

Did she know those people? Homer watched as Jack Markey turned his head and glanced at her. Was that a nod of recognition? Now Jack was leaning forward again, while Mimi put her big pocketbook on her lap and crossed her legs. She seemed unaffected by the heat. Probably she was coated with some sort of lacquer that protected her like a space suit.

Then Homer caught a glance between two opposites. Roger Bland's mild eye, exploring the audience, encountered the scowling stare of Oliver Fry. What a mistake! Roger winced and looked away. A sob of laughter rose in Homer's throat. How Roger must fear poor old Oliver! And rightly so. In a fair contest Oliver Fry would devour him like a python swallowing an egg. Homer closed his eyes and tried to control himself, imagining the cracking shell, the breaking of the tissued bones, the pitiful wriggling on the way down.

The meeting was about to begin. The board members leaned toward each other, joking among themselves. Some were dressed in proper business shirts, but they had rolled up their sleeves and wrenched loose their ties. Others wore short-sleeved polo shirts and shorts. Big sneakers shifted under the table. One member of the board, Isabelle Moseley, was late. She came hurrying in and sat down, her face red, her breast heaving with the effort of running upstairs in the heat. The recording secretary opened her notebook. Roger Bland glanced up at the clock over his head and called the hearing to order.

"Mr. Markey? Would you like to begin your presentation?"

Jack came forward and unzipped a portfolio. He removed a large plot plan of Walden Green, set it up on an easel, and began to talk.

He was smooth and brisk, but there was a smiling excitement in his manner. Homer guessed that the whole layout was his. The access road through the farm off Fair Haven Road and the bridge over the railroad track, all, all were his. It was a Grandison enterprise but a Jack Markey project from beginning to end.

"Am I right in thinking, Mr. Markey," said Roger Bland, "that the site you propose is now a high school playing field?"

"That's true," said Jack, "but as you will hear in a moment from Mrs. Bowman of the school committee, we have their blessing. She will demonstrate that the present lacrosse field is unnecessary to the high school athletic program. The playing fields nearer to the school buildings have been declared perfectly adequate. I must point out that the tennis courts here"—Jack touched the chart with his pointer—"will remain just as they are."

Homer glanced at Oliver. The man was choking. He was beside himself. Homer remembered Mary's cautious suggestion that he do his damnedest to keep Oliver in check. He patted Oliver's knee.

The plot plan disappeared and was replaced by a handsome watercolor rendering of Walden Green, an oblong sward of grass surrounded by white houses. Sunlight slanted through the pale spring foliage, making long strokes of shadow across the grass. Concord citizens strolled in twos and threes along the circling paths of this land of Beulah.

Swiftly Jack ran through his list of promises—the low-income housing units, the day-care center, the extension of the sewage line, the gifts of the transfer station and Titcomb's Bog and the Burroughs farm, and last but not least, the perpetual flow of tax dividends into the town treasury.

The list was impressive. But not to Oliver Fry. Leaping to his feet, Oliver thundered in a voice of doom, *"Timeo Danaos et dona ferentes,"* warning of Greeks bearing gifts. He shook his fist at Jack.

But the planning board members had not read their Virgil. Roger Bland frowned. "Oliver, I must ask you to refrain from such outbursts. Later on there will be an opportunity for comments from the floor."

Fuming, Oliver sat down, his chest heaving. At the table where the board members sat, Isabelle Moseley modestly kept her eyes down. She was drawing a portrait of Oliver Fry on the pink cover of her zoning bylaws. Her fellow board member Brad Woodrow glanced at it and tried to control an outburst of laughter. The picture was Oliver Fry to the life. The burning eyes! The wild hair! The shaking fist!

Homer Kelly pitied his friend. He was beginning to see Oliver Fry and Jack Markey and Roger Bland and the entire planning board in their relation to something Thoreau had said about snowflakes. They were the product of enthusiasm, he had said, the children of ecstasy.

The product of enthusiasm! Well, here it was in real life, surrounding Homer on all sides—enthusiastic Oliver on the one hand, the child of ecstasy, tempestuous for the right, and Jack Markey on the other hand, enthusiastic in the pride of his creation, eager for the wrong.

And there in the middle sat Roger Bland, neither right nor wrong, the soul of moderation, stroking his chin.

What good did moderation ever do in this world? wondered Homer bitterly, sensing the passionate throb of Oliver's heart as he shuffled his feet under his chair. You had to go whole hog if you wanted to accomplish anything, and clash with the hogs on the other side. It was passion that built things up and tore them down. To hell with moderation.

36

We have built for this world a family mansion, and
for the next a family tomb.
Walden, "Economy"

Ananda bought himself a secondhand car, an enormous old boat of an Chevy Impala. Its parts were in doubtful health. It vibrated at rest and shook in motion, and the muffler fell off the day after inspection.

It had cost him the rest of his nest egg, but he was making enough money at the hardware store to live modestly on his earnings. His father had written to inform him that on his twenty-first birthday he would receive a monthly income from a trust fund established at his birth, but Ananda didn't really believe in it. He expected nothing.

Mary Kelly instructed him in the fine points of driving on the right side of the road, and he drove with extreme caution on his way to Oliver Fry's house to rent a room.

To his pleasure, the house reminded him of his family's summer home in Simla. That house, too, had been wrapped in verandas, it had been gloomy with the same stygian darkness. Ananda recognized the fireplace of glazed brick and the window seats and the meandering back halls through which bearers carried trays of *nimboo-pani* and iced tea.

But there were no bearers in this house, no cook, no gardeners, no chauffeur, no chowkidar to guard the premises—only Hope Fry in the kitchen, making a sandwich. Hope licked a dab of mayonnaise from her finger and turned in surprise as Oliver ushered Ananda through the pantry with a courtly, "After you."

Oliver had been too cowardly to ask his daughter what she would think about renting a room to Ananda Singh. Now he looked at her guiltily and explained. "All those empty bedrooms," he said, flapping his hand in the direction of the hall stairs, "which one do you think . . . ?"

Hope thought with horror of the bedrooms upstairs, bleak chambers that hadn't been freshly painted since the Second World War. They were brown with dark-varnished doors and closets, dreary with Mission rockers and swaybacked beds in which great-aunts had died. "Wait," she said, panic-stricken, "just let me take a look," and she rushed upstairs.

The only possible choice was the south bedroom with the bay window bulging out over the driveway. Hope threw open the door, plunged past the bed, snatched up the drying rack on which bras and panties were hanging, and hurried it into her own room. Then she hoisted up her pretty up-holstered chair and lugged it back across the hall. On the return journey she carted away the sewing machine. Next she whisked off the bedspread, which was gray where the cat had been sleeping, and replaced it with the clean white one from her own bed.

She was charging across the hall with a floor lamp when her father appeared at the top of the back stairs with Ananda in his wake.

"This way," said Hope breathlessly, pointing with the floor lamp.

Ananda was charmed with the room. "It is perfect," he said.

"The bathroom's right across the way," said Oliver proudly.

"Oh, whoops," cried Hope, remembering the state of the bathroom, feeling trapped in the midst of domestic disorder. "Don't go in there yet." Having yanked open the linen closet, she grabbed out an armful of clean towels and lunged into the bathroom to hang them up. Swiftly she dabbed at certain grubby corners. "Okay," she said, gasping, "you can come in now. Oh, I'm afraid you can't take a bath if the dish-washer's on. What you do is, you tell everybody you're going to take a bath, and then we're careful not to use any water at the same time."

"I see," said Ananda humbly, delighted with everything.

Hope left them and went downstairs, her head in a whirl. Life had taken a dizzying upswing, and she was filled with tremulous excitement. What would happen now?

37

Sarah Peel had vowed to return to Concord, and return she did. Counting up the money Marjorie Bland had thrust at her as she got on the train, Sarah bought ten one-way tickets to Concord and passed them out freely at the Women's Lunch Place on Newbury Street in Boston.

They were like the seed scattered by the sower in the parable. Some fell on stony ground and withered away, and some fell amid thorns and the thorns choked them, but some fell on good ground and brought forth fruit a hundredfold.

Francie Morris, for example, was stony ground. Francie was sleeping off some kind of trip, with her head down on her folded arms. When she woke up, she stumbled out without noticing the ticket Sarah had put beside her plate.

Eloise Wordsworth simply wandered away, befuddled, and afterward Sarah retrieved her ticket from the floor.

But Dolores Marshall took two tickets, one for herself and one for her eight-year-old daughter, Christine.

The silent woman, Audrey Beamish, always sat in the corner with her back turned. She wouldn't look at Sarah, but she accepted the ticket when Sarah put it in her hand.

The hysterical Bridgie Sorrel took one.

Almina Ziblow took one. Almina was an elderly black woman who wore a checkered woolen cape even in the heat of summer.

Bobbsie Low didn't take off her earphones, but she looked with interest at the ticket in Sarah's hand and accepted it.

Poisonous Doris Harper looked at hers suspiciously and

demanded to know what the fuck Sarah was trying to do, get her the fuck out of town? What was all this shit? So Sarah took the ticket away, and then Doris shouted at her, "Asshole! That's mine!" So Sarah gave it back.

When she gathered her flock together on Dartmouth Street, Sarah still had two tickets left. On the sidewalk she handed them to a couple of men, Carl Browning and Palmer Nifto.

Carl was an old man who had never been able to get the hang of the welfare system, but Palmer was something else altogether. Palmer was a forty-year-old college-educated engineer who had lost his job, his wife, and his children, and vanished into the street to live by his wits, avoiding child support, taxes, and alimony. Looking at the ticket Sarah offered him, Palmer took it cheerfully.

"We'll have to go to Porter Square," he said. "Come on, we'll take the Green Line to Park Street, okay? Nothing to it."

They made a long parade up Dartmouth Street, carrying with them their life-support systems, their emergency arrangements for camping out in strange places as unwelcoming as the Arabian desert. On the plush seats of the Boston and Maine train they all sat back and enjoyed the ride, looking out at the back streets of Cambridge and Belmont and Waltham and the rural landscape of Weston and Lincoln, glimpsing the blue water of Walden Pond through the trees.

Sarah's excitement mounted as she approached closer and closer to Pearl, her own beautiful horse, but as the train pulled into the Concord depot the others felt the return of uncertainty, the challenge of fashioning each day out of nothing, nothing at all.

On the platform they all stood silent for a moment, watching the train disappear around the curving track in the direction of Fitchburg. Then Sarah said, "This way," and led them around the depot to Thoreau Street.

At once Palmer Nifto took command. Palmer had been

a wide receiver on the football team at Belmont High, and his school had often played in Concord. He knew his way around. "Forward," he cried playfully, lifting the briefcase in which he carried his small store of possessions.

"Hey, where the fuck you going?" demanded Doris Harper. "What the shit's all this?" But she moved along smartly after Palmer, not wanting to miss anything. Audrey Beamish said nothing as usual, but she trailed after the others. Christine Marshall held her mother's hand and stared at the big comfortable houses on Main Street. An orange cat emerged from a hedge and rubbed against her legs. "Oh, kitty," cooed Christine, and picked it up.

"No, no," said her mother, who lived in fear of the diseases of the street. "It's probably got germs."

The only one who didn't accompany the procession up Main Street was Sarah Peel. Unnoticed, she slipped away and hurried across the street to the Nashawtuc bridge. From there she could see her horse in the pasture across the river.

Pearl was looking at her intently, waiting for her, just as Sarah had known she would.

Mimi Pink usually spent part of the afternoon visiting Corporate Gifts. Today, approaching the glittering Lucite door, she had to step over a bulky string bag. An odd-looking woman with dyed orange hair was leaning against the shop window, obscuring the display of talking alarm clocks.

Mimi went at once to the rear of the store and called the police.

The fire and police station was only a block or two away on Walden Street. An officer appeared almost at once. Mimi watched as he bent over the offensive object slumped beside the door. She watched him help the woman up and hand her the string bag.

The woman was the hysterical Bridgie Sorrel. In a moment she was screaming and striking the officer with her fists.

There were two customers in Corporate Gifts, a pair of

well-dressed women from Dedham. They turned blank white faces toward the disturbance. Their button earrings trembled, their bifocals flashed with indignation.

"How dreadful," said the first woman, who had been examining a digital yo-yo.

"That person should be locked up," said the second woman, fondling a giant hourglass.

They craned their necks as the officer bundled Bridgie out of sight, still yelling.

The episode was so disconcerting, the two women left the shop without buying anything, and Mimi was furious.

Palmer Nifto was more successful with the two women from Dedham. While the other expatriates from Boston distributed themselves here and there among the shopfronts like shells washing up on a beach, Palmer was more subtle. Conscious of his own air of respectability, he at once put into practice a stratagem that had worked for him many times before.

Approaching the two prosperous-looking women, he stopped short and began ransacking his trouser pockets and slapping his seersucker jacket. "My billfold," he cried, "it's gone."

The two women stopped, too, and looked at him sympathetically. "It's those people," said one of them, glaring in distaste at Audrey Beamish, who was sitting on the broad step in front of the drugstore, her head bowed on her knees. "They picked your pocket."

"My God," said Palmer Nifto. "I don't know how I'm going to get home. All my credit cards are gone, my driver's license." He groped again in his trousers pocket and brought out a penny. "I can't even make a phone call."

The poor fellow was really quite good-looking. "Here, dear," said one of the women from Dedham, handing him a five-dollar bill.

"Oh, I couldn't," said Palmer Nifto.

"No, no, you must. I insist."

"This too," said the other woman, not to be outdone, proffering ten dollars.

Palmer thanked them profusely, wrote down their names and addresses conscientiously, and walked away, pocketing the fifteen dollars. It was a useful tactic, especially in a new place.

The two women hurried back to their car, vowing never to return to Concord.

"The town has certainly changed," sighed one.

"What a shame," agreed the other.

Sarah had some candies in her pocket, a bag of M&M's. She put a few on the flat of her hand, and Pearl took them neatly. It felt funny when the horse's big teeth picked them up, but it didn't hurt. Sarah fed her the whole bag.

Then she stood back and looked calculatingly at Pearl with the shrewd eye of the expert rider she had become on the merry-go-round at the fairground beyond the Ring and Flange Company. The horse had no saddle, but her back was smooth and strong-looking. There was a deep swaybacked hollow in front of her projecting hipbones. One day Sarah would try it. Then she and Pearl would circle the pasture, and they would plunge and surge forward, and plunge and surge forward, as though the cymbals were clashing and the drums were beating and the horns were playing the "Skater's Waltz."

38

*If you are going into that line,—going to besiege
the city of God,—you must not only be strong
in engines, but prepared with provisions to
starve out the garrison.*
Thoreau, Letter to Harrison Blake,
December 19, 1853

Homer took his convictions about Pond View to Police Chief James Flower.

"It's just too many things at once," he told Jimmy. "Four deaths, two obviously criminal attacks on Julian Snow, one near electrocution, and one house fire."

"When you put it that way," said Jimmy, "it certainly looks bad, but you could put it another way, too. Three of those people died from natural causes, and the other one was probably an accident. And so was the house fire, and so was the electric iron. They're old, those people. They have accidents."

"That still leaves the hole in Julian's gas line and the sabotaging of his machine at the landfill. Those things weren't carelessness. They were deliberate."

Jimmy sighed. "Well, I'll send somebody over to talk to Mr. Snow and take a look. The truth is, Homer, we're really strapped for manpower. I've got my one and only inspector doing traffic duty. Work on it yourself, why don't you?"

"I am, but, look here, those people are in danger. They're *all* in danger. Somebody's trying to finish off everybody in the park."

"Look, even if it were true, what am I supposed to do, put a squad of police officers at Pond View around the clock? I told you, we haven't got the staff. Do you know how many motor vehicle accidents there were in Concord last year? Go ahead, guess."

"I don't know. A hundred or so?"

"Nearly seven hundred. And we had almost a hundred B and E's, three hundred and fifty cases of larceny, and over a hundred incidents of domestic violence. We can't keep up."

Homer was surprised. "I thought this was such a polite little law-abiding town."

"It is, compared with some. But, believe me, Homer, those figures are God's truth."

Homer went away, humbled and enlightened, and spent the afternoon in his vegetable garden.

Next morning he dropped off a bag of summer squash at Oliver Fry's house and stayed to enjoy a second breakfast.

Oliver too had a midsummer harvest to display. "Look

here," he said proudly, displaying a basket of greenery. "I got these pitcher plants in Gowing's Swamp."

"Gowing's Swamp?" Homer was fascinated. "You mean that quaking bog that sucks you down?"

"Not if you exercise reasonable care." Then Oliver explained the cannibal mechanics of pitcher plants, which were notorious for being carnivorous. "My biology class will get a kick out of these."

"Flies, right?" said Homer nervously. "Pitcher plants digest flies?"

"Flies, and anything else that wanders in."

"Oh, ugh," said Homer. "You know what? They remind me of Jefferson Grandison. He's the pitcher plant, damn him, and the town of Concord is the fly. Right now we're all perched on his detestable carnivorous lip, ready to fall in."

Oliver's face fell. His enthusiasm faded, and he dropped onto a chair. "I'll bet he's some kind of crook. What do we know about him, anyhow? He's got a lot of money, that's all we know."

"Oh, I don't think he's a crook," said Homer dolefully. "Probably every low-down thing he does is strictly legal. He doesn't make a move, probably, without an army of lawyers." Homer banged down his coffee cup. "Tell you what, I'll see what I can find out. I'll beard Grandison in his den."

"Oh, hello, Homer!" Hope burst into the kitchen, fresh from the shower, a tall girl in a baggy blouse, her brown hair misty with drops of water like dew on a flower, her fingers wrinkled and pink.

Oliver looked at his daughter tenderly. "Hopey dear, is our boarder coming down for breakfast?"

Hope turned away and began fussing with the coffeepot. "Oh, I think he's moving around up there."

And then Ananda appeared, smiling radiantly. "It is very comfortable, my bed. Oh, good morning, Mr. Kelly."

"Coffee, Ananda?" said Hope in a strangled voice.

"That would be splendid," said Ananda heartily.

"Thank you, Hopey dear," said Oliver, grateful to his daughter for so politely disguising her antagonism toward the unwelcome guest at the table.

Homer had bitten off more than he could chew. His teaching duties in Cambridge were no joke, and the plight of the people at Pond View had become his responsibility alone, since Chief Flower seemed to have washed his hands of the whole thing.

And now he had promised Oliver Fry that he would look into Jefferson Grandison's empire and try to find some loophole in the legitimacy of his dangerous assault on Concord's woods and fields.

The teaching duties came first. In the next few days the final papers of the summer semester came flooding in, followed by stacks of final exams. It took Homer a week to work his way through them. Not until he had graded them all could he turn his attention to his promise about Grandison.

As usual Homer failed to adopt the sensible approach of going through channels. Instead he simply flung himself at the problem, starting at the top, making a random attack with a blunderbuss.

He made no appointment. He appeared at Grandison's door.

It was his first ride in the glass elevator. For a man with a child's pleasure in sensation, it was a stunning surprise to find himself hurtling upward from the dark chasm of the city street into the bright sky. Stepping out into the blaze of noontime sunshine on the seventieth floor, Homer felt dizzy and vaguely discomfited, manipulated by demons of the air.

The lobby of Grandison's office was an enormous cube. At first glance it looked empty. It occurred to Homer that emptiness was the best sort of conspicuous display in a building where every cubic yard was of stupendous dollar value.

Squinting, he detected a human being at the far end, and he approached her at once, his feet sinking into the white carpet. Halfway across the pure expanse he looked back to see if there were footprints in the snow.

The woman at the desk was, he guessed, some sort of high-class receptionist. Probably an executive vice president. She was dressed in the apogee of fashionable taste. To Homer, who identified high fashion with the shiny exaggerations of Mimi Pink, it was a revelation. She had gone past the artifices of Mimi Pink, way past Mimi's glossy surfaces and football shoulders. Her face was unsullied by makeup. Her blond hair was long and flowing. Her dress was of a white gauzelike material draped on her lank body in loops and swags. She was telephoning.

As Homer approached, she put down the phone and scribbled something on a sheet of paper. Only then did she look up at him and smile.

"Good morning," said Homer genially. "My name is Kelly. I wonder if I could see Mr. Grandison?"

The woman put one pale hand over her sheet of paper. "What do you want to see him about?" Her gaze was frank, her accent impeccable. Three centuries of Brahmin ancestors had scattered umlauts in her speech. Her name, decided Homer, was Abigail Saltonstall.

He shuffled his shoes on the rug, depositing mud from his great-grandfather's potato field in Ireland. "I'm doing an article on Mr. Grandison for . . . ah, *Harvard* magazine. They're running a series on prominent graduates of the Harvard Business School." Homer smiled ingratiatingly, wondering if Grandison had ever been to the business school.

"I see. Won't you sit down?"

Homer looked around for a chair. He could see nothing but a small cumulus cloud. "Oh, is that a chair? Well, all right, here goes." For an instant he was lost in its cushiony folds, but then the chair recoiled and bounced him to the surface. "Perhaps you could give me a little background before I take up any of Mr. Grandison's valuable time. Then I could get right to the heart of things with the man himself. Of course we'll want a picture or two, not just the usual captain of industry kind of thing. Mr. Grandison with his dogs, perhaps? Mr. Grandison in his boat in foul-weather gear?"

Abigail Saltonstall was obviously won over. "What would you like to know about Mr. Grandison?" A little breeze from some remote ventilating duct fluttered her gauzy dress.

"Well, perhaps you could just run down for me what it is that Mr. Grandison actually does. That is, what is his firm engaged in from day to day?"

"His firm? Well, actually it's not just one firm. Mr. Grandison has interests in many conservation organizations, enterprises concerned with environmental development, idealistic real estate."

"Idealistic real estate?"

"Development that preserves the landscape, housing that respects the natural setting, that sort of thing."

"Could you give me the names of these firms?"

"Certainly." Abigail pulled open an ethereal drawer and handed him a sheet of paper.

Homer ran his eye down the list. "Does Mr. Grandison actually run all these outfits?"

"Oh, no. He's on the boards of the charitable institutions. He takes personal charge of a few of the commercial enterprises. And of course he's always creating more. Mr. Grandison is a man of the broadest vision, Mr. Kelly. He has an outlook that's really incredibly immense." Throwing out her arms, Abigail displayed the huge canvas of Grandisonian interest, extending from sea to sea and pole to pole.

"Well, what's this one, for instance," said Homer, "Breathe Free?"

"The name is perfectly clear. It represents Mr. Grandison's concern for clean air, his anxiety about toxic waste, his hope for—"

"How about Egret Country?"

"Florida real estate. It's a retirement community in the Everglades. Individual luxury apartments with hospital, golf course, concert hall, art museum."

"They got any egrets?" said Homer crudely.

"Why, of course. The heart of the community is an untouched piece of wetland, with blue herons, egrets, pelicans, alligators. I've been there myself. It's just beautiful."

For a moment Homer was swept away. He pictured himself standing on a greensward holding a golf club, with a blue heron nudging his golfball. He was wearing golf knickers, diamond-patterned socks, and big shoes with fringed flaps. "Move over," he said to the blue heron, and smacked the ball high into the air. It soared and soared, taken by the wind, and landed with a splash far out to sea.

He woke up as a buzzer sounded on Abigail's desk. "Oh, here's Mr. Grandison." She flicked a tiny switch. "His meeting is over."

A door opened on the other side of the gigantic room, and Abigail got to her feet. So did Homer, sucked upright by awe. Slyly he took the opportunity to put his hand on the piece of paper on which Abigail had been scribbling. Casually he slipped it under the list of Grandison's enterprises. Folding the sheets together, he tucked them in his pocket.

"Oh, Mr. Grandison," said Abigail, "this is Mr. Kelly. He's doing an article for *Harvard* magazine, part of a series on prominent business school graduates."

Homer strode forward and extended a hearty hand. "I hope, Mr. Grandison, you'll permit me an interview."

Homer had seen Jefferson Grandison at the Concord Planning Board hearing, but then the man had been seated, crowded in among sycophants and hangers-on. Standing alone, he had an even more majestic presence. His head was large and imposing, gushing a sublime flow of whisker. He had probably spent the morning speaking to Moses from a burning bush.

"Ineffable Industries has canceled out," said Abigail dreamily.

"Well, in that case," said Grandison, "my time is at your disposal, Mr. Kelly. Come in."

Homer followed him into his office, wondering why he was thinking of flies drowning in pitcher plants instead of Dante at the summit of Paradise.

The office was staggering. The view in three directions made Homer gasp. The entire metropolis lay before him, an alabaster city undimmed by human tears. Well, maybe there were a few tears down there somewhere, but they were invisible from the seventieth floor of the Grandison Building.

Homer lowered himself into another cumulus cloud, took out his notebook, and began asking gentle questions, beginning with simple ones about Jefferson Grandison's childhood.

Mr. Grandison seemed flattered. He told all. Homer scribbled a few things down, to give the impression he was taking notes.

Happy childhood, death of dad, mom remarries, cruel stepdad, sorrow in luxury, prep school, college, marriage, Harv Bus School, onward, upward.

So far, so good. Facts were facts. But when Homer inquired about the progress of the great man since graduate school, he could catch at nothing to write down. He could make neither head nor tail of the language that came out of Grandison's mouth. It was all flabby phrases—*speaking candidly, tangential maximization, in terms of, as far as, analogous polarities, as it were, prevailing utilization, depending on the parameters*—and then Grandison would plunge into sets of interlocking parentheses, plummeting deeper and deeper into the swamp of a sentence and working his way up again, unlocking the parentheses one by one, finalizing brackets, bursting to the surface at last with the verb in his teeth.

Homer's mind fuzzed over. After an hour of his own

increasingly befuddled questions and Grandison's increasingly amorphous replies, he emerged from the office in a daze, nodded vaguely to Abigail Saltonstall and fell to the earth in the glass elevator, closing his eyes in terror. As he drove home to Concord he was troubled by a humming in his ears. Feeble phrases undulated in his head, tumbling over and under, and under and over.

By the time he got home he was in a state of frantic deprivation. He wanted nouns, short Anglo-Saxon words like *ax, rake, dog, horse;* he wanted meaningful prose. He went to Thoreau's journal as to a medicine cabinet and opened the second volume at random.

> As I climbed the hill again toward my old bean-field, I listened to the ancient, familiar, immortal, dear cricket sound under all others, hearing at first some distinct chirps; but when these ceased I was aware of the general earth-song, and I wondered if behind or beneath this there was not some other chant yet more universal.

Ah, that was speech. That was English speech.

Mary was not at home to complain to. Warmed by the tonic of Thoreau's language, Homer got back in his car and drove to the parking lot at Walden Pond. Striding across the road into the woods, he found his way to the place that had once been the beanfield. It was covered now by the successors of the trees Thoreau had planted when he left the pond.

Homer leaned against one of them and listened. Above him he heard the creaking of the trunk, the wind in the leaves making a sound like the sea. There was no birdsong, no thrilling unfamiliar note that might be a wood thrush. But the crickets were making their midsummer chant, their strong mutual pulse, all in the same rhythm. It was older than he was, older than Thoreau, older than Walden Pond, older perhaps than the great chunk of ice that had hollowed out the basin and filled it with water. In the broad sweep of

Walden Pond

geologic time, the small human turbulences afflicting these
few square miles of Massachusetts were nothing. Someday
all the people shouting so angrily at each other in the woods
around the pond would be gone. But the crickets would still
be there, singing their earth-song, telling of antediluvian and
everlasting things, praising the brightness of the moon, the
light of the stars, the survival of insects.

As the door closed behind Homer in Jefferson Grandison's
office, a buzzer sounded on Grandison's desk. He picked up
the phone.

The voice was familiar. It belonged to Archibald Pouch,
of Pouch, Heaviside and Sprocket, a firm of attorneys hired
to intimidate Grandison. As usual Pouch was vulgar, im-
perious and threatening, demanding the instantaneous removal of Lot Seventeen. The conversation was disagreeable.
Grandison threatened court action in return.

When he put down the phone, he stalked into the reception lobby to dress down his secretary-receptionist, Martha Jones, for putting the call through. Martha complained that Pouch had been so insistent, threatening her personally with litigation, she had had no choice.

Back in his office, Grandison made a call of his own. This time he used a pattern of speech totally unlike the tormented language he had inflicted on Homer Kelly. There were no parenthetical remarks, no elliptical parameters, no aforementioneds, no supplementary conditionalities or affiliated relationships.

The exchange was short and sharp.

"Get on with it," said Grandison.

"Right you are," said Jack Markey.

39

There is no remedy for love but to love more.
Journal, July 25, 1839

Hope Fry didn't know what to do about Ananda Singh. Here he was in her own house, sleeping in the room across the hall. He was exquisitely courteous, but he seemed more like a colleague of her father's than someone her own age.

And he was so shy and old-fashioned, so conservative in his behavior with girls! And yet, Hope knew, there were temples in India covered with sculptured images of love-making. She had seen pictures of them, exotic female deities with narrow waists and swelling hips and breasts as round as melons. Oh, it was so difficult, falling in love with some-one from another culture, not knowing what things meant, perhaps making awful mistakes.

He would not allow her to do anything for him. Was it insulting to have a woman do your laundry? Ananda washed his own clothes and hung them on the back porch. Sometimes Hope went out on the porch and put her face against one of his shirts when no one was looking, except the owl with its ferocious yellow eyes.

Most of the talking at the supper table was between Ananda and her father. It was all Thoreau, Thoreau, Thoreau, alter-nating with Oliver Fry's angry denunciation of the town boards, his rage at the callow ignorance of the citizenry, his sorrow at the fate of prophets without honor in their own country. The prophet was supposed to be Henry Thoreau, but it was plain he was thinking about himself at the same time.

And Ananda would nod and smile and look down at his plate.

Privately Hope slipped a copy of *Walden* out of the bookcase and took it to her room. She had read some of it before, in high school, but it had seemed odd and cranky, and she had given up. This time she would try, she would really try. Solemnly she turned to page one.

> When I wrote the following pages, or rather the bulk of them, I lived alone, in the woods, a mile from any neighbor, in a house which I had built myself, on the shore of Walden Pond. . . .

As for Ananda, he was equally disturbed by the presence of Hope Fry. Seeing her in her flannel bathrobe and fuzzy slippers crossing the hall in the early morning, her hair flooding down over her shoulders and the sunlight slanting in upon her from the window on the landing, he was captivated. It was so odd that the first girl he had spoken to in the United States should be keeping him awake at night, thinking of her lying softly in her own bed across the hall. As usual Ananda was ashamed of his thoughts, which had become more intense as he grew older. It seemed hypocritical to dress so circumspectly in the morning and exchange so few words with this girl at breakfast, after the wild visions of the night. He remembered that Thoreau had written of his own "rank offenses." Had he been troubled in the same way?

There was to be a dance at the Concord Armory. Hope had seen the poster. It was too good a chance to miss. Casually, as if it were the most ordinary thing in the world, she invited Ananda.

He was delighted. He could imagine no pleasure greater than holding this statuesque girl in his arms. "I'm afraid I don't know anything but the steps they used to dance at the club in Simla," he said apologetically.

"The club?" said Hope. "That sounds so British."

"I did not go there often."

The armory was only a few blocks away. Together they

walked down Everett Street. Hope didn't care how Ananda danced. In the noisy immensity of the enormous room she closed her eyes as he held her carefully and maneuvered her across the floor in a sort of two-step while the band crashed and smacked and everybody else gyrated and swayed without any body contact at all.

And then, suddenly, it was over. Bonnie Glover moved right in. She came running up as Hope and Ananda sat between dances at one of the tables arranged along the wall.

Bonnie wore a skinny black dress held up with narrow strings over the shoulders.

"Hello again, you two," she said cheerfully.

Ananda looked at her vaguely, as if she were a stranger. At once Bonnie pulled him to his feet and steered him out into the seething middle of the floor.

Hope gave up. She followed them and yelled at Ananda, "I'm going now. Do you know the way home?"

Ananda looked at her blankly. Bonnie saw her chance. "I'll take him home," she shrieked. "I've got my car."

Then Ananda pulled himself away from Bonnie. "Don't go," he said, coming to his senses. Ananda was not a fool. It was plain to him that Bonnie belonged to a cruder order of being than Hope Fry. Hope was like the girls he had grown up with, the kind his mother was always writing him about, trying to entice him home.

But Bonnie, grinning, took his arm again, staking a claim.

Weakly, full of shame, Ananda watched Hope battle her way to the door.

Hope, looking back, caught a glimpse of his green face looking at her anxiously. As she slipped outside, it changed to purple.

Lying in bed at home, she couldn't sleep. She turned and tossed. When at last Bonnie's headlights shone on the ceiling, Hope sat up, waiting for the slam of the car door and Ananda's step on the stairs.

Oh, God, there was no slam, no step on the stairs. Hope fell back on the pillow and closed her eyes. For half an hour she lay still, picturing them entwined on the front seat, kissing, groping, perhaps even—

She had never been so wretched in her life. What a fool she had been to think Ananda too pure and high-minded to be obsessed with sex. If only she had exploited her opportunities like Bonnie! If only she had crushed herself against him, too! Let him compare Bonnie's endowments with her own in the melon department, she thought bitterly.

At last the car door slammed. Bonnie drove away. Ananda ascended the stairs. Lying rigidly in bed, Hope heard him stop outside her room. There was an electric pause, then a light tap.

With her heart throbbing, Hope got out of bed and opened the door.

They stood looking at each other, two dark shapes.

"I just wanted to be sure you got home safely," whispered Ananda.

It's taken you a while to worry about it, Hope wanted to say, but she didn't. "Here I am," she whispered instead.

"Well, good night."

"Good night."

Next morning Hope and Ananda sat silently eating their bowls of cold cereal while Oliver talked excitedly about the new bee in his bonnet.

"I'm going to run for selectman," he announced, beaming at his daughter.

Hope was shocked. "Selectman! Who would you be running against?"

"So far, it's just Roger Bland. This is his last term on the planning board. There's going to be a special election in October to replace people who have resigned in midterm."

Hope stared at her father in dismay. "But you'll never beat Roger Bland."

Her father looked at her defiantly. "Why not?"

Hope didn't know how to reply. Her father would make a fool of himself, that was what she wanted to say.

"But we will help," said Ananda eagerly, looking at Hope for support.

Hope tried to explain. "It's just that Mr. Bland is a fixture in town government. You know, for years and years."

The phone rang. Hope jumped up.

"Hi!" said Bonnie Glover. "Is Ananda there?"

Wordlessly Hope held out the phone to Ananda. He was astonished. He raised his eyebrows and pointed to his chest. No one had ever telephoned him before in the United States. Flustered, he stood up and took the phone and turned to the wall and stared at the toothed gears of an eggbeater that had hung on the same hook since 1937.

Hope couldn't bear to listen. She left the kitchen and ran upstairs.

Later she had a phone call of her own. It was Jack Markey. He was coming out to Concord to show the revised plans of Walden Green to Roger Bland and Judy Bowman. "So how about we have dinner and see a film?"

"Well, okay," said Hope stiffly.

So when Ananda asked her shyly if she would like him to prepare for supper a couple of special Indian dishes, *rajma* and *keema*, she answered airily, "Oh, sure, that's great. I won't be here, but I'm sure Father would enjoy it."

Ananda's face fell. He had never actually cooked a meal in his life, but he thought it was merely a matter of mixing together the proper ingredients and heating them on the stove. But the pleasure had gone out of it, if Hope would not be there.

The restaurant chosen by Jack Markey was cunningly mock historic, mock regional. Waitresses in mobcaps ran to and fro. Big cutouts of comic-book minutemen lined the walls. Hope toyed with her scampi in marinara sauce, wishing she were eating Ananda's Indian specialties instead.

The phoniness of the setting irritated her. While Jack talked enthusiastically of the improvements to his design for Walden Green, a passage from *Walden* kept running through Hope's head. "I sat in my sunny doorway from sunrise till noon, rapt in a revery, I grew in those seasons like corn in the night."

At the theater she tried to forget herself, to be swallowed up in the film, but the words kept running through her head—"like corn in the night, like corn in the night."

It was a Finnish film, artistic and full of sex. During one heavy-breathing episode Jack put his arm around Hope and reached under her shirt.

"Oh, Jack, for Pete's sake."

"Oh, Hopey, come on."

Hope stared at the screen. It pulsed and throbbed. In spite of herself she was excited by the groping hands, by Jack's lips on her neck.

A tall silhouette moved past them, walking up the aisle. Hope could feel the brilliant light of the screen bouncing off her own face in the dark. The reflection of the Finnish actress's bare skin flooded her, it flooded Jack.

The man in the aisle was Ananda Singh. His head turned toward her, then turned away. Without a word he went on up the aisle.

Hope pulled away from Jack and shook herself angrily. Through the rest of the film she sat beside him, no longer paying attention to the flashing images on the screen. She kept turning her head, looking up the aisle for Ananda, but he didn't come back.

Life was a lie, really, thought Hope bitterly. It was all false. Look at the way people carried on their ordinary lives, going to school or working at their jobs or shopping or getting supper, while underneath it all was this shaky foundation, sex, this volcanic, titanic force. Everybody knew it, but nobody said anything.

> . . . *in dreams we never deceive ourselves,*
> *nor are deceived.* . . .
> Thoreau, *A Week on the Concord and Merrimack Rivers*
> "Wednesday"

Homer Kelly would have put it differently, but he might
have come to a similar conclusion. Looking out at the shining
surface of the river, he saw it as a screen for a different
reality. Hidden beneath the slow-moving water a battle was
forever taking place, a continuous savage fight for life—the
perpetual craving of the carnivore for its prey, the shrinking
recoil of the victim. The beauty of nature, all this plenteous
multiform glory that meant so much to him, was only part
of the story.

It was an old dilemma for Homer, the lovely variousness
of natural forms on the one hand and their menace on the
other. And Jefferson Grandison, that august carnivore, was
a similar enigma. There he sat, presiding over his glittering
high rise, seventy stories of gossamer glass—what was hidden
behind that blinding surface? What lay buried in the mud
and slime in which its foundations were imbedded?

Homer meant to find out. Climbing into bed at midnight
on the day of his swooping ascent and plunging fall in the
glass elevator, he ran over in his mind the names of the
elements of Grandison's empire—the names on the list given
him by Abigail Saltonstall on the seventieth floor of the
Grandison Building. The first fifteen were obviously building
projects—Egret Country, Woodland Mall, and the like. If
something wasn't done to stop it, Walden Green would soon
be added to the list.

The rest were more mysterious:

Breathe Free
Serene Harbors
Seashores Unlimited
Mountain Lake Environmental Services
Blue Skies
Ah Wilderness
Dreams of the Maine Coast

What exactly did they represent, all those poetical adjectives and nouns? Drowsily Homer went to sleep, gathered into one curve with his sleeping wife.

But instead of dreaming of serene harbors and mountain lakes, he was circling in a crepuscular darkness, dancing in a slow, heavy-footed ring with shadowy people he could dimly recognize. They were Jefferson Grandison, Jack Markey, Ananda Singh, Oliver Fry and his daughter, Hope, Roger Bland and his wife, Marjorie. And who was that shapeless woman whose hand was so limply clasped in Marjorie's? It was the homeless woman he had seen in Copley Square. And look at all those others, the residents of Pond View—Julian Snow and Charlotte Harris and Stuart LaDue and Honey Mooney. The big-shouldered woman was Mimi Pink. What a clumsy ring-a-round-rosy! There was no music, and even the tramp of their feet made no sound. Homer shuffled around clumsily, shuddering as he made room for two more. They were Alice Snow and Shirley Mills, wrapped in fluttering grave cloths, awakened into lethargic life. Around and around they all went in a sluggish gavotte, the alive and the dead together.

Homer woke up in the airless room and lay in the dark, staring at the ceiling. In a moment the languid figures of his dream were gone, leaving only an image of their joined hands, all those lumpish fingers clasped in a ring.

He turned over and whispered in Mary's ear, "A ring is a ring is a ring."

"What, Homer?"

"Nothing." Now even the shreds of his dream were gone, leaving only something about a ring. A ring? Homer closed his eyes again. It was strange the way dreams seemed so important when you were having them and so meaningless when you woke up.

Next morning Homer ate his breakfast, worrying about Julian Snow and his friends at Pond View. It had been days since he had spoken to Julian. Perhaps no news was good news. Perhaps the succession of violent events at the trailer park was over.

Homer stirred his coffee and looked at his wife with an expression of pathos. "My dear, you're so good with the telephone."

The toaster went pop and tossed up a blackened piece of bread. "Damn," said Mary, jumping out of her chair. Dropping in another slice, she glanced at him warily. "Why are you looking at me like that?"

"It's just that I really admire the way you hold the phone to your ear with such a wonderful iron clasp."

"Come on, Homer, tell me what you've got in mind. You want me to call somebody?"

"Not just somebody." Eagerly Homer whipped out his list. "Look, you see all these high-sounding foundations and grandiose charities and bighearted companies? They all belong to Jefferson Grandison. I want to find out what the hell they really are."

Mary examined the list. "You want me to look up their phone numbers and call them and ask what they actually do?"

"Exactly. My sainted wife." Homer shook his head in wonder. "I often ask myself how you got to be so perfect. I mean you were obviously born like that. For you it's just plain natural. Whereas if I were to try to be perfect, it would be a tortuous process of trial and error, I'd be bumping into trees and falling off cliffs and struggling back up, while you just roll serenely along as though there were nothing to it. It's amazing."

Mary groaned, turning the list over. There was more on the back. And there was a second sheet. "What's this?" She held it up. "This isn't part of the list."

Homer looked at it. "Oh, my God, I forgot to look at it." Swiftly he ran his eye over it, then read it aloud.

MR. GRANDISON, YOU'VE HAD ANOTHER THREATEN-ING CALL FROM ARCHIE POUCH, THE ATTORNEY INTERESTED IN THE DISPOSAL OF LOT 17. HE WAS MOST INSISTENT! HE SPOKE OF DIRE CON-SEQUENCES!

"Homer," said Mary disapprovingly, "you can't go around stealing papers from people's desks."

"You're right, of course," said Homer. "I'll never do such a naughty thing again." For a moment he sat staring at the piece of paper he had filched from Abigail Saltonstall. What did it mean? This attorney, Archie Pouch, was threatening Jefferson Grandison with some sort of dreadful catastrophe unless he did something or other about a mysterious entity called Lot Seventeen. "I wonder what she means by Lot Seventeen?"

"Maybe it's something that's being auctioned off, like rugs or works of art."

"Well, maybe. This lawyer Archie Pouch is obviously very much interested in its disposal, whatever disposal means. I wonder if he's in the phone book."

"Oh, Homer, you're not going to call him up? What good would that do? No lawyer is going to tell you about the concerns of a client."

"No, I suppose not," said Homer dreamily. "Still, I think I'll just take a look at the Yellow Pages."

And then Homer had no trouble finding Archibald Pouch

in the listings under "Lawyers." He was not only *in* the phone book, he was *all over* the phone book. There were four large half-page ads recommending the services of Pouch, Heaviside and Sprocket. One of the ads showed them in person, lined up side by side, three rapacious-looking characters in three-piece suits. Their areas of expertise were listed in full:

> PERSONAL INJURY
> MEDICAL MALPRACTICE
> DEFECTIVE PRODUCTS
> NEGLIGENCE
> SLIP AND FALL
> TOXIC INJURIES
> UNDERGROUND STORAGE TANKS
> 21-E HAZARDOUS WASTE
> LEAD PAINT POISONING
> DRUNK DRIVING

And finally, as a general catch-all invitation:

> LITIGATION

The implicit message of all the ads was the same—"Consider yourself aggrieved? Sue the bastards!"

For a while Homer sat musing, staring at the three drooping mustaches on the three faces of Pouch, Heaviside and Sprocket. Then he stood up, slammed the Yellow Pages shut, picked up the Boston phone book, and dumped it in front of his wife, who was finishing her breakfast and reading *Barchester Towers*. "Your turn, Mary dear. Good luck. I'm off to the city to bag Mr. Pouch."

Mary shook her head in a gesture that meant, *Homer dear, you're out of your mind*. But she licked the butter off her fingers and kissed him good-bye. And at midmorning she got to work on the list of Grandison's enterprises. With one finger holding her place in *Barchester Towers*, she dialed the number for Ah Wilderness.

"Please hold," said a faraway recorded voice. Mary held the receiver with its canned music away from her ear and lost herself in the machinations of Mr. Slope and the tyranny of Mrs. Proudie. Now and then the recording informed her that all lines were occupied. At last a human voice abruptly cut off the music. "Ah Wilderness Incorporated, may I help you?"

"Oh," said Mary, still caught up in the affairs of Barchester, "good morning. My name is Mary Kelly. I wonder if you could tell me what it is you do about wilderness?"

"Pardon me?"

"I mean, what does your name mean, Ah Wilderness?"

There was a chilly pause. "Who, may I ask, is calling?"

"I told you. My name's Mary Kelly. I live in Concord, Massachusetts. I'm trying to find out what your company is for." Mary drummed her fingers on the table, thinking that Homer would have done better. He would have invented some plausible untruth, whereas she was incapable of lying.

"What, may I ask, is your interest in wilderness?"

"I don't have any particular interest. I'm just looking for information."

"I think perhaps you should speak to Mr. Thor."

"Mr. Thor? Well, all right. Could you transfer me?"

"Mr. Thor is in conference."

"Well, could he call me back when he's finished?"

"What is the nature of the subject you wish to discuss with Mr. Thor?"

Mary spent the morning fighting her way out of similar paper bags.

Seashores Unlimited was closed for the day. Dreams of the Maine Coast put her on hold and forgot her. Breathe Free told her to call back between four and four-fifteen. Serene Harbors transferred her to five different departments and at last informed her that the individual to whom she wished to speak had left for the day. Save the World Services wanted her to punch buttons with which her old-fashioned telephone was not equipped. Birdsong Incorporated put her on hold.

By midafternoon Mary had come to the chapter in *Barchester Towers* in which the gown of the overbearing Mrs. Proudie is ripped by the sofa of the ravishing Signora Neroni, and she was almost irritated when Pride of the Earth awoke from its musical slumber and asked her what she wanted.

"Oh, hello! My name is Mary Kelly, and I wonder if you could tell me what Pride of the Earth means, what it is exactly that you people do."

"May I ask the nature of your interest?"

"Just curiosity. The name sounds so grand, I just wondered what it means."

"Do you represent the media?"

"The media? Oh, no."

"Well, I'm afraid we are too busy here to respond to random questions."

"Too busy doing *what?*"

The phone went click.

41

Every maggot lives down town.
Journal, October 15, 1840

The offices of Pouch, Heaviside and Sprocket were housed in a pink marble building on Federal Street. The luxurious lobby, too, was lined with marble. It was obvious to Homer that Pouch, Heaviside and Sprocket were doing well. Other people's personal injuries were their personal happy times, the sordid miseries of litigious customers their chuckles and merriment. Some poor wretch fell off a scaffolding and broke his back, and Pouch, Heaviside and Sprocket rubbed their hands with glee.

Homer took the elevator to the seventh floor, chastising himself for his disdain. Somebody had to help people out when ghastly things happened to them, and why not Pouch, Heaviside and Sprocket?

POUCH, HEAVISIDE AND SPROCKET
ATTORNEYS AT LAW

said the brass plate on the door. Homer walked in and flinched. What was the matter with him? He had become absurdly sensitive to high-toned swank. He blamed it on the year he had spent in Florence, surrounded on every side by perfection of proportion and effortless grace. He would have to get over it, if he was going to go on consorting with the likes of Jefferson Grandison and Archie Pouch.

Homer tried to avoid looking at the extravagant flossiness of the waiting room. He concentrated instead on the receptionist. She was very different from Abigail Saltonstall.

Something about her plucked eyebrows and the abandon with which she was chewing gum made her look like a film star of the 1930s.

"You can't see Mr. Pouch without an appointment," she said, her jaw going around and around. Her gum was pink. Homer hoped she would blow a bubble.

"Oh, I think Mr. Pouch will see me," said Homer. "My name is Kelly, Homer Kelly. I'm Mr. Jefferson Grandison's attorney." It was only half a lie. Somewhere in Homer's attic lay a mildewed diploma from Suffolk University Law School.

The girl was impressed. Her jaw stopped rotating. She hoisted herself from her chair, pushed open a door, and disappeared.

Homer occupied himself while she was gone by picking up an old *Celebrity* magazine from an immense glass coffee table. The magazine fell open at a picture of a goodlooking young man stepping into a limousine in New Delhi under the heading THE TEN MOST ELIGIBLE BACHELORS IN THE WORLD. Homer gasped. It was Ananda Singh.

The receptionist came back. "Okey-doke," she said, like a true thirties movie star, "you can go right in."

Archie Pouch too seemed a throwback to the silver screen of days gone by, as he came striding forward to shake hands with Homer. His suit was sharp, his tie was white, his shirt was black. "Mr. Kelly, pleased to meet you. Now maybe we can get this whole can of worms straightened out, the whole ball of wax, right?"

"Well, of course Mr. Grandison certainly wishes to do the right thing." Homer was surprised to find himself sounding stuffy and dignified, as though he were genuinely concerned with the best interests of Grandison Enterprises.

"Okay, so tell me, when does old Jeff plan to give the heave-ho to Lot Seventeen? That's what this bummer's all about, right? Let's get something straight right from the start. Grandison thinks he's an eight-hundred-pound gorilla, right?

Well, so what? So's my client. Me, I'm a thousand-pound gorilla." Archie Pouch thumped his chest with both fists like King Kong. "My client paid your client spot cash to deep-six Lot Seventeen. Grandison's got to give it the bum's rush, understand? My client's fed up with the way he just sits there on his butt."

Aha, thought Homer gratefully, so Lot Seventeen wasn't something Grandison had bought, it was something he had been paid to take away. So much for Mary's notion that it was rugs and works of art! What kind of thing would someone be paid to remove? It would have to be something nobody wanted. Something toxic, putrid, poisonous, radioactive, evil-smelling. Homer gazed piously at the ceiling and phrased a careful response. "The toxic characteristics of Lot Seventeen are disputed in scientific circles."

"Toxic!" Archie Pouch stared at Homer in disbelief. "Nobody's pretending Lot Seventeen is toxic." He guffawed. "It's just in our fucking way."

"May I ask," ventured Homer, groping in the dark, "how much of your client's space it now occupies?"

"Jesus, Grandison knows how much space it occupies. Forty acres, that's how much. It's the biggest specialized dump in New England. The stuff's gotta go." Pouch leaned forward and put his nose close to Homer's. His breath smelled of mint wafers and gin. "Get that shit out of there."

"Forty acres? Forty acres of . . . of . . . ?" Homer waited encouragingly for Pouch to elucidate the nature of Lot Seventeen.

But Pouch was suddenly on his guard. "What the hell, Kelly? You mean you don't know?" He leaned still farther forward, and Homer had to arch his back to keep the Pouch nose away from his chin. It was easy to picture the man intimidating witnesses in a courtroom.

Adopting a hoity-toity manner, Homer tried to bluff his way out. "I'm afraid Mr. Grandison has treated this matter as a strictly legal problem. He has not divulged to me what it is that he has contracted to remove. I'm afraid I don't—"

"Oh, Christ." Pouch put his hand on Homer's chest and shoved him toward the door. "What are you, some kind of media? Sprocket," he shouted, "hey, Sprocket, come in here."

Homer looked over Pouch's shoulder uneasily, expecting a thug in a fedora hat and double-breasted suit. Sprocket turned out to be a healthy-looking kid in baby blue suspenders, with overhanging brows like some small-brained early hominid, *Australopithecus*, or something like that. But small-brained or not, Sprocket had obviously passed the Massachusetts bar, and now he took Homer's arm in a mighty grip and dragged him out of Pouch's office.

"Never mind, Sprocket," said Homer, shaking himself free, speaking through his teeth, trying to retrieve some shred of dignity. "I shall leave of my own free will."

At home he found Mary still lost in the internecine affairs of the cathedral city of Barchester. Looking up from her book, she admitted to Homer her failure at extracting information on Grandison's enterprises by telephone. "It was zilch all the way, I'm afraid. I can tell you all you want to know about the state of the Anglican church in nineteenth-century England, but as for Mr. Grandison's undertakings, I haven't got a clue. They're all wrapped in veils of awful music and answering machines and sullen switchboard operators who don't know anything, and the people who do know something are in conference and can't be disturbed until Tuesday."

"It's Grandison's celestial conglomerate," said Homer darkly. "You can't expect to reach God on the telephone, nor anybody sitting at his right or left hand. When you get down on your knees to say a prayer, the angel Gabriel puts you on hold." Then he confessed his own humiliating failure in the pink marble sanctuary of Pouch, Heaviside and Sprocket. "I did find out one thing, however," he said, pouring himself a drink. "Lot Seventeen isn't Oriental rugs and Rembrandts, it's something putrid Grandison has agreed to remove."

"Well, good, that's some kind of progress." Mary ran into the kitchen to take a pot off the stove, then poked her head out again. "Listen, I've been thinking. What about Jerry Neville? Remember Jerry? Jerry knows everything."

Homer's gloom vanished. "Jerry Neville, of course. How could I have forgotten Jerry?"

Jerry Neville was a criminal lawyer who had given up practice in the courts to pursue a personal investigation of the inner workings of the commonwealth of Massachusetts at the end of the twentieth century. His book, if he ever had the audacity to publish it, would scandalize the nation. Jerry had been working on it for years.

When Homer reached him on the phone, Jerry was pleased with the nature of the problem. "Sure, sure, I know exactly how to go about it. I've got ten thousand file cards on the interlocking interests of big operators in this state. Read me the list."

Homer read the names on the piece of paper he had stolen from Abigail Saltonstall, and Jerry took them down, chuckling now and then.

"What are you snickering about?" said Homer. "I mean, that was what I'd call a knowing snicker, if ever I heard one."

"I'll tell you later," promised Jerry.

When he called back next day he was laughing. "Oh, Homer, thank you. I never enjoyed myself so much in my life. I should have guessed it. Jefferson Grandison has taken up the noble cause of toxic waste disposal. It's a terrible problem in this state. No kidding, it really is. Nobody wants it in their backyard, especially the kind that emits low-level radiation. But the stuff has to be got rid of somehow, so Grandison obliges. For the right fee he'll take any kind of crud and dispose of it for you, no questions asked. He's the hazardous-waste king of New England, the emperor of toxic trash. God knows what he does with it. That Lot Seventeen of yours must be something highly undesirable."

"You mean Ah Wilderness and Breathe Free and Save the World and so on, they're all just disgusting bilge of one kind or another, putrid petroleum gushing out of dirty pipes, raw sewage, that sort of thing?"

"Worse stuff, probably. Well, that's our century for you, a hundred years of swill. Translate all those pretty words of his into their proper names, and you get Foul Water instead of Seashores Unlimited, and Contaminated Air instead of Breathe Free. But give the man credit. The putrid stuff is there, and somebody has to dispose of it. The only question is how. Do you trust him to get rid of it safely? I don't."

"But, listen, Jerry, it's not toxic. That's all I could get out of Archie Pouch. Lot Seventeen isn't toxic, it's just in the way."

"In the way?" Jerry was silent for a minute. "That's strange. Hey, what's that noise?"

Homer laughed. "Can you hear it? Well, I'll tell you what it is. It's Birdsong Incorporated, it's Pride of the Earth, it's Dreams of the Maine Coast. It's Canada geese, that's what it is. They're back already. They're flying over the house making a hell of a racket."

"Oh, I see. Well, so long."

Homer hung up and went out on the porch to watch the long straggling line of Canadas flap low over the river. They were calling to each other hoarsely, gliding with widespread hovering wings, coming to rest on the water and rocking up and down.

42

*I perceive that we partially die ourselves through
sympathy at the death of each of our friends. . . .*
Journal, February 3, 1859

"Homer? This is Julian Snow." Julian's voice was quiet
but intense.

"Just a sec." Homer looked at his watch. It was five-fifteen
in the morning. Unsnarling the telephone wire, he put his
legs over the side of the bed. "Something else has happened,
hasn't it?"

"It's Porter McAdoo. He was changing a tire, and the
jack collapsed, and the car came down on him. I've called
the police ambulance, but it's too late."

"I'll be right over."

When Homer drove into Pond View, people were standing
around in a gloomy half circle—Honey Mooney in a tur-
quoise wrapper, Pete Harris in an enormous bathrobe, Stuart
LaDue in a nightshirt, his old man's bow legs bare, Eugene
Beaver with a winter coat buttoned over his nakedness, Julian
Snow fully dressed in shirt and jeans.

Who was missing? Homer ran over the list in his mind.
Only Charlotte Harris. He got out of his car and stood with
the others, watching a couple of paramedics from Emerson
Hospital slam the ambulance doors on Porter McAdoo.

"Who found him?" said Homer.

The residents of Pond View shuffled uneasily and looked
at each other. "It was Charlotte Harris," said Stu LaDue.
"She *said* he was already dead." Stu rolled his eyes to imply
that Charlotte's word was not to be trusted.

They stood back to let the ambulance turn around and
drive away. Julian looked at Stu LaDue angrily. "The am-

bulance guys, they said he'd been dead for a while. It didn't just happen this morning."

Stu shrugged, Pete Harris shook his head sorrowfully, Honey Mooney wiped her eyes, and Eugene Beaver huddled down in his raincoat. Then they all drifted away. The day threatened to be sticky and hot.

Homer and Julian inspected Porter's shiny Ford Taurus. There was nothing much to look at. It had been hoisted high on the jack again so that Porter's body could be removed.

"Bumper jack, I see," said Homer.

"Why didn't he shore up the wheels with those big stones?" said Julian. "See those white rocks, there in his flower bed? Porter was a careful kind of guy. I don't understand it."

"Why didn't anybody discover him sooner? It must have happened last night."

"Real late, probably. Porter was a night owl. He used to wash his car at midnight. Sometimes he mowed his lawn by the light of the moon."

Julian looked at Homer reproachfully, and Homer felt a stab of guilt. Somehow, some way, he should have been on hand when Porter McAdoo was jacking up his car.

"Mr. Kelly, Mr. Kelly!" Homer turned to see Honey Mooney running toward them, waving her arms. Her turquoise wrapper flapped, her slippers flip-flopped on the pavement. She was puffing and out of breath. "My curtains, somebody set fire to my curtains!"

"Jesus," said Julian. They hurried after Honey and followed her into her big mobile home, one of the largest in the park.

"Somebody must have set fire to them while I was out just now." Honey gestured at the pair of dripping charred curtains hanging on either side of her bay window. She had drenched the smoldering ruffles with a kettle of water. "I didn't lock my door. I just ran out. Look at my entertainment center! It's all wet. I'll bet my TV won't work anymore." Leaning down, she turned on the switch. At once the set

flickered into life, and there on the screen were Vanessa and
Angelica pulling each other's hair. "Well, at least the picture's still nice and sharp."

Julian recognized the curtains. They were the ones he had
given to Honey after Alice's death. "It's strange," he said.
"Both sides are burned the same amount."

"That's right," said Homer. "You'd think a fire would
catch one side and burn it all the way to the top before the
other side started. It looks as if somebody touched a match
to one side and then the other." He looked at Honey. "You
didn't leave a cigarette burning in an ashtray under the
curtains?"

Honey looked offended. "I don't smoke."

"But who could have done it? All of you were there together
beside the ambulance. All of you except——" Homer glanced
at Julian, who looked away.

"All of us except Charlotte Harris," said Honey in triumph.

"Why don't I go talk to Charlotte?" mumbled Homer,
excusing himself. Outside on Honey's lawn he shook Julian's
hand and said good-bye. He couldn't think of anything else
to say, except "Watch out for yourself, be careful, you're all
in danger," but Julian knew that perfectly well.

Homer knocked on Charlotte's door. She opened it at once
and seemed glad to see him, but she looked embarrassed as
she invited him to come in and sit down. Homer guessed
that her style was cramped by the presence of her husband,
who sat impassively on the sofa like a toad.

"May I ask how you found Porter this morning, Mrs.
Harris?"

"I went out very early to sprinkle the lawn, because there's
been so little rain lately, and I saw him right away, pinned
under his car." Charlotte's eyes filled with tears. "He was a
fine man." She glanced at Pete, who lifted his shoulders and
raised his eyebrows, as if to say "He was okay, I guess."

"Did you happen to go into Honey Mooney's while the
others were all at the other end of the park just now?"

Charlotte looked at him blankly. "No, I was right here, looking out the window."

"Did you see anyone else go into Mrs. Mooney's?"

Charlotte shook her head.

"What's the matter?" said Pete. "Somebody steal something?"

"No," said Homer gravely. "Somebody set fire to her curtains."

"Fire!" said Charlotte. "Not another fire?"

"I'm afraid so. Somebody around here seems to be fond of setting fires. What about last night? Did you notice any strangers around here last night?"

"No. I always step outside before going to bed, just to look at the stars. But I didn't see anything unusual."

Homer thanked her and went away to talk to Honey again, and to Eugene Beaver and Stu LaDue. They had all been watching the happy colors of television jiggling on the screen. They had heard nothing else, they had seen nothing.

Homer drove away and headed across Route 2, wondering why the remaining Pond View people didn't seem more concerned for their own safety. Only Julian Snow had the sense to be afraid. As Homer pulled into the parking lot beside the fire and police station, he saw Julian's sober face rise up against the background of the shining red fire engines parked in the open air.

"That's two more things," he told Police Chief Flower. "Porter McAdoo's death and Honey Mooney's fire. You can't ignore it now. Somebody's trying to eliminate everybody at Pond View."

Chief Flower obviously felt a little guilty. He didn't look Homer in the eye. He rocked back on his chair with his short legs off the floor and stared out the window at the little hollow where the Mill Brook ran trickling toward the center of town. "Like I said, elderly people, they have accidents all the time. Take the old folks in Peter Bulkeley Terrace. Just the other day we had a fire and a burglary there the same day. But the fire was this old woman's hair dryer blew up, and the burglary was another old lady, she forgot where she put her pocketbook."

"But Porter wasn't elderly, and neither is Honey. I tell you, Jimmy, those people need protection. What about posting somebody there at night? One man, just one?"

"Jesus, Homer, where you been? I told you, we haven't got the manpower for private security. We've had to cut our staff twenty percent. There's no way I could justify taking anybody off regular duty to guard a bunch of elderly folks around the clock, people who are probably dying of accidents and natural causes. No way in this world."

Roger Bland's interest in the future of Pond View had blossomed since the death of Alice Snow. The termination of the trailer park was now even more desirable. Roger had been asked to help effect certain changes at whatever time in the remote future the park at last became empty of residents. The legal ramifications would be tricky, and the social uproar horrendous, but Roger was inclined to think the town should keep its options open.

"Only six of them left," he said, reading the obituary notice for Porter McAdoo in the *Concord Journal*. He looked at his wife in triumph. "Four of them retired to Florida, so now it's only six."

"Six what, dear?"

"Never mind."

"Oh, Roger, dear, did you remember the tickets?"

"Tickets?"

"The plane tickets. For Nantucket. Our vacation, remember?"

"Oh, the plane tickets. No, I'm sorry, Marjorie, I forgot."

"Honestly, Roger, it just shows how badly you need a rest. Promise me, dear, you'll call the travel agency tomorrow morning first thing."

43

*Every day or two I strolled to the village to
hear some of the gossip. . . .*
Walden, "The Village"

The same issue of the *Concord Journal* that listed the death
of Porter McAdoo published the warrant for the special town
meeting in October.

One of the warrant articles was highly controversial—the
proposed zoning change to allow a mixed-use complex on a
site belonging to the high school. Jack Markey's scenic watercolor rendering was printed on the front page. Soon everybody was talking about Walden Green and the sacrifice of
the high school land.

"I must say," said Marjorie Bland, meeting her friend Jo-
Jo Field on the Milldam, "I think the picture of Walden
Green is awfully attractive, don't you?"

Jo-Jo was shocked. "But it's another insult to Walden
Woods. When is it going to end?"

"Oh, Jo-Jo, didn't you read the article? Grandison Enterprises has promised to finance a transfer station at the
landfill. Roger says the huge hole in the ground will disappear
at last. You know, where they pile all those old washing
machines."

"It's bribery," said Jo-Jo, frowning and folding her arms.
"I don't like being bribed to do something wrong."

"But, Jo-Jo, dear," said Marjorie, laughing, "Roger says
that's the way things are done these days. And anyway he
thinks the pretty little square with its houses and shops will
be an asset to the town. And Roger thinks"—Marjorie
stepped over a recumbent form on the sidewalk—"he thinks
the affordable housing will fill a need."

"Well, of course anything Roger says is gospel truth to me," Jo-Jo said earnestly. "We all swear by Roger." She nodded her head significantly at the man huddled in the entrance to Hugo's Hair Harmonies and whispered, "But what about that poor old man? Will he be able to live there?"

Marjorie looked down at the man in surprise. "Good gracious. You know," she said, hurrying away with Jo-Jo, "one of those people keeps turning up at my house. She hides in the stable with Carmencita."

"Carmencita?"

"Wally's horse, Baronesa Carmencita de Granada. She's got a Spanish name because she's a Paso Fino. You know, the Spaniards brought them to the West Indies way back in history."

"A Paso Fino, isn't that the horse with the lovely smooth gait?"

"Right, but she's too small for Wally now. And anyway she's been so skittish lately. I've been thinking seriously, Jo-Jo, of having her put down."

"Put down! Good heavens."

"Honestly, Jo-Jo, it would be such a relief. She tried to bite me the other day." Marjorie displayed a bruise on her arm and stepped over another sleeping person on the sidewalk.

"Listen," said Jo-Jo, getting back to brass tacks, "what about that homeless woman in your stable? Have you called the police?"

"The police? Oh, I don't know. Perhaps we really should." Marjorie said good-bye to Jo-Jo and rushed away without explaining that Roger was hoping to become a Harvard overseer, and therefore he couldn't possibly throw a homeless person out on the street. It was a perfectly good reason, but it was just so difficult to explain.

Oliver Fry's response to the front-page picture of Walden Green was his usual choking fury. But an item on one of the inner pages distressed him even more.

It was an interview with Judy Bowman, the chairperson of the Concord School Committee. Judy was answering a question about the committee's plan for reducing their budget by the ten percent required by the finance committee. "We hate to do it, but we've got to. We're going to close the libraries in the primary schools, restrict interschool athletic competition, and reduce the teaching staffs at the high school in the departments of language and biology. It's a shame, but I don't know what else we can do."

". . . and reduce the teaching staffs at the high school in the departments of language and biology." The paper slipped out of Oliver's fingers. He was about to lose his job. Judy had warned him it might happen, but he had chosen not to think about it. "It will only be for a year or two, Oliver," Judy had said. "If this Walden Green zoning change passes, there'll be money to burn, and we'll hire you back."

It was an ironic blow from the hand of fate. It was bad enough to lose his job, but to have it restored thanks to a shopping mall in Walden Woods was inconceivably awful.

Anxieties crowded in upon Oliver. Hope had another year of college ahead of her. He had been saving for years to put her through school. If he put together all his savings and some unemployment money and a little something from his pension plan, there'd be enough to allow the girl to finish her education. But what would they live on in the meantime? What if he couldn't find another job?

At the moment Oliver couldn't face it. He couldn't make himself begin looking for a new teaching position. Instead he threw himself into the race against Roger Bland for the opening on the board of selectmen.

"It's not as if the selectman's job paid a salary," said Hope to Jack Markey. "All those people on the town boards work for nothing."

Hope was sorting bottles on the back porch under the fierce scrutiny of the owl, throwing them into paper bags. Marjorie

Bland's bottle-sorting campaign had swept the town, and Hope was doing her best to cooperate. *Crash* went the green bottles into one bag, *smash* went the clear ones into another.

Jack Markey thought about the two candidates. It was easy to guess that the fire-eating Mr. Fry would be an easy victim for sober, solid Roger Bland. "I don't suppose your father will win anyway," he said truthfully.

Hope opened a second bag for her father's whiskey bottles. "It's just so embarrassing. He's going to have bumper stickers. Did you ever hear of a candidate for a town office handing out bumper stickers? And listen to this, they won't say 'Vote for Oliver Fry,' or anything sensible like that. He's going to use a quote from Emerson." Hope took a mock heroic stance and waved her hand at the wooden ceiling of the porch. " 'The rapt saint is the only logician,' how do you like that?"

"What?"

" 'The rapt saint'—oh, never mind. It's just so ridiculous."

"I suppose your, ah . . . tenant is supporting your father," said Jack, feeling a twinge of jealousy at the thought of Ananda Singh.

"Oh, well, naturally." Hope laughed bitterly. "Those Thoreau freaks all stand together." She felt an odd discomfort as she said it, because it was for Ananda's sake that she was reading *Walden*. Passages from the book had oozed through the cracks in her defenses like slippery snakes, inserting themselves in soft passages in her brain: "I grew in those seasons like corn in the night. . . . The greater part of what my neighbors call good I believe in my soul to be bad. . . . Only one in a hundred millions is awake to a poetic or divine life."

"Hey," said Jack, "who drinks all the booze around here? That's a hell of a lot of whiskey bottles."

"My father, of course. Who do you think?" Hope pushed the bags of bottles together with her foot and shrugged. Rays

of afternoon sunshine were pouring through the wooden lattice of the porch, illuminating Jack's blond curls. Hope
couldn't help thinking by contrast of Ananda's sallow skin,
his dark eyes and black hair. At the moment he seemed odd
and foreign.

"You mean your father drank all this stuff? My God, what
is it, a year's supply?"

"This? Oh, no. It's a couple of months, maybe. Less than
that." Hope took a melancholy pleasure in exaggerating her
father's indulgence in drink. Actually she couldn't remember
taking bottles to the dump since last Christmas.

A glimmer of a good idea came into Jack's head. "I've got
some errands to do. Why don't I take this stuff to the landfill?"

"Oh, say, that would be great. You'll have to use Father's
car. Yours doesn't have a dump sticker. It's okay, he won't
be needing it. He's off somewhere on his bike."

Jack and Hope carried everything out of the house and
packed it in the back of Oliver's ramshackle station wagon
—the sacks of newspapers, the plastic bags of trash, the paper
bags of bottles. Then Jack took off with a clash of gears
because he wasn't used to a standard shift.

On the way to the landfill the bottles rattled and jingled.
Turning in at the gate, Jack followed the sign to the recycling
area to drop off the newspapers and hurl the wine bottles into
the glass-collecting dumpster. The three bags of whisky bottles stayed in the car, clinking against each other as he drove
down the uneven dirt road to get rid of the plastic bags.

Pulling up at the drop-off point, he stopped beside three
men who were standing next to a glittering new machine.

Jack recognized it at once. It was a compactor, the kind
manufactured by one of Jefferson Grandison's enterprises.

"Hey," he said, getting out of the car, "where do I throw
my stuff?"

"Hold it," said one of the men. "Hey, Julian, here's our
first customer. Look," he said to Jack, "just throw it right
down there. See? Right there." He pointed at the huge con-

tainer buried in the ground, an empty bin of shining steel.

"Brand-new gadget," said the second man as Jack hauled Hope's plastic bags out of the car and dropped them in the bin. "New compactor. You're the first guy to use it. Is that all you've got? Okay, Julian, let her go."

The skinny man in the visor hat hesitated, then disappeared into another part of the machine high above the open container. There was a whining sound. Jack watched as one wall of the bin began moving forward, shoving the bags toward the other side. Slowly the moving wall ground them into the maw of the machine. For a moment there was a crumpling, crushing noise, and then the ram pulled back with a shriek of metal on metal.

"Holy shit," said the first man.

"See, like it squeezes all the trash together," said the second guy, "so the stuff don't take up so much space."

"Right," said Jack.

The man called Julian came down from on high and looked at them. His face was pale. His hands were shaking. "My God," he said, "you've got to watch it like a hawk. It's dangerous, I tell you."

"Oh, for shit's sake, Julian, we're just trying it out." One of the other men grinned at Jack. "It's just an experiment. It can't handle all the stuff comes in here."

"Well, thanks for letting me be your first customer," said Jack. He backed Oliver's car around and drove out of the landfill and headed across town to the bridge over the river at the foot of Nashawtuc Hill. There he parked the car and got out and carried the three bags of whisky bottles around the corner to the house of Roger Bland.

Roger was spraying his roses, wearing a mask over mouth and nose. The spray had a nasty smell. Roger's horse had retreated to the far side of the field. It was rearing and plunging dangerously.

"I've got something to show you," said Jack, walking bravely into the spray.

Roger put down his pump and pulled off his mask. "Well, okay," he said. "Come on inside."

Jack's eyes watered. He turned his back on the poisonous cloud drifting over the river and followed Roger across the terrace into the house.

In the kitchen Jack took the bottles out of the bags and lined them up in a long row on the counter. "Do you know what these are?" he said dramatically.

"No," said Roger Bland. "What are they?"

"They're the downfall of Oliver Fry, that's what they are."

44

*No man stood on truth. They were merely banded
together, as usual one leaning on another, and
all together on nothing. . . .*
"Life Without Principle"

Roger Bland was too sensible to make a public display of
Oliver Fry's whisky bottles. Nor did the matter surface at
any of his neighborhood meetings in the living rooms of the
voters of Concord.

That sort of direct revelation was unnecessary. It could be
left to itself. Marjorie Bland began it, when her friend Irma
Draper called to confess that she was thinking of deserting
Roger in this election. "I hope he'll forgive me," she said,
"but I just can't support his stand on Walden Green."

"But, Irma, you know who's running against him, don't
you? Oliver Fry."

"Well, what's the matter with Oliver? Oh, I know he's
a crusty sort of a nut case, but his heart's in the right place.
We can trust him to protect the town against commercial
development, if we can trust anybody."

"Oh, well, I suppose that's right. But what about"—
Marjorie lowered her voice—"Oliver's drinking problem?"

"His what?"

"Didn't you know?" Marjorie's tone expressed her sorrow.
"The poor man, he's been an alcoholic for years."

"An alcoholic? Oliver Fry? No kidding? Good heavens, I
had no idea."

And then Irma met Granger Pond in her yoga class, and
she passed on the news on the way to the parking lot. And
of course Granger told his wife.

Thus the news flitted around town at high speed. It did
not need to be typed up and copied and folded and stuffed

into envelopes and sent out in a town mailing to six thousand households.

It didn't matter that no one had ever seen Oliver Fry intoxicated. The merest hint that he had a drinking problem was enough to condemn him. It was so easy to imagine him in a sodden condition, his speech slurred, his head lolling, his eyes half-closed, his hand clutching a bottle.

Hope Fry was surprised to find herself the recipient of little sympathetic pats and embraces. "My dear," said Marjorie Bland, running into her in the Star Market, "have you thought of AA?"

"AA?" said Hope, confused. "You mean in case I have a flat tire?"

"A flat tire?" They parted, mutually bewildered.

The wildfire spread of the rumor did much to promote the candidacy of Roger Bland for the empty place on the Concord Board of Selectmen. Roger's bid to become one of Harvard's overseers was not so easily handled.

Those candidates were far more formidable than Oliver Fry. They were leaders of the nation. Roger labored over his personal history, the short paragraph of biographical information that was to accompany his picture on the ballot. Should he mention that he had been active in the election campaign of a recent Republican governor of Massachusetts? Or would that turn off all the Democratic alums? Better say nothing about it. How about his term as director of the Concord Country Club? No, strike that. Well, what the hell *could* he say?

Roger quailed at the thought of all the thousands and thousands of alumni and alumnae who would read his words of self-praise, detecting the hollowness of his claim on the one hand and the strength of his desire on the other.

45

Our relation was one long tragedy. . . .
Journal, March 4, 1856

Given enough time, the essential quality of a man or woman reveals itself. Presidents fail because one massive flaw works its way to the surface and stands revealed. Marriages reduce themselves to the clash of defects unguessed at in the beginning.

The married life of Pete and Charlotte Harris suffered from Pete's total lack of imagination and Charlotte's stubborn refusal to bend. She would not, she could not, accommodate herself. This evening, while Pete watched his favorite game show, Charlotte turned her back on him and read the *Concord Journal*. Tight-lipped, she examined the front page. She learned about the selectman's race, she read the letters to the editor, she looked with horror at the prices of real estate, she examined the police log:

VAGRANTS: Milldam shopkeepers report vagrants occupying the sidewalk. Warnings have been issued, but so far there have been no arrests.

When Pete switched off the television set, Charlotte put down the paper with relief. It was time for the night shift in the kitchen of Emerson Hospital. Behind her she could hear the starched rustle of his white cook's jacket as he heaved himself into it.

Rebellion started up in Charlotte's breast. "I won't," she said.

"You won't what, baby doll?"

"I won't take any wooden nickels."

Pete was nonplussed. He hesitated in the doorway, unable to utter his ritual farewell. Robbed of speech, he descended the steps and let the screen door bang behind him.

Charlotte took a deep breath. Her lungs expanded. Her spirit spread out to fill the trailer. She poured herself another cup of coffee and picked up her book. In the deepening twilight she sank down into the final chapters of *The Mill on the Floss*.

After a while she could no longer see to read. She stood up and turned on the light, then paused for a moment to look out at the other mobile homes. Their glowing windows were comforting, as always. Behind the blinds of the trailer next door, Eugene Beaver would be washing his supper dishes. Honey Mooney's curtains were new, replacements for the ones that had burned. Beyond Honey's mobile home Charlotte could see Norman Peck's lighted windows.

Sitting down again, she picked up her book. Then she lifted her head from the book and stood up.

Norman Peck was dead. His trailer was empty. Why was a ray of light streaming down on the long grass around it, the grass nobody had cut since his death? What was going on in there? Perhaps Norman's daughter Fran was showing the old Landola to a prospective buyer. Stu LaDue said she was trying to sell it for a lot more than it was worth.

Charlotte opened her door, walked softly down the steps, and crossed the driveway to take a look.

There were no cars parked at Norman's place. His daughter wasn't there. But someone was inside. Charlotte saw a woman sail past the window and out of sight, then whirl past it again. She was dancing! She was wearing earphones and dancing with her eyes closed, bobbing around, turning in circles, dipping and swaying.

Charlotte watched for a moment, wondering what to do. Then she walked to the end of the driveway, climbed the steps to Julian's door, and knocked. At once she hurried down the steps again and stood on the pavement. She didn't want him to think even for a moment that she was invading his privacy.

When Julian opened the door, Charlotte turned away at once and pointed. "Norman's place, there's someone in there."

"There is?" Julian came down the steps and they walked together back to Norman's trailer.

"There she is," whispered Charlotte. They stood still, watching the woman with the earphones. She had stopped dancing. She was reaching up into Norman's kitchen cupboard, taking out a jar, running her finger around the inside, sucking the finger.

"Jam," murmured Charlotte. "I guess Fran didn't clean out the shelves."

Moving away, they stopped beside Charlotte's mobile home to talk it over.

"I don't know what to do," said Julian. "Who do you suppose she is?"

"Probably one of those homeless people. I've seen them on Main Street near the hardware store."

"Jesus." Julian looked back at Norman's windows.

"I suppose she shouldn't be there," said Charlotte, "but it seems silly to leave it empty when people are sleeping on the street."

"Right," said Julian. He stood irresolute for a minute, then shrugged his shoulders. "So let's just forget about it, shall we?"

"Good." Charlotte watched his thin shape move away, merging with the deepening darkness. Aching a little, she went back inside.

Next morning Julian looked out at the little street of mobile homes, wondering if Norman's was still occupied. The pale trailers nosing this way and that along the driveway looked a little seedy this morning. The turquoise plastic shutters were supposed to make the long narrow houses look like colonial dwellings, but Julian thought the shutters were ridiculous.

There were no lights in Norman's trailer, but of course there wouldn't be, not in the daytime. Only later, as Julian set off for the landfill, did he encounter the woman with the earphones. They were dangling around her neck.

"Hey, mister," said Bobbsie Low, "what's the matter with my sink? I got no water."

"You're disconnected," said Julian. "Wait a minute." He went back indoors to find his toolbox, then accompanied Bobbsie back to Norman's. "How'd you get in?" he asked her, but then he saw how she had done it. She had smashed the glass louvers of the locked door, probably with one of the white-painted rocks around Porter McAdoo's yard next door.

Later on when Julian came back from the landfill, eager for a shower, he encountered an outraged Stu LaDue.

"Fucking homeless," hollered Stu. "Three or four of 'em, they've moved in. They're in Norman's place and Shirley's and Porter's. Somebody even moved into old Jane Peacock's place, back there behind the laundry shack, the one's been empty for three years. We gotta get 'em outta here. I'm gonna call the police."

"Oh, Stu, what the hell difference does it make? Those old rigs are empty anyhow."

"You think we ain't got enough crime around here already?" whined Stu. "You wait. They'll steal everything's not nailed down."

But when the police came, the four trailers were empty once again. Stu yelled and waved his arms and complained, but there was nothing to be done. The patrol car left, with Stu standing in the driveway, shouting after it.

Julian waited until Stu went back indoors, and then he whistled into the woods behind his house to inform Dolores Marshall and her little girl, Christine, and Bobbsie Low and

Carl Browning and Almina Ziblow that the coast was clear. They came straggling up the hillside with their baggage.

"You can move back in now," said Julian, "but don't turn any lights on this evening. And I'm afraid you'll have to leave in the morning. The police will be back. Stu LaDue will see to that. Hey, wait a minute. Come on in. I made a bunch of sandwiches."

Next day, regretfully, they left Pond View—Dolores and Christine, Bobbsie and Carl and Almina—and trudged back to the center of town to take up their places on the sidewalk. The younger shoppers on the street ignored them. Healthy young legs in sneakers stepped over them, passing in and out of Mimi Pink's Den of Teddies or Hugo's Hair Harmonies or the Unique Boutique. But to the older customers they were a threat, a menace, a warning—and of course Mimi Pink herself was in a continuous hissing state of rage.

"I'm sorry, ma'am," Chief Flower told her again and again, "there's nothing we can do about it. They're not breaking any law. It's a case for the churches. Why don't you talk to one of the reverends?"

Sarah Peel was not among those who occupied Concord street corners and shopfronts. Sarah had found her way home. She had settled down in Marjorie Bland's recycling studio next to Pearl's cozy stable. Oh, she was careful. Whenever Marjorie and Roger Bland were at home, Sarah lay low. But when both cars were missing, she moved around and enjoyed herself. She and Pearl were in constant communion. Sarah tended the horse with devotion. She curried her dappled gray coat with the rubber bristles of a hard brush she found in a basket. She petted her and fed her wormy fruit from the apple tree behind the house. She pulled up carrots from the vegetable garden and gave them to Pearl. She fed her candy. She looked with longing at the saddle hanging on a rack on the wall of the stable, but when she tried to put it on Pearl's back, it slipped under the horse's belly. There was some trick to putting it on.

Well, it didn't matter. Sarah was sure she could ride bareback. Pearl was her very own horse, and sooner or later Sarah would ride her far, far away.

Every now and then Marjorie surprised Sarah by walking into the recycling studio. Then Marjorie would squeal, "Oh, no, not again," and shriek at her to go away at once. So Sarah would stuff everything back into the stroller and depart. It puzzled her that she was never troubled by an officer of the law. Without an official warning she felt perfectly comfortable returning to Pearl and settling in night after night among the stacks of newspapers and the bags of bottles and the plastic bags of trash and the empty boxes from J. Crew and Lord & Taylor and Saks.

One day, peering through the hinge crack of the door into the stable, Sarah saw something interesting. Marjorie was teaching a young teenager how to care for the horse. "Fresh water every day," Marjorie told the little girl. "Sweet feed twice a day, but only this much. A can of pellets. This much grain, no more. We're leaving next Saturday, so you'll take over from then on. Now promise me, Emily dear, you won't try to ride her. Promise!"

And Emily promised.

As for Sarah's friends, they too were resourceful. For a while they holed up in the First Parish Church. In the basement there were splendid bathrooms and a large, well-equipped kitchen. Bridgie Sorrel found a big jar of sauerkraut in the refrigerator. Doris Harper opened a box and discovered a giant cake.

After supper they went out the back door of the church into the drowsy summer dusk and stood on the little wooden bridge over the Mill Brook. Young Christine took off her shoes and waded in the water. She picked black-eyed Susans and Queen Anne's lace in the weedy grass. When it grew dark they went back inside and climbed the stairs to the sanctuary and lay down on the long rosy cushions in the pews. Every pew boasted a rack full of hymnbooks and questionnaires for newcomers to the church services. "Would you like the pastor to call?" inquired the questionnaire.

"Yes," wrote Bobbsie Low.

"Fuck you," scribbled Doris Harper.

Next they bedded down in the Concord Public Library. It was simple. They hid in the stacks until the library closed for the day, and then the whole place was theirs. The big entrance hall was furnished with comfortable sofas and a lot of white marble statuary. Almina and Dolores did their laundry in the staff rest room, then hung their wet clothes over the balcony railing to dry. That madcap Palmer Nifto tossed some of Almina's underwear onto the busts of Ebenezer Rockwood Hoar and Amos Bronson Alcott, and then he draped one of Dolores's skirts over the shoulders of the big seated statue of Emerson. The others all screamed with laughter.

Bridgie Sorrel was not with them during their days in the church and the library. Somehow she became detached from the rest. She hitched a ride to Burlington, but she didn't like it there, and it took her a week to get back. Sarah came upon her one day limping up Main Street in tears. Bridgie had just been evicted from the Den of Teddies by Mimi Pink, who had given her a tongue-lashing.

"It's okay, Bridgie," said Sarah. "Listen, I've got an idea." Putting her arm around Bridgie, she walked her down Lexington Road to the Concord Museum.

The museum was a large brick building with a triangle of pretty garden. "We'll wait here a while," said Sarah, settling Bridgie down on a garden bench. Adroitly she stowed their possessions behind the stone wall. Then she sat beside Bridgie and waited for the right moment.

"Look," said Sarah, "a tour bus. It's stopping here. Now, listen, Bridgie, do just as I say."

People were flooding out of the bus and starting across the lawn. "Now," said Sarah, rushing Bridgie to the front door.

There were two women at the door, Dolly Smith and Carolyn Lahey. "Can I help you?" said Dolly, looking doubtfully at Sarah's too many layers of dingy clothing.

"Oh, look, the bus is here," said Carolyn as people streamed toward them across the grass. "It's the golden-agers from Salem."

"We just want to use the ladies'," said Sarah urgently. Her arm was around Bridgie Sorrel, who was holding her hand over her mouth. Bridgie's wild stare made it clear she was about to throw up.

"Oh, dear me," said Dolly Smith. "Quickly, come this way." She ran ahead of them to point out the right door, then rushed back to deal with the flood of newcomers from the chartered bus.

Not until closing time did Dolly remember the odd-looking pair of bag ladies who had come in to use the rest room. "Did you see those two women go out?" she asked Carolyn.

"No," said Carolyn. So they went to the ladies' room and looked in. It was empty. "They must have gone out through the gift shop," said Carolyn, and then they locked all the doors and turned on the burglar alarm and went home.

Upstairs in the eighteenth-century bedchamber Sarah went to the window and looked out. "It's okay now," she said.

The two of them had been lying flat in the canopy bed under the puffy spread.

Bridgie smiled and sat up.

"I've got some doughnuts here," said Sarah, pulling out a bag from an inside pocket and sitting down comfortably on the edge of the bed.

After that Sarah and her friends tried the other historic houses in Concord. They didn't get anywhere at Hawthorne's Old Manse, or at Orchard House, where Louisa May Alcott had written *Little Women*. But behind Orchard House stood Bronson Alcott's School of Philosophy. It was a real find.

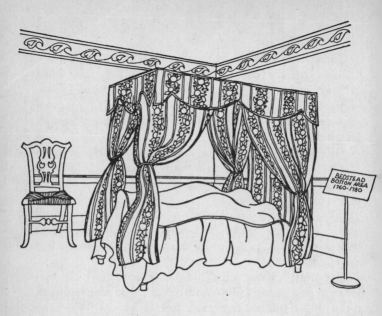

There were windows at ground level in the back, and Carl Browning had one of them open in a jiffy.

The School of Philosophy lacked comfortable sofas and upholstered chairs, but it was delightfully airy and open. Emerson was there again in plaster effigy. The floor was uncomfortable to sleep on, but the place had an exalted aura, and they all enjoyed it.

Palmer Nifto was the cleverest at finding a home away from home. A place had occurred to him immediately, the instant he saw the destination on the ticket handed him by Sarah Peel.

It was a one-person dwelling. Palmer kept it in the back of his mind until they were thrown out of the library and the School of Philosophy. Then he resolved to try it.

But first he gave himself a present, a splendid meal at the Colonial Inn, paid for with the piece of broken glass he kept in his pocket. The piece of glass had worn out its welcome in Boston, but out here in the boondocks it awaited its debut.

The hostess found him a table in a prominent part of the big dining room, he looked so interesting and respectable in his seersucker jacket. His twenty-five-cent Morgan Memorial tie was limp, but it had begun life at Brooks Brothers. He looked like a young professor of the shabby genteel variety.

The Colonial Inn specialized in hearty old-fashioned food rather than trendy gourmet stuff. Palmer ordered a charcoal-broiled steak.

"Baked potato or mashed?" said the waitress.

"Mashed, please," said Palmer craftily.

When his steak and mashed potatoes were put in front of him, he smiled at the waitress and struck up a conversation. "Not many places like this left," he said, plying knife and fork, taking his first bite of steak, then shaking his head in appreciation. "Mmmm-*mmm*. Dee-licious."

Therefore when Palmer found a piece of glass in his mashed potato, his disappointment was profound. He beckoned the waitress to him, his face long with woe, and displayed the mashed-potato-smeared piece of glass, which he had pushed delicately to one side of his plate. "I must say, I'm surprised," said Palmer sorrowfully.

The waitress was stunned. She summoned the hostess. The hostess was horrified. She hurried out and returned with the manager. The manager was appalled. He spoke soothingly to Palmer and asked if he was hurt in any way at all. When Palmer said no, he was only very much surprised, the manager assured him that he, too, was completely astounded, because nothing like this had ever happened before in the entire history of the Colonial Inn. There would of course be no charge for the meal, and would he like anything else from the menu, courtesy of the inn, of course?

"Well, that's very kind of you," said Palmer courteously. At once he examined the menu and ordered a second meal, even more luxurious than the first.

Later on, as he consumed his lobster thermidor, the manager hurried over with a bottle of champagne in a bucket of ice. "With our compliments," he said, getting to work on the cork. There was a resounding pop. Heads turned. People smiled.

Ah, there was nothing like virgin territory. What innocence, what charming naïveté in this idyllic rural town!

After dinner Palmer walked off his heavy double meal. It was two long miles to Walden Pond. Was the little house still there?

It was. The house was a replica of the one Henry Thoreau had built on the northern shore of the pond. The replica occupied a similar spot on the shore of the parking lot.

The door was open. The parking lot was empty of cars. There was heavy traffic on Route 126, but all those people were going somewhere else. No one would notice a tourist walking into the house and not walking out again.

The summer dusk cast a pleasant green shade through the

Replica of Thoreau's Walden house.

windows. Except for the fireplace the room was bare. There was no stove, no bed, no table, no electricity, no plumbing. But there was something else, a faint whiff of the spirit of the man called Henry David Thoreau. Palmer had taken a course in American lit at Boston University. He had even written a paper on Thoreau's poetry.

Now he had a sentimental idea. Before going to bed he went out into the woods and gathered fallen branches. When he arranged them in the fireplace and touched them with a match, they flared up brightly.

Palmer lay down and stared at the fire, remembering a verse of Thoreau's:

> Go thou my incense upward from this hearth
> And ask the gods to pardon this clear flame.

46

When heaven begins and the dead arise, no
trumpet is blown. . . .
Journal, March 13, 1842

A wood thrush was singing beside one of the Andromeda ponds as thunder rumbled over the town of Concord. It was still singing as a ray of sunlight shot out of the clouds and threw a millionfold spread of color over the eastern sky.

Homer missed the wood thrush, but he saw the rainbow as he came out of the Concord Public Library. He stood for a moment, gaping at it, and then it faded, and he walked to his car.

If he had stayed in the library five minutes longer, he would have missed it. The trouble with nature's spectacles was that they didn't employ a public address system. Nobody leaned out of a cloud and boomed:

NOW HEAR THIS: KINDLY DIRECT YOUR GAZE TO THE EASTERN QUARTER OF THE SKY AND YOU WILL SEE SOMETHING RATHER ATTRACTIVE, IF I DO SAY SO MYSELF.

Actually Homer had stayed an hour longer in the library than he had meant to. He was late for the party at the Badgers' house. As he parked in the Badgers' driveway, Mary saw him from the porch, and she ran out and hauled him inside.

"Everybody's asking for you. Where were you?"

"I just stopped off in a bar for a couple of quick ones. You know that famous saloon, the Concord Library."

"Well, come on in. Henry Badger is making a speech."

Homer ducked under the lintel of the French doors and joined the modest crowd.

"In short," said Henry, concluding his speech, "We've all got to do what we can to support Oliver Fry in his campaign, if we want to save Walden Woods from the bull-dozers of the developer. Am I right, or am I right?"

"You're right," cried Homer.

"You're right," cried everybody else.

Oliver Fry stood beaming in the middle, happily drinking his third glass of wine punch. The speech was over. The noise level rose.

Homer looked around the room with satisfaction. These people were friends from way back. They were just what he needed, a captive audience for his investigation, prese-lected for their true-blue support of conservationist causes. There were loyal Thoreauvians among them, members of the Audubon Society, the Appalachian Mountain Club, the Environmental Defense Fund, the Wilderness Society, the Concord Land Conservation Trust.

He buttonholed them one after another, while they laughed and filled their glasses and shouted to make themselves heard. Homer asked what they thought about Pond View. Did they think the state of Massachusetts should speed up the last days of the trailer park by moving the remaining residents out?

"Oh, no," said Elizabeth Bates, "they couldn't do that. Those people were promised life tenancy. That would be terrible."

"Well, I don't know," said Marcus McDowell, "they don't bother me. It's the landfill that gives me a pain."

"Leave them lay," said Steve Freiburg. "Bunch of old codgers. They're not doing anybody any harm."

"Let sleeping dogs lie," said Wendy Chin. "Old saying of Confucius."

"Get them out of there by hook or by crook," cried Oliver Fry. But Oliver was Oliver, and he didn't count.

. . . trade curses everything it handles . . . though
you trade in messages from heaven. . . .
Walden, "Economy"

The rainbow that dazzled Homer Kelly was within Jefferson Grandison's line of vision when he came to town with Jack Markey.

If he had been looking up at the sky, he would have seen the arching bands of color glowing behind the steeple of the First Parish Church. Unfortunately Grandison was staring at the sidewalk, where Carl Browning was taking a late afternoon nap. When Grandison walked into the fragrant ambience of Mimi's Parfumerie, followed by Jack Markey, he was in a sour mood.

But he was ready to do his duty. He had agreed to address Mimi Pink's Consortium of Concord Boutiques, and address it he would.

Mimi came forward to meet him, her hand outstretched. "Mr. Grandison, we are so honored."

Grandison's glance flicked over Mimi and flicked away. Then he looked back at her uneasily, reminded of something disturbing. Putting the thought aside, he took his place among the mirrored shelves at the rear of the store, while everyone stood up from the rows of folding chairs and clapped.

"Mr.—Jefferson—Grandison," said Mimi. No other introduction was necessary. The applause mounted, and then they all sat down and listened reverently.

Grandison cleared his throat, opened his mouth, and began to speak. He spoke of his faith in the town of Concord, a population center where the standards of consumption were high, a village attracting customers from a wide geographic area, a suburb with potential as a world-class resort, inspiring a confidence on the part of the knowledgeable observer in the economic future of the locality which—for a moment the sentence seemed too entangled to be resolved. Grandison cut the Gordian knot and started over. "Concord, in my opinion, will someday be classed with St. Moritz, Vail, and Monaco."

Monaco. There were gasps. Excitement spread from breast to breast. They were all part of something important, something immense. They had known it dimly before. Now they were sure of it.

Mimi led the standing ovation. Then, as her distinguished guest slipped out of the shop with Jack Markey, she darted after him and touched his arm. "Oh, Mr. Grandison, I wonder if I could have a private word?"

The great man was annoyed. This afternoon he had already endured a conversation with the shyster lawyer who kept calling him about Lot Seventeen: "You hear me, Grandison? Time is going by. Would you like us to deposit Lot Seventeen on Huntington Avenue, Mr. Grandison? Because that's precisely what we have in mind right now, Mr. Grandison."

"Well, what is it?" said Jefferson Grandison, glowering at Mimi. He was already doing as much for the woman as she deserved.

"It's simply a matter of cash flow." Mimi went on to explain that people were reporting to her who were taking great personal risks, who, it was perfectly natural, deserved substantial financial reward. She didn't speak for herself, although she had certainly done her part.

"Certainly, certainly," said Grandison smoothly, gliding away. Behind him Jack Markey grinned at Mimi, rolled his eyes comically, and followed his master to the car.

But Mimi wasn't finished. Leaning out the door of the Parfumerie, she called after Jefferson Grandison, "Oh, Mr. Grandison, give my regards to your *wife*."

He pretended not to hear. Then, flustered, he tripped over

the outstretched leg of a woman sitting on the sidewalk. If Jack hadn't caught him, he would have fallen.

"Where the fuck you think you're going?" cried Doris Harper.

Regaining his balance, Grandison raised his eyebrows at Jack and murmured, "What's all this?"

"I don't know what the hell." Then Jack quickened his steps, because another shapeless person was leaning against Grandison's Mercedes. The man looked asleep on his feet.

Ignoring him, hoping he would wake up and go away, Jack unlocked the door for Grandison, then went around the car to let himself in. The person leaning against the radiator did not stir, although the car dipped heavily under Grandison's weight and then under Jack's.

Jack started the engine. Still the object failed to move. "Sticky wicket," murmured Jack. Slowly, very slowly, he edged the car forward. The object collapsed and disappeared.

"Oh, shit," said Jack. He stopped the car and got out. So did Grandison. Together they lifted Carl Browning from the street and deposited him beside the twisting candy stripes of the barber pole in front of Hugo's Hair Harmonies.

On the way back to Boston, Grandison went to sleep at once, but Jack remained alert. It was a terrible journey. Unseeing, he sped down Route 2, heading for Route 128 and the turnpike, driving mechanically, suffering from a conviction that had overpowered him many times before. It had been imprinted upon him during his Bible-reading infancy, this apocalyptic sense of approaching doom, of the coming end, of last and final things. "Babylon the great is fallen, is fallen, and is become the habitation of devils." Those people on the streets of Concord were a sign. The whole thing was going to collapse. It wasn't going to work. "And I looked, and behold a pale horse; and his name that sat on him was Death." It was ridiculous, Jack told himself, this sort of premonition. It had nothing to do with reality. It was only a loathsome regurgitation of the mad incantations of his youth.

He pulled himself together, but his driving was erratic. On the turnpike he kept changing lanes, dodging in and out. He almost sideswiped another car. It was a good thing Grandison was asleep.

Mimi Pink observed the departure of Jack Markey and Jefferson Grandison from the window of the Parfumerie. She saw Grandison trip over a homeless person, she saw another dreadful-looking old man leaning on his car. She was deeply disturbed. Once again she called the police.

"Well, I'm sorry, ma'am," said the officer on duty, who had taken complaints from Mimi many times before, "what do you suggest we do with those people?"

"Might I suggest jail? They are obstructing the free passage of pedestrians in and out of the commercial establishments of the town. Surely that is an infringement of the law."

"I've told you, ma'am, it's a matter for social workers, not the police. I understand the churches are working on it."

"I suppose you mean the Open Table at the First Parish on Thursday nights? That free meal? I want you to know I regard the Open Table as an attractive nuisance. People come from miles away to hang around town and wait for a handout. Some of them wouldn't be here at all if it weren't for the free food."

"Well, I don't know."

"I pay a considerable sum in taxes in this town, and I expect police protection. I want those people off the street."

"I'm aware of that, ma'am," said the officer dryly.

Mimi hung up, dissatisfied. It was embarrassing that Jefferson Grandison had witnessed this plague on the streets of Concord. It was important that he should not discover the falling off of business in all her shops, the reduction in the number of well-groomed customers.

It wasn't only the trashy people who were to blame. This

morning Mimi had been deceived by an attractive man in a good-looking sport jacket. He had stood at the counter in the Parfumerie as if he were ready to buy the most costly fragrance in the shop.

It was his wife's birthday, he said, and she loved some sort of perfume, but he couldn't remember the name. He'd know it when he smelled it, because it was sort of like his wife's trademark.

Then he and Mimi spent an amusing quarter of an hour sniffing at this and that. But suddenly the man asked if he could use the rest room. Normally Mimi didn't permit customers to use the little lav tucked in at the back of the store, but this man was so charming and sexy, she agreed at once and led him behind the scenes.

And then he didn't return. He nipped out the back door, taking with him a flagon of French perfume from the shelf in the storeroom.

Actually this scam by Palmer Nifto wasn't his own invention at all. He had borrowed his sudden need for a bathroom from Sarah Peel and Bridgie Sorrel. It didn't matter whose idea it was. In a matter of survival it was share and share alike.

48

The life in us is like the water in the river. It may
rise this year higher than man has ever known it,
and flood the parched uplands . . .
Walden, "Conclusion"

The rocking seesaw of Hope's emotional life went up and down all summer.

Hearing the bang of the screen door and Ananda's light step on the stairs of the back porch, she would run out to say hello, her pulse quickening, and see in his face the bright reflection of her smile.

But Jack Markey was a powerful presence, too, with his obvious competence. There was a forcefulness of argument in his professional success, in knowing that he was an important person in an important concern. Ananda Singh was not, after all, one of the richest bachelors in the world, or he wouldn't be working in a hardware store.

The fact that Ananda was her father's friend and Jack Markey his enemy was upsetting, and Hope preferred not to think about it. But she was her father's daughter. Her mind and heart and lungs, her ankles and knees, were steeped in the essence that was Oliver Fry. It was the element in which she had been raised. Turn against it as she would, she couldn't get rid of it. It was part of her.

But Jack was wearing her down. Lying beside him on the warm grass of the sloping ground above the North Bridge, Hope felt herself drifting into the acceptance of anything, anything, as he kissed her and kissed her.

"Oh, look," she murmured over his shoulder, "a falling star."

And then to her surprise he stopped kissing her and sat up and stared at the sky.

"There's another one," said Hope.

Jack seemed shaken. "I'll take you home," he said, getting to his feet.

"Well, all right," said Hope, wondering what was the matter.

For a lot of people the first week in August was the beginning of vacation. A great many Concord people went away. They were vacationing on Cape Cod, or sailing in Maine, or cruising among the Norwegian fjords, or digging up pottery shards in Mozambique.

The town was left to the small grubby band Sarah Peel had brought with her from Boston and to tourists in brilliant summer togs.

But one day Mimi Pink stood in the doorway of the Porcelain Parlor and beckoned to Bonnie Glover. "Come here a sec, Bonnie."

Bonnie obeyed.

"What's different today?" said Mimi.

Bonnie looked up and down the street and shrugged her shoulders. "God, I don't know."

"Can't you tell? Doesn't it look better? They're gone. They're all gone."

"You mean . . . ?" Bonnie brightened. "You're right. I don't see a single homeless person."

"Let's hope they've gone back where they came from."

"How fabulous."

It was true. Sarah Peel was gone, and so were all her friends. They had not gone back to Boston. They too were taking a vacation. Theirs was a holiday from sleeping in Monument Square and bedding down in suburban garages, it was a vacation from barking dogs, a furlough from surviving without help from anyone except the good women of the Open Table, who by now had increased their schedule of free meals from one day a week to three.

On the morning of the first day of August, Marjorie and Roger Bland drove to the airport and flew to Nantucket. On the afternoon of the same day Sarah and her friends moved into the spacious house on Musketaquid Road.

It was securely locked, but locks didn't stop Sarah Peel. Sarah had a way of leaking in through the cracks. She could dissolve herself on the outside of a building and rematerialize within.

This time she got in through a cellar window.

There was a washing machine under the window. Sarah heaved herself down to the floor and called to the others, "Wait a minute. I'll open the front door."

Obediently they ran around the house and walked into the front hall as Sarah grandly swung the door open.

"Oh, isn't this nice," said Dolores Mitchell. "Look, Christine, they've got a piano."

Christine sat down at once on the piano bench and played Chopsticks. The rest of them dispersed all over the house. It was a dream of sudden possession like the granting of three wishes, like winning the lottery.

Palmer Nifto had a nose for good things. He ferreted out the liquor cabinet right away, because it was locked. The lock was no problem. Palmer went downcellar with Carl Browning to look for a crowbar. In the basement they found Roger Bland's well-appointed workshop, with a drill press, a shaper, a couple of fancy table saws, a band saw, and a planing machine. A row of bins held lumber.

"Hey, this here piece is teak, I'll bet," said Carl. "And look at this one, bird's-eye maple."

The tools hung neatly on a pegboard. Palmer found a crowbar, took it upstairs, inserted it under the padlock of the liquor cabinet, and gave it a couple of strong jerks. The cabinet opened with a wrenching squeal.

"Hey, Carl, look at this," said Palmer, reaching past the

wrecked door. "Nothing but the best. Beefeater, Jack Daniel's, real Russian vodka."

There were cries of rapture from upstairs, where Almina Ziblow had unzipped a garment bag in Marjorie Bland's closet and discovered a mink coat. Almina came down the stairs majestically, her hand sweeping the banister, the long coat flopping behind her on the stairs.

Dolores and Christine and Bridgie and Bobbsie settled down in the family room in front of the TV to watch a soap opera. "Oh, I remember her," said Dolores. "That's Vanessa. What's happened? She must be sick."

They all stared avidly at Vanessa, who was lying unconscious on a hospital bed. Her boyfriend, Dirk, was shouting at the doctor, insisting on her right to die, but the handsome doctor refused to pull the plug because he had fallen in love with Vanessa himself. Well, no wonder. She really did look beautiful, lying there with her long lashes sweeping her cheeks and her lovely hair tumbled on the pillow.

The doorbell rang. Everybody froze. Dolores switched off the TV. Sarah went to the door and opened it cautiously.

A little girl stood on the porch. "Oh, hi," she said. "I'm Emily. Hasn't Mrs. Bland gone yet? I'm supposed to take care of her horse."

"Oh," said Sarah, thinking fast, "didn't she tell you? I'm house-sitting for them and taking care of the horse. And, you know, the plants and all."

"Oh, okay." Emily looked pleased. "That's great. My best friend, she invited me to Lake Winnipesaukee, only my mother said I can't go because Mrs. Bland was counting on me. Oh, boy, now I can go after all. Gee, thanks."

Sarah closed the door and grinned at the others in relief. "Hey, everybody," said Palmer Nifto, coming in with a bottle and a tray of glasses, "how about a little Chivas Regal?" Then he looked up. "Good Lord, who's that?"

Somebody else was coming down the stairs. It was Audrey Beamish, the silent woman. Audrey had discovered a bureau drawer full of Marjorie Bland's nightgowns and negligees. She had torn off all her clothes and gowned herself in the laciest, the filmiest. She had pulled her hair out of its prim little clips.

"Well, say now," breathed Palmer, handing her a glass.

49

What is the price-current of an honest man and
patriot to-day?
"Civil Disobedience"

"I've got the whole town to myself," said Oliver to Ananda. "My opponent is vacationing in Nantucket. Why don't I start my campaign?"

"Excellent," said Ananda. "What can I do to help?"

"Write a letter for me. We'll get out a town mailing."

So Ananda spent a couple of days composing earnest paragraphs at the dining room table, surrounded by a gloomy sideboard, a wicker plant stand, a tarnished tea service, an iridescent art nouveau vase, and two large brown pictures of the Colosseum and the Roman Forum.

There were helpful interruptions by Oliver. "Hold it," he would cry, running in with another passage from Henry Thoreau. "You've got to get this in."

"Of course," Ananda would say. "How splendid, how appropriate."

In the end they handed the letter to Mary Kelly, who cut it in half. Then Homer got busy on the phone, rounding up signatories, a nicely balanced selection of West Concord and Concord Center citizens, old residents and young professionals, people from the temple and all the churches, a good mix of town employees, and one very special farmer.

The farmer was Paul Rivelli, whose father had come to Concord from Italy in the 1920s. Paul's signature was so valuable, Homer buttonholed him in person at his produce stand on Bedford Street. Paul turned out to be an admirer of Oliver Fry's, and he agreed at once. Homer brought the signature back to Oliver's house with a sack of Paul's early corn.

"Here," said Homer, "this is your half. Has Ananda ever tasted corn on the cob?"

Ananda hadn't. At suppertime he sat at the dining room table with Oliver while Hope rushed in with a platter of corn plucked from a pot of boiling water.

"You roll them in butter like this," explained Oliver, "then sprinkle them with salt and pepper."

"How interesting," said Ananda politely, picking up a steaming ear.

Oliver had consumed two preprandial whiskeys. He was euphoric. "I'm going to win this election," he said, brandishing the salt shaker. "You see if I don't."

"Oh, Father, how can you be so sure?" Hope sat down at her place with a thump. It was another hot day. Her face was flushed from bending over the kettle. Her feet were bare. She was wearing shorts. Her plump thighs and long calves were hidden under the table, but Ananda was aware of them. He listened to Oliver's cocky exuberance and tried not to think about Hope's legs. When she leaped up to run back to the kitchen for more corn, he got a good look, but when she came back he riveted his attention on Oliver's rubicund face.

"What about the young people, Hopey dear?" said Oliver. "What about all your friends? And Ananda my boy, what's the name of that girlfriend of yours? The one who keeps calling? Bonnie somebody? Do you think she . . . ?"

"She is not my girlfriend," muttered Ananda, casting an agonized glance at Hope.

"But doesn't she work in one of those fancy stores on the Milldam? She could get after all those shopkeepers. That woman Pink, for instance."

Ananda's embarrassment turned to melancholy. "Alas, I fear the woman Pink is hopeless."

Oliver beamed. In his cups he was indomitable. "Oh, my

young friend, I love the way you say 'alas.' I haven't heard anybody say alas for thirty or forty years."

The phone rang. Hope leaped up to answer it, and Ananda got another look at the twinkling legs.

It was Bonnie Glover. "It's for you," said Hope, handing him the phone with cool fingers.

After supper Hope went grimly upstairs and opened the door to the sleeping porch. She felt terrible. She batted the hammock. A cloud of dust flew up. Climbing in, she lay on her back, her hands folded over her copy of *Walden*, her eyes gazing at the big hooks from which the hammock hung. Then she wrenched herself sideways and stared at the porch screens. They were black and bulging.

Languidly she opened the book and turned to the chapter called "Higher Laws."

> . . . the spirit can for the time pervade and control every member and function of the body, and transmute what in form is the grossest sensuality into purity and devotion.

Purity and devotion! Hope was filled with bitter cynicism. How much transmuting of sensuality into purity and devotion was Ananda practicing, that eager disciple of Henry Thoreau?

Faintly from the deep well of the stairs the phone rang once again. It rang and rang. Why didn't somebody answer it? Slowly Hope got up and pattered downstairs, expecting to hear Bonnie's voice on the line.

It wasn't Bonnie, it was Jo-Jo Field.

"Hope, this is Jo-Jo. How are you, dear? I'm calling on behalf of Roger Bland. I'm helping with his campaign for the opening on the board of selectmen. You know, in the special election in October."

"Oh, right."

"Now I know, Hopey, that your dear father is running

against him. But a little bird told me you might actually be supporting Roger."

"Well, I don't know. I haven't thought about it much."

"Of course not. But we loyal campaign workers have to busy ourselves so early. We have to collect signatures for a town mailing. Now, dear, might I read his letter over the phone? It's not very long."

"Well, okay, I don't see why not."

Roger Bland's letter was very different from the one concocted for Oliver by Ananda Singh and Mary Kelly. Roger's was the standard candidate's letter, reciting his solid qualifications, his devotion to the town and its history, his concern for the preservation of its rural character, his awareness at the same time of the fiscal crisis in the commonwealth, affecting all the cities and towns in Massachusetts. It was a time, said Roger's letter, when state support for local needs was at rock bottom. Thus it was a time for imaginative responses to modern pressures. Roger's supporters too quoted Henry Thoreau—oh, that was clever of them, thought Hope—"Alert and healthy natures remember that the sun rose clear. It is never too late to give up our prejudices."

"So you see, Hope, dear," said Jo-Jo, "it's really the same things your father stands for, but with—forgive me, dear— just a bit more practicality. We feel Roger will accomplish more in the long run, if you see what I mean."

"Oh, yes, I see."

"Now, to get to the point," said Jo-Jo, suspecting that Hope's resistance was softening, "we just wondered if by any chance you would lend your name to the others." Swiftly Jo-Jo ran through the list of highly respected Concord citizens who had already agreed to sign Roger's letter.

There was a pause. Hope thought it over. Actually she wasn't thinking of the different points of view of the two candidates. She wasn't even thinking of her father. She was thinking angrily about Ananda Singh. "Well, okay, I guess so."

"You darling! You're sure now? We can really use your name?"

"Why not?" said Hope, recklessly burning all her bridges, taking up a sledgehammer to destroy those made of stone, tearing apart with savage fingernails the cobweb threads she had flung out into empty air.

50

> *There is indeed something royal about the month
> of August.*
> *Journal*, August 18, 1852

Roger Bland's campaign letter was ready, but Jo-Jo Field
knew better than to send it out. Too many Concord people
were away. The town was deserted.

But only by two-legged citizens. The raccoons of Concord
had not abandoned their favorite garbage pails for faraway
realms of milk and honey. Wood thrushes remained in res-
idence, singing to proclaim this or that patch of forest as
their own. Coyotes loped along woodland paths. White-tailed
deer plunged out of roadside thickets and paused in the middle
of Lowell Road to stare at oncoming cars. In the open fields
Monarch caterpillars inched along milkweed stalks to feed
among the fragrant flowers. Cutworms ravaged neglected
tomato vines, beetles wandered unchecked among the beans,
borers tunneled into fattening ears of corn.

At the high school the lacrosse field lay quietly waiting
for whatever action might be taken by the voters in October.
In anticipation of the vote at Town Meeting, tens of thousands of bricks were stacked on pallets in Marlboro. At a
cement factory in Chelmsford limestone rattled down chutes
to be crushed into powder by steel drums and heated in kilns
and cooled and poured into sacks. Screaming saws in Oregon
milled logs into clapboards.

The land itself lay dormant, warm beneath the August
sun. The backhoe had a flat tire, and it leaned to one side
with feathery heads of grass springing up between the bucket
and the hydraulic cylinders. A sweater Jack Markey had torn
off his back one broiling July day lay forgotten in the woods.

Below the playing field the train roared between Boston and Fitchburg thirty-six times a day. Traffic on Route 2 was perpetual, clogging the highway during morning and evening rush hours. One hot morning a black snake laid a clutch of eggs in the sandy kettle hole where Thoreau had once seen the carcass of a dead horse. Before the day was out a raccoon ate the eggs, only to be killed a moment later on the highway. At once a crow flapped down to examine the crushed furry object on the road.

Another predator was hard at work in the commercial center of Concord. Mimi Pink was not taking a vacation. Every day she laid cunning traps for the tourists flooding the streets. The homeless people who had disturbed the smooth flow of pedestrian traffic were still missing, and the turnover of merchandise in Mimi's stores was brisk. People from New Jersey and Michigan and South Carolina and California visited the old North Bridge and Orchard House, then drove back to the Milldam to buy ice cream at Brigham's and saunter among the gift shops.

Roger and Marjorie Bland stayed only a week on the island of Nantucket, but they came away refreshed. Driving back

to Concord from the airport, they avoided the cluttered center of town and approached Nashawtuc hill by way of Simon Willard Road. Marjorie was nicely tanned. A patch of pink showed under Roger's thinning yellow hair. His knees were fiery red.

During the week, tumult had prevailed in the house on Musketaquid Road. Sarah Peel's friends had made good use of every room. The master bedroom was Doris Harper's as her own fucking right. Dolores and Christine Marshall slept in the bedchamber belonging to Wally Bland. The three other bedrooms were occupied by Carl Browning, Bobbsie Low, and Almina Ziblow. Bridgie Sorrel slept on the daybed in the family room, and Sarah settled down on the living room sofa. Audrey Beamish and Palmer Nifto shacked up together in Roger's den.

"What the hell's going on in there?" said Doris Harper, staring at their locked door. "What kind of shit is that?"

But nobody else seemed to mind that Audrey and Palmer were happy.

The house was a mess. For a while Sarah Peel tried to keep things under control, but it was soon beyond her power to tidy things up. Before long she abandoned the attempt and lived for the moment like the rest of them, giving no thought for the morrow.

Fortunately Bridgie didn't disconnect the freezer in order to plug in Marjorie's blow dryer until they had all gorged themselves on the four gallons of ice cream—chocolate chip and black raspberry and butter pecan and strawberry swirl. When little Christine dropped a dish of chocolate chip into Roger's compact-disc player, Dolores did her best to swab it clean, but the player didn't work very well after that.

The freezer warmed up so fast that everything thawed before they knew what was happening, but Almina got to work and cooked up a storm with the sirloin roast, the turkey, the leg of lamb, and the six cans of lobster meat. Nobody bothered to clean up the kitchen afterward because Marjorie had an awful lot of dishes, and they just moved on from Lenox to Royal Copenhagen.

Something crucial happened to the washing machine when the soap powder ran out and Doris Harper did her laundry with bubble bath. The teeming bubbles rose up in airy towers and filled the cellar with frothy foam. After that everybody had to wash their stuff by hand.

And it didn't do the dining room table any good when Audrey Beamish dropped a big bottle of perfume on it, the Parfum Shalimar that Palmer had stolen from Mimi Pink.

In fact, everything was going to hell. But Sarah was content. Her dream of living in the country was fulfilled. She spent hours every day sitting on an overturned bucket, just looking at Pearl. She fed her and watered her and brushed her coat. When Pearl was tormented by flies and stamped her feet and flicked her gray-white hide, Sarah borrowed one of Marjorie's filmy negligees and draped it over her back.

Sarah was happy. Pearl was happy. Never again would they be parted.

The next happiest squatter in the Blands' house was Palmer Nifto. Not only had Palmer found himself a girlfriend, he was also the best-equipped person among them to exploit the contents of the house. In Roger's workshop, for instance, he knew how to use the equipment. There were great whanging and screaming noises from the basement. Palmer and Carl Browning tracked sawdust upstairs and down. They soon had the teak and bird's-eye maple cut up into interesting shapes. Palmer made holes with the drill press and screwed the pieces together into a sort of sculpture.

And Palmer was the only one who understood Roger's personal computer. He was delighted with it. Palmer had been a computer hacker in high school, a whiz kid who had sent a virus raging through the files of the Worcester Trust Company. Now he penetrated Roger's memory bank, and before long he had the key to Roger's connection with his broker. Inquisitively he ran down the record of all Roger's recent transactions.

"Look at that," he said to Audrey. "He's been selling Boeing, but wait a sec, look at this." Palmer punched a couple of keys and brought up on the monitor the latest figures from Standard & Poor's. "Transports are going up, way up, you see that?"

He shook his head in pity for poor Roger Bland, who was not at home to guide his fortunes from day to day. The man needed help. "I'll take care of his portfolio for him," Palmer said. "It's the least I can do while he's away." In a jiffy he figured out how to send a buy order to the broker. And then his first transaction gave him such a feeling of power that he began frolicking among the rest of Roger's accounts, consulting the daily listings in *The Wall Street Journal*, selling this and buying that. It was exhilarating.

For Doris Harper the use of the telephone was equally stimulating. Doris made a lot of long-distance calls. Her limited vocabulary of four-letter words flashed across the nation at the speed of light to acquaintances in San Francisco, Juneau, Honolulu. Once when the phone rang only a few seconds after she put it down, she snatched it up and shouted at her old boyfriend in Sausalito, "Bullshit! Shut your fucking trap," only it wasn't her old boyfriend, it was Wally Bland, calling his parents' house from Camp Watcheehatchee in Maine, where he was a counselor.

"Hey, who's that?" said Wally.

Doris rolled her eyes at Sarah.

Sarah took the phone. "Who did you want to speak to?" she said cautiously.

"My parents," said Wally. "Is Mrs. Bland there?"

"No Blands here," said Sarah. "Sorry, wrong number."

Wally hung up. When the phone rang again a moment later, they all stared at it and let it ring.

"No more phone calls," said Sarah firmly, glowering at Doris.

But Doris made an awful fuss. Palmer Nifto shouted at her to shut up, for Christ's sake, and Doris screamed back at him, and Dolores told her not to say things like that in front of Christine, and then Doris fell silent and looked at them evilly, and later they found the yellow brocade upholstery of the Sheraton sofa slashed front and back. Goose down floated in the air and settled on everything.

At the moment when Roger and Marjorie returned from their vacation and drove up to the house on Musketaquid Road, all the squatters happened to be quiet. Only the television set was making a lot of noise. It was "The Young and the Reckless" once again. Vanessa had awakened from her coma, but then the doctor became her lover, and pretty soon Vanessa was pregnant, and then she had an abortion, and now she was undergoing severe postpartem suicidal depression, which involved a lot of screaming. The actress who played Vanessa was giving it all she had. Scream after scream rent the air of the Blands' family room and shrilled out the doors and windows onto the lawn.

"Good heavens," said Roger, "what's that noise?"

Marjorie stared dumbfounded at Baronesa Carmencita de Granada. The horse was trampling the flower bed, eating the petunias, draped in Marjorie's best boudoir gown, a delicate garment of mousseline de soie and Belgian lace. While Marjorie looked on in horror, Carmencita stepped on a trailing end and ripped the gown from neck to hem.

Trembling, Marjorie got out of the car and faltered up the front steps and stood behind Roger as he grimly threw open the door.

51

Our whole life is startlingly moral.
Walden, "Higher Laws"

"For you," muttered Mary, reaching the telephone across the bed. It was six o'clock in the morning.

Homer groaned and rolled over. "Homer Kelly here."

"Homer?" It was Police Chief Jimmy Flower. "Hey listen, I wonder if you'd do me a favor."

"Well, I don't know," murmured Homer, getting up sleepily on one elbow. "What kind of favor?"

"We've got some people here, locked up for breaking and entering, malicious destruction of property. What they need is counsel. You know, somebody to act for them, arrange bail."

"Listen, Jimmy, it's true I've got a law degree, but I haven't practiced in years. Why pick on me?"

"Because you're such a goddamned famous old-fashioned liberal, everybody knows that."

"What's being a liberal got to do with it?"

"Well, it's these homeless. It's a typical bleeding-heart case. Everybody else in town is mad at them, mad as hell. You know what they did? They moved into Roger Bland's house while he was on vacation and wrecked the whole place. Bunch of freeloaders. Welfare Cadillac types, if you ask me. Just your meat."

"Now wait a minute." Homer sat up in bed. "You mean we've got homeless people here on the streets of Concord?"

"Homer Kelly, where have you been? Haven't you been downtown lately? Haven't you seen them on the Milldam? I tell you, the merchant community is giving me a hard time. That Ms. Pink, she calls me every day, wants 'em run out of town."

Homer was dumbfounded. He couldn't speak.

"Homer? Are you still there?"

"Of course. It's just that I didn't know we had people like that here in Concord. I guess I've had my head in the clouds. I've been listening for wood thrushes. You know, stuff like that." Homer sat up and rubbed his frowsy head. "Well, okay, I'll come over and talk to them."

At the police station on Walden Street he found the ten of them sorted into three lockups. Little Christine was officially too young to be locked up, but she had been permitted to stay with her mother.

At first Homer talked to Palmer Nifto, who was by far the most presentable and articulate. But in the end it was Sarah Peel who commanded his attention. Homer liked her laconic truthfulness. Her speech was not encumbered with excuses, fanciful stories, and elaborate sociopolitical jargon like Palmer's.

"We've got no place to sleep," said Sarah.

It was enough. The words rang in Homer's head like a gong. *The foxes have holes, and the birds of heaven have nests, but the Son of man hath no where to lay his head.*

"That's terrible," he told Sarah, and she said nothing, she just looked at him, while the others jabbered and told their stories. The worst was Doris Harper, with whom it was difficult to feel any sympathy. In a few minutes Doris had exhausted all the obscenities in her repertoire—religious, excretory, sexual—and now she was repeating herself. Somebody should invent a new religion, decided Homer, just to give Doris new words to swear with.

Before Homer left the police station he promised to arrange bail for all ten of them, volunteered to be their public defender, and obtained the immediate release of Dolores and Christine Marshall. "I'll be back," he said earnestly to Sarah Peel, but she just looked at him silently.

Homer felt an urgent need to talk to Oliver Fry, but first he delivered Dolores and Christine to his astonished wife. Then he drove back into town and pulled up beside Oliver's back porch. It was eight o'clock in the morning.

Homer was in distress. Until today he had been juggling only two things in his head, the splendor of the natural world on the one hand and its bloody teeth and claws on the other. Now there was this huge third thing to worry about, the fall of man, and Homer couldn't handle it. How could there be any excuse for preserving these lovely fields and forests in the face of all this human need? Let them build low-income housing all around Walden Pond, and erect cheap apartments on Thoreau's sacred cliffs, and comfortable dwellings along the river all the way from Sudbury to Bedford. He could no longer find it in his heart to fight against such things.

But, oh, God, those places were so precious, so sacred. Homer burst into Oliver's kitchen, full of doubt. "We can't do it, Oliver," he proclaimed, while the alarmed owl screeched at him. "We've got to drop the whole thing."

Oliver was eating breakfast with his daughter Hope and Ananda Singh. They looked up in surprise as he poured out the news about the helpless people in the police lockup.

Oliver fought back. "Drop it? Never," he thundered, lowering his mighty brows. He stood up and prodded Homer with his forefinger. "Those homeless people don't have anything to do with whether or not we should save the countryside. They're beside the point. We can take care of them and save the land, too. Those developers, you think they're going to do anything about homeless people? Hell, no."

Ananda listened in dismay. The existence of people without homes of their own was not new to him. With his own eyes he had seen the teeming streets of Calcutta. He had seen lepers lying among open sewers. It was terrible that such things should be.

Hope listened, too. Silently she set a fourth plate of pancakes on the table. Ananda leaped up and pulled out a chair for Homer.

"Oh, thank you," Homer said, breaking off in midshout. He sat down, attacking the pancakes hungrily, and let Oliver pummel him with furious protestations. Then he stopped listening. An idea had occurred to him. He calmed down. The ugly housing he had built in imagination around the shore of Walden Pond faded, and the trees returned. The moment of ethical crisis was over. He knew what to do.

"Look here," he said, changing the subject, putting down his fork, and turning to Ananda, who was, he remembered, one of the ten most eligible bachelors in the world, "where shall we go next?"

"Go next?" said Ananda blankly.

"Following in Thoreau's footsteps, where shall we go now?"

Ananda's stricken face cleared. He smiled. "Have you ever been to Gowing's Swamp?"

"Never. It's a quaking bog, right?"

"Oh, no," said Hope, "you're not thinking of going there?"

Homer adopted the idea at once. "Of course we are. What about some day next week? Oliver can tell us how to get there."

"You'll need rubber boots," exulted Oliver, "because you'll sink in up to your knees. Ananda, I'll loan you mine." Then he gave them a lecture on the nature of quaking bogs. "Sphagnum moss grows over the surface of a pond and gets thicker and thicker, and things grow in it, so that it looks like solid ground, but there's water underneath, so you have to be careful."

"I'll come, too," said Hope, flinging off restraint, the seesaw of her alternating affections flinging her high in the air.

Ananda beamed at her, and she turned away, smiling, to wash the dishes at the sink. Dumping them on the drainboard, she was pricklingly aware that Ananda was looking at her back, which was engulfed in a huge sweatshirt. In the competition with Bonnie Glover, Hope had fiercely made up her mind to be herself. The more lusciously Bonnie exposed the curviform parts of her anatomy, the more stubbornly Hope draped herself in her old clothes, the more violently she pulled back her hair into a tight pigtail.

Ananda looked at her bony little skull and longed to caress it. He jumped up, snatched a damp dish towel, and dried the dishes, setting them down in the cupboard with extreme care, each chipped dish touching the one below with the most delicate of clinks.

Tags from *Walden* ran through Hope's head, and she wanted to say them aloud, to impress Ananda. But she couldn't fit them into the conversation. "I love the wild, not less than the good"—it didn't go with washing dishes.

"Thank you for helping," she whispered as Ananda picked up the last cup and wiped it around and around with the towel.

"You are most welcome," he said softly, hanging it tenderly on its hook.

52

*I saw . . . some worldly miser with a surveyor
looking after his bounds, while heaven had taken
place around him, and he did not see the angels
going to and fro, but was looking for an old post-
hole in the midst of paradise. . . . I saw that the
Prince of Darkness was his surveyor.*
                                                    "Walking"

Archie Pouch was back on the line. "Ten days, Grandison.
You've got ten days to take Lot Seventeen off my client's
hands. Or else."

"Or else what?" said Jefferson Grandison.

"Or else you'll find it on your doorstep."

"Are you threatening me? May I remind you, sir, that I,
too, have legal representation? Intimidating threats are, I
believe, a felony in the state of Massachusetts."

"Legal representation? *You've* got legal representation?
You call that stuffed shirt legal representation?" There was
a loud guffaw from Archie Pouch's end of the line, and he
hung up.

Grandison looked sourly at Jack Markey, and Jack
laughed. "Is that true? Are threats really a felony?"

"I have no idea," said Grandison loftily.

They spent the next hour spreading maps on the table,
pulling out drawers to find other maps, leaning over them
to study specific areas in greater detail, buzzing Martha Jones
in the outer office to find certain files and bring them in at
once.

What they needed was a temporary holding facility for Lot
Seventeen. At last they assembled a reasonable list of pos-
sibilities, and Grandison sat down and grasped the phone.

Jack collapsed onto a chair, closed his eyes, and listened,

his head drooping on his chest, his face relaxing into dejection.

Call after call failed in its object.

"Totally impossible," said the town manager in Malden.

"Good God, think of the abuttors," said the town counsel of Stow.

"That parcel is in full view of the town green," said the Nashoba town planner.

"You must be kidding," said the mayor of Lawrence.

At last Grandison put down the phone and turned to Jack, who had apparently fallen asleep.

Actually Jack was wide awake. He had heard every word. He had heard other words as well: "And when he had opened the fifth seal, I saw under the altar the souls of them that were slain for the word of God. And they cried with a loud voice, saying, How long, O Lord, dost thou not judge and avenge our blood on them that dwell on the earth?"

"Jack?"

Jack sprang out of his chair and gave a jocular salute. "Sir?"

"It's still in your hands, I'm afraid. Can't you hurry it up a little?"

Then Jack began talking about money. "I hope, Mr. Grandison, you're not forgetting what you owe to me personally? I understood I was to receive a percentage of the profits, which were, I believe, turned over to you some months ago?"

Grandison sighed and turned on Jack the look of one with the weight of the world on his shoulders. They dickered and agreed at last on a figure. But then Grandison craftily added a piece of extortion. "That sum is, however, to be shared with the others."

"The others! Well, how much, for shit's sake?"

"I leave that entirely to you and Ms. Pink. Please do not swear on these premises."

"Christ."

Then Jack had to call Mimi and make some sort of bargain. It was not pleasant. She was a fierce negotiator. They haggled. Jack shouted. Mimi threatened. Jack capitulated. "Well, all right," he said in a steaming rage. "I'll bring it out on Wednesday afternoon. Where will I find you?"

"In the Porcelain Parlor. I'm always there on Wednesday afternoons."

53

What is it to be born free and not to live free?
"Life Without Principle"

Sarah Peel's people were back on the streets of Concord.
Homer found them a bail bondsman, and they popped out
of jail and trailed up Walden Street to the center of town and
settled down again in nooks and corners.

As usual Palmer Nifto landed on his feet. Blithely he
walked into the theater at 51 Walden, where the Concord
Players were casting *The Madwoman of Chaillot*, and tried
out impulsively for one of the principal parts.

"You're marvelous," cried the casting director. "Will you
be our leading man?"

"Why, sure," said Palmer cheerfully. "Hey, listen, I don't
suppose any of you people would let me stay with you? See,
I live in Worcester, and it's kind of hard to get here for re-
hearsals."

In a trice Palmer had three offers, and in no time he was
installed in a charming bedroom belonging to the Whipples,
an old Concord family. At once he sneaked Audrey into the
house to share his room. Audrey lay low.

In the meantime Roger and Marjorie Bland struggled to
recover from the vandalism to their house. It wasn't as hard
for Roger as it was for Marjorie. Roger had not yet discovered
Palmer Nifto's interference with his computerized financial
affairs, and therefore, being naturally of a phlegmatic dis-
position, he took the whole thing in stride.

But Marjorie couldn't get out of her head her first glimpse
of her lovely living room with the sofa slashed and the goose

down floating in the air and all those awful faces staring back at her. One of the women had been wearing Marjorie's mink coat, even though the temperature was in the nineties.

Roger had bravely taken charge. He had marched solemnly to the telephone and called the police. Some of the interlopers leaked out of the house before the cruiser arrived, but they were soon picked up.

It was left to Marjorie to repair the damage. First she summoned a team of housecleaners, then she sent the sofa out to be reupholstered and the dining room table to be refinished. She junked the CD player and the washing machine, replaced them, paid the horrendous telephone bill, hired a carpenter to repair the liquor cabinet, replenished its contents, and refilled the freezer.

"Of course it's the spiritual damage that's the worst," said Marjorie to Jo-Jo Field. "We felt"—she paused dramatically—"raped."

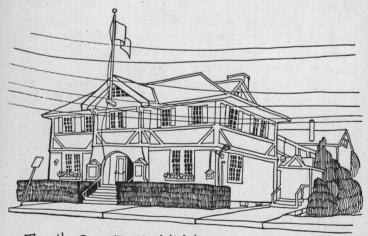

The theater at 51 Walden

"Oh, Marjorie dear, how dreadful. You've been so brave."

There was still the problem of the horse. Marjorie called the vet and asked him to give Carmencita a good once-over. When he came, she sat down with him and called a spade a spade. "It's a wonder no one was hurt. She's been so aggressive lately. She does her best to bite me whenever I come near. Roger and I have been thinking"—Marjorie looked at the vet soberly—"of having her put to sleep."

"Well, she's an old girl," said the vet sympathetically. "Sometimes they turn nasty. Let me know when you make up your mind."

54

The telephone was like a part of Bonnie Glover's body. She tucked it between ear and shoulder and chattered away, doing her nails at the same time or leaning over a mirror to stroke mascara on each individual eyelash. She had begun the telephone habit in junior high school, when she and all her friends had discovered this way of being perpetually together.

Today she was doing something forbidden. She brought the phone out to the counter in the Porcelain Parlor and called Ananda Singh.

"What's it really, really like, living with the Frys?" Bonnie wanted to know.

"What is it like?" Ananda was puzzled. "Oh, it is very nice. It is a good house. Very comfortable."

"But how about—you know, I mean Mr. Fry has a drinking problem. It must be kind of, you know, pretty gross sometimes, just really incredible?"

"Oh, but that is calumny."

"Calumny, what's that?" Bonnie laughed. "Oh, Ananda, you're so intellectual. My girlfriend said to me, 'Isn't he just so incredibly intellectual?' And I'm like, 'God, you should see him sometimes.' " Bonnie's chuckle was sultry.

"But I am an eyewitness. Mr. Fry is not—I assure you, it is not so."

"Listen, there's another eyewitness, his own daughter,

Hope, that darling friend of yours. She told Jack Markey, you know Jack Markey? She told him her father drinks a quart of whiskey every day, I mean it's all over town."

Ananda was stunned. For a moment he had nothing to say.

Bonnie went on babbling. When a customer came into the shop Bonnie turned her back and hugged the phone tighter to her shoulder. "His own daughter, how do you like that?"

The customer stared at Bonnie's back. "I wonder if I could interrupt you?" she said in a frosty voice.

Bonnie turned farther away, crouching lower over the phone. She was alone in the universe with Ananda Singh. Behind her back she heard the customer leave the shop. The glass door sighed as it puffed open and slowly swung closed. "You don't believe me? It's the truth, honest to God."

Once again the door puffed open, and there was a sharp clack of heels across the floor. Bonnie turned to behold her boss, Mimi Pink.

"Put—down—that—phone," said Mimi.

"Oh, sorry, I gotta go," said Bonnie, pushing the hang-up button.

Mimi's voice was edged with ice. "I have just met Mrs. Alexander Whittier on the sidewalk. She told me she drove all the way from Ipswich this morning in order to purchase the signature Lladro golden eagle for her husband's birthday. It happens to be the most valuable piece of porcelain in the shop. She told me she was not able to get your attention."

"Well, I'm sorry, but I had this fabulously important phone call."

"You—are—fired."

Bonnie left in tears, and Mimi took over. She polished the glass counter. She wiped a speck off a porcelain madonna. She rearranged the golden eagle on its pedestal. Business in the Porcelain Parlor was slack.

Then suddenly there was another crisis. Mimi's assistant

in the Den of Teddies came running in to report that a giant stuffed bear had been stolen by one of the homeless people.

"How could such a thing possibly happen?" said Mimi, scandalized.

"I don't know," sobbed the assistant. "One moment they were there, the mother and daughter, you know, and the next they were gone. By the time I noticed the big bear was missing, they were nowhere in sight on the street."

Mimi was outraged. Once more she called the police, but she knew it wouldn't do any good, and it didn't. Then later in the afternoon business picked up.

The afternoon was always the best time. Customers from other towns never shopped in the morning, they came after lunch. Today it was a handsome older couple from Cohasset. First they fell in love with the porcelain ballerina. Then they got excited about the golden eagle.

Marjorie Bland came into the shop, too, looking for a wedding present. She was in no hurry. She stood at the counter gossiping with Mimi about the homeless problem. Mimi told her about the theft of the teddy bear. Marjorie told Mimi about the vandalism to her house.

"And you won't believe this, but that crazy old lady keeps coming back. I think she's in love with my horse."

"Can't you have her arrested?"

"Oh, well, the problem won't be with us much longer. The vet's coming over Thursday night. We're putting the horse to sleep."

There was a squeaking noise from the front of the shop. Marjorie and Mimi turned to see Sarah Peel staring at them with her mouth open.

"That's her," whispered Marjorie. "That's the very one I was talking about."

Mimi looked at Sarah sternly. This particular bag lady had been forbidden to enter the Porcelain Parlor. She was the most dangerous one of the lot, because her stroller bristled with appendages—an umbrella, a bulging plastic bag, a pillow, a pile of clothing, a blanket, an overflowing basket. There was even a folding chair.

"No," cried Sarah, "you can't do that to Pearl."

It was the last straw. "Out," cried Mimi, striding forward. "Out with you! Out, out!" Grasping Sarah by the arms, she turned her around and dragged her out the door. Sarah fought back. There was a furious tussle. The golden eagle rocked on its pedestal, and fell, and smashed on the floor, followed by the ballerina. The Cohasset couple were spattered with chips of broken china. Sarah's stroller, abandoned in the middle of the floor, rolled this way and that.

It was at this moment that Jack Markey walked in, carrying a pink plastic bag. Dodging the stroller, he put the bag on the counter, then turned abruptly and walked out again, tripping over the stroller, which sailed across the floor and slapped against the counter. The pink bag fell off the counter into the stroller and nestled between Sarah's umbrella and the folding chair.

Regaining his balance, Jack marched out to the street, ignoring Mimi Pink, who was standing on the sidewalk shouting angrily after the shambling figure of Sarah Peel.

Mimi didn't notice his departure. She was too angry. She tramped back into the shop, crunching underfoot the splintered pieces of the porcelain eagle. Her breast heaved, adrenaline coursed through her body. She stared at the stroller. It was a hideous blot, a foreign object in her glittering store. One hand grasping the handle, she rushed it through shop and office and back door into the alley beside the Mill Brook, where a dumpster was parked. Violently she hurled the contents of the stroller into the dumpster. By the time she had tossed the stroller in after the basket and the umbrella and the folding chair and the coats and the blanket and the pillow and the pink plastic bag, she was shaking, she felt really ill. She stood for a moment, gasping for breath, and then she stalked back into the shop to apologize to the couple from Cohasset.

They were gone. Marjorie Bland was gone.

It was typical, absolutely typical of the chilling effect those homeless troublemakers were having on local trade. The time had come to take the case to court.

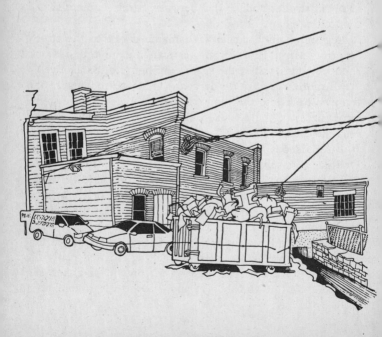

55

*I am like a feather floating in the atmosphere; on
every side is depth unfathomable.*
Journal, February 21, 1842

Charlotte Harris woke up at five o'clock in the morning
to find herself alone. The other side of the bed was not sagging
under her husband's weight. The room was gray with dawn
light. Where was Pete?

It wasn't like him to be late. Whenever he had night duty
at the hospital he came home exactly at four in the morning
and ate a dish of Wheaties and came to bed, making a lot of
noise, talking to Charlotte, waking her up so completely she
couldn't get back to sleep.

Charlotte got out of bed and looked out the window. Pete's
car was not parked at the edge of the driveway. She called
the hospital. "May I have the kitchen? Mrs. Heppleman?
This is Charlotte Harris. Is Pete still there?"

"Why, no, Mrs. Harris. He left at his usual time. You
mean he hasn't come home?"

"I suppose he stopped off for breakfast somewhere. Well,
thank you."

But they both knew there was no place in the neighborhood
to get breakfast in the middle of the night. Charlotte hung
up, aware that Mrs. Heppleman would assume the Harrises
were having marital troubles.

She called the police.

"How long has he been missing, Mrs. Harris?" said the
sleepy voice of the officer on duty.

"Well, he left the hospital at quarter of four, and it's five-
thirty now. He always comes straight home."

There was a pause. Once again Charlotte knew what the

man was thinking—*marital problems.* "Tell you what, Mrs. Harris. If your husband is still missing tomorrow morning at this time, call us back. We don't usually issue a missing person bulletin until somebody's been gone for several days."

"Well, all right." Charlotte put down the phone and took a deep, shaky breath.

A mile away from Pond View in Oliver Fry's house, just up the street from the police station, Ananda Singh came downstairs at seven-thirty and saw a letter lying open on the table. The heading at the top was clearly visible, and he couldn't help reading it:

TO THE VOTERS OF THE TOWN OF
CONCORD FROM THE COMMITTEE TO
ELECT ROGER BLAND

Ananda was not an American citizen, not a voter, and therefore the letter was not addressed to him. But he didn't think he would be invading the privacy of Hope and Oliver Fry by reading it. After putting a kettle on the stove, he sat down at the table and looked at the sheet of pale green paper. Behind him the shrews scrambled in their cage. The snakes writhed in the aquarium.

The letter too was a snake, and it bit his hand. At the end of the printed text was a list of Bland's supporters. At the head of the list was the name *Hope Fry.* Ananda closed his eyes in pain.

Hope came running into the kitchen. She was cheerful and excited. She threw open the refrigerator door. "Isn't this the day we're going to Gowing's Swamp? I'll make a picnic lunch. There'll be four of us, right?"

Ananda stood up in torment. "Only three, I'm afraid. I cannot go. I am not—feeling very well."

Hope turned in surprise. "Oh, I'm sorry." She watched as he crumpled a piece of paper, threw it in the wastebasket, and left the room in silent dignity.

At once she went to the wastebasket, extracted the paper, recognized it for what it was, and read her own name at the top of the list of Roger Bland's supporters. Overcome with misery and shame, she sank into a chair.

From his bedroom window Ananda watched her open the back door of Homer Kelly's car. She was carrying a bag of sandwiches and a pair of rubber boots.

"Where's Ananda?" said Mary, smiling at her from the front seat.

"He's not feeling very well today," said Hope stiffly.

Looking down from above, hearing his own falsehood, Ananda winced. He watched them drive away and murmured good-bye to Hope Fry. The girl who had attracted him so strongly with her open face and lovely smile was not the person he had thought her. That person had never existed.

He was alone in the house. When the phone rang, he picked it up with a sense of desolation.

"Ananda?"

It was Bonnie Glover. Ananda cringed and muttered, "Hello."

Bonnie was in tears. "She fired me. I don't know what I'm going to do. I can't pay my rent."

"Oh, I'm sorry."

Bonnie's sobs stopped, and her next words were perfectly clear. "So I'm moving in with you."

"No, no, you can't do that!"

"But I can't afford to be by myself!" The sobs began again, running up into a high squeal.

"Wait, wait." Ananda thought rapidly. "I'll find a place. But not here. You can't come here."

"Because of Hope, right?" sneered Bonnie. "Your precious Hope."

Ananda was suddenly so full of anger, he didn't trust himself to speak.

Bonnie sensed her mistake and began sniffling again. "Okay, okay, that's fabulous. I'll be waiting. Kiss, kiss."

Ananda hung up, his life collapsing around him.

56

The devil goes on exacting compound interest . . .
Walden, "Economy"

Jack Markey had had enough. He had been clever, he had been responsible, he had done whatever was necessary, he had delegated the job whenever it was possible to do so and performed it himself when it was not. But this was the last goddamn time.

The body of Pete Harris was so heavy, Jack had to drag it by the feet along the path beside Gowing's Swamp. By the time he got it down beside the watery margin of the bog, he was worn out. He shoved the carcass under a bush, and ventured into the muddy water. Sinking down, hanging on to the brittle branches of dead trees, he heaved himself toward the middle of the swamp. Jack had not bothered to find a pair of rubber boots. His shoes were mired in mud. His pants dragged at him, soaked to the hip.

He had no eyes for the strange beauty of his surroundings, no interest in the bird singing somewhere above him—only a desperate desire to lunge forward until he found the hole in the middle of the quaking bog, the place where people shot horses and watched them sink.

Then he saw it, a small pool of open water in the middle of the encircling sphagnum. At once he turned and struggled back to the shore for the body of Pete Harris.

God, it was impossible. First Jack tried hoisting Pete up on his shoulders, dragging him by the arms, bending himself double. But their combined mass was so great that his feet plunged too deep in the slimy mud and he nearly lost his balance. Then he let the enormous weight slip down his back until it was half-submerged. Grasping the feet again, he tried floating it behind him. The effort was almost more than he could handle. The body kept snagging on fallen trees and the roots of straggling bushes.

The worst was yet to come. The big-bellied carcass was a spongy pneumatic mass of air cavities, and it floated high above the surface. It wouldn't sink. Jack had to slosh back to the shallows and return with a water-soaked log. And then he barely had time to drop it on Pete Harris and retreat, because there were voices in the woods.

They were near, very near, a man talking loudly, a woman laughing. Christ! Jack hauled himself back to the shore, catching at twigs, tripping and splashing up to his chest in muddy water. Full of dread, he crawled high on the bank and hid himself in a grove of pine trees, slumping down exhausted in the low undergrowth of blueberry and fern.

He was only just in time. Soaked through and shivering, he watched through a gap among the whippy stems of buckthorn. What the bloody hell were they doing?

Oliver had told Homer how to find his way in. With Mary and Hope slogging behind him, Homer led the way through the watery moat to the carpet of sphagnum moss supporting the bog garden in the middle of Gowing's Swamp. Silently they stood gazing.

"Better not all stand in one place," whispered Mary, and they moved apart. The mossy surface billowed beneath their feet.

It was not a place for talking. Slowly they walked around the green-gold garden among the dwarfed larches, the panicled andromeda, the swamp azalea and summersweet. Cotton grass lifted puffs of white on wiry stems.

"Listen," said Mary. They all looked up as a watery warbling began in the woods, a bell-like melody. A moment later it was repeated in a higher register, the last notes rising out of hearing.

They didn't need to be told what it was. Homer looked at Mary. The singing stopped, then began again, a little nearer.

Hope listened, too. She was inundated with waves of regret. With the song of the wood thrush in her ears, she kept seeing the anguish on Ananda's face as he crumpled the letter to which she had signed her name.

Then there was a new sound, a blare of music from the direction of the housing development off Lexington Road. The thrush stopped singing. The boom box shouted, "Do it, do it, do it . . ."

"Oh well, hell," said Homer, and they turned to go.

Again he led the way. With his arms held high before his face, he pushed through the surrounding barrier of thorny bushes, holding them aside for Mary and Hope. "Watch out for this one. Wait a sec, this way's easier."

And then, turning for a last look at the Garden of Eden, he saw a hand rise up and sink among the dwarfed trees.

"Shit," whispered Jack Markey, watching from the shore.

"Wait for me." Homer turned around and started back and looked again. The hand was gone. Had he been mistaken? Now there was nothing in Gowing's Swamp but miniature larches and green moss and cotton grass and the tyrannical vibrations of the world's loudest radio.

"Homer?"

"Wait a minute." Homer turned and stared at the green pool where the body of Pete Harris was now rolling slowly, floating just under the surface. Homer saw only the half-submerged log that held it down. The log bobbed slightly and lay still.

"Come on, Homer."

"Coming." Homer shrugged his shoulders and made his way out of Gowing's Swamp, following Mary and Hope along the woodland path to the car. For the rest of the morning he tried to put the mirage of the disappearing hand out of his mind. But later in the day he had a call from Julian Snow.

"Pete Harris is missing," said Julian, his voice sounding faint and far away.

"He is?" Homer thought about it. "Do you think he walked out on his wife?"

"She doesn't think so. She says this isn't like him at all."

"Well, thank you, Julian. I guess I'd better speak to the police again."

"Okay, good." Julian's voice faded as though he were calling from the moon. "So long. I just thought I'd let you know."

So Homer told Police Chief Flower about the hand he had seen in Gowing's Swamp. Maybe, he said, it belonged to a man named Peter Harris who was missing from Pond View.

At first Jimmy Flower pooh-poohed it, but at Homer's urging he agreed to walk around the corner of the building and speak to the fire chief, because some of the fire fighters were scuba divers. It turned out that the divers were pleased to have an honest-to-God reason for putting on their rubber suits and testing their equipment. But when Homer told them what the problem was, they lost their enthusiasm. And then it took the rest of the afternoon because they had to borrow underwater lighting equipment from Cambridge.

It wasn't until late in the day that two divers from the Concord Fire Department eased themselves into the hole in the middle of the quaking bog with a lot of breathing apparatus and submersible lamps and grappling hooks.

The whole thing was embarrassing. The divers found nothing in Gowing's Swamp at all, not even a dead horse. Homer was mortified.

57

I am stranded at each reflux of the tide . . .
Journal, January 17, 1841

At Pond View the news of Pete Harris's disappearance ran swiftly from one mobile home to another.

Charlotte could feel the instantaneous loss of respect. A deserted woman has no dignity. She has been judged and found wanting. She could guess what they were thinking. Pete had run off with somebody else, somebody who appreciated him more than his snobby wife.

"There, dear," said Honey Mooney, coming over to comfort her. But there was condescension in Honey's sympathy, and Charlotte didn't want it. Instead of falling into Honey's arms, she turned on the electric broom. It made too much noise for shared intimacies. Honey shrugged and went away. Outside in the driveway she raised her eyebrows at Stu LaDue and rolled her eyes. That Charlotte! You know what she's like.

Charlotte gave the whole trailer a thorough cleaning. She scoured the bathroom sink and polished the toaster and washed the windows and emptied the wastebaskets, feeling a little guilty, aware of her own trembling relief that Pete was not there. When all the rooms were sparkling, she took the trash bag across the grass to the two big barrels behind the laundry shack.

As she tossed her bag into one of the barrels, she looked up to see Julian Snow approaching with his own small bag of rubbish. "Hello, Charlotte," he said softly. "Has Pete come back?" But Julian was sure he hadn't.

Charlotte shook her head and clapped down the lid of the

trash can. "Use the other one," she said curtly. "This one's full."

"Thanks." Julian wrinkled his nose. "Awful smell."

"Yes," agreed Charlotte, turning away.

"Oh, Charlotte," said Julian, his heart going out to her. But Charlotte was gone.

Oh, Lord, why couldn't they talk to each other? Ever since Julian had seen her half killed by the defective iron cord, his tenderness had magnified. This morning her desperate coolness in the face of disaster was like a match to his fuse. If Charlotte had shrewdly calculated how to work on his feelings, she couldn't have done a better job.

But she was not shrewd and calculating. She was merely preserving her self-respect.

Left to himself, Julian lifted the lid of the empty trash barrel and dropped in his paper bag. Then he looked at the other one. It was part of his routine. Full barrels had to be emptied into the dumpster. None of the other people at Pond View had the willing muscle to do it. If Julian didn't take care of it, the collection area would overflow with trash, and then the stuff would blow all over the park.

He took the metal barrel by its two handles, meaning to lift it to his shoulder. But it wouldn't lift. It was too heavy.

Julian prided himself on his wiry strength. What was so heavy that he couldn't lift it? Removing the lid of the trash can, he took out Charlotte's bag and a couple of other small kitchen trash bags, then turned his face away from the overpowering smell of decay.

There was only one other bag in the can, a single enormous awkward-looking bundle. Actually it was two bags attached to each other with staples and mailing tape.

Julian was swept by a feeling of repugnance. The bulky package was folded on itself in a way he didn't like. With his pocket knife he tore an opening in one end of the bundle and exposed the contents, then turned away with a moan.

It was Pete Harris, with a hole in the side of his head.

At once Julian thought of Charlotte—Charlotte, who had told him to use the other trash can; Charlotte, who had been "unhappy as Pete's wife my whole married life."

Quickly Julian picked up the small bags he had tossed on the ground and dropped them back on top of Pete. He didn't know how Charlotte could have lifted her two-hundred-and-fifty-pound husband into a trash can, but his heart misgave him.

"Oh, ugh," said Honey Mooney, coming up behind him. "What's that smell?"

"Meat papers, I guess," said Julian, feeling sick.

Honey too had a sackful of rubbish to throw away. "Not here," said Julian, clashing down the lid of the barrel. He lifted the top of the other one. "Here, this one's empty."

"Thanks," said Honey.

Julian walked stiffly around the laundry shack, then broke into a run.

Charlotte seemed surprised to find him at her door. Her freckled face flooded with color as she stood back to let him in.

"I've got to talk to you," said Julian.

"Well, fine. Come in."

Julian sat down on the built-in sofa and looked around. He had always liked Charlotte's place. It was sensible and neat, comfortable-looking without being crowded. Charlotte settled herself on a chair and looked at him with apparent calm.

He returned her look keenly. "Where's Pete?"

"I don't know," said Charlotte steadily.

"You really don't know where he is?"

"He's been away almost a whole day. I can't imagine what's become of him."

Julian stood up uneasily. "Have you got a stapler? And some of that heavy tape for sealing packages?"

Charlotte stood up, too. "Tell me what's happened."

In spite of himself Julian was disarmed. Taking her by

the elbows, he lowered her gently to the sofa. "I'm sorry, Charlotte. Pete's dead."

"No, no." Charlotte shook her head in disbelief. "He can't be, he can't be. It isn't true."

"It's true. He was shot. He's dead."

Charlotte gasped and put her trembling hands to her face as Julian told her what he had found in the trash barrel.

"What I'm afraid of," he said huskily, "is they'll think we had something to do with it. Because of—you know."

"Because of my letter." Charlotte said it bravely, but then she lowered her eyes and began to cry. Her dreadful letter —once again the whole world hung on that single impulsive mistake. The letter had been like a tap on a tiny drum, and now the whole sky echoed it like thunder.

Charlotte had wanted desperately to be free from Pete, but not like this, never like this. Her tears gushed, bursting the dam of her warring and impossible feelings. She couldn't stop. Julian sat down beside her and put his arm around her. She leaned against him and sobbed.

Over her shoulder Julian gazed out the window at the empty trailer that had once belonged to Norman Peck. Nothing was left of Norman now but the prize cup his pug dog had won in days gone by. Norman's daughter had probably thrown the cup away. Nothing was left of people when they died, nothing at all.

The woman weeping on his shoulder was mortal, too. Enfolding Charlotte, Julian kissed her hair and murmured her name. Charlotte went right on crying, but she clung to him and said, "Julian, oh, Julian."

Stuart LaDue burst in without knocking. "Oh, right," he shouted, staring at them. "Oh, yeah, wouldn't you just know. Well, I seen you. Honey told me, she says look in the trash can, I seen it with my own eyes. We already called the police."

Charlotte raised her head from Julian's shoulder, but Julian held her tightly against him. "Fuck off," he told Stu. "You don't know what you're talking about."

Stu backed out, still shouting. "I seen you. I'll tell them I seen you."

This time the Concord police had no choice but to take the matter seriously. Homer Kelly's story about the body in Gowing's Swamp had been a ridiculous and expensive false alarm, but this was a gruesome actual murder, and no mistake. The fact that the body was soaking wet and dripping with fragments of sphagnum moss was not associated with Homer's story until later, much later. But within the hour the investigating detective sergeant found a stapler in Charlotte's possession, one that matched the staples holding together the plastic bags in which Pete's body had been found. And in one of Julian's kitchen drawers he uncovered a roll of mailing tape exactly like the tape reinforcing the staples. In another drawer Julian kept a package of trash bags of exactly the right kind.

Only now did Chief Flower take seriously the possibility that Alice Snow too had been a homicide victim. It was beginning to look very much like a couple of lovers killing off their inconvenient spouses. Seldom had he seen such an open-and-shut case.

Stu LaDue's crude evidence was additional proof. "Hugging each other on the sofa," he said with malicious pleasure. "I seen them."

"Is that so?" said the arresting officer, writing it all down.

Roger Bland heard about the murder of Pete Harris and the arrest of the two suspects on the evening news.

So there were only five residents left. "And if the two suspects go to jail, that will make three. Think of that! Only three people left in the whole park!"

"How marvelous!" cried Marjorie.

58

*Let us settle ourselves, and work and wedge our feet
downward through the mud and slush of opinion
. . . till we come to a hard bottom and rocks in
place, which we can call* reality. . . .
Walden, "Where I Lived, and What I Lived For"

Once again Homer Kelly was called upon to arrange bail.
This time it was for his two favorite people at Pond View,
Charlotte Harris and Julian Snow. By late afternoon he managed to spring them from the same lockup where Sarah Peel
and her friends had been incarcerated.

Afterward Homer and Julian and Charlotte sat in Charlotte's kitchen and had a couple of drinks apiece and talked
the whole thing over. Julian told Homer about the discovery
of Pete's body in the trash can. Charlotte was silent, but after
Homer polished off his second whiskey, she smiled at him
and said, "Call your wife. Tell her to join us for supper."

"Well, thank you very much," said Homer, heaving himself out of his chair. "She'll be delighted."

Mary was willing, if not delighted, but first she wanted
to know where in the hell he had been. Homer explained,
and she was mollified. "I'll be right over. Would Mrs. Harris
like some tomatoes from the garden?"

Charlotte said yes, she certainly would, and Homer sat
down again. Then Julian held up one finger and looked at
him solemnly. "Listen, there's something else I've been
meaning to tell you. Maybe it's nothing, I don't know. The
other day I was in Honey Mooney's house because the air
conditioner in her bedroom wasn't working, and I saw something in there. She's got one of Alice's lamps."

"Honey Mooney? That little round woman?"

"Right. Well, of course she's got a bunch of Alice's other

stuff, too. I gave her a couple of things after Alice's death. But I never gave her the lamp. I mean you couldn't miss it, it was a flouncy one Alice bought from some catalog."

Homer looked at him, uncomprehending. "So Honey stole a lamp. Is that all?"

Julian looked troubled. "It's just that it has a heavy round base. I couldn't help wondering . . ."

"I see." Homer's face brightened. "You think it might have been used to kill your wife? The round base would fit the round depression on the back of her—" Homer glanced at the bereaved husband and winced at his own clumsiness. "Well, good for you. I never was happy with the idea that she struck her head on the edge of the step."

Julian threw out his hands in a helpless gesture. "I haven't got any idea why Honey would do such a thing, but suppose, just for the heck of it, that she did. And then she was afraid the lamp was all covered with her fingerprints and bits of Alice's hair and—"

"I know," said Homer. "All sorts of microscopic evidence that could be used against her after it was analyzed in some laboratory."

"Right. So she took the lamp away from my place to her own house."

Homer was baffled. "But why on earth didn't she get rid of it?"

"I know why." Charlotte turned away from the counter with an onion in her hand. "Honey likes pretty things. She couldn't bear to throw it out. She showed me the curtains you gave her, Julian, and that doll on the wall, and the lamp with the ruffled shade. She said you gave them all to her."

"Not the lamp," said Julian grimly. "It's funny I didn't even notice it was missing until the other day when I saw it in Honey's house."

"Wait a minute." Homer held up a warning finger. "What if Honey bought one just like Alice's from the same place?"

Julian shook his head. "No, this is my wife's lamp all

right. Nobody but Alice would decorate the damned thing with artificial flowers. She pinned them all over the lampshade. I remember them particularly, because they really gave me a pain."

"You shouldn't talk that way, Julian," said Charlotte, but she smiled as she unhooked a frying pan from a rack on the wall.

"After supper," said Homer, "you know what we're going to do? We're going to pay a call on Mrs. Honey Mooney."

59

*What is the singing of birds . . . compared with the
voice of one we love?*
Journal, April 30, 1851

Hope Fry was back in the hammock on the sleeping porch.
It was pitch dark on the porch, so dark that the ugly mesh
of the black screens was invisible. Low in the western sky
she could see the slender crescent of the new moon.

Across the hall Ananda was moving around. Hope could
hear his hurrying footsteps going up and down the stairs again
and again.

She was eager to tell him she had heard the wood thrush
singing in Gowing's Swamp. But she was angry with him
for not being at home for the lovely supper she had made
with such special care. If he had been too sick to go with
them to Gowing's Swamp this morning, he should have been
too sick to go out for supper. He had spent the day with
Bonnie Glover, that was obvious. Hope wasn't about to coo
at him about birds, not when she was so cross at him, so
disappointed.

And miserable, just miserable. It wasn't only that Hope
was in love with Ananda Singh. It was something more than
that. She was beginning to see the world through Ananda's
eyes. She saw him moving along a path strewn with pine
needles, waving aside a swarm of black flies, climbing a
hillside lush with ferns, growing to the dimensions of a white
oak tree, his arms poised like branches, his hands fingering
out into leaves. Oh, what was he doing, running up and
down the stairs like that?

There was a grinding noise outdoors. Hope sat up suddenly, and the hammock nearly dumped her on the floor.

She knew that noise. It was Ananda's car. He was leaving.

Oh, but she had to talk to him, she had to. She had to tell him about the singing bird and the garden in the swamp. Hope rushed down the back staircase, not stepping on each stair but dropping down in the controlled fall she had learned in childhood.

Her father was alone in the kitchen. "Oh, where is he going?" cried Hope.

Oliver Fry looked at her in surprise. "He told me to say good-bye to you."

"He hasn't gone for good?"

"Well, yes, I guess he has."

"But where? Where is he going?" Hope strained at the jammed screen door and jerked it open.

Oliver Fry stared at his daughter. "He's moving in with a roommate. They found a place on Belknap Street."

Oh, it was Bonnie, of course it was Bonnie. Ananda was moving in with Bonnie Glover. A lump swelled in Hope's throat. She cast a desperate glance at her father and ran out of the kitchen. The owl shrieked. The door of the porch banged shut.

Oliver's pity went out to his daughter. He wanted her to be happy—one's children should not be wretched—but her present misery seemed better to him than her former bitter pride.

Outdoors in the driveway beside the house, Hope stopped short. Ananda's car was still there. The noisy engine had been turned off. The driver's seat was empty. In the glow from the kitchen window she could see the suitcase on the front seat, the boxes of books in the back.

Ananda had been about to drive to Belknap Street, and then he had changed his mind. He was nowhere to be seen. Where was he?

Hope ran out to the sidewalk and looked left and right. Then she saw him in his long white Indian shirt. He was pumping a bicycle, moving away toward the center of town.

She followed him. She couldn't help it. As the narrow moon dropped out of sight behind the houses on Everett Street, Hope began to run after the dim white figure rising and falling on her father's old bicycle, wheeling slowly in the direction of the Milldam.

> *. . . sometimes it has rained flesh and blood!*
> *Walden,* "Spring"

The Madwoman of Chaillot was opening in the theater at 51 Walden Street. The first act had been a smash hit. At intermission the audience flowed out into the open air and milled around on the sidewalk in front of the theater, smoking, sipping white wine from plastic cups, grinning at each other, looking conspicuously jolly the way one is supposed to look at such times, happy with an enviable gaiety that makes other people wonder why their own lives are so drab.

Jo-Jo Field and her husband were there, talking rapturously to Roger and Marjorie Bland. Roger would just as soon have spent the evening at home, because theatrical productions bored him, but Marjorie had explained that he had to be seen by the voters, he had to introduce himself to strangers and be amiable to all and sundry. Besides, lots of these people were probably Harvard grads, too, Marjorie said, and they'd be helping to choose new overseers. So Roger was doing his best to be a hearty good fellow.

Jack Markey and Jefferson Grandison were there for similar reasons, beaming and affable, true members of the Concord community, not menacing outsiders. Grandison had even brought along his wife, a nondescript little woman with dyed red hair.

Ananda Singh saw the crowd on the sidewalk as he rode up Walden Street on Oliver Fry's bicycle. At once he slowed to a stop and put one foot down on the pavement. Ananda was in no mood to see or be seen. He didn't want to ride into that flood of light, that worldly glare—not when he was so wretched, not when his life was disintegrating around him.

There was a path beside the theater, leading off into the darkness. Ananda dismounted, bumped the bike up on the sidewalk, left it leaning against the fence beside the path, and hurried out of the light, head down.

The path was narrow, but it led straight away from Walden Street between the theater and the savings bank next door. Apple trees lined the path. Ananda's feet kept kicking the hard little knobs of green fruit littering the ground. To his

surprise the path took him to a narrow wooden bridge. At once he guessed that the water flowing beneath it was the Mill Brook. Long ago the little stream had been dammed to make a millpond. The pond and the mill were gone, but Main Street was still called the Milldam.

The bridge was a surprise, a sanctuary in the middle of town. Ananda stopped on the bridge and leaned on the railing, looking up at the clapboarded rear wall of the First Parish Church. Above it the gold dome of the lighted steeple rose into the dark sky. Then he stared down at the black water. Along the edges of the stream, nature had crowded forward, filling every niche. Wild vines reached across it into empty air. The water itself was invisible, but he could hear it purling, moving secretly toward the river.

When he heard voices, his misery returned. People were approaching along the path. Ananda hurried to the other side of the bridge and lowered himself into the thick growth of weedy shrubs lining the shore. Boldly he stepped into the shallow water and waded upstream.

"Here," said Jack Markey, stopping on the bridge, and running his hand along the railing. "No one will bother us here."

Jefferson Grandison moved up beside him, and together they looked down at the water. "Well?" said Grandison.

Jack took a deep breath. "I'm resigning," he said. "Well, of course I'll carry on with Walden Green, but as for everything else, I'm sorry, sir, but I'm quitting. As of right now."

There was a pause. Then Grandison spoke very softly. "Whatever for?"

Jack couldn't tell him the real reason, his sense of ill fortune to come, of the approach of the last days. I heard an angel flying through the midst of heaven, saying with a loud voice, Woe, woe, woe. "It's just that I've had enough." He turned to look at his chief, but Grandison's face was invisible in the darkness. Only his glasses glimmered at Jack.

"I think, sir, I've done all you asked of me without question or complaint."

Jefferson Grandison spoke without emotion, his face still blank and dark. "I'm not sure you understood me when I turned over those funds to you the other day. Not only were they to be shared with your subordinates, they were for services not yet rendered."

Again there was a pause. "What do you mean," said Jack, "not yet rendered?"

"I mean services still to be performed."

"No," said Jack. His voice trembled. He was overcome with a sense of injustice. "No more. There won't be any more." Angrily, almost weeping, he related in detail the hideous difficulties he had encountered in disposing of the body of Pete Harris. "Oh, killing him was nothing. A gun to the head in a dark corner of the hospital parking lot in the middle of the night, nothing to it. The river was right there, so I tossed away the gun. And then I shoved Harris into the trunk of my car. But, Christ, next morning when I tried to dump him in the open place in the swamp, that asshole Homer Kelly came along and saw him there, so I had to haul him out again. The damn carcass must have weighed two hundred and fifty pounds. Two hundred and fifty swollen, stinking pounds. And then I had to figure out what to do with it. Well, what the hell would you do? I'll tell you what I did, I—"

"The landfill," said Grandison at once, interrupting, grasping Jack by both arms.

"The landfill?" Jack gaped at him.

"The compactor. They've installed one. It's one of ours."

Jack shuddered. He was filled with horror. He had a mental image of the bloated body of Pete Harris being crushed in the compactor, exploding into hideous, foul-smelling fragments. "Oh, Christ," he said, pulling away from Grandison.

Then they both turned their heads and stared at the water. There had been a noise, a splash, an exclamation.

"What was that?" said Grandison.

Jack peered into the dark and whispered, "Who's there?" Something was rising out of the brook, something long and thin and white. Ananda, who had been balancing himself on the muddy edge of the stream, had slipped and fallen on his back. Standing up in the water, he looked back at the two men on the bridge, and Jack saw his face clearly in the light from the floodlit steeple and the glittering golden dome.

He knew him at once. It was the kid from India, the foreign kid living at Hope's house, the one she was so crazy about—Jack had guessed it before Hope did herself. Once again the sense that he was present at a day of judgment boiled up in Jack. He was lifted out of himself. When Grandison thrust a cold object into his hand, he took it without question. Vaulting over the railing into the shallow water, he plunged upstream.

Ananda stared at him and stumbled backward, putting one foot in a hole. Jack came at him with the gun held high over his head. Before Ananda could regain his balance, Jack brought the butt of the gun down on his narrow skull once, twice, three times.

Ananda fell to his knees in the water, but Jack hauled him upright and held him sprawling in his arms. He turned to stare up at Jefferson Grandison.

"I trust you see what to do now?" whispered Grandison, leaning over the railing, his face still in deep shadow. Only the metal frames of his glasses sparkled at Jack like rings of gold.

"No, Mr. Grandison," cried Jack, careless of what happened from one moment to the next. "What the hell do I do now?"

"The landfill, you fool, the landfill. Take him to the landfill."

Like Ananda before her, Hope Fry slowed down at the theater, exhausted with running, shy of passing the crowded steps so thick with elegantly dressed people all talking and laughing at once. She could no longer see the lanky boy crouched over the handlebars of her father's bicycle. Where was he? He must have turned the corner onto Hubbard Street.

She was about to run across the street to the other side when she saw the bicycle leaning against the fence beside the path to the Mill Brook.

There was no question whose bicycle it was. Oliver's old Raleigh was an old-fashioned bike with upright handlebars. Nobody but Hope's father rode that kind of old thing anymore. Hope could feel her heart beat as she went up to it and touched the narrow saddle. It was still warm. Ananda must be walking along the path to the bridge.

Peering into the darkness, Hope could see someone silhouetted against the lighted church. She turned into the path. Now that she was so close to Ananda, she didn't have the faintest idea what she would say to him. Slowly she trailed along the path, trying to think of something, running things over in her mind.

She was just in time to see Jack Markey pluck Ananda out of the water, just in time to hear Jack's furious question and the other man's reply. Hope wanted to cry out to Ananda and scream at Jack, but a panic-stricken intelligence possessed her, and she ducked back under one of the apple trees.

Jefferson Grandison walked blindly past her. He found his wife waiting for him on the porch in front of the theater. Intermission was over. Everyone else had gone inside. The music of the second act was noisy from within.

"Where's Jack?" said his wife.

"He had to leave," said Grandison, firmly taking her arm.

"Why don't we go too? Please, Buzzie?"

"Nonsense, Annie. Of course we're not leaving." Urging her ahead of him, Grandison walked back into the theater.

"He's back," people whispered, turning their heads and staring, as Mr. and Mrs. Jefferson Grandison walked forward and took their conspicuous seats in the front row.

61

*The guilty never escape, for a steed stands ever ready
saddled and bridled at God's door, and the sinner
surrenders at last.*
Journal, January 31, 1841

Sarah Peel was late. Bridgie Sorrel had made a scene in
Melanie's Lunch Room, and Melanie didn't know what to
do, so she went out and found Sarah and brought her back
and asked her to handle it, and Bridgie was really having a
fit, so by the time Sarah could detach herself it was dark.
She ran as fast as she could down Main Street and panted
across the Nashawtuc bridge.

What if she were too late? What if the vet had already
shot lovely Pearl or stuck her with a poisoned needle?

But then Sarah saw the horse leaning over the paddock
fence, just as usual, a looming dark shape against the spot-
lights illuminating the house. Pearl was reaching out her
long neck as if she were looking for Sarah.

Thankfully Sarah scrambled down the bank and went up
to Pearl and stroked her nose and fed her a handful of candy.
The candies were expensive Swiss chocolates Palmer Nifto
had picked up somewhere. They were laced with brandy.
Pearl ate them daintily and nosed at Sarah, asking for more.

"No more, sweetie. That's all I've got."

Beyond the paddock Sarah could see the vet's big van in
the driveway. He was there all right. He was probably in
the house having a drink with Mr. and Mrs. Bland. Then
he'd come out and murder darling Pearl.

There was no time to lose. Sarah hurried around to the
gate and opened it. Then she came back to Pearl and stepped
up bravely on the first rail of the fence. "Now hold still,
Pearlie," she said.

Pearl always did what Sarah wanted. Obligingly she edged her rump closer to the fence and stood quietly while Sarah stepped on the second rail, then to the third, and teetered with her shins against the fourth. Pearl moved encouragingly a little closer and looked around at her.

"Okay, girl," murmured Sarah. Boldly she flung one leg over the broad back, then plopped herself down with a thump, smack in the middle.

Pearl stood very still while Sarah adjusted her several skirts and wriggled until she was comfortable. It felt wonderful. It felt right. It felt like being a queen. It was so high!

Pearl looked around at her again, as if to say "All right now?" And then she took a tentative step forward.

Sarah buried her fists in Pearl's mane and hung on tight as the horse began to walk gently around the yard. Sagging a little to the left and a little to the right, Sarah clung to the horse's belly with her legs. There was nothing to it. She had known it, she had always known it! Once a person knew how to ride, they never forgot. The horse's head bobbed up and down, the fresh damp smell of the river floated up to Sarah's nose, and a pretty scrap of moon hung in the sky above the trees. Gallantly Sarah dug her heels into Pearl's sides, just to see what would happen.

Sure, thought Pearl, why not? Picking up speed, she hurried around the yard with the same easygoing single-footed gait. Joyfully Sarah prodded her again, and once again Pearl obliged. Around and around they cantered at high speed, Sarah leaning forward against the horse's neck, her legs flopping up and down. On the third time around the yard they sailed right through the gate past Marjorie Bland and the dumbfounded veterinarian.

Away went Pearl with Sarah Peel on her back, straight as an arrow along Nashawtuc Road, straight across the Nashawtuc bridge, straight through the red light at Main Street, while cars veered to the side and screeched to a stop and the drivers leaned out to shout. Away they went straight down the middle of Thoreau Street in the dark of the summer night, free of Roger and Marjorie Bland, free of the vet, free of being put to sleep.

They were an astonishing vision, the gray-white horse and Sarah in her layers of clothing all bleached the same gray by the sun. The wind of the running horse blew everything back, Pearl's mane and tail, Sarah's fluttering skirts and streaming scarves.

"I'll get her back," cried the vet, a stern-jawed man of action, leaping into his van. With a roar it swerved around the gravel drive, spitting pebbles over Roger's and Marjorie's flabbergasted legs, and then it stormed out onto Nashawtuc Road.

But Pearl was already out of sight, racing through another stoplight, heading with abandoned recklessness for Route 2 with its thick speeding traffic, two lanes tearing east in the direction of Boston, two more charging westward, whizzing hellbound the other way.

62

As my own hand bent aside the willow in my path,
so must my single arm put to flight the devil
and his angels.
Journal, January 29, 1841

There was no one outside the theater when Hope mounted her father's bicycle and began pumping up Walden Street, ramming her feet down on the pedals, throwing all the strength of her thin body into propelling the bicycle forward without benefit of multiple gears.

She was alone on the street, except for Jack Markey's car. Its taillights were moving swiftly away from her, but she knew where it was going. Hope raced after it, standing up because the seat was so high she couldn't sit down. On the steep approach to Route 2 she leaned forward, struggling, sobbing with effort, filling her lungs with strangled gulps of cool night air. Oh, God, why hadn't her father ever bought himself a new bicycle?

Jack Markey was unaware that Hope was following him. He was unaware of anything but his own seething fury. This was the last time he would ever do Grandison's bidding. It was the last time, the very last time. The sense of last times crowded in on him. It pressed inward from the dark sky. It churned in his digestive tract and constricted his breathing.

From the backseat there was a slight sound, a groan from Ananda Singh. For a moment Jack lost control of the car, and it veered to one side and bumped up and down on the rough shoulder. Wildly he brought it back onto the pavement and raced across Route 2 as the yellow light turned red. Turning into the landfill, he began mumbling under his breath passage after terrifying passage from the book of Revelation. The evil verses had meant nothing to him when he had learned them as a show-off little kid, jumping out of his tiny chair to recite, while everyone smiled and clapped and the pastor put his big hand on Jack's head and blessed him. "And the stars of heaven fell unto the earth, and the heaven departed as a scroll when it is rolled together." And then there were the verses about the horsemen, and Death, and Hell following after.

The compactor was a shapeless large object halfway up the dirt road. Jack parked beside it, turned off the engine, switched off the lights, pulled on the brake, and sat for a minute, trying to accustom himself to the darkness. Then he heaved himself out of the car and looked up at the sky. At once a pair of stars dropped from the zenith, and Jack cried out and fell to his knees. They were only Perseid meteors, a couple of burning rocks from the swarm of flying stones encountered by the earth every summer in its orbit around the sun, but Jack didn't know about the Perseids, he only knew about the dread warnings in the book of Revelation.

After a moment he came to his senses. The heavens had not departed like a scroll rolled together. The sky was still there, with most of its faint stars. Shakily Jack got to his feet and told himself to get the thing over with. He opened the back door of the car, took hold of Ananda Singh, and hauled him out by the shoulders.

Ananda's body was limp. Jack had no stomach for what he was about to do. It took all his strength to drag Ananda to the pit and tip him over the edge. At once he jumped in beside him and covered the prostrate body with miscellaneous refuse and a big sheet of cardboard.

Climbing out of the pit, Jack was so weak he could hardly stand. His stomach was churning, saliva poured into his mouth. He barely had time to climb the steps to the controls of the compactor and push the button, before his gorge rose. Then he tumbled down the steps and fell to his knees. The contents of his churning stomach spewed out of him in volcanic spasms as the grinding noise of the machine started up behind him. He didn't see Hope Fry leap down into the pit, he didn't hear her scrambling among the rubbish, looking for Ananda Singh.

At once Hope was caught in the undertow of the sucking tide. As the far wall of the machine began shoving against everything in its path, she was lifted by the thick moving flood and propelled forward. Frantically she scrabbled with her arms and legs, feeling for Ananda. It was like trying to find a drowning man. Oh, God, where was he? Then a broken bottle gashed her hand and Ananda's head rolled against her leg. Frantically she reached for him. Plastic bags pressed against her, rose and tumbled over her face, blocked her breath, burst and released their contents all over her, while the moving wall of steel ground forward, whining, mashing the contents of the pit against the jaw at the other end, to be crushed and pulverized and turned into pulp.

Hope hauled and tugged. For a moment she had Ananda by the waist. But then once again she was knocked down by buckling cardboard boxes. Squashed bags roiled around her, an avalanche of catalogs fell on her, the handle of a broom struck her chin. Once again she surfaced and heaved at Ananda.

Oh, thank God, he was beginning to help her. His hands came alive. They gripped hers feebly as she waded to the side of the narrow pitching cavity. With a last effort she hoisted Ananda's legs over the edge and rolled him free, so that he lay safely above her on the ground. At once he pulled himself up and reached down to her, and she clutched at his hands, but her foot was caught. Her leg twisted and snapped.

Her cry of pain was overpowered by the grinding of the machine and the crushing of cereal boxes and the chewing and tearing of a thousand plastic wrappers and sticky paper plates and wads of computer printouts and broken toys and torn underwear and smashed dishes and wastebasketfuls of miscellaneous rubbish. With a violent effort that tore the ligaments around her fractured bone, Hope wrested her foot from her captured shoe, and Ananda pulled her free, as Jefferson Grandison's compactor crushed and swallowed the household debris of a hundred Concord families and solidified it into a grisly welter of flattened fragments, to be hauled away and buried somewhere in the town of North Andover.

They lay still, side by side, with their faces pressed into the dirt and Ananda's arm thrown over Hope. The machine was shuddering to a stop. The droning whine died away. In the sudden quiet they could hear Jack Markey weeping.

At least, thought Hope, he had the grace to take it hard. Poor old Jack, he thought Ananda Singh had been ground up into little pieces, and it caused him pain. Angrily Hope pressed closer to Ananda, and he squeezed her tighter, and she prayed that Jack Markey would climb back into his car and drive away without checking to see if a random arm or leg was sticking out of the jaw of the machine, unconsumed.

They lay still, listening, as Jack's snuffling became a torrent of sobs, as if he had been holding back tears all his life and were letting them out now in a single flood.

Jack's weeping went on and on. At last it petered out into gulping sobs. They could hear his stumbling footsteps. The car door slammed. The engine purred. The car moved softly away, jouncing on the rough dirt road.

Slowly, hardly daring to think themselves safe, they sat up. Ananda's head was swollen and aching, Hope's leg was broken in two places.

"I heard a wood thrush today in Gowing's Swamp," murmured Hope.

Tenderness welled up in Ananda, and he took her in his arms.

As Jack Markey turned out of the landfill onto Route 126, he was too anguished to remember to turn on the headlights. He wanted only to get away. Violently he pressed his foot on the accelerator. The car leaped forward and plunged along the road in the direction of Route 2.

But he couldn't get away from the falling stars, which were still catapulting from the heavens. In the narrow band of sky between the overarching trees he saw one star drop, and then another. Jack screamed, and screamed again, as a pale horse rushed upon him, pounding toward him with Death on its back and Hell following after.

Sarah and Pearl didn't know anything terrible was happening. Miraculously they had negotiated the crossing of Route 2 by arriving at the intersection just as the light changed to green. Gaily they plunged straight across in front of the stopped traffic, and galloped down the road. The darkened car that careened toward them was a shock, and Pearl was so surprised she dug in her forelegs and stopped cold. Poor Sarah was tossed forward, and she banged her head hard on Pearl's neck, but she wasn't really hurt.

But Jack Markey completely lost control. Screaming, he drove off the road and struck a tree with shattering force. Instantly he was crushed between the smashed windshield and the crumpled hood.

Sarah was oblivious of death and destruction at the side of the road. The noise of the impact of Jack's car against the tree was lost in the tremendous accelerating roar of the trucks starting up at the traffic light on Route 2. Sarah righted herself on Pearl's back and clucked at her, and they started off again. Soon they were cantering smoothly along Route 126, keeping to the narrow shoulder, and they didn't slow down until they came to a house with a vegetable garden, where Pearl stopped of her own accord and began helping herself in the dark to some juicy carrot tops.

Far behind them at the scene of the accident, a police ambulance came streaking through the night, its siren wailing, and pulled up beside the shattered car.

There was nothing the two men in the ambulance could

do to help Jack Markey. Instead they picked up a couple of young people who hobbled up to them, supporting each other, barely able to walk. In spite of their obviously traumatic injuries the two kids were grinning hugely.

"Were you in the car?" said one of the medical technicians, helping them into the ambulance.

"What car?" said Hope.

"That car, over there against the tree. You mean, you had nothing to do with the accident?"

"What accident?" said Ananda.

It was very strange. In the milling confusion of puzzled medics, and police officers routing traffic around the ambulance, and cruisers with blinking lights, and the loud blatting of the intercom, and the shouted questions of inquisitive people leaning out of passing cars, nobody understood it at all.

In the ambulance Hope and Ananda lay on two cots, smiling at each other.

"Excuse me," said the medic, stepping over their clasped hands to apply a splint to Hope's leg.

"*Pyar karta ho,*" said Ananda in Hindi, squeezing her hand tightly.

"What does it mean?" whispered Hope.

"It means, 'I love you.' I have never said such words before."

"Oh, ouch," said Hope. "Oh, Ananda, I'm so glad. I love you too."

"Excuse me again," said the irritated technician. In the performance of his duties he had never before been hindered by love.

63

GO DIRECTLY TO JAIL.
DO NOT PASS GO,
DO NOT COLLECT $200.
Chance card, Monopoly

Mimi Pink had a habit of tippling a little too much on Saturday nights. After a hard week of running from one store to another, keeping things moving along smoothly, poking a little here, scolding a little there, trying to keep things under control while uneasy rumblings grumbled below the surface, Mimi felt she deserved a glass of wine, and then another and another.

Tonight something was vaguely lurching and yawing at the back of her consciousness, but she couldn't put her finger on it. Muzzily she polished off the bottle of Chianti. It was only after she dropped off to sleep right after supper and awoke two hours later in total darkness with her head on the table that it struck her with an awful jolt what it was.

The money—what had happened to the three hundred and fifty thousand dollars Jack Markey had promised to deliver yesterday afternoon? Oh, God, he had come, he had certainly come, he had walked right into the Porcelain Parlor, he had given her a significant look, and he had set something down on the counter.

But she had been in the middle of that awful fracas with the mad-looking ragged woman with the stroller. And then when the confusion was over and things settled down, Jack was gone, and Mimi had completely forgotten him because she was still so furious about the unspeakable creature who had violated the sanctity of her pretty shop and smashed an important piece that had cost her nine hundred dollars wholesale.

Mimi sat in the dark trying to order her thoughts, which were tumbling over each other, bright flashes of perfect recall intermingled with foggy lapses of memory. Had Jack Markey brought her the money or hadn't he?

Her head swarmed with sodden recollections of other temper tantrums, old half-forgotten explosions, like the time Lee-Ann had shrieked with gloating laughter and snatched at Mimi's Monopoly money and screeched, "That's mine! You landed on Park Place! You did! It's mine, mine, mine, all mine!" And it had been so awful, so unbearable, that once again Mimi had slapped her hard and thrown the whole game on the floor.

Then with a sharp pang of dismay, Mimi remembered what had happened. Jack Markey had been carrying something pink, a pink plastic bag, and he had set it down on the counter. Mimi closed her eyes in the dark. By a supreme effort of concentration she summoned up a crystalline image of the dumpster behind the Porcelain Parlor. She saw herself hurling the bag lady's stroller into it with all its contents. She had a vivid recollection of a conversation with the driver of the flatbed truck that came once a week to transport the dumpster to the landfill. He had come this very morning, and they had exchanged a few sharp words.

"I will thank you not to litter my premises," Mimi had said.

"I got no interest in littering your premises," shouted the driver, leaning out of his cab. "Just don't fill the goddamned thing so full."

And then he had maneuvered his truck out onto the busy street. The last Mimi had seen of the trash she had thrown out during the week was a pink bag wobbling on top of everything else. A pink bag! It was Jack Markey's pink bag, it was Mimi Pink's pink bag, trembling and jiggling on top of the dumpster as the driver whirled the steering wheel and the big truck lumbered out of sight around the curve of

Walden Street, heading for the other side of the highway and the Concord landfill.

Mimi didn't stop to gather her wits. She didn't stop to think. She didn't put on flat-soled shoes for walking or gloves for burrowing, she didn't bring a shovel for digging. Emptyhanded she tore out of her condominium apartment, clattered down the stairs in her high-heeled shoes, leaped into her car, and sped down Route 2. As she turned the corner on Route 126 she had to slow down, because a tow truck and a couple of police cars were occupying half the road. An ambulance moved past her with flashing lights, and a traffic policeman beckoned her forward. Mimi hoped they were all too busy to see her turn into the entrance to the landfill.

The place was new to her. She peered into the dark as her car bobbed up and down on the dirt road. Where in this godawful place would the dumpster have been emptied? Blindly she passed the compacting machine and headed for the mountain of rubbish at the top of the rise. Surely the pink plastic bag containing her three hundred and fifty thousand dollars was somewhere in that colossal pile.

Jumping out of her car, Mimi hurried over the uneven ground, staggering on her stiletto heels. Swiftly she clawed her way to the top of the mountain, her hands digging into the soft covering of dirt, her heels puncturing the plastic bags just below the surface. At the top she stood up, balancing with difficulty, and looked around, feeling desolate. She was alone, all alone. There was no one in the whole world to help her now.

Somewhere below her lay the pink bag of money. She must find it, she must. Bending over, Mimi began the search, thrusting her fingers through the layer of dirt, clutching at one of the submerged bags. Her sharp fingernails pierced a hole, and at once her ankles were engulfed in a tumble of cat-food cans. Before long she was down on all fours, reaching for bag after bag, and then she lay full length on the hill of debris, hauling bags aside, dragging out one bag after another, seeking a smaller one, a paler one, a pink bag stuffed with money. One of her shoes came off and lost itself in a sea of damp paper towels. Her delicate panty hose were ripped from hip to toe. She was engulfed in smelly fish papers and greasy wads of aluminum foil and sticky jam jars and noisome tissues and prickly chicken bones and oily butter wrappers.

The daily effluvium of Concord's domestic life was different in detail from the expensive schlock lining the shelves in all her sumptuous stores, but not in its essential nature. Mimi's merchandise was not toxic to human life, but it was still pollution. In the mounded trash of the Concord dump she found at last the Park Place and Boardwalk that were hers by right.

For two desperate hours Mimi crept and crawled and slithered among the sedimented rubbish without finding the pink bag full of money. At last, shaking with frustration, she gave up. Trembling with anger and self-loathing, she tottered to her knees and made her way, slipping and sliding, back down the hill of mounded garbage to her car.

She did not drive back to her condominium. Jerking the car into action, she bucked it out onto Route 126, darted left and then almost immediately left again into the Pond View Trailer Park, and pulled up with a squeal of brakes beside one of the mobile homes. Leaping out, she stumbled in her wrecked stockings up the steps, and pounded savagely on the door.

Lee-Ann opened it and stared at her sister. Mimi's hair was in strings, her face was streaked with dirt, her clothes were grimed with filth. There was scrambled egg in her ear, dog food crusted on her blouse, nameless slime stuck to her from head to toe.

"Christ, Mimi," said Lee-Ann, "there's people here. Jesus, what happened to you?" Then she took Mimi by the shoulders and shook her, and whispered, "My money! Did you bring me my money?"

Mimi pushed violently past her sister. She had no regard for the people who were visiting Lee-Ann. "No," she shouted, "I didn't bring your money. There isn't any money. Where the hell do you think I'm going to get any money?" And then she reached out her foul hands with their broken fingernails and scratched the pink pudding of Lee-Ann's face.

Lee-Ann fought back. "What do you mean," she whimpered, grabbing Mimi's hands in a fierce grip, "there isn't any money?"

"Because there isn't," wept Mimi. Jerking her hands free, she shoved Lee-Ann to the floor and fell on her.

Homer Kelly and Julian Snow jumped out of their chairs and pulled them apart. Mary Kelly dragged Honey Mooney to her feet. Charlotte Harris hurried into Honey's kitchen and dampened a paper towel and dabbed at Mimi Pink's face and hands, while Mimi sobbed and blubbered.

It was just like always. Mimi was in the wrong. She always got the blame. Nobody knew what she had been through. Nobody understood. Lee-Ann always won, Mother's little honey-child.

64

Goodness is the only investment that never fails.
Walden, "Higher Laws"

In her furious rage against her sister, in her vengeful anxiety to destroy her, Mimi told everything. She stood amid the smoking ruins of her life, shaking her fist. Oh, it had been good to Lord it over Lee-Ann, to keep her on a string and tell her what to do, to dole out money in dribs and drabs. Now everything was smashed up, but it didn't matter, as long as Lee-Ann was smashed up, too, and so was Buzzie, and so was Annie.

Look at Buzzie Grandison! Just look at him now! He had married Annie Finney, not Mimi, and then he got rich, and after that Annie turned up her nose at Mimi, and only the other day she had passed Mimi on Newbury Street in Boston as if she didn't recognize her at all, only of course she did, because Mimi saw that little flicker in her eyes before Annie looked away.

Mimi did not merely talk to Homer Kelly, she babbled, she gushed, she spouted, she divulged everything.

Homer listened and tried to make sense of the deluge, as he sat in Mimi's condo apartment, which was all white, with puffy white sofas and pictures that were white on white and lampshades white as the driven snow. "You're telling me your sister poisoned Shirley Mills?"

"Exhume the body," cried Mimi. "You'll see. She did it! Lee-Ann did it!"

"And Alice Snow? Your sister struck her with that heavy lamp?"

320

"Oh, she's strong," gibbered Mimi. "I've got scars, the things she's done to me."

"Wait a minute." Homer remembered Dr. Stefano's missing files, and he framed his next question carefully. "Your sister killed Alice Snow first, although Alice was an invalid, and everybody thought she didn't have long to live anyway."

Mimi smiled wickedly. "That woman wasn't sick, she was just lazy, she liked being waited on. I had private information."

"Private information? You mean Dr. Stefano's files?"

Mimi laughed, flaunting her cleverness. "Oh, yes, that was me. I was sitting there in the waiting room and his receptionist asked me to cover for her while she went down the hall to use the public phone. I saw my chance, and I pulled out all the Pond View files and stuffed them in my attaché case. So I knew she was lying, Alice Snow. I knew she was healthy as a pig."

"So it's true, your sister was picking on the younger ones. I remember telling her to be careful for her own safety, because she was the youngest one in the park." Homer smiled grimly. "So those burned curtains of hers were just an act, to make herself look like one of the targets."

"Naturally."

"But what about the hole in Julian Snow's gas pipe, and the sabotage to his machine at the landfill? What about Porter McAdoo's collapsing jack? What about Charlotte Harris's electric iron and the fire in the Ryans' place, what about the bullet that killed Pete Harris?"

"Don't ask me," said Mimi, shrugging her big shoulders. "Ask her."

"Now just let me be sure I've got this straight." Homer shifted his big frame among the white pillows on the white sofa. "The point of this entire exercise was to remove all the residents from the trailer park, to free it up so that it could be acquired from the state of Massachusetts to be used for another purpose? What was that purpose? It wasn't just the restoration of the natural landscape? Your sister isn't an enthusiast for the forest primeval?"

"Ask her!" Mimi leaped up, exultant. "Ask Jack Markey! Ask Buzzie Grandison!"

"Buzzie . . . ? You mean Jefferson Grandison? He wanted this property, too? Not just the high school land, but Pond View, too? He wanted to develop Pond View?"

And then Mimi made the hierarchy clear. Lee-Ann Mooney had taken orders from Mimi Pink, Mimi had been in partnership with Jack Markey, and Jack had answered to Jefferson Grandison. "I don't know what the hell Buzzie wanted to do with the place. Ask him, go ahead, ask him." Mimi ended with a shriek of laughter. "And give him my love! Give him all my love!"

The final result of Homer's interview with Mimi Pink was the indictment of her sister, Lee-Ann "Honey" Mooney, for the homicides of Alice Snow and Shirley Mills. Mimi herself was indicted for conspiracy to commit homicide, even though she had never harmed a hair on anybody's head.

Then, while her shrewd defense attorney sweated over her case, Mimi disposed of all her properties on Walden Street and the Milldam, turning in all the playing pieces of her private Monopoly game, all the little green houses and red plastic hotels. The dice vanished, too, the ones she had tossed and tossed and tossed—and at last the playing piece called Mimi Pink disappeared altogether from the board.

. . . he has set his trap with a hair spring . . . and
then . . . got his own leg into it.
Walden, "Economy"

Homer Kelly was fascinated by the multiple collapse. Jefferson Grandison's descent was especially calamitous. Homer heard about it at second hand from Abigail Saltonstall—or rather, from Martha Jones, but even Martha hadn't witnessed all of it.

The day of reckoning was the Tuesday after Labor Day. Martha Jones heard the mounting noise on Huntington Avenue, she looked out the window and recoiled with shock, and then she burst into Grandison's office without knocking.

"Mr. Grandison, Mr. Grandison! It's Lot Seventeen, Mr. Grandison! It's here!"

"Here?" Grandison looked up and started out of his chair. "What do you mean, here?"

Martha's hair was wild. Her white dress dragged where she had caught it in the door. She pointed at the window and tried to get the words out. "Look," she cried, "just look!"

Grandison strode to the window and looked. He couldn't see the street directly below the seventy-story building, but he could see its approaches northeast and southwest, he could see the crossing streets and Massachusetts Avenue and the turnpike. They were all choked with trucks. Other traffic was at a standstill. Even from this height he could hear the lumbering roar of the diesel engines, the honking of furious cars, the shrilling of police whistles. There was gridlock as far as the eye could see.

He turned with bulging eyes to Martha Jones. "Did you say it's Lot Seventeen?"

"That's right. I just had a call. He warned us last week, remember? Mr. Pouch, he said they'd dump it at our front door. Well, that's what they're doing, they're dumping it on the sidewalk."

Grandison was ashy pale. He staggered and clutched at a chair. Then he snatched up a phone. "I'll get an injunction, a restraining order."

There was a pounding at the door.

"What shall I do?" cried Martha Jones. "Mr. Grandison, what shall I do?"

Grandison dropped the phone and ran heavily to another door, the one that opened on the stairway. Without a word he began hurrying down the stairs.

Martha looked over the railing at his disappearing back, the bald top of his head. "Good-bye, Mr. Grandison," she cried, knowing in her heart that she would never see him again. "Good-bye, good-bye!"

Seventy flights of stairs were a great many flights. Jefferson Grandison descended the last of them in a state of collapse, slipping and sliding down whole staircases, losing track of where he was, ending at last on his back on the floor of the second basement, where a couple of men with sooty faces were cleaning one of the enormous furnaces.

Heat buffeted him as he lay gasping, trying to catch his breath. The two men climbed out of the furnace and helped him to his feet. Choking, nearly fainting, he made his way up two flights to a service exit at the back of the building and stumbled outside.

He could hear tumult in the street. Something came rolling around the corner of the building and knocked him down. It was a rubber tire. Grandison sat up dizzily and stared at it. Then he heaved himself to his feet and limped to the corner and peered around at the street.

The noise was deafening. Fifteen-ton trucks were lined up for blocks, their diesel engines roaring. An entire squad of police officers shouted and pointed and blew their whistles, and one of them hung on to the cab of the truck that was now discharging its contents on the sidewalk. The policeman yelled at the driver, but the driver had a piece of paper, he was flourishing it. He had a permit, some sort of permit, and all the other drivers were waving their permits, and they were all taking turns backing their trucks into position and hauling on the levers that lifted the hydraulic cylinders so that the truck beds rose in the air and the contents slid out with the pull of gravity and piled higher and higher against the gleaming glass facade of the Grandison Building.

It was tires, rubber tires, hundreds of thousands of automobile tires, truck tires, giant tires from eighteen-wheelers—they careened gaily down the street, they wobbled and rolled and bounced and collided and ricocheted against cars, and the cars honked their horns and tried to back up, and bumped into other cars that were trying to back up, while still more cars tried to go forward in the snarl of tires and trucks and entangled traffic. Whistles shrilled, the tires piled up on the sidewalk of Huntington Avenue and spilled over into the street and rolled and wallowed all over the intersection with Harcourt Street and tumbled up against the shimmering walls of Copley Place and pyramided in mountain ranges of rubber, choking the approaches to the Prudential Center, blocking traffic in the center of Boston for three solid days.

Jefferson Grandison disappeared. He simply vanished, along with his wife, Annie. There were sightings, rumors that he had been seen pumping gas in Illinois or running a casino in Las Vegas. The cost of the cleanup of the tires and their storage in temporary emergency facilities here and there around the countryside was absorbed by the city of Boston and charged against the sale at auction of the assets of Grandison Enterprises.

The final destiny of the tires was unknown too, since burning them had become illegal and depositing them in a landfill was illegal and shipping them to Bolivia was out of the question. The disposal of Lot Seventeen became an election issue for the mayor of Boston—but that is another story.

Of course it was to be expected that Grandison's undertakings in the town of Concord would now be broken off. No proposal to change the zoning of the high school land would ever come before Town Meeting. Jack Markey's charming mixed-use commercial village, Walden Green, with its toy church and mock Town Hall, its condominiums and its underground parking lot for a thousand cars, would never be brought into being. The backhoe was trundled away, the survey stakes were removed, and before long the high school kids on the lacrosse team returned to their old playing field and raced up and down on the grass and scooped up the ball in their rackets and flung it at the goal.

The other Grandison project in Concord was scuttled, too, the one in which Jack Markey and Mimi Pink and Lee-Ann Mooney had been so heavily involved. It probably wouldn't have worked anyway. Even if the land had suddenly become available, even if all the remaining residents of Pond View had died peacefully in their beds, it was doubtful that the place could ever have become an annex to the landfill, a disposal site for Lot Seventeen, with a deep cement-covered pit for a hundred thousand rubber tires. Even with an expert on his payroll—a famous technical adviser on the protection of groundwater—even with Roger Bland in Grandison's pocket and the director of public parks in the State House very much in his debt, it was doubtful that he could have brought off this last, worst insult to Walden Pond.

Surely, thought Homer Kelly, surely this time there would have been a genuine uproar in the town of Concord, a protest too overwhelming even for the likes of Jefferson Grandison. "It couldn't possibly have passed Town Meeting," said Homer to Oliver Fry.

Oliver wasn't so sure. "All it takes to persuade the people of Concord to do something stupid is a few town fathers calling it sound fiscal policy. Then they keel over and vote for it, every single time."

Poor Oliver was in a dejected state of mind. He had been defeated at the polls, and he was taking it hard.

He had not been licked by Roger Bland. Both Oliver and Roger lost the selectman's post to a woman named Betsy Beaumont, the mother of eight children. Betsy was neither a rapt saint like Oliver nor a cautious middle-of-the-roader like Roger. She was a down-to-earth woman of conviction. "Anyone who's brought up eight children without any of them landing in jail," she said firmly—it was her winning argument—"can handle anything that comes along."

Defeated candidate Roger Bland was in worse shape than Oliver Fry. At least Oliver was going to get his job back, through the mysterious magnanimity of an anonymous philanthropist, whose gift to the high school was to be expended solely for the teaching of natural science.

"Isn't it wonderful," said Hope. "Who do you suppose it could possibly be?"

"I don't know," said Ananda, smiling wisely at his future wife, keeping his own counsel.

Roger Bland was in serious trouble. Not only did he lose the local election, he lost the hoped-for seat on the Board of Harvard Overseers as well. Bleakly he examined the pictures of the winning candidates. They were a mixed collection of men and women who had somehow juggled their autobiographies so that they looked like compassionate people with their feet solidly on the ground—Boy Scout leaders who were investment analysts, full-blooded native American insurance executives. Roger's timid curriculum vitae never had a chance.

But these two blows to his self-esteem were not the worst. In September Roger received a statement from his broker, informing him that his account was worth five hundred thousand dollars less than it had been the previous month. Roger was sure there must be some mistake. He called up the broker and learned the truth.

"But it's not my fault," complained Roger bitterly. "Somebody must have broken into my software. It was those people who occupied my house last month. One of them must have bought all that worthless stock and sold my blue chips. It wasn't me."

"I'm sorry, sir, we were only obeying the orders that came over the line. It isn't our problem if someone other than yourself is permitted to use your private account and personal identification numbers."

"Permitted!" Roger's mild nature was incapable of responding adequately to this catastrophe. He didn't know how he was going to tell Marjorie that they would have to sell their heavily mortgaged house and live more simply.

Poor Marjorie! When she learned the truth, her niceness was sorely tested. It turned out, as might have been expected, that vitriol accumulates in nice people like poisonous sediment in the bottom of a jar. Marjorie had sour words to say to Roger. She was no longer happy as the day was long. When Mary Kelly came to her with the suggestion that Sarah Peel should keep the horse called Pearl, which was at that moment cropping the weedy grass around the Kellys' house, Marjorie said furiously, "Honestly, I don't give a damn what happens to the goddamned horse," which didn't sound like Marjorie at all.

As for Sarah herself and her phalanx of homeless friends —Palmer Nifto and Audrey Beamish and Almina Ziblow and Bridgie Sorrel and Bobbsie Low and Doris Harper and Carl Browning and Dolores Marshall and Dolores's daughter, Christine—all of them landed more or less on their feet.

Homer Kelly was their advocate in court. Most of them turned up for sentencing. Only Palmer and Audrey jumped bail and took off for parts unknown. The rest humbly pleaded nolo contendere, with Homer looming protectively alongside.

The judge didn't know what the hell to do with these perpetual indigents, one of whom was a small child, and he let them go with a severe talking-to.

66

Ah, bless the Lord, O my soul! bless him for
wildness, for crows that will not alight
within gunshot!
Journal, January 12, 1855

It was mid-autumn in Concord. Sugar maples flamed along
Walden Street. The swamp maples had already lost their
leaves, revealing on the ends of their bare branches the dirty
clotted handkerchiefs of tent caterpillars. Petunias disappeared, chrysanthemums came on strong. Yellow buses lumbered to and fro, carrying the children of Concord to schools
called Alcott and Thoreau and Sanborn, Willard and Pea-
body. Along Route 2 the farm stands were colorful with
baskets of red apples and mountains of orange pumpkins.
Flocks of red-winged blackbirds settled in the trees around
Gowing's Swamp, just passing through, and one day the
myrtle warblers stopped over in Concord, fluttering between
branches, soaring in dipping arcs, lacing the trees together,
then rising all in a body to migrate farther south. And all
over town the Canada geese flew back and forth from pond
to pond, keeping up a restless shout, informing each other
that winter was coming.

If it was coming for the Canada geese, it was coming for
Sarah Peel and her friends. Something had to be done about
them right away, but what? Like the judge in the county
courthouse, Homer Kelly didn't know what the hell to do,
but he threw himself into the task of figuring it out. While
Sarah and Dolores and Christine and Doris and Almina and
Carl and Bobbsie and Bridgie were passed around among the
Kellys' long-suffering friends, Homer made a study of the
Hugh Cargill land, a large triangular parcel near the center
of town.

"It used to be the Concord poor farm," he told his wife. "Hugh Cargill left it to the town in 1798 for the benefit of the poor."

"I remember the house before it was torn down," said Mary. "It was right there on Walden Street across from the police station."

"Right. And you remember what happened. The trustees sold off most of the property and used the profits to build affordable housing elsewhere, because most of the Cargill parcel is wetland. But look at this." Homer unfolded one of the maps he had been using in his explorations of Thoreau country. "This little piece right here, that's not wetland. Why couldn't they put a bunch of house trailers right there?"

"House trailers?" Mary gasped. Then she laughed.

Homer looked at her in surprise. "What's so funny?"

"It's Roger Bland and all those other people. People like us, good conservationist types, you have to admit we've been looking forward to the eventual closing down of Pond View, which is the trailer park we've already got." Mary went off into another gale of laughter. "And here you are, putting another one right in the middle of everything. I tell you, Homer, it won't be easy."

And it wasn't. While Sarah and her friends were gently shifted from house to house, and Doris Harper wore out her welcome with one hostess after another, Homer befriended the Hugh Cargill trustees, he pleaded with the affordable housing commission, he pressured the planning board and the board of appeals, he hounded the finance committee, he pestered the Concord Public Works Department. As a result of his efforts a new zoning change was inserted in the warrant for the April town meeting, along with an article for a change in the bylaws to permit subsidized housing in the shape of mobile homes.

The town meeting was stormy. "What about sewage?" demanded Roger Bland, rising from the audience to protest. "Those trailers will contaminate the town well."

"If you will examine the rest of the warrant," said Homer, speaking from the rostrum, "you'll see another article requesting that the town sewer be extended across Walden Street from the courthouse. That will take care of the town well."

Roger was on his feet again, waving his hands, hardly able to express his outrage. "What's to prevent all the homeless people in Boston from coming out to Concord and expecting to be housed?"

"What indeed?" murmured the chairman of the finance committee to Selectwoman Betsy Beaumont.

Oliver Fry leaped up. "If all the suburban towns around Boston act as responsibly as we're doing, that won't happen." There was huge applause. One of Betsy's eight children was old enough to vote at Town Meeting, and he whistled through his teeth.

The sewage proposal passed. So did the change in the bylaws, by a narrow margin. The zoning change was the trickiest, since it required a two-thirds vote. Homer Kelly gave an impassioned speech. People shot out of their seats and waved their arms to be recognized and spoke with irrefutable logic on both sides. The discussion went on and on. When the moderator at last called for a voice vote, there was a tremendous clamor of ayes, followed by a huge chorus of nays.

The moderator frowned around the hall and declared himself in doubt. "Will the aye voters please stand? Tellers, will you record the vote?"

It was a near thing, but it squeaked by. "The motion is passed," thundered the moderator, whamming down his gavel and moving on to the next item on the warrant. "Article fourteen, public works, the purchase of a snowplow. Does anyone wish to speak to this motion?"

67

> *There are no larger fields than these, no worthier*
> *games than may here be played.*
> *Walden*, "Baker Farm"

Sarah Peel and her friends were homeless no longer. Seven trailers were quickly set up on the Hugh Cargill land, the sewer pipe was rushed across the street, and on the first day of May everybody moved in. Next morning little Christine walked right across the field to the Alcott School, where all the fourth-graders in Concord were gathered under one roof. Sarah's horse, Pearl, began nibbling the grass on acres of pasture.

The only one who was dissatisfied with the new living arrangements was Doris Harper. "What the fuck?" she said angrily, after inspecting her brand-new mobile home. "Sarah, she's got wall-to-wall carpeting. What've I got? Shitty hardwood floor."

"But, Doris," said Sarah mildly, "you've got a cathedral ceiling and a bow window. Do you want to trade with me?"

"Oh, now I get it," responded Doris, "you're trying to get my cathedral ceiling. Well, fuck you."

So everybody stayed put.

At Pond View, the other Concord location for mobile homes, only four were left. They belonged to Charlotte Harris, Julian Snow, Stu LaDue, and Eugene Beaver. When Stu died of apoplexy in August, there were only three. Then Eugene went to live with his son in Atlanta. That left only Charlotte and Julian.

Pond View looked moribund. Bird-watchers and environmental enthusiasts congratulated themselves on the approach of the day when this trailer park, at least, would be no more.

Roger Bland was one of those who was counting down. Keeping track of the shrinking of Pond View was one of the few satisfactions left in his diminished life. Coming home every day to his small rented cottage in West Concord was depressing. Marjorie was grumpy. The house was dark and inconvenient.

But Pond View was petering out. "There's only a couple of them left," Roger told his wife. "Surely those people can't last long."

"Well, who gives a damn anyway?" said Marjorie.

Certainly Julian and Charlotte had no intention of giving up and fading away. "Let's spite them all," said Charlotte. "Let's live to be a hundred."

And they did. Sometimes they lived in Charlotte's place, sometimes in Julian's. The commonwealth of Massachusetts offered to buy them out, but they refused to sell, and since their two mobile homes were at opposite ends of the park, the whole thing had to be preserved just the way it was.

Far into the next millennium they had the run of the place. One day during the first decade Charlotte, a woman of taste, did something surprising. She bought a pair of orange plastic flamingoes and stuck their wire legs into the grass facing Route 126. All the Thoreauvians and bird lovers had to look at them as they trudged by. Later on, Charlotte added a couple of gnomes and a whirly windmill.

Charlotte and Julian went right on living at Pond View until they were very, very, very, very old.

In the commercial center, the part of town where Walden Street intersected with the Milldam, all the boutiques were gone. No one regretted their departure. When Taylor Baylor heard that Mimi Pink had sold out, he abandoned his retirement in Florida and came roaring back to Concord. Before long his old shoe store was back on the Milldam, occupying the former premises of Hugo's Hair Harmonies.

But perfection is elusive. The Concord landfill was still a

vast hole in the ground. Five thousand people went right on
trailing across Route 126 on torrid summer days to swim in
Walden Pond. And every piece of private unoccupied land
in the town was up for grabs. Fifteen houses went up on the
Burroughs farm, to be offered for sale at a million dollars
apiece.

And therefore Oliver Fry still found it necessary to do
battle for Thoreau country. Sometimes his fellow citizens
wished Henry Thoreau had been born in some other town,
some village far away. Then Henry would have written *Winnipesaukee*, or *Moosehead*, not *Walden*, and Oliver Fry would
have left them all alone.

Unfortunately Thoreau had been born right here in Concord. It was a simple fact, and they were stuck with it.

Sometimes when Oliver was oppressed with the hopeless-
ness of it all, sometimes when he saw bulldozers assaulting

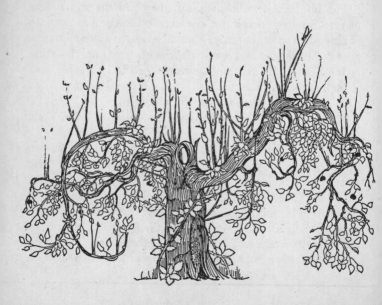

a new piece of virgin Concord soil, Homer Kelly took him by the arm and led him back, back, back, through tangles of catbrier and honeysuckle and buckthorn, to an abandoned orchard not far from his own house. Red cedars towered among the bristling apple trees. Homer and Oliver had to force their way in, torn by prickling blackberry canes, inhaling the fragrance of the air—ah, such smells!—the heady aroma of fox grapes, the hot perfume of sunlit leaves, the thrilling scent of wild apples dangling from neglected boughs, and now and then, faintly from far away, the whiff of a passing skunk.

And sometimes, once in a while, they heard again the song of the wood thrush. But whether its singing amended any human institution in the world, even in the town of Concord, Massachusetts, was still very much in doubt.

Author's Note

What about Thoreau's wood thrush? Was he mistaken? Was he really listening to the song of the hermit thrush?

In the 1906 edition of Thoreau's journal, edited by Bradford Torrey and Francis Allen, there are doubting footnotes to some of Thoreau's entries about the wood thrush.

Here, for example, is Thoreau on April 27, 1854:

The wood thrush afar,—so superior a strain to that of other birds . . . This is the gospel according to the wood thrush. He makes a sabbath out of a week-day. I could go to hear him, could buy a pew in his church.

And here is the footnote:

Probably it was the hermit thrush, not the wood thrush, for which the date is too early, whose song he had been praising.

One might add a cautionary footnote to the footnote: Thoreau was such a keen observer and wrote so often about both the hermit thrush and the wood thrush, perhaps he was not mistaken after all.

But in this book I have gone along with the notion that he was indeed wrong, that the heavenly note of his wood thrush was really that of the hermit. Therefore, when Homer Kelly hears it at last, "a watery warbling, a bell-like melody . . . repeated in a higher register, the last notes rising out of hearing," it is a description of the hermit thrush's song as I have been introduced to it in Concord by my friend Walter Brain.

The setting of this book more or less resembles the actual town of Concord, Massachusetts, but all the shops are imaginary. The Walden Street house of Oliver and Hope Fry is real however—in some of my children's books it was home to the family of Frederick Hall.

There is a trailer park in Concord, but in this story its residents and their mobile homes are invented. So are the members of town government, as well as the various building projects and real estate enterprises that come before them. In fact, all the characters in this book have no connection with actual people, although some are descended from certain residents of Anthony Trollope's cathedral city of Barchester.

There is no seventy-story Grandison Building on Huntington Avenue in Boston.

I can't close without thanking Tom Blanding and Anne McGrath for spreading so generously their knowledge and enthusiasm for the work and the landscape of Henry Thoreau.

WARNING: Quaking bog enthusiasts are advised not to go unaccompanied into Gowing's Swamp. Titcomb's Bog, on the other hand, is perfectly safe, since it does not exist.

FOR THE BEST IN PAPERBACKS, LOOK FOR THE

In every corner of the world, on every subject under the sun, Penguin represents quality and variety—the very best in publishing today.

For complete information about books available from Penguin—including Pelicans, Puffins, Peregrines, and Penguin Classics—and how to order them, write to us at the appropriate address below. Please note that for copyright reasons the selection of books varies from country to country.
